A Superhero Needs No Cape

A Remarkable Story of
Dreams, Dedication and Desire

Andy Lipman

PublishAmerica
Baltimore

First printing

At the specific preference of the author, PublishAmerica allowed this work to remain exactly as the author intended, verbatim, without editorial input.

ISBN: 1-4137-3152-X
PUBLISHED BY PUBLISHAMERICA, LLLP
www.publishamerica.com
Baltimore

Printed in the United States of America

Table of Contents

Acknowledgments

I want to thank the following editors for their assistance on this project:

Melanie A. Lasoff Levs, Richard Etchison, and John Allen

I want to thank the following Major League Baseball players for taking the time to answer my questions.

John Smoltz, Chipper Jones, Johnny Estrada, Adam LaRoche, John Rocker, Jim Poole, Joe Simpson, Blaine Boyer, and Nick Green

I especially want to thank Mr. Smoltz who called me up and talked with me for fifteen to twenty minutes. It was a thrill of a lifetime to speak to my Ricky "The Jet" Kilmer.

I want to thank my friends and family and especially my wife Andrea and my daughter Avery who have given my life new meaning.

This book is dedicated to my mom and dad who taught me how to step up to the plate on and off the field.

The Recurring Dream

It is finally his turn. It must be 100 degrees out here under the scorching sun, just another summer in Atlanta. From inside the dugout at Turner Field, his hometown baseball stadium, Paul Morgan can feel the sweat pouring down his back under his red and blue uniform.

He grabs his trusty wooden Louisville Slugger and puts his batting gloves on one at a time. His hands shake as he places his helmet on and strides out of the dugout. On instinct, he looks up into the stands and spots his family in the crowd, standing and frantically waving at him with huge grins on their faces.

He takes his place in the on-deck circle, listening to the steady din of the crowd as he waits for his opportunity to be announced. After the player in front of him strikes out, he hears the public address system squawk out his name.

"Now batting: Paul Morgan."

He takes a few practice swings before approaching the batter's box, then takes his stance at home plate: elbows up, feet shoulder-width apart, bat pulled back. But just as Paul is ready for the first pitch, the strangest thing happens.

A young man emerges from the stands and walks toward him. Does anyone else see him? Paul doesn't recognize him. He's wearing some type of mask but other than that, the stranger is dressed just like any other young guy at a summer baseball game—denim shorts, blue polo shirt, sneakers. He steps close to Paul and whispers advice on how Paul can realize his life-long dream: to get a base hit that wins the game in his first Major League at-bat.

The man disappears as strangely as he appeared—just walks away from the plate and disappears back into the crowd. Paul stands in the batters box, perplexed. Who was that guy? Why was he giving him advice? Should he take the advice? And, most importantly, will he get a hit to win the game?

He tries to shake off his questions and take his stance again. The crowd noise grows louder as diehard Braves fans begin chanting and moving their arms in the familiar tomahawk chop motion. Flashing "LET'S MAKE SOME NOISE!" the scoreboard exalts the fans into further frenzy. Cameras are at the ready, anticipating a monumental sports moment.

Paul eyes the pitcher, signaling his readiness for whatever the tall, lanky southpaw is about to throw his way. But there's that odd beeping noise again...

Ah, yes, his alarm clock.

Chapter 1
A Losing Season

To most, it was a typical sticky summer night in September at Turner Field. To a 40-year-old father and his teenage son, it would hardly be just another night watching America's pastime.

The smell of peanuts and cotton candy filled the air. This was the last home series of the season for the Atlanta Braves, their favorite baseball team, which unfortunately owned the worst record in the National League. The vast stadium seemed empty—only the hardcore fans remained, maybe 12,000 people, since the team had been out of the pennant race since July. Instead of the electricity of a playoff atmosphere, there was a resigned calm in the stands. It was about half an hour from game time and you could see people just milling about, chatting, some with binoculars pressed against their faces, straining to make out the expressions on their favorite players' faces. It was Hank Bowers Night and the first 1,000 kids in the ballpark received a Hank Bowers autographed baseball.

To many fathers and sons, taking in a baseball game was more than watching two teams compete on the diamond. It was a chance to catch up on life, to exchange funny anecdotes and on this night, for Greg and his father, it was a long-awaited chance to reveal a tale that would change their relationship forever.

"Dad, why is Hank Bowers still taking batting practice?" Greg asked, as he shifted in the cramped blue plastic seat. As season-ticket holders for years,

Greg's father made sure they sat close so they could observe all the action. "Shouldn't he be in the dugout by now?"

"Relax, Greg," his father said, smiling and taking a sip of his soda. "It's the last home-stand of his career and he's just trying to enjoy every minute on the field. Did I ever tell you that Hank is six-feet, three-inches tall? It says in the program he's six-feet, four-inches, but he's an inch shorter."

"You always tell me that, dad. Who cares if he's an inch shorter?"

"It's funny how something as small as an inch can change someone's life, Greg."

Greg looked a section to their right and 2 rows back and noticed a dark-haired man, probably in his late twenties to early thirties, looking at his father.

"Dad, why is he staring at you? Do you know him? It's kind of creepy."

"I don't know, Greg. He doesn't look familiar to me. Don't worry about it."

Greg's father, nursing a slight cold, could feel a coughing fit coming on and knew he needed to move around a bit. He put his drink on the ground, stood up and wiped his hands down the front of his gray T-shirt and navy blue shorts. He glanced over at his son, with his full head of dark, curly hair, slim build and—surprisingly for an adolescent—smooth skin.

"Do you need anything while I'm up?"

"Can I have a chicken sandwich and some peanuts?" Greg asked, as he grabbed his soda and started chugging.

"I'll get you another soda, too, kid." He winked at his son as he took off. "Growing boys need their fuel!"

Greg's father noticed the same man looking in his direction as he walked up the stairs. He chose to ignore the stare and grab some food for his boy. Greg's father normally didn't get hungry until the later innings and that's when he would get his mandatory ballpark meal—a juicy hotdog and some Cracker Jacks. Strolling through the massive food areas, he heard the peanut vendor, Ernie, shouting at him.

"Mr. M, how are you?" Ernie bellowed.

"Great!" he yelled back, amazed that Ernie recognized him every time he came to the ballpark. As he made his way over to the hotdog booth, he realized the vendors saw him coming and had his dog and Cracker Jacks ready to go by the time he got to the window.

"Actually guys," he said with a grin, "I'm just here to get my son a meal."

"No problem, Mr. M," said Charlie, a balding vendor about his age, who'd been there almost as long as he had. "We thought it was a little early for you."

"What do you mean?" he asked.

"Sir, you show up at 9:15 on the nose every night. Did you know that?"

Greg's father laughed, slightly embarrassed, and ran his fingers though his own dark, slightly-thinning curls.

"I wasn't aware."

"Hey Mr. M, how tall did you say Hank Bowers is?"

"Six-feet, three-inches, but the program says six-feet, four-inches."

Charlie laughed. "You would know, Mr. M. You sure would know."

Greg's father gathered up his son's food and thrust some extra cash at Charlie as he turned around and headed back to his seat.

"Thanks for the refreshments, Charlie. See you in a couple of hours."

As he approached the ticket-taker in their section, a sensation came over him. It was one he was all too familiar with. Suddenly, his throat felt clogged as if a wad of tissue had been stuffed in his esophagus. The only way he could breathe was by letting free the hacking monster that was tormenting his chest. He tried to find an isolated place where he could clear the phlegm out of his throat.

It was too late. A coughing spasm gripped him and went on for about thirty seconds. Soon after, he grabbed a ruffled tissue from his pocket and covered his mouth. Sometimes he'd hope he could avoid these loud outbursts, but they were about as preventable as a sneeze for someone with allergies.

"You okay, Mr. M?" asked Charlie. From Charlie's face, Greg's father could tell that he was concerned.

"Fine, Charlie. Thanks again," he said, his voice now considerably more hoarse than before. He always ran away from people when he was having an attack. He was normal in everyone's eyes until that hacking occurred. Then people would stare at him as if he needed to be hauled off on a stretcher.

Composed again, he returned to his seat and handed Greg his food. Then he grabbed his binoculars and looked out toward the field. He pointed toward home plate, as had become his superstition, and pointed his left index finger at the blue left field wall 335 feet away. He smiled and squeezed the antique silver pendant hanging around his neck.

Greg noticed the same guy as before pointing and staring at his father. His father also noticed the strange man steering his finger towards him. "Who was this guy?" he wondered, "and why is he staring at me?"

Trying to forget about the strange pointing man, he asked Greg how his sandwich was. When he looked at Greg, though, he noticed that his son hadn't touched his food. Instead, he was gazing at the ground, looking dejected.

"What is it?" he asked Greg. "You okay?"

"Dad, I didn't want to tell you this, but I got cut from the baseball team today." Greg hung his head in shame and slouched down in his seat.

"It's okay, son," he said and gave a couple of consoling pats to Greg's jeans-covered leg. "We'll practice more this off-season. We'll go to the batting cage every weekend and play catch in the yard during the week."

His father's consolation didn't cushion the blow at all. Greg sighed and stared at the field.

"You don't understand, Dad," he said, flustered. "The other guys are just too talented. I'm not going to try out next season. It's a waste of time."

"Are you kidding?" his father said, turning toward him to put his hand on Greg's shoulder. "Now, what kind of attitude is that? I'm a bit disappointed."

"I knew you'd be disappointed if I didn't make the team," Greg mumbled, looking away from his father's probing eyes.

"Greg, I'm not disappointed because you didn't make the team. I'd be disappointed if you didn't try and give it your all."

"I'm not good enough, Dad."

Hearing him say that hurt his father's heart—the kind of ache only a caring father who hates to see his son disappointed could feel.

"Hey, Greg," he said, trying to soothe the pain they both felt for each other. "No one can tell you what you can or cannot do. Only you can decide your fate."

Greg looked up into his father's eyes again.

"You don't know what it's like to play against people that are so much bigger and better than you," he groaned, making those adolescent assumptions that parents couldn't possibly understand. "Some of the girls are even bigger than me."

"Quitting is not the answer when things are tough. You can never be afraid to fail," his father replied.

"I guess I'm not brave like you, huh?" he said, with a slightly sarcastic tone.

"Bravery has nothing to do with it," his father shot back, with an edge to his words.

They sat silent for a while, neither knowing what to say to the other. He thought about reminding his son how the Braves left fielder was only six feet, three inches, but he knew how that irked the boy. As the Braves players, in their red, white, and blue home uniforms took their positions on the field to the tune of John Fogerty's *Centerfield*, Greg's father realized he couldn't bear to hear his son talk like that. Sitting there in their favorite ballpark, the first-pitch excitement building around them as what was supposed to be a meaningless game was about to be played, Greg's father decided now was the time to tell his son the story he'd been wanting to tell him his whole life.

"Greg, look at me," he said.

Greg looked up at him with a frown still pulling his cheeks down.

"At this moment, you have no earthly idea what you can do or how good you can be. I can prove it, too. I want to tell you my story."

Chapter 2
Life Needs a Little Kick

Paul Morgan was ten years old when he first saw his classmates playing kickball in the schoolyard. Watching the boys knock knuckles with each other after one kicked the purple ball high into the air, he instantly wanted to play, thinking it would be a great way to make new friends.

Paul didn't have many friends because he missed a lot of school fighting bacterial infections. His mother didn't want him around other kids' germs while he was sick and he was a little embarrassed by his lack of friends. Paul's only real playmate was his two-year-old black lab, Delta, who got her name because she was found near the airline's home, Hartsfield Airport, later known as Hartsfield-Jackson Atlanta International Airport. Delta was much faster than Paul and enjoyed running circles around her friend.

That Saturday morning, Paul convinced a few neighbors to let him join their kickball team since one of the kids had moved away a few weeks ago. Paul pleaded his case until the boys finally relented—even though they really didn't want to add a sick kid on the team, they needed another player.

That afternoon Paul's team challenged the kids from Happy Hollow, the neighborhood next to his, to a kickball game. Most of the games were played in the acre-and-a-half lot behind Paul's house, the largest yard on the block. The only hazard was a two-foot deep, snake-infested creek that separated his yard from his neighbor's. No one really worried about the snakes, only the unlucky soul who occasionally kicked the ball into the water. Then the poor fellow had to retrieve it, with no backup like Indiana Jones's whip. Every now and then some twelve or thirteen-year-olds were brought on as ringers but for the most part, the kids were about Paul's age.

Paul didn't kick the ball very well the first few games but playing with his friends made him happy. His mother was at the mall most of the day, so he wasn't worried about getting caught disobeying her orders. He thought it was kind of unfair that she insisted that he stay home all the time after school, anyway. It further alienated him from his would-be buddies and made him feel like life was meaningless.

Paul admitted to himself that he wasn't the best player in the neighborhood, but he wanted to be—some day. Success in sports translated into popularity at school and that was always in the back of Paul's mind. He was determined not to let the fact that he had a life-long lung illness, cystic fibrosis (CF), slow him down.

CF is a genetic disorder, meaning it was passed on to him by his mom and dad, who each had the gene that caused it. When each parent has the gene, there is a one-in-four chance the child will have CF. Paul was a member of that 25-percent club. CF made his body produce thick, sticky mucus that clogged his lungs, making it difficult for him to breathe at times and causing serious bacterial infections in his lungs. The gunky mucus also affected his pancreas, which made it harder to digest food. And, because it can harm the reproductive system in some people, there was a very good chance he wouldn't be able to have children later in life, but he probably wasn't worried about that, yet.

But it tormented other kids worse than him—at least, that's what his mother insisted. Paul was doing just fine except for being the skinniest kid in school—not a muscle on him. The worst episode he'd had with the disease was when he had a cold in second grade. He missed two weeks of school. Not that he complained. He never understood why his teachers would freak out when his mom walked in the first day of every school year and told them her little boy had CF and that he had to take his pills before every meal.

Like a lot of boys his age, Paul loved comics. Often sick in bed with nothing to do, he'd flip open a comic book and live vicariously through Superman's adventures. He tried hard to be a regular kid, but more than anything he wanted to be a hero like his comic book idol. For now, he found his best chance to be a hero was on the kickball field.

Late that spring—with summer vacation only a week or two away—Paul had a showdown with Josh Wilson. Josh was the stud of the fourth grade. He lived about two miles from Paul and because he was such a great athlete, he was the closest thing to a celebrity in his neighborhood. Josh's father, who was a Little League baseball coach, called him "The Human Highlight of Happy Hollow." Josh had never lost a kickball game. Or any game for that matter. He was an all-star in football, baseball, soccer, and basketball. He was even ranked in the top-ten in the twelve-and-under tennis league.

In fourth grade, kickball was as big as an Olympic sport at Paul's school— classmates discussed every kick and catch over lunch. Josh stood five-feet, two-inches tall, a giant among his fellow classmates. He was the kid who dated the prettiest girl in class and was student council president. With his sandy blonde hair, blue eyes and stylish clothes, Josh had everything going for him. Paul didn't have much going for him except a cool Superman lunchbox. But, that was about to change.

Paul had set a goal for when he returned to the fifth grade in September. He wanted to be picked first when his classmates were choosing sports teams. A lot of kids had that desire, but it felt like Paul's whole life back then, especially since he usually finished last at everything else. He couldn't run very fast or far. Thanks to his illness, he had been held out of most athletic competitions. He ran out of breath a lot, but he figured most kids his age did, too.

The only way to impress his teammates was to beat the towering giant— the great Josh Wilson. The Human Highlight. That, he knew, would ensure they'd pick him first next year.

Things couldn't have played out any better for Paul during that early May game. The bases were loaded, with two outs in the final inning, and it was his turn to kick. He stepped to the plate, squinting under the blinding sun and wiping sweat off his brow. Paul's team trailed 1-0 as Josh had bragged the whole game that no one could score on him.

A base hit was all Paul needed to be Superman. Paul did not have one good kick in four games, but all his failures would be forgotten if he came through in this pivotal plate appearance.

He waited for Josh to roll the ball towards the plate. He could feel his body dragging a little from some new medication he had just started taking. But, he shrugged it off as it just felt like a small cold.

Crouched behind home plate, the catcher, Bobby Jarvis, got Paul's attention before Josh could release the pitch.

"Hey Paul," he whispered. "Josh told me he was going to roll the ball to the outside corner of the plate. If you stand closer to the plate, then you can run up to the ball quicker and hit it up the middle."

Paul eyed him suspiciously.

"Why are you telling me this?" he asked, knowing that while they were classmates, they rarely talked. He hung out more with Josh and his popular crowd.

"Josh is a jerk," Bobby said, as if spitting a bad taste out of his mouth. "I caught him beating up on my little brother after school yesterday. I'd love to see the shock on his face when you kick."

Paul turned back toward Josh, who looked smug in his designer shorts outfit. He didn't know if Bobby was telling the truth but he sure did want to make that kick mean something. He had nothing to lose because he'd faced Josh several times before and never reached base. Sure enough, Josh rolled the ball as hard as he could to the outside part of the plate.

With all his might, Paul smacked the ball dead-center with his Nike tennis shoe. The ball shot off his foot, headed straight over the pitcher's circle. Josh jumped as high as he could, but his outstretched fingertips were still six inches below the ball. Two runs scored and Paul's team won the game.

Suddenly, the playground erupted. Paul jumped up and down in his Atlanta Braves replica jersey and navy blue running shorts as each of his teammates ran up and slapped him on the back and high-fived him.

"I won!" he shouted. "I won!"

Through the crowd of dirty, sweating boys, he saw Josh Wilson. "The Highlight" stared at the ground as he slowly walked off the field in the other direction. He had finally been beaten. Even more miraculously, it was the skinny, out-of-breath boy with CF who took him down.

For the rest of the day, everyone wanted to be Paul's friend. He was a hero, like Superman, and he lapped up the attention like a thirsty dog. He realized he'd reached his goal—there was no doubt in his mind now that he'd be the first pick on any team as a fifth-grader. That night, his parents took him and his brother, Garey, out to the local Pizza Hut to celebrate, with Paul wearing a huge smile all night. That was the tastiest slice of pepperoni pizza he'd ever eaten.

It was the first time that he'd really felt like he'd accomplished something. He was tired of being known as the "sick" kid and he hoped his kickball success could finally change that stereotype.

The next day at lunch, people were still talking about the game. Everyone in his class wanted to know how he got that kick. He never admitted that Bobby told him what the pitch was going to be. All that mattered was that he had the game-winning kick.

The game grew to legendary status in just a few days. Paul heard accounts of the story from kids who weren't at the game, who said he kicked the ball so far that it went into a neighbor's yard two houses over. The story changed depending on who you talked to, but there was one constant: Paul was a hero.

One kick changed his life. When school started that fall, as Paul predicted, he was picked first for teams in gym class. During lunch, Bobby invited him to sit with his crowd at the popular table. Marvin, another one of the popular kids, asked Paul if he wanted to hang out after school and go dirt-biking.

But the best part of the day was when Debbie Adams asked him how it felt to beat Josh. Debbie Adams was the most popular girl in school. She had long brown hair and pretty green eyes. She always smelled like peppermints. That afternoon, she wore a pretty pink dress that made Paul's heart beat a million times a minute.

She was dating Josh and they'd had a fight the night before and broken up. Paul wanted to think it was due to his kickball prowess. He couldn't believe Debbie actually talked to him. They'd been classmates and next-door neighbors for four years and this was the first time she'd said a word to him. He wasn't sure she knew his name until today. He was sure that by the sixth grade they'd be going steady. She'd certainly drop Josh for the new Superman of the neighborhood.

Like any kid who might become popular overnight, the success went straight to Paul's head and he couldn't help but imagine what it would be like to be a hero in front of a crowd of millions. You couldn't be in front of millions playing kickball, but you could do it in baseball.

Paul's favorite baseball team, the Atlanta Braves, were competing for their first division title in nine years and were trying to become the first National League team to go from worst-to-first in just one year. He watched every game with Garey that season. The excitement of the pennant race turned Paul into an avid fan.

He asked his parents if he could play baseball over the summer and, even though his mother protested, his dad convinced her that it was okay and signed him up. Paul could sense that kickball was only the beginning for him.

But there's no way he could have predicted what was about to happen.

Chapter 3
Dreams to Nightmares

He began having the dream a couple of nights after his heroic kick. In the dream, he comes to the plate for his first big league at-bat with the game on the line. He doesn't think he can get a hit off of the pitcher but then the masked man comes over to give him some advice. Just as he's getting ready to hit, he wakes up.

He's questioned so many parts of the dream: Who is the masked man? Did he end up getting the hit to win the game? Could he really be a big leaguer?

The morning after the first dream, he woke up with a shooting pain in his legs. When he tried to get out of bed his legs crumbled under him. He fell on his chin and cut it wide open.

"Help me!" he screamed at the top of his lungs as blood fell from his chin and onto his Atlanta Braves flannel pajamas. Delta ran into the room and started licking his wounds, prompting him to scream even louder.

Paul's mother heard the screams from the laundry room. She ran to the bedroom only to discover her son face-down on the floor with blood gushing from his chin all over the beige carpet.

"Oh my God!" she screamed as she frantically searched for the phone and called 9-1-1.

Paul trembled as the ambulance came for him that rainy morning. Everyone hears the sirens scream in the distance, but it's always for someone else. Not this time. Paul heard it wailing all the way down the street until it stopped in front of his house.

The sirens must have awakened the entire neighborhood. His panicked mother threw a mask over his nose and mouth to protect him from spreading germs in the ambulance. The emergency medical technician put him on a stretcher and carried him through the rainy front yard to the big box with lights still flashing, his parents running alongside and getting soaked. The pain was excruciating now. Not so much in his legs, as they were now numb, but the cut on his chin was really stinging.

He saw the neighbors covering their children's eyes as if to shield them from the sight of his gory face and the unsettling nature of it all. These were the same kids who were congratulating him a couple of days ago for his game-winning kick, and now they were afraid of him. The worst was when he saw Debbie Adams, wearing a red and yellow sundress, retreat inside her home as if she'd seen the ugliest monster in the world. Not that it compared to the pain he was in, but knowing he'd lost any chance at dating the most popular girl in school was pretty devastating.

The ambulance doors closed and it whisked him away to the hospital. His father followed them in his metallic silver Lexus, still with a broken headlight that Paul's mother begged him to fix weeks ago. He could hear his mother murmuring to him and to the EMT, but Paul didn't answer her. He was in pain; moreover, he was afraid. What was wrong with him? Why couldn't he walk? How were his friends going to react the next time they saw him? Were they going to run away like Debbie? He stared at the metal ceiling of the ambulance as they flew through the traffic, siren screaming, tears trickling down his cheeks.

When they arrived, he could hear the EMTs' radios blathering away as they hurriedly wheeled him in. He was still wearing his blood-spattered Braves pajamas.

"His chin's sliced up. He can't walk, either," one of the EMTs yelled into the radio as he and another EMT loaded him into the elevator.

His mother, now escorted by his father, chimed in, "He is on Pancrease, Zithromax, and many other medications. He can't be given any anesthesia. He has cystic fibrosis. He…"

She was cut off by a blast from the radios.

"Let's get him into surgery," a crackly voice responded.

"His mother says he has cystic fibrosis," the EMT shouted back.

"Copy on that," the disembodied voice said, "We'll be really careful with this one."

A nurse stitched up his chin gash and left Paul, still on the stretcher, and his parents in one of the ER rooms until they could figure out what to do with him.

"What do we have here?" a tall, gray-haired ER doctor asked Paul's parents as he strode into the cramped room after Paul had been stitched.

His parents' faces were ashen, and they just sat there looking from Paul to the doctor, willing him to tell them what was wrong. Dr. Peters started poking and prodding the boy. He immediately ruled out paralysis, since Paul had feeling in his legs.

After a few hours and a bunch of tests—X-rays, an MRI and other fairly painless procedures—Dr. Peters looked at Paul's chart and had an answer.

"Mrs. Morgan, is Paul on Averpril?"

"Yes," she quickly responded.

"Well, that's the culprit then," he told Paul and his parents as they huddled together in the tiny ER room. "The drug has caused his legs to lose ligament strength. This is very rare, but there have been a few cases where this happened. This is a relatively new drug. Did his CF doctor put him on it?"

"Yes," his father responded, "He read us the list of side effects and was hesitant to prescribe Averpril, but we felt the potential positives far outweighed the negatives."

"Can he go off the medicine?" his mother interrupted.

"I would not recommend Paul going off the medication, because without it he will only get sicker. It's not the type of drug that you can start and suddenly stop. Averpril stays in your system for several months regardless if he stops taking it or not. He will have to deal with this side effect, unfortunately."

"What does that mean, doctor?" his dad asked calmly, checking out Paul's reaction from the corner of his eye. "Will he walk again?"

The doctor asked Paul's parents to confer with him outside the room. Paul was visibly concerned. He knew the doctor wasn't telling them something.

"Mr. Morgan, all of Paul's signs look good for a quick recovery, but as I noted before, we've had a few cases like this and anything can happen."

Paul's father asked about the other cases, so Dr. Peters recalled what he had read.

"One patient was able to walk within months. Some, it took a bit longer, but there are others who…"

"Who what?" Paul's mother interrupted.

"Who never walked again, but they still were able to lead a relatively normal life and I don't think Paul will be one of those individuals."

Paul's father was devastated. He knew that Dr. Peters was trying to be as positive as he could, but Paul's father, being a great athlete, wanted children who could share his passion for sports. Garey was an exceptional athlete. Paul, on the other hand, would potentially be handicapped for the rest of his life. Paul's parents embraced and agreed never to share the worst case scenario with their son. They wanted to keep his hopes up, but seeing their expressionless faces, Paul knew they were distraught over whatever the doctor told them.

Since Paul needed the medication, Dr. Peters advised that he use a wheelchair for a while.

After Dr. Peters left the room, Paul started crying again.

"This is so not fair!" he wailed. Disturbing thoughts crossed his mind. Now he wouldn't be a hero at school—he'd be a disabled person in a wheelchair. He'd have to endure ridicule from his classmates. What 10-year-old wants that? "I'm not going back to school," he announced as he clenched his fists around the bed sheets. "Why would God do this to me?" he demanded. "What did I do wrong?"

"Honey, Paul," his mother quickly said, to cut off Paul's tirade, "we'll deal with this. I promise you we'll get you physical therapy, anything we can do to see that you're walking before you start school next year."

Paul's mother was trying to convince herself as much as she was trying to persuade him that he'd walk again. She blamed herself for her son's predicament. She believed she was not protective enough, which in Paul's mind, couldn't have been further from the truth. Maybe she should have done research on that medication before her son started taking it. She blamed herself for having the gene that contributed to her son having cystic fibrosis. Her guilt tore her up inside.

"And if any kids make fun of you, we'll deal with that too," she said.

Paul knew what that meant. Because he was sick, his mom was so overprotective. She'd been known to call school to make sure he'd eaten his corn beef sandwich and vegetable soup at lunch and gone to the nurse to get his medicine before class. His mom was the one who did his postural drainage every morning, since his dad had to be at work at 6 a.m. every day. Postural drainage was the procedure where his mother would cup her hands and hit him on his sides, back, and front for thirty minutes a day to loosen the phlegm that filled his lungs.

Much like his mother, Paul's dad also felt guilty about his condition. Since he was responsible for the other gene that caused the dreaded ailment in his son, he blamed himself. Paul had overheard him one time telling his mother how sad he gets every time he thinks about what his son has to go through—the medicines, breathing exercises, coughing fits and pain.

Paul and his father realized they had little in common—his father played basketball, football and baseball in high school but Paul wasn't much of an athlete. Paul's father had more in common with Garey, who he would always talk baseball with or discuss who would win the Super Bowl. With Paul, it was "how are you feeling?" and "did you take your medicine?"

Those types of questions depressed his youngest son. "What does Dad think of me?" he asked his brother.

"Paul, dad loves you, but he is very protective of you," Garey replied. "Almost as protective as mom, if that's possible. We just have two over-protective parents and we have to deal with that."

Garey, though, wasn't like his parents. Six years older than Paul, Garey was always giving his younger brother pep talks and pushing him to be a better person. He brightened a little when he thought of him helping Paul get out of the wheelchair. While his parents didn't want Paul to hurt himself by trying too hard, Garey always told him to work for everything he wanted, regardless of the pain he endured. He stressed that if his little brother put in the effort, he would succeed.

Paul sure needed to succeed in the next couple of weeks. After all, baseball season was right around the corner.

Chapter 4
The Puzzle

Three years later, Paul was still in a wheelchair. Playing baseball was no longer an option. While there were some kids who were friendly to him, he was considered "unique" because he was the only kid in school with a wheelchair. Paul didn't need a dictionary to know that to teenagers, "unique" was never good.

His lack of ligament strength perplexed the doctors. After all, he'd been off of Averpril for two years now and if he was going to walk again, he should have been at least on crutches by now. They blamed his slow recovery on his lack of exercise. Well, "who could exercise from a wheelchair?" Paul lamented. He knew he wasn't motivated. He would roll his wheelchair up to the sliding glass door and silently watch as his neighbors played hundreds of baseball games in his backyard. Delta would sit along side and lick his arm. Paul would let Delta run around the yard as he recalled the days when he could run along side his dog.

He had given up playing outside with the kids in the neighborhood, even though there still were many things he could do. Because he always looked so sad and angry, he became the outcast of the neighborhood. No one remembered the game-winning single off Josh Wilson anymore.

Paul also was the only kid in school who had to report to the principal's office for medication, since his mom was afraid he'd lose his pills. He coughed so much that kids sitting next to him used to ask him if he was going to die. Kids can be cruel in middle school. There was no subject that was off limits—not even death. The scary thing was that Paul didn't know anything about his life expectancy. He was too afraid to ask his parents, or even the doctors. A lot of times he would come home from school crying because he started to believe what the kids were saying. Maybe he *was* going to die. In the past three years, he'd become increasingly out of breath and was noticeably sicker. Doctors not only blamed it on his lack of exercise but on the progression of cystic fibrosis.

One kid in particular made sure Paul knew he stood out. For some reason, Biff Goolson hated him. At 14 years old, six-feet tall and 200 pounds, Biff, with his brown buzz cut and constant black clothes, was literally the biggest bully in school. He'd make a point of going up to other guys, gripping their bicep and be able to touch his fingers to his thumb while doing it. He'd laugh hysterically like it was some big joke that other 13-year-olds didn't have grown-men muscles like he did. He would steal your lunch and then, his lust for humiliation not fully sated, flush your head in the toilet. This teenage scourge had joined Ross J. Goldman Middle School toward the end of last year.

On the first day of seventh grade, outside the building before classes started, a crowd of students gathered to snicker as Biff put rocks under Paul's wheelchair so he couldn't move.

"Leave me alone!" Paul shouted, trying in vain to push Biff's broad shoulders away from him. Then Biff threw eggs in Paul's face and called him names like, "Puzzle," because, like a puzzle, Paul had fallen to pieces. There was nothing Paul could do. He was embarrassed that he was so weak. Biff finally ran off when some teachers came out to see what all the commotion was about. Mrs. Donnelson, the playground monitor, brought Paul a wash cloth and removed the rocks. He would smell like frustrated omelet the rest of the day.

One day Biff was even more sinister. On the playground, he asked Paul to do ten pull-ups. He knew Paul couldn't do anything physical, much less pull-ups.

"Come on, Puzzle," he chided him. "Every girl in our class can do ten pull-ups."

Everyone started laughing at Paul, including Debbie Adams, who hadn't spoken a single word to him since the day she saw him bloodied and hauled off in an ambulance in fourth grade. Paul was completely humiliated and more alienated than ever.

"I hate this stupid wheelchair," he mumbled to himself. "I hate it!"

Suddenly, Biff toppled Paul and his chair over, spilling Paul on the ground. Then the heartless monster grabbed the wheelchair and started riding in it himself, giggling as he tore around the blacktop.

"Look at me! I'm Paul the Puzzle!" he shouted. Sitting helplessly on the ground, Paul started to cry. He had never hated his life more than he did at that very moment of spirit-crushing humiliation. He was sick of being pushed around and ridiculed by some bullying jerk.

Problem was, there was nothing he could do about it. If he told adults, Biff would be punished and torment him even more the next time. If he told no one, he was still going to be bullied everyday. He glanced at the faces of the other students standing around. Although they looked at him with pity in their eyes, they did nothing to help. "Why won't you help me?" he shouted in disgust. None of them responded. He felt so helpless and alone. Biff rode the wheelchair over next to Paul, still crumpled on the ground. Staring Paul straight in the eyes, he shoved the chair down the hill next to him. It rolled several hundred feet, gaining speed on the way down, before crashing into an oak tree. On impact, one of the wheels flew off.

Paul wanted to punch him right then, but he had about as much strength in his whole body as Biff had in his little finger. Then Biff threw a rock that hit Paul right between the eyes on the bridge of his nose. Blood spewed from Paul's nose as Biff yelled, "You'll never get out of that wheelchair! Game over!"

Paul never forgot those words. "Game over" was Biff's credo, his version of "I always win."

Paul was lying on the ground, face in the grass, while blood continued to ooze out. He didn't know which was worse, the pain or the fact that he was embarrassed to ever show his face at school again. From out of nowhere—which is always where teachers seemed to be when Biff was around—Mrs. Donnelson ran over asking what happened. Rather than risk further torture from Biff, Paul told her he fell. Her doubtful look told Paul she knew better, but she helped him up and into the broken wheelchair, rushing him away from the blacktop into the nurse's office. It was a bumpy ride not only for his body, but also for his self-esteem as the whole episode flashed through his mind again.

Paul never told his teacher or his parents the truth about what happened. He knew his mother would pull him out of school and he'd just end up an outcast somewhere else. He did tell Garey, though. He was the only one he could tell because he knew he wouldn't tell their parents. After school, he lay in bed and listened to Garey scream at Biff on the phone to leave his younger brother alone. Paul appreciated his brother for sticking up for him, but it didn't stop Biff from bothering him. In fact, it probably made it worse.

Every day for the next two months Biff sought him out for more punishment. In P.E., he would do ten pull-ups, and then ridicule Paul by offering what he knew was the impossible challenge to match him. The kids would look at their scrawny classmate and laugh. Paul hated going to school each day. He dreaded seeing Biff in the halls. Whenever their eyes met, Biff would give an evil smirk and sometimes slap him on the top of the head.

"You have your brother fighting your fights for you, huh, Puzzle," he would say.

The worst was that although they didn't have any of the same classes, they both went to lunch at the same time. Biff would grab Paul's lunch and eat it in front of him, then pour the vanilla pudding over his head. Every day, he would end up in the boy's bathroom rinsing the gooey yellow mess out of his hair. It became a cruel ritual. And because Paul was wearing more lunch than he was eating, he got skinnier by the day.

There were a few people who didn't laugh at him. Kevin Oates and Tony Romano would come to his rescue when Biff Goolson was in a torturous mood, if they happened to be around.

Kevin was known as the smartest kid in school. That made him an outcast of a different sort—kids made fun of him because he was brilliant. He even left school during the day to take classes at a nearby college. He was short and blonde, and wore a pair of glasses with frames the size of Michelin tires. The kids called him Ralphie because he looked like the kid from the movie, *A Christmas Story*. He most likely helped Paul because he knew all too well what it was like to be ridiculed.

Tony was different, though. Popular and athletic, he was the biggest guy in their class, after Biff. Tony's long brown hair, muscular arms, and dark complexion made him a hit with all the girls. He was on the baseball team with Biff and even though Paul could not play, he and Tony loved to talk sports. They traded baseball cards every Sunday at Tony's house or Paul's house, whichever had the best snacks. Tony usually got the better end of the deal, but Paul often did that on purpose so his buff friend would continue to hang out with him. Tony kind of felt sorry for Paul because his own younger brother was in a wheelchair, paralyzed from a car accident two years earlier.

With his daily—sometimes hourly—hardships and humiliations, it was a wonder Paul made decent grades but he did. He knew he could do better but feeling sorry for himself made it tough to study sometimes. Besides, he'd shrug silently to himself, he didn't think his grades were going to get him a good job because he was a skinny kid in a wheelchair, anyway. Who would hire him? Heck, he couldn't ever leave his parents' house because his mom did his postural drainage everyday. Therefore, he couldn't go to overnight camp or spend the night at a friend's house—not that he was ever invited to.

He was always depressed. He blamed kids like Biff for hurting his feelings. He blamed doctors for giving him the medication that prevented him from walking. He blamed his parents for having him. He blamed his only two friends in the world, Tony and Kevin, for not always being there when Biff beat him up. He blamed God for making him what he was.

His mother constantly reminded him that most people as sick as he was lived in the hospital. Therefore, so he wouldn't end up there, he had to be cautious and could never afford to risk his health. He had a note from his mother that basically prevented him from doing anything strenuous due to his "condition." It was embarrassing to Paul. Perhaps even worse—he began to accept it. During P.E., which he used to love, he'd sit on the sidelines and watch the other kids play baseball—the game he had such a passion for.

"Throw it here," he'd hear them roar to each other. Occasionally, a tear would appear in the corner of Paul's eye as he'd wonder how good of a baseball player he could have been. He knew more about baseball than his physical education teacher, Coach Moxley. To try and keep Paul's spirits up, Coach Moxley would quiz him about baseball facts but he could never stump him. The coach felt bad that while the other kids played, Paul couldn't do much. His classmates knew it, too. He'd sit there on the sidelines and often wonder why kids like Biff Goolson could smell his weaknesses like a Doberman that senses fear in a surprised burglar.

Oh, how he dreamed of playing baseball, literally. That same dream had stayed with Paul since he was ten years old. Since he was now stuck in a wheelchair, playing baseball in the major leagues seemed an unreachable dream, yet he still had it several nights a month. But every time he woke up, he was still the sick kid in a wheelchair.

One afternoon, after a particularly hurtful Biff Goolson episode, during which Biff told him "You'll always be the Puzzle," Paul wheeled himself into the boy's locker room to be alone. School would be over in twenty minutes and he wanted no one else to make fun of him that day. He began questioning what the point of life was and why he'd been treated so unfairly. He knew he was too young to be worried about the meaning of life.

That's when Biff walked in and spat out his most ominous warning yet.

"I've had absolutely enough of you, Puzzle. You need to leave my school. I'm going to kick your butt all over this locker room!"

"Leave me alone!" Paul shouted as he slowly backed away in his chair. "I never did anything to you!"

"Well, I'm about to clean your clock you little runt." Suddenly, Biff drew back his right hand, made it into a fist, and punched Paul's left cheekbone just below his eye socket. The haymaker landed with such force that Paul tumbled to the ground while his wheelchair crashed into the locker. His eye swelled shut almost instantly. He couldn't get up. Biff grabbed his legs and dragged him like a sack of garbage to a green trash can that was already half-full of old food and used paper towels. With a straight face, Biff threw Paul in the can as nonchalantly as if it were kitchen trash his mother had ordered him to take out.

It all happened so fast. Thinking he'd escaped the rest of the day without any more torment, Paul found himself stuffed in a trash can like useless waste. His vision was blurred from the shot he took to the face and the blow to the head he got from hitting the floor had him nearly unconscious.

Biff attached a note to the garbage can and rolled it outside as carpools started to arrive. All the kids saw the spectacle and stopped to read the note on the trash can.

"My name is The Puzzle. I can't do ten pull-ups and some day soon I will die because I'm a pathetic piece of trash!"

As if that wasn't bad enough, that's when the pain kicked in. Not the pain from being hit in the face, falling on his head or being dragged across the floor, but something far more excruciating. His chest started stinging and heaving, like someone had just thrown darts all over it. He gasped for air and began to cough uncontrollably. Panicked, he tried to scream for help.

"Help me, please!" he blurted out. One of the parents from the carpool line pulled him from the can and tried to calm him down before Coach Moxley finally showed up and called 9-1-1.

Soon, the familiar sound of sirens arrived at Ross J. Goldman Middle School. As he lay in the ambulance, his eye black and blue, his chest feeling like the ambulance had parked on it, staring at the ceiling for the second time in three years, Paul thought again about dying. He began to shake uncontrollably. What was happening to him? The EMT tried to calm him down.

"Has this happened to you before? Are you allergic to any medications?" the EMT asked.

"No," Paul gasped. "But…but…" he struggled to turn over his emergency medical bracelet so the EMT could read it.

"Cystic fibrosis!"

Chapter 5
The Hospital Stay

Paul arrived at St. Luke's Memorial Hospital as a 13-year-old for what he thought would be a brief visit. But days turned into weeks. Weeks stretched into months. Months agonizingly became years.

Room 205 was his home for two years. One bright spot was Nurse Ingrid Johanson. She had huge blue eyes, long blonde hair and curves in all the right places. Back home in Sweden, she told him, she had been a swimsuit model. He saw Nurse Johanson, whom he thought to be in her mid-20s, almost every day. He had a major crush on her. She might have known, but then again, she was nice to everyone.

Nurse Johanson also took care of Paul at home as a favor to his family, with whom she had grown very close. She even took Delta for long walks when Paul's mom was too tired. The one week or so a month he actually got to stay at home, she would come and see him every day, adjust his medications, fluff his pillows, tend to his needs. As much as he enjoyed seeing a swimsuit model every day, he would have traded it just to have a "normal" life that didn't make him feel like a failure.

Days at the hospital were tough. There wasn't much to do but watch lousy daytime TV, work on lessons the school sent home to his mother and read comic books. He also spent a lot of time inside his head. He posed the most horrible questions to himself. "Am I going to live to see my 20s? When can I get away from this place? Why was I put in this position?"

By the time he was 15, the weight of it all had sunk him into a serious depression. He wished he could enjoy life like everyone else. Most of his old classmates were shooting hoops, going to school dances and thinking about which college they might attend. Paul, on the other hand, sat in his hospital room and moped all day. The most excitement he had was when the hospital served red Jell-O instead of green. He would sarcastically tell his visitors he was serving a prison term with an occasional parole for good health.

Paul thought back and realized he had been nine when he really understood how bad cystic fibrosis was. One night, he was lying on his parents' bed channel surfing. A talk show was on TV, and the host had just introduced a boy with cystic fibrosis, Dave Compton. The boy was twelve and had a tube in his throat and an oxygen tank to help him breathe. He looked pale and gaunt, and was as slender as a rope. He spoke in a hoarse, laboring voice about how, after his recent lung transplant, the doctors had told him he might not live another year. During the show's ending credits, a message flashed across the screen.

"Dave Compton passed away from cystic fibrosis two weeks after this show was taped. May he rest in peace."

After the show, Paul ran straight to his room and cried. He knew he had cystic fibrosis. Only then did he know he had a disease that could rob him of his life. That night in the living room he screamed at his parents.

"Why did I have to find out from some stupid talk show that I'm going to die?" he yelled. "Why didn't you tell me?"

Although his mother had always tried to control herself in front of him when talking about his illness, she suddenly started bawling.

"We're s-s-sorry, P-Paul," she sputtered between sobs. "We wanted to tell you. We j-j-just didn't know how. We always thought that they'd find treatments or a c-c-cure and we'd never have to go through this moment."

That was unacceptable, even to a nine-year-old. He couldn't think of words to describe the fear and intense anger he felt, so he said the words that he knew would hurt his parents.

"I hate you!" he shouted. "I hate you! I hate you!"

His outburst hit home. His mother looked at him like he'd slapped her. Too shocked to respond, she whirled around and sprinted upstairs. His father just stood there, gaping at him. Paul thought his dad was trying to tell his son that he was sorry, but he couldn't move his lips to form the words. Then he saw a few tears fall from his father's eyes. Paul felt slightly guilty standing there, but his rage kept him from finding any words, either. Instead, they both just stood there, looking at each other, sizing each other up. After what felt like an eternity but was in reality only a minute, the silence was broken.

"Go to your room, son," Paul's dad said softly, trying to calm the situation. "We'll talk about this later."

Later never came. Paul kind of convinced himself that his cystic fibrosis was not as bad as the kid's on TV. He was different, he thought. That was before everything happened, from being handicapped to the pulsating pains in his chest. He would later find out the chest pains were caused by a hiatal hernia—another obstacle in his life that he believed he would never overcome. Now he just accepted the fact that cystic fibrosis was the disease that was going to steal his life away from him.

Paul had to take a lot of medicine, including pills with every meal to help him digest food since his pancreas needed the help. Daily, he endured pains in his chest and stomach, like having heartburn every moment of his life, not something many adolescents can relate to. He also had occasional bacterial infections—he would get a bad cold, and it weakened his lungs, which let in more bacteria. Most people take a week or less to get over a cold, but it would take him several weeks. Some days his throat hurt so much he had trouble swallowing. When that happened, he didn't want anyone near him because he felt so frustrated and cranky. Sometimes the pains in his body would get so agonizing that he needed a pill just to sleep.

Every day, he had to do what was called chest therapy for thirty minutes. He would put on a vest that vibrated to shake up the mucous in his lungs. The machine looked like something from a science-fiction movie—it had a metallic skeleton with piping on the inside. One of his old roommates at the hospital called it, "The Monster." The thing sounded like a speedboat taking off from the dock. This was a new device, put on the market a few years before, which would assist people with pulmonary difficulties. As much as he hated using the machine, it was better than the alternative –his mom furiously hitting the back, sides and front of his torso in several different places for thirty minutes a day. Postural drainage was kind of painful, especially when his mom forgot to take off her wedding ring, not to mention that he could not watch his favorite television shows while his mom pummeled him.

The vest was very expensive and only a few families could afford it. His parents planned on having one for him at home during his one-week visits, within the next few months. After he used the vest he would hack up wads of mucous, and then examine them to make sure it wasn't blood. Sometimes, he'd close his eyes, spit in the toilet, and flush because he didn't want to know

what color the mucous was. Paul was so scared to look at it for fear it would
be red. It sounds gross, but the colors he had to look for were like a traffic
light: if his mucous was green or yellow, he had to be careful. If it was red, he
had to stop whatever he was doing and call his doctor. Paul found it
disgusting and, at times, agonizing to have daily mucous examinations. But
such is the life of someone with CF.

All in all, Paul swallowed about forty pills per day. He used to joke that on
New Year's Eve, while most people shouted "Happy New Year," he
celebrated by popping his fourth antibiotic. But he wasn't very responsible
when it came to taking his pills. He would forget sometimes or just didn't
want to be burdened with opening the dresser drawer to get them at other
times. Because he was not taking his pills the way he was supposed to, the
food was not digesting correctly and he would have terrible stomach aches.
But sometimes he felt it was a small price to pay. The way he looked at it,
none of his old school friends had to take medications, so why should he? If
pain was the price for normalcy, well, then Paul was willing to endure the
anguish.

Meeting people with cystic fibrosis was not an option for Paul as his
parents prohibited it. There were cases in cystic fibrosis camps where
patients spread bacterial infections to each other that remained in their
systems and eventually killed them. As if it wasn't bad enough to have a life-
threatening disease, it was tougher for Paul that he had no one to empathize
with him. He felt like he was part of a leper colony. The Internet was a huge
help to him, because he could talk to other CF kids his age and they knew what
each other was feeling. One person he met online was Michael McBride from
Carson City, Nevada. He was six months younger than Paul and had eight
siblings. They met in a CF teen chat room and began e-mailing and instant-
messaging every day. They agreed to meet one day when there was a cure for
cystic fibrosis. Michael was by far the stronger of the two emotionally as
evidenced by his online moniker, CFdestroyer1.

"We should meet on Oprah's show," he once IM'ed Paul.

"Oprah?" Paul wrote back, a little surprised. *"You like her?"*

*"Sure! What's not to like? She's rich, she gets all the coolest guests and
she's on during the day when there's barely anything else to watch when
you've got that vest on. Right?"*

Paul laughed. There weren't many people who understood what it was
like to wear an inflatable vest for half an hour. He had his own dream about
where he'd meet Michael. Actually, it was a general fantasy, but he liked the

idea of them meeting while Michael was in the stands of his first Major League Baseball game. Before all the medical setbacks, Paul thought he might actually make it to the bigs some day. Now, he knew there was a better chance he'd sprout wings and fly. But Michael had just received a lung transplant and was recovering. His spirits were high, even though the odds of survival decrease after a lung transplant. In general, though, Michael had a very positive attitude about life and if anyone could survive a lung transplant, it was CFdestroyer1.

Paul wasn't on the list for a lung transplant, though. You could only get on the list if your lung function was a certain number on a scale, and Paul's numbers were low, but not low enough that the doctors could recommend a transplant. Every couple of months he had to test his lung function to update his numbers. He had to blow into a tube as hard as he could five times and afterwards he would have to inhale as quickly as possible. By the fifth blow, he was usually pretty light-headed. No matter how hard he tried, his numbers seldom got better. Garey would try a little sarcasm to cheer him up.

"Dude, you need to exercise," his brother would chide.

"How am I supposed to do that when I'm hospitalized in a wheelchair twenty-four hours a day? Should I do wheelies around the nurse's station?" Paul would snap back with an obnoxious tone in his voice. Garey would roll his eyes and chuckle, then tousle his younger brother's hair. Garey didn't mind Paul's sarcastic retort. What upset Garey was Paul's pessimism and lack of effort to have a better attitude.

From his room in the hospital, Paul could see Turner Field, the brand new baseball stadium near downtown Atlanta. It was built to host the 1996 summer Olympic Games and eventually converted to the home of the Braves. He dreamed about it before it was ever built—the recurring dream he had of getting that game-winning hit. When he fell asleep he never had nightmares. His biggest nightmare came when he woke up to see what his life had become.

Chapter 6
Stan's Plan

Two years in a hospital took a toll on Paul's body. His eyes were always glassy because pain wouldn't allow him to sleep. His pale skin and bony frame made him look like he had just pulled an all-nighter for a mid-term chemistry exam. When the doctors helped him stand up, he was 5-feet, 6-inches tall but weighed a meager 110 pounds. He was so emaciated he was embarrassed to wheel himself around the hospital because he couldn't bear the looks people threw at him. He cried a lot, but not just for himself. Being in the hospital two years seeing other kids come and go meant he had to deal repeatedly with losing hospital roommates who became friends.

He never forgot Stan Blue. Stan was a great guy, his first roommate in 205. He was fourteen years old and had cancer.

"I'm going to be an astronaut," Stan declared one day when they were talking about what they wanted to do when they got out of the hospital.

"Dude, the day you become an astronaut is the day I become a Major League Baseball player," Paul said with a rare laugh. Maybe he shouldn't have made fun of him, but Paul believed he was being totally unrealistic.

He grinned at Paul. "Deal," he said. Though Paul was only kidding, Stan considered it a pact. "You'll see me in a space suit when I come to watch your first game."

One morning, Captain James McTavish, a NASA astronaut who had just been on a spacewalk two weeks before, came into their room. Stan was so excited tears welled in his eyes and he shook all over.

"When you're released, son, I'm going to take you flying," the larger-than-life astronaut told Stan as he sat on the edge of his bed. There was no trace of pity in his voice—he sounded like he really meant it. He handed Stan a space helmet that he wore on one of his missions to put on his dresser. As Captain McTavish left, Paul noticed a man with him who wore a nametag that read, "Make-A-Wish Foundation."

Paul's mom later told him that the Make-A-Wish Foundation grants wishes for children, usually when they don't have many wishes left. Paul never told Stan that—he was too thrilled by the visit and Paul didn't want to upset him.

"See? I'm going to go flying when I get out of here," Stan said, beaming to his roommate. "I'm going to fly with Captain McTavish. I'll fly to watch you play in the Majors."

Paul was impressed with how Stan tried to take care of himself and kept such a good attitude. He did pushups and sit-ups. He'd walk a lot around the hospital. When Paul saw how enthusiastic he was, he began to believe Stan would orbit the earth someday, too.

Part of Paul wanted to believe in himself. If Stan could do it, he wondered, why couldn't he? Then he noticed Stan's hair was falling out, from the cancer treatments. Then he heard the doctors say "terminal" when referring to Stan's case. Then Paul's mom told him what terminal meant. One month later, Stan went into a coma. They were just hanging out in the room, and Paul looked over and it looked like his roommate was sleeping. But all of a sudden, a group of doctors burst in and frantically started poking and prodding Stan. Finally, they came to the conclusion that he was in a coma.

A week later, when Paul had left for his one week of Nurse Johanson catering to his needs at home, he heard from one of the patients across the hall that Stan died. All he could think of was Stan up there, orbiting the earth like an astronaut.

Before he even had the chance to mourn his fallen roommate, another one moved in.

Every time one died, his hopes dwindled even more. Watching a friend die is one thing, but losing four friends before your sixteenth birthday is another. They all had similar outlooks—there wasn't much time left, and they wondered why they were born this way. Every time he'd lose a roommate the hospital would send in some counselor to talk to him but Paul never wanted to, and they'd gradually just go away.

As the months passed, Paul had a hard time believing that he'd be the first kid from Room 205 to be released, but he learned that some of the patients were jealous of him because his case was not as severe as many of theirs. He wasn't even on the transplant list yet. They'd urge him to work harder and tell him he could overcome some of the obstacles that CF put in front of him. He'd read the statistics though, and he'd seen the sad stories on the news of kids with CF who lost the fight. So if he was going to lose anyway, he wondered, why fight in the first place? The statistics and stories had brainwashed him into believing he would be just another casualty in the war against cystic fibrosis.

His doctors showed him statistics and articles on why it was so important to stay in good shape. When he first arrived at age thirteen, the doctors had tried encouraging Paul but now their strategy was to show him the awful things that happen to kids with CF when they don't take care of themselves. While they thought scaring Paul would motivate him, quite the opposite happened. He became apathetic and gave up on his life. He saw Stan work hard like the doctors asked him to, yet he fell short. Why would it be any different for him?

Paul's memories of Biff Goolson also depressed him. He couldn't shake the feelings the bully brought out in him, like he was the biggest loser in the world and couldn't do anything. He had heard that Biff was expelled from school for hitting a teacher, but no matter how far away he was, his menacing face and the words "Game over!" were still fresh in Paul's memory. And he couldn't get the word "Puzzle" out of his mind. Just hearing that word sent chills down his spine like hearing a set of fingernails slowly scratching a chalkboard.

Lying there in St. Luke's he just wanted the terrible pain to end. He coughed so much one time that he broke a rib. He started thinking that if death was the only escape from the pain, well, he wasn't exactly turning away from the issue.

His parents and the doctors all tried to help but he became too depressed to eat. Instead, the doctors put tubes in his arms to give him nutrition. He lost fifteen pounds in two months. He was a living, breathing skeleton. He lost hope almost as quickly as he dropped pounds. His doctors told him and his parents he had to gain weight or there wasn't much they could do. Instead of thinking they were trying to help, Paul thought the doctors were trying to absolve themselves of blame. He could see the obituary already:

"Paul didn't eat, so he died from CF. Doctors are not liable, since they told him that's what would happen."

He still used his wheelchair to get around the hospital. That depressed him even more, because he knew that it wasn't CF that was the reason he couldn't walk. It was still the side effect of the medication he took when he was ten. Due to complaints from parents like Paul's, Averpril was taken off the market. But back then, putting Paul on the new drug seemed to be a no-brainer. It was a breakthrough treatment that had a great effect on several cystic fibrosis patients. Doctors said this complication happened to one out of every 5,000 patients. He wished he'd played the lottery that day instead.

Despite visits from Nurse Johanson, his family and the occasional classmate who was guilt-tripped into visiting by his parents, Room 205 was a very lonely place. His phone never rang and he didn't have anyone he felt like calling. When his family wasn't in the room, his only solace was watching his Atlanta Braves on TV in the spring and summer.

While eating lunch one afternoon, he turned on the TV and saw that the Braves were playing the Chicago Cubs at Wrigley Field. The Jet was pitching. Ricky "The Jet" Kilmer was in his seventh year with the Braves and was the best pitcher he'd ever seen. He'd led the league in strikeouts and wins over the last six seasons. The Jet was his idol. He had 100 baseball cards of just him. His old friend, Tony, who he still traded baseball cards with once in a while, once asked if Paul would trade the Jet's rookie card for a Babe Ruth card. "No way!" he shouted. That was the end of that.

When The Jet pitched, Paul didn't allow anyone to bother him, except Garey, who appreciated the game of baseball as much as his little brother. He required complete silence as he watched the master at work. He would get out his scorekeeper's book, a gift from Garey, to keep track of all of The Jet's pitches. He wasn't sure why he loved The Jet so much. Part of it may have been because he helped his Braves win three division titles. Maybe part of it was that he was breaking records that had lasted several decades. But most likely, the Jet's mound mastery kept Paul's mind off the fact that he was losing the battle to cystic fibrosis.

He continued to have that dream—of playing in the Majors and getting a base hit in his first official at-bat to win the game at Turner Field. Maybe the masked man was an assistant coach for the Braves, he started thinking. Maybe he knew a lot about the pitcher. Paul just couldn't figure out why he'd be wearing a mask. As always, he woke up in the same old hospital bed, very disappointed, with no answers.

He loved watching baseball, but it couldn't compare to playing in that amazing stadium he watched being built before his eyes. As Turner Field came together, he fell more and more apart. He'd think that watching baseball from a hospital bed, watching a stadium being built, was all he was ever going to do. All he'd ever wanted to do since he was ten was play baseball.

Kids are often told to think about their future, but they rarely concern themselves with what life has in store for them. Ironically, Paul thought about his future everyday, but it was doubtful that he'd ever have one.

Chapter 7
Special K

Aside from Braves games and Nurse Johanson, the only thing Paul looked forward to in the hospital was visits from his brother, Garey. He was Paul's best friend, always there to cheer him up. He would stroll in, give his little brother a hug and immediately tell one of his famous "Killer Creek" jokes. That's where he went to high school, and where Paul would be going if he wasn't confined to room 205. The Killer Creek basketball team hadn't won a game in four years—a streak of 115 straight losses. And Garey had about a hundred jokes about the team's futility.

"Hey Paul," he would say, "Where do drums go when they can't be used anymore?"

"I don't know, man," Paul would answer with a smirk, waiting for the punch-line.

"The Killer Creek basketball team's locker room. They don't beat anyone!" Garey would shout. He would always have his little brother hysterical.

Garey wasn't just a comedian; he was a mentor, too. He was the only person Paul told about being tipped off on Josh Wilson's kickball pitch that glorious day in fourth grade.

"That was a bogus hit," Garey said without hesitation when Paul confided his secret. "In this world, we can't depend on others—we have to depend on ourselves first."

"How'd you get to be such the philosopher?" Paul would joke, while still taking his brother's comments seriously.

Garey was also a superb storyteller. Since he was in college and in a fraternity, he would often regale his brother with tales of fraternity shenanigans. Paul loved those stories. He could live vicariously through his older brother. He told Paul that one time one of his fraternity brothers was expelled for indecent exposure during a football game when he mooned a referee for making a bad call against his team. Paul never laughed so hard!

It was because of Garey that Paul was interested in baseball. He was a starting pitcher for the University of Georgia for three years running, rated the best pitcher in Division I-A college baseball by almost every magazine. He had acquired the nickname "Special K" because of the way he struck out batters, since a strikeout is recorded as a K in a scorekeeper's book. He didn't just strike batters out; he made them look especially bad. Some batters would end up in a heap at the plate after spinning themselves into the ground trying to catch up with Garey's fastball, which was clocked in the high 90s. His little brother wished he could be his catcher—even more than he dreamed of being The Jet's catcher.

Garey told him the story of how he and his Georgia team faced the Jet in an exhibition game in Orlando last February. Garey faced The Jet twice and struck out on six pitches, but his claim to fame was that he did meekly foul off two pitches.

When Paul lost his voice from his medication right before his fifteenth birthday, Garey bought him a birthday present—a magnetic board—on which he could spell out messages. He always kept it by his side at the hospital. Garey also gave him 500 magnetic letters since, as he said, "I know you love to talk." The board came in handy when Paul had to tell a nurse he had to use the bathroom—all he had to do was put a "P" on the board!

Garey was his little brother's hero, but he told Paul that one day he would get out of his wheelchair and become a superhero. He'd been telling his little brother that since the day he'd lost the ability to walk. They had watched the movie *Superman* on TV together when Paul was ten years old, and he had told Garey in the way that 10-year-olds have of thinking everything they see on TV is real, "That's what I'd like to do someday. I'd love to fly. I'd love to be a superhero."

"Ok, little man," he said. "You're going to beat CF and you'll fly. I will see to it that you are the greatest superhero that the world has ever seen."

Paul didn't know if he believed him, but Garey was dead serious. He would scold his little brother when he talked negatively. Secretly, Paul was glad Garey kept trying to pump him up.

His big brother had three goals they talked about every time he visited his little brother in the hospital: Paul would beat the disease and become a superhero, they would both become Major League Baseball players and Paul would get that first hit to win a Major League game just like in his dream.

Paul's favorite pastime when Garey visited was to trade baseball cards and memorize the stats of their favorite players. Paul and Tony used to trade cards, but Tony stopped coming to the hospital several months ago. He had hinted to Paul that the hospital scene depressed him. Thanks to Garey, Paul hardly noticed his friend's absence. Garey would grill his brother on the Braves players.

"What was The Jet's ERA in August?" he'd ask.

"2.12," Paul shot back before Garey's last syllable escaped his mouth.

"How many homeruns did Fred McGriff hit in May?"

"Seven. Eight if you include the one that was taken away due to a rain-postponed game," his little brother said proudly.

"Nice," Garey would answer. "How many times did the Braves lose two in a row this season?"

"Fifteen," he answered. If only life was this easy, Paul thought to himself.

No matter how hard he tried, Garey couldn't stump Paul on anything to do with his beloved Braves. Some days Garey came by 205 just to watch a Braves game with him. He would bring hotdogs and Cracker Jacks, and, decked out in their Braves shirts and hats, they would scream at the television like they were in the nose-bleed section of the stadium. His roommates in 205 would usually laugh but then close the curtain between them, allowing them their fun. One time, a nurse came in to see Paul's roommate and shook her head at them with an annoyed look on her face, as if they'd gone a little overboard. To lighten the mood, Garey asked her if she could get them some cotton candy. They laughed like loud hyenas that entire day.

Garey came in early one day, about two hours before a big Braves-Mets game. It wasn't that the game meant a lot in the standings; it's just that The Jet was shooting for his twelfth straight win. Garey brought in their traditional hotdogs and Cracker Jacks. He also had a bag with a ketchup bottle, a mustard jar, and two packets of relish. That day he showed his little brother how to create a scrumptious hotdog. There was way more to it than simply squirting some ketchup and mustard on the dog. Oh, no, there was actually a science to creating the perfect dog. Step by step, Garey led him through the process. It all started with a small plastic knife.

"First, you cut the foil to remove the hotdog," he said as he slowly sliced open the aluminum wrapper that kept the dog warm, allowing the aroma of the hotdog to fill the room. "Then you spray a line of ketchup along the topside of the hotdog. Next, you spray a line of golden mustard along the lower section of the dog."

Paul was eating up the drill with as much fervor as he would the dog itself.

"Finally, you squirt two packets of fresh relish until they are both empty," Garey's tutorial continued, building to a taste-teasing climax. "You close the dog, but you don't re-wrap it in foil because the foil takes most of the condiments off and makes it really messy to eat. Just put a napkin under it."

"What's next?" Paul asked, his mouth starting to water in anticipation.

"You bite into it and the result is the best hotdog you've ever had," Garey said, proudly. And after one bite, Paul agreed. Hotdogs and Cracker Jacks became as much a part of baseball to Paul as ball and bat. Learning to dress a ballpark frank was one of the best times he'd had with his big brother.

Garey sent Paul a baseball from every game he won in college. Because of that, Paul had about 60 baseballs in a big glass case that he kept under the bed in his room at home. He had arranged them in order by the significance of the game. Garey would autograph and write the game's storyline on each ball. Paul's number-three ranked ball was from Garey's no-hitter against the Florida Gators in a Southeastern Conference tournament game in Tuscaloosa, Alabama. His number two-ranked ball was from the second round of the NCAA tournament in Houston, where he struck out ten Tennessee Volunteers. His number-one ball was the one he shut out the Oklahoma Sooners with in the National Championship Game.

Everyone knew Garey was destined to become a famous baseball player. Their father, an avid Braves fan, named him after Gary Mathews, a star outfielder for the Braves for many years. Dad loved the way Mathews flew out from under his helmet when he sprinted out of the batter's box. He changed the spelling to Garey because he'd never seen the name spelled that way, and he wanted Garey to know that he was one of a kind. One day, Garey said, he would pitch along side The Jet.

"Can you imagine a double-header rotation of The Jet and Special K?" he asked.

"Sure, I could," Paul smiled. "Maybe my doctor will let me out of the hospital that day to go and watch."

"When I get to play with The Jet, I'll get you his autograph and I'll make sure he comes to visit you," Garey assured Paul.

Though Paul tried to act excited, deep down he began to wonder if he would be around to see his brother pitch in the big leagues. A coughing spasm immediately ensued; a constant message from cystic fibrosis that it was in control. And at that moment, a little bit of depression seeped in and the questions that tortured him worse than Biff Goolson crept back into his mind.

Why am I sick? Why is life so unfair? What did I do wrong?

Right before Garey returned to the Georgia campus in Athens, he learned that he was projected to be a top-ten pick in the college draft. That meant a signing bonus of over one million dollars! No way could he turn that kind of money down, so he decided to turn pro instead of returning for his senior year at Georgia. He told Paul the first thing he'd do with the money was give half to the Cystic Fibrosis Foundation, and then he would get a big-screen TV for 205 so he could watch him pitch. He said he'd make sure the television had Picture-In-Picture so he could watch two games at once. He told him it would come in handy that rare occasion when he and The Jet pitched the same day on different channels.

Paul got a letter every day from Garey when he was away at college. When Paul was in so much pain that his shaking made it impossible to read the letter, his mom read it aloud for him.

Dear Paul,

I pitched a two-hit shutout today against the Wildcats. We won, 3-0. I saw a scout from the Cubs in the stands. He wrote something on his little pad each time I let a pitch go. The Cubs have the first pick in the draft, so I'm hoping they take me. I'm sure that Mom and Dad would be upset if I moved to Chicago, but I could always go to Atlanta as a free agent some day. I promise you that I will send you a baseball for every game I win at the Major League level. Those baseballs are a part of me and I want you to have them.

How is everything? Did they serve you the meatloaf again today? Dude, that meatloaf walked on its own, last time. Hey, if the meatloaf can walk, then so will you some day. Stay motivated and push yourself. Keep taking your medications. How are Mom and Dad? I miss you pal. Don't give up hope. When you're a superhero, don't forget about your big brother.

Hey, the Braves have the third pick in the draft. If they draft me, I'm going to get you released from the hospital so you can meet all the players in the dugout. Then you can watch the game from the dugout, and get autographs from the whole team. I bet you can't wait to meet The Jet. How does that sound?

I love you, Paul.

From your older brother,

Garey Ethan Morgan

The letters would always end with:

"I love you, Paul. From your older brother, Garey Ethan Morgan"

He always wrote out his full name. When Paul became a superhero or Major League Baseball player one day, Garey explained, he didn't want his little brother to forget his brother's name. They'd both heard that fame changed people but it would never change the relationship he and his brother had.

Fame was something Garey was used to. Something that happened when he was eleven years old made him a neighborhood legend. One summer afternoon, the neighbor from three houses down, Mr. White, knocked on the Morgan's front door. He had this smirk on his face along with an expression that made him look both surprised and amused at the same time.

"Your son hit a baseball that broke our window to pieces," he told Mrs. Morgan.

She put her hands to her face and said, "Oh, Ed, I'm so very sorry. I won't let Garey into your yard again."

"Well, actually," Mr. White began to explain with a smile and awe-struck expression, "that's the amazing thing. You see, he hit it from *your* yard."

"That's about 250 feet, isn't it?" their mom asked, incredulous.

"Sure is," Mr. White replied, turning to head back home. Then, over his shoulder, "You don't have to pay me for the window. Just slip me a percentage of his signing bonus when he makes it to the big leagues."

By the time Garey was fifteen, pro scouts were already watching him. Heck, he could even outrun Delta, who ran circles around everyone else. Paul at age fifteen was trapped in a hospital bed. Sure he envied Garey's life, especially the potential future that he had. But his jealousy didn't stop him from rooting for his big brother to succeed, since he took such good care of his little brother.

What Paul really loved about Garey was that he never felt sorry for his little brother. Whenever he cried to his big brother, Garey told Paul that when he overcomes his obstacles, he would be stronger for it. Garey said Paul wasn't special because he had an illness, but because he fought the illness.

He didn't really fight the way Garey wanted him to, though. Garey always told him to push himself so he could become that superhero. Paul just didn't have much fight in him but that didn't keep Garey from trying. He bought his little brother a subscription to *Pro Bodybuilding* magazine.

On the first anniversary of Paul's hospital stay, when he was fourteen, Garey sent him a box wrapped with blue paper and a green ribbon. He thought it was a barbell or something—another way Garey was pushing him to work out. He realized by holding it that it was far too light to be any type of weight. When he opened it, he was surprised to find a pendant shaped like a baseball. The pendant was silver on the outside, and when you opened it up, there was a silver "K" inside, representing his nickname. Their names were inscribed on the vertical line of the "K." Paul's eyes flooded with tears as he read the accompanying letter.

Dear Paul,

Enjoy the pendant. When you can't reach me, rub that pendant and know that I'm thinking of you. I bought myself a pendant that looks just like the one I gave you. That way, when I'm on the mound, I'll rub it on television so you can see that I'm thinking of you. If you see me rubbing it, maybe you can rub yours too. It will be our way to communicate secretly. I think that's pretty neat, don't you?

The draft is right around the corner. I hope to go to the Braves so I'm closer to you. Just remember to never forget me when you become a superhero. I love you, Paul.

From your older brother,

Garey Ethan Morgan

Paul wore the pendant every day in the hospital. He'd sooner take off his clothes in public than remove his new treasure. Sometimes he felt like it protected him. It was like having Garey with him all the time and that was better than any medication a doctor could ever prescribe.

Chapter 8
The Life of a Failure

Those two years in Room 205 gave Paul a lot of time to think. And it wasn't good thinking.

"I must have been born this way for a reason," he'd say to himself. "Maybe God saw me as a bad seed. Maybe I did something wrong in a past life."

Lying there all by himself staring at the ceiling, the florescent lights staring back down at him, he felt so broken. Maybe he felt fragile because he had a mother who treated him like a delicate soufflé in the oven that would implode if she made the slightest noise. Maybe it was people like Biff Goolson who made him feel so weak. Maybe he felt vulnerable because he had an illness that doctors predicted would take his life much too soon. Any of these reasons alone would make someone feel hurt but to have dealt with all three, it was no wonder why Paul's will to live was wearing thin.

He remembered when a doctor brought some medical school students to look in on patients on the second floor during daily rounds. Paul heard him whisper to the group that this was the "chronically ill" level. A herd of five or six of these trainees, who didn't look much older than Paul in their ill-fitting white lab coats and awkward smiles, gathered around his bed in the middle of the room. A random doctor from the second floor read from Paul's chart.

"Paul has cystic fibrosis. His pulmonary numbers have slowly declined since he was first admitted. He cannot walk due to a medication he took. Paul's been here for over three years now."

Paul got sick of hearing his chart read to every new group of interns. Sometimes he just wanted a doctor to say, "He has CF, but he'll be fine." In the hundreds of walk-throughs that physicians and medical students made, he never heard those words. He felt like a goldfish trapped in a bowl as the fresh-faced students stared at him and said things they must have thought would make him feel better.

"Wow, you're so inspiring! You're so brave." He would smile back cynically—how amazing that he could inspire people just by lying in a hospital bed. Really, he'd rather inspire them by hitting a four-hundred-fifty-foot homerun into the upper deck of Turner Field.

He didn't feel like any of those interns genuinely cared about his name or what his hobbies were. As far as they were concerned, he was just the sick kid in room 205. Garey nicknamed Paul "205." He said he would ask Major League Baseball if he could be the first player to wear a three-digit number on his uniform to honor his little brother. Paul knew he didn't say that to depress him. His big brother wanted him to know how much he meant to him. Each time Paul received another letter from his brother, it gave him a little hope.

Dear Paul,

I arrived in Baltimore today. I'm going to ask Mr. Sanders if I can propose to Jennifer. I can't believe it, Paul. Can you? Me, a married man? All of my teammates are telling me that when I get to the Majors, I'll get a chance to meet so many women. I told them I don't want anyone else. I really love her, Paul. I hope you do too. Mr. Sanders tells me he hopes I go to the Orioles so his daughter can be close to home. I told him I don't have much control over that.

I hope you're feeling better, Paul. Just remember to take your pills and push yourself. We need you to get stronger. Did you get the recent edition of "Pro Body Builder's Magazine"? They said crunches can strengthen your entire body. Maybe they could help your leg strength. You have to fight, Paul.

Tell everyone I said hello. Hey, when you become a superhero, maybe you could fly to see one of my baseball games. When I see you hovering overhead, I'll try to strike out the batter for you. I love you Paul.

From your older brother,
Garey Ethan Morgan

Paul loved his brother very much, but even all his encouragement couldn't get him out of the slump he'd been in for most of his young life. His brother was about to get a major league contract and was soon going to be engaged to a beautiful college cheerleader. Paul was stuck in a hospital room. His only moment of glory was a kick when he was ten. And if that wasn't bad enough, the kick was tainted because the catcher tipped him to what was coming.

Paul wanted to scream as loud as he could sometimes, but he couldn't even do that because he'd lost his voice as a side effect of one of his stronger antibiotics—it hurt too much to talk. All he knew was sickness. All the weightlifting magazines Garey had gotten him landed, unopened, in his dresser drawer. He thought a lot about the trips he wanted to go on, the places he wanted to visit like the Grand Canyon, Disney World, or the stadium across the street. One time he joked with a nurse that hospitals were his hotels and he didn't get exceptional room service or the current Spectrovision lineup. Paul wanted to be free. He wanted to be able to help people instead of always having to be helped.

Michael, his friend from Nevada who also had cystic fibrosis, could relate.

"I'm sick of being sick," Paul told him as the big white phone cord dangled off his hospital bed. "I'm sick of being called heroic because I can deal with a disease. I'd rather be called heroic because I can make a diving catch or hit a game-winning homerun."

"Paul, you can't change who you are," replied Michael, with his deep raspy voice Paul found so comforting. "We fight cystic fibrosis to give other people hope that they too can overcome obstacles. I don't like dealing with cystic fibrosis everyday, either, but that's how it's going to be. One day when there is a cure, we'll meet on a talk show and reminisce about these tough times."

"Michael, you've always been the more positive of the two of us," Paul conceded. "I hope there's a cure soon, too."

Garey and Michael always had so much faith in Paul. He wished he believed as much in himself as they did. He once told Garey he thought his big brother was the guy in the dream helping Paul out before his at-bat. Garey would chuckle and tell his little brother that's a great dream but to remember his baby brother had to be a superhero someday, too. Garey hated when Paul told him he was giving up. Paul, on the other hand, didn't know if Garey could truly empathize as Garey didn't know what it was like to take tests all the time. Tests that weren't pass or fail, but life or death.

Paul thought of a line from a book he'd read a while back: "Life is a gift. Just because you're breathing doesn't mean you're living." Paul remembered that line because he felt it perfectly described him. He was just breathing, not really living. Life may be a gift to some people, but to him it was a curse.

It was 4 p.m. when Dr. Knotts walked calmly into Room 205. Dr. Knotts, with his wild Albert Einstein gray hair, big black glasses and lanky frame, had been Paul's doctor for the last three years. He was a cystic fibrosis specialist. Dr. Knotts was always very honest when Paul asked him about his condition, but he liked to tell his patient a corny joke from time to time to coax a smile from his solemn patient.

That afternoon, with the sun peeking through the window and casting a shadow across his bed, Dr. Knotts told Paul another one of his "funny" jokes before letting Paul know his pulmonary function test results would be back today.

"I know you're worried, Paul, since, when you took this lung function exam last year, there was a bit of a decline," he said as he moved the stethoscope around Paul's chest to listen to his lungs. "Your chest sounds a bit tight. You have been doing your vest everyday, right? You're taking all of your medication?"

"Of course," Paul said. "I am very responsible."

"Then you should be fine," Dr. Knotts reassured him.

The truth was that Paul skipped his meds quite often and missed a chest therapy at least once a week, but he didn't need Dr. Knotts piling on him like everyone else seemed to do.

"Well," Paul said sheepishly with a shrug, "I haven't really exercised at all and I am always out of breath." It was like waiting to see your grade on the history test you know you flunked.

"Young man, you can't give up," Dr. Knotts said with a wink, and then was off. Then it was time to wait. Paul knew that it would take a miracle for the results to be positive so he prayed for good news.

A few hours later, after he'd flipped through just about every TV channel at least a hundred times, his favorite nurse arrived. Nurse Johanson leaned over him to fluff his pillows and he could smell the sweet flowery scent of her perfume. "Ah, another reason to hope," he sighed to himself.

"Good evening, Paul," she said in her soft, sweet voice with a trace of Swedish accent. "Dr. Knotts is on his way back in." Just then, he got that nervous feeling in his stomach that the news was not going to be very positive. He said another quick prayer for encouraging news. That seemed to trigger a long coughing spasm. He hoped that was not an omen.

There was a knock at the door and in walked his goofy doctor. He was carrying an X-ray and his old, battered Mead notebook that he often joked had seen more ink than the Bible. Paul glanced into his doctor's brown eyes and saw something dark and grim, something he had never seen. He sucked in what little breath he could manage, coughed a couple of times and waited for Dr. Knotts to speak.

"Paul, we've looked at your tests," he said. No silly jokes this time to soften the blow. "Your parents thought it best that I told you."

"Told me what?" Paul inquired, resigned to what he knew was going to be bad news.

"Son, your X-rays show a lot of congestion in both of your lungs. We want to take some more tests to see if you have a bacterial infection. But, what I'm trying to say is, according to the tests, it's not looking good."

"What, what?" Paul cried, distraught and anxious now. Never, not even in his imagined worst case scenario, did he think the news would be this bad.

"Just tell me—am I going to die? How much time do I have?"

Chapter 9
Time Running Out

Dr. Knotts was always honest with him so Paul knew that he would get an answer. He was not sure he wanted an answer or to know how bad off he was, but he knew he couldn't just sit there with his mouth shut. Dr. Knotts' eyes lightened a little but Paul could see they did not hold good news.

"I hate to give numbers like that," he stammered. "But if you're asking— I'd say four to six months. I'm sorry, son."

Paul was stunned. Four months! What did he mean? Four months to *live*? He honestly thought Dr. Knotts would say two or three years, maybe more. His face grew hot as he glanced from Nurse Johanson's sympathetic smile to Dr. Knotts' furrowed brow. Paul had never *lived* a day in his life. His life was a freakin' joke! All he did was lie in a hospital bed with tubes dangling from his arms, watching an occasional baseball game and sitting in the dark. Suddenly he thought of that creep Biff Goolson, who used to chase him and steal his lunch. Biff would have smiled to see the nickname he coined for him, The Puzzle, still holding true.

Paul looked through the window into the dark early evening, just barely seeing the large group of trees that thankfully blocked the view of the asphalt parking lot. Turner Field, while dark, was still in his line of sight. He was never going to play an inning there. His parents would have to prepare for a funeral before they prepared for Garey's wedding, he thought, as he heard raindrops fall and the soft rumbling of thunder.

The thunder inside him also brought a flow of tears. When he turned away from the window, the doctor and nurse were still standing there. It made him so mad he just started screaming, yelling as loud as he could until his faulty lungs could produce no more air to sustain his outburst. The bearer of bad news and the sympathetic nurse just stood there and let him yell until he fell back against his light blue feather pillow. A few gasps of air later he managed to whisper, "Do my parents know?"

"Yes," Dr. Knotts said softly. "They wanted to tell you but your mother was so distraught, she didn't want to break down, and felt it was best coming from me."

Paul stared at him, realizing he was probably right but feeling his anger build inside just the same.

"So now what?" he spat. "What happens now?" He was now wheezing and coughing from exerting more energy than he probably had in the last six months. Nurse Johanson handed Paul a tissue to release some of the mucous clogged in his throat. Dr. Knotts tried to smile. Paul almost hated him for that.

"Well, Paul, your dad contacted a foundation that grants wishes for ill kids, and they said they'd get you front row seats for a Braves game in a few weeks at Turner Field. A representative will come in a week or so to meet with you. How does that sound?"

The only wish Paul wanted was getting his life back. He didn't want to die like Stan. He didn't realize it until that second, but he didn't want his life to end. He sat up in bed and opened his eyes wide.

"Tell those 'wish' people not to come," he said flatly. "And while you're at it, Doc," he began to ask, trying to take the edge out of his voice, "what about a lung transplant? My friend, Michael, had one of those and his lung function is better than it was before the operation."

"Paul," Dr. Knotts sighed, moving around to the other side of his bed and nodding at Nurse Johanson that it was okay to leave. Seeming relieved, she backed out of the room and quietly shut the door. "Getting you listed for a lung transplant takes several months and then finding a donor can take years. We don't have that kind of time. Most individuals with cystic fibrosis slowly lose their lung function and we have time to list them, and then get them a transplant. Unfortunately, your numbers plummeted too rapidly."

That was too much—Paul had wanted to give up, and now that it seemed like it had worked, he realized that wasn't what he wanted at all. He snapped. He picked up his cup of water, crumpled it up violently and flung it at the wall across the room, flinging water everywhere. Dr. Knotts jumped to avoid the unwanted shower.

"It's your fault I'm going to die! Get out! Leave me alone," Paul shouted at him.

"Paul, this is why I don't like to give numbers," he said calmly, as he checked the tubes in Paul's arms to make sure his tantrum hadn't pulled them loose. "You can work at this and disprove my diagnosis." Then he got up and without saying another word backed out of the room and closed the door.

Was he kidding? Disprove his diagnosis? Paul couldn't even pull the IVs out of his own arms. He coughed again, hard—deep, phlegm-filled coughs that shook him to the core. So that was that, huh? He remembered the kickball game in fourth grade he won against Josh Wilson, his one crowning achievement. How sad! He'd won one stupid kickball game. He remembered all the times Biff picked on him. He remembered all of the doctors who told him he was underachieving. He remembered his dream of playing baseball. That wasn't going to happen.

He decided to call the one person who could help him.

"Hey, Garey," he said, choking back sobs. "They've told me I have four months to live. Can you believe it? It's not fair. It's not fair!"

"Paul, calm down. I know you're upset but you have to motivate yourself to fight," Garey said in his soothing voice. "Don't listen to the doctors. Start exercising! I told you that if you didn't exercise, your health would pay for it."

His brother's voice never wavered. How was he so calm, Paul wondered?

"I'm never going to live your dream, Garey. I'm never going to be a superhero. You're about to propose to your girlfriend and I'm not even going to be at the wedding," he lamented. "I'm never going to live any of my dreams, either. I can't get stronger. I just can't!"

"Paul, you *will* be a superhero. You will," Garey said reassuringly. "Now, I'm going to get Jennifer's dad's permission while I'm here in Baltimore, and the first decision I've made about the wedding is that you'll be my best man. So you have to fight, bro, so you can stand, and yes I said 'stand,' alongside me."

Instead of cheering Paul up like it always did, Garey's enthusiasm and optimism were just making him angrier. Paul wrapped the phone cord around his fingers and squeezed the plastic.

"I don't need one of your unrealistic motivational talks," he said, irritated, and slammed the phone onto its carriage. For the first time in his life, he had hung up on his big brother. He didn't want to hear that Garey's "I told you so," that if he had done what he was supposed to do—exercised and kept a positive outlook—he probably wouldn't be in this predicament. He pulled on the sliding table next to him that held his laptop, and sent an instant message to Michael, hoping his CF friend could calm him down.

Hey, Michael...what's up?

Twenty minutes later, he finally received a response from CFdestroyer1.

Paul, is that you?

Yeah, man...I need to talk to you. What took you so long to respond?

This is Maureen, Michael's mom.

That was strange, Paul thought. Michael's mom was never on the computer. Michael told him computers scared her. Why would she be using Michael's e-mail account?

Is Michael there? Paul asked this question with apprehension, concerned that the answer may not be the one he wanted.

I'm so sorry to have to tell you this way. Michael's new lungs rejected his body last night. He died this morning. I'm so sorry. We are all having a really tough time dealing with the situation. I'm e-mailing all his Internet friends this morning to tell them the sad news. The funeral is tomorrow. He really cared for you, Paul. You were like a brother to him.

Paul pushed the computer table away, stunned. His only friend who knew truly what it was like to live with cystic fibrosis was gone. The two of them would never meet face-to-face. He laid his head back against his pillow and pushed the button on his bed that threw his room into complete darkness. Just like he felt. Though he tried, he was physically unable to cry anymore. He was sick of the misery he experienced, the pain in his stomach every time one of his friends died. As much as he felt alone, betrayed by God, he didn't want to call Garey or talk to anyone who might help him. It took him hours before he fell asleep.

The next morning, Nurse Johanson told him that his parents wanted to visit him. He told her he didn't want to see them, not after they made Dr. Knotts tell him the bad news. Where were they when I needed to be comforted, Paul thought?

Garey called from Baltimore but Paul pulled the phone out of the wall and asked the nurse to take it away. For three days he kept that chip on his shoulder—wouldn't talk to anyone, wouldn't look at anyone, wouldn't let anyone visit him. All he could think about was his life and how little he had really lived. The nurses wordlessly brought him food trays but he just dumped them in the trash. He stopped taking his medications and refused his treatments. He wouldn't do his chest therapy, causing the gunk in his lungs to grow thicker. Without his antibiotics, he grew sicker. His cough resembled the hack of a six-packs-a-day smoker. His phlegm resembled thickened anti-freeze, a sure sign of infection. Anytime he talked, he could hear the wheezing in his chest. The way he looked at it, the sooner he died the better. Nothing mattered anymore.

One night he lost control and began sobbing uncontrollably. "I hate my life!" he shouted repeatedly. Moments later, Nurse Johanson rushed in but he yelled at her to leave him alone. For once, he didn't want to see her. His chest was still hurting from the news that he wouldn't be around by year's end. He was never going to have a girlfriend let alone a family. He would never see his big brother play baseball in the big leagues. He would never walk through the gates of Turner Field much less get a hit in the big leagues. He would never know who the masked man in his dream was.

New tears were falling down his already soaked cheeks like ants crawling toward a picnic basket. His ribs ached from all the coughing. He couldn't catch his breath at all anymore. Nurse Johanson tiptoed back in and handed him two pills.

"Take these," she whispered. "They'll make you sleepy."

A few minutes later his eyes—red and burning from too many salty tears—started drooping. His cough finally slowed down. He took the deepest breath he could manage and let go.

Chapter 10
Disaster

Paul woke up the next morning thinking the past few days were the worst of his life. He had the dream again where he was playing baseball at Turner Field and the man in the mask is trying to help him hit the ball. Maybe it was an angel helping him get to heaven, he thought. He used to think it was more than a dream but with four months to live, he doubted he'd ever be visiting Turner Field, much less batting there. Oddly, there was one variation to this dream—when he looked into the crowd, he saw his parents as always but his brother was nowhere to be found.

As soon as he awoke, he tried to assess the dream. He didn't like that Garey was missing. Although he hoped he was making one of his stops at the hotdog stand, he worried that the reason he vanished was because he was mad at his little brother for not taking his phone calls. The first thing Paul did when he woke up was call Garey on his cell phone to apologize for hanging up on him. He got his voice mail and left him a long message.

Garey, it's Paul. I'm so sorry that I hung up on you the other night and I'm sorry that I didn't return any of your phone calls. I've had time to think and I'm feeling better now. I hope it went well with Jennifer's dad last night. I just know he approved of you. How could he not? Call me later to let me know how everything went. I love you, Garey.

The sad truth was that while he tried to make his message sound hopeful, he wasn't feeling better. In fact, he'd never felt worse emotionally or physically. He was still coughing violently, still wheezing every time he breathed, and his ribs continued to throb from the incessant coughing. He just didn't want to ruin the most important weekend of his brother's life. It was the first time he'd lied to Garey about anything.

Twenty minutes later, Nurse Johanson came in with a phone under her arm, looking distressed. She sat down next to him, and sighed deeply.

"Paul, I need to tell you something," she said, her lilting Swedish accent apparent even as she tried to steady her trembling voice. "Your brother, Garey…" she stopped, stood up and plugged in the phone. "You need to talk to your dad," she said softly as she dialed. She handed him the receiver and quickly left the room.

"Hello?" he heard his dad's booming voice at the other end, sounding strained.

"Uh, hi dad," Paul stammered. "Nurse Johanson said I should call you. Listen, I'm sorry about the other day. It's just…"

"Paul, it's fine," his dad said, sounding worn out. "Son, I have to tell you something." Paul swallowed hard but couldn't find any words. He'd never heard his dad so tired, sounding so hopeless. "Paul, you know Garey was in Baltimore over the weekend. Mr. Sanders gave Garey his blessing to marry Jennifer, and Garey was so excited that he took Jennifer's brother, Jason, out on the town to celebrate."

Paul strained to hear something else in what sounded like good news. Before he could express his happiness that his brother was going to be engaged, his father continued.

"Garey and Jason were returning from dinner when Jason dropped his wallet on the street beside them. Garey stepped onto the street to pick up the wallet. Just when he'd picked it up, a car came zooming toward him. Garey tried to get out of the way but instead he slipped and the car hit him and sped away."

"What? Dad, no! Is he okay?"

He heard his mother bawling in the background and his father's voice broke as he continued. "Jason tried to revive him. He's at a hospital in Baltimore and…and…he's not doing well." Paul didn't respond, so his father kept talking. "Son, we love you very much. We're so sorry that you've had to endure so much pain lately." Then silence, except for his mother wailing in the background. He heard his dad put the phone down, speak to his mother in a hushed, soothing voice, then come back and pick up the receiver. He sighed, trying to compose himself. "Paul, we are going to Baltimore this afternoon and I don't know when we'll be back."

"Dad, is he going to be okay?" he sputtered. "Did they catch the guy who hit him?"

"I don't know, son. They didn't catch the driver but Jason described the car and we'll just hope for the best on all counts. That's all we can do. We'll call you when we know more. Take care of yourself, Paul."

There was no need to say goodbye. When the phone clicked on his dad's end, Paul just dropped the phone and started sobbing. He didn't think he had any tears left, but he cried all day and all night. He prayed, though he had lost faith in prayer through his tribulations at St. Luke's, and asked Nurse Johanson to ask the entire second floor and all the nurses to pray for his brother, too. He couldn't imagine life without Garey. He had just lost his friend, Michael. God wouldn't take someone else away from him! His brother was lucky, though, he thought, and he was always positive and upbeat. Luck could get him through this. Garey, with his bright hazel eyes like Paul's, his dark brown hair and freckles, huge grin and athletic build, was destined to be the next Babe Ruth.

His mother called the next morning. It was the first time he'd heard her voice in almost a week.

"The doctor says there's a ten percent chance he will survive, and if he does, he could be paralyzed," she said, sounding exhausted and defeated. "He's lost a lot of blood." Paul could hear the rustling of tissues and blaring intercom in the background, all those familiar hospital noises.

"We're all praying for him in Atlanta. Bring him home soon," he said, trying to maintain a steady voice. He just couldn't comprehend Garey lying in a coma, near death. Garey was always there when he needed him, with a wide grin and positive words of wisdom. But now Garey needed his little brother and Paul couldn't be there for him.

His mother called back four hours later to report that after an operation, Garey was still in critical condition. His chances of survival had improved only slightly.

"Mom, he's going to make it. You'll see," he re-assured her. His brother was the strongest person he knew. One of them had to be strong and realize their dreams, and he knew that out of both of them, it would be Garey. He wouldn't let Paul down. He'd recover from surgery and eventually walk again. He bet he'd still find a way to defy all the odds and play for the Braves, Paul thought, now trying to re-assure himself.

His mom called again eight hours later. Between sobs she told Paul his only brother, his best friend, the guy who had always been his strongest supporter, was gone.

He sat there in his bed, a million feelings flying through his head all at once, so many that he couldn't grasp any one of them—denial, shock, anger, sadness, fear and every other negative emotion human beings are capable of. He couldn't be dead! Losing Garey was like losing his own heart. Garey was the only person who gave him faith that he could beat this disease. He was supposed to be the greatest baseball player ever. He was supposed to send Paul a baseball for every Major League game he won. He was supposed to get married and raise a family. All of his dreams were gone, simply because he was helping Jason pick up his wallet. Why do bad things always seem to happen to good people, he wondered?

What would he do without Garey? He wouldn't have any dreams if it hadn't been for him. He was the one who got Paul interested in baseball. He was the one who told him he could be a superhero. He was the one person who knew just what to say when his little brother needed to hear it. He thought about his last dream and not seeing his big brother in the stands. That's how his life would be from now on. He no longer had his best friend in the stands to support him.

He was reminded of how Garey ended each and every letter.

I love you, Paul.

From your older brother,

Garey Ethan Morgan

He touched the baseball pendant around his neck, the one Garey gave him when he was ten years old and his medication made it impossible to walk. Each time something reminded Paul of his brother, he felt for the pendant, which always reminded him of Garey and the unwavering faith he always showed in his little brother. He used to tell Paul not to forget him when Paul was a superhero but that was when they assumed Paul would go first. Garey told him he would be a superhero and fly but Paul knew what he really meant was that when he went to heaven he would be free of all pain. Now, it was his older brother who flew in heaven. He hoped Garey would never forget his little brother.

Paul probably should have thought of all the great times they had together, but all he could think of were the times that he and Garey would no longer share. The two brothers would never again watch a Braves game together. He'd never get to hear another one of Garey's Killer Creek jokes. Worst of all, he'd never be able to hear his voice or hug Special K ever again.

It broke Paul's heart knowing the last time he spoke to Garey he had hung up on him. Garey was only trying to help, as usual, and Paul didn't want to hear it. Paul thought, "I was always a failure, but now I am a horrible person, too." He cried harder than ever before. He kept seeing visions of his brother. He imagined him picking up the wallet, he envisioned the car crashing into him and disappearing into the night. He pictured him bleeding to death and calling out Paul's name to help him. Suddenly, Paul couldn't take it anymore. He started shouting and screaming anything he could think of to describe how he felt about himself.

"I'm a selfish jerk! I don't deserve to live!" Nurse Johanson came busting into his room. "I don't want to live anymore!" he yelled, and ripped the pendant from his neck and threw it to the floor. He snatched the plastic knife from his dinner tray and tried to slice his wrist with it. "Let me die!" he shouted. Blood slowly seeped from his wrist.

In one smooth motion, Nurse Johanson grabbed the knife away from him and stuck him with a syringe. Suddenly, he felt light-headed and fell back on the bed. Things turned hazy. He saw a couple of doctors rush in and everyone talking all at once, moving in slow motion. He heard one say, "His brother just died," and another say, "He's been angry and feeling hopeless," and "Poor kid."

In all the commotion, he just wanted to die. He didn't have much time left anyway, and now that Garey was gone, what little time he had meant nothing anymore.

In his stupor, he saw Nurse Johanson's eyes gazing sympathetically at him through her signature red-rimmed glasses. He could feel her hand putting pressure on his swollen wrist. That's all he remembered before everything went black, again.

Chapter 11
Make a Wish

He woke up groggy. Everything was blurry. He rubbed the sleep out of his eyes and the first thing he noticed was that his wrist was healed, with no sign of his crude cuts. How could that be? Was medical science that good? Was he in heaven? Probably not, since it still looked like familiar 205.

Standing in the back of the room, with his hands folded, was a man with short, brown wavy hair, wearing a blue blazer. He was tall and thin. From his bed, Paul could tell the man smelled like the baseball mitt Garey gave him for his twelfth birthday. Was this what God looked like? Paul stared at him as the man walked over near his bed and whispered, "Paul, today is your lucky day."

"Are you God?"

The man sat down in the chair next to his bed and smiled.

"No, my name is Gregory Hartman. I was sent to you to give you one wish."

Paul chortled and said, "One wish? Is this a joke? Are you from the Make-A-Wish Foundation? Is this because I'm dying?" His anger building, Paul pointed at him and yelled, "Forget it! Get out! I told Dr. Knotts I don't want you here."

"Wait, let me explain," the man said in the same soothing, calm voice he'd been using, basically ignoring Paul's anger. "I'm from more of a *special* type of Make-A-Wish Foundation."

"What do you mean?" Paul asked, his tone still cross. "Besides, there's no way you can make my wish come true."

"Let me guess," Gregory said. "You want your life back, right?"

"Of course!" he shouted, agitated at Gregory's statement of the obvious. "Everyone has that wish."

"Paul," he said urgently, moving closer as if about to share a secret. "I can help you in more ways than you can imagine. There are no limits to the wishes I can grant."

Now the guy was starting to give Paul the creeps. It was time for him to go. "Ok," Paul said, trying to steady his voice. "Here's my one wish. I wish for you to leave!"

"Don't believe me?" Gregory asked with a wry smile. "Ok, watch this!" He looked at Paul's wheelchair, produced what looked like a magic wand, and said, "Aliana Morani Inilog, turn his wheelchair into a frog."

Suddenly, the wheelchair turned green and Paul watched it grow frog legs, croak, and hop right out the door. Paul shook his head, shocked. Was I on that many drugs, he wondered? Yeah, that must be it, he thought, but he'd play along.

"That one was on the house, Paul," Gregory said, still wearing that odd smile and tapping the wand against his leg. He stared into Paul's eyes and Paul could see flecks of all the colors of the rainbow in Gregory's mesmerizing orbs. "Now," he cooed, "do you have a wish or not?"

"All I have to do is make a wish?" he asked, trying to look away from Gregory's probing eyes. "Any wish? And it will come true?"

The strange man smiled again and nodded.

"So," Paul began, trying to be nonchalant. "Gregory, is this heaven?"

"No, this isn't heaven," he replied. "It's kind of the last stop before heaven. And there's one catch—your wish cannot change any person but yourself."

"What do you mean?"

"Your wish can only affect you, so you tell me the kind of person you want to be, and I'll make you that person," he explained.

Paul raised himself up on his pillows and really thought about what he wanted to be. He knew he didn't want to be himself. He'd always had two dreams: to play Major League baseball and to be a superhero. Well, the superhero one was more Garey's dream for him than his own. But perhaps he owed it to Garey to be a superhero. Though he couldn't bring him back, he could fulfill Garey's dream.

All of a sudden, it dawned on Paul again what had happened, that his brother was gone and never coming back. He hung his head in his hands and started sobbing. A slow coughing spasm ensued. He missed his older brother so much.

After a few minutes, he wiped the tears from his face. Gregory was still sitting there patiently with a dreamy, half-smile on his face. For some reason, Paul found it almost comforting now. But he had one question for the strange man before he made this wish.

"Why me?" he turned toward Gregory and asked. "Why do you want to help me? There are millions of people in the world who are sick. I'm not special. Why would you choose me?"

Gregory patted his leg and handed him a tissue from the nightstand.

"I guarantee one day you'll figure it out, Paul, and it will all make sense."

So this was Paul's chance. He imagined the elation having super powers would bring, especially after being the "sick kid" for so long. Plus, as a superhero, the Major Leagues were well within reach. He could have his own crime-fighting identity. What would he call himself? Suddenly, he began brainstorming. He could've called himself "Futureman," since Dr. Knotts told him he had no future left. He could've called himself "Special K," since that was his brother's nickname, but that didn't really fit him, either. He could've taken "The Jet" as his name, after his idol, Ricky Kilmer. But then it dawned on him that Biff had nicknamed him "The Puzzle" because he was falling apart and could not be put back together; and because the doctors didn't know what was wrong with him when he lost the ability to walk. Well, now "The Puzzle" would be put back together. He'd become..."The Solution!"

"Well," Gregory asked. "Have you made your decision?"

"I want to be a superhero," Paul declared, still with a slight wheeze in his chest. "I would like to be called The Solution."

"Okay, would you like a uniform?"

Paul thought about that for a second. "Sure, why not?"

"Would you like to be able to fly?"

That was a no-brainer.

"Would you like to be stronger than any human and be rid of cystic fibrosis?"

"Absolutely!" he blasted. No more sick kid for Paul Morgan.

For the next thirty minutes, Gregory instructed Paul how to fly—"Just flap your arms and when you ascend over the clouds, point yourself in the direction you want to go."

It sounded easy enough, Paul thought. Then Gregory told him never to doubt his strength. Things he couldn't do before, he'd be able to accomplish now, he explained.

"Your wish will come true at midnight, Paul. I'll be back to check on you then," he said, before he strode out of the room into the hallway.

Paul hadn't realized it was night already, so it seemed like Gregory just faded into the distant darkness of the dimly-lit hall after he walked past a couple of nurses.

He suddenly got this huge grin on his face. This was the first good news he'd received since he was carried through the front doors of St. Luke's. But, part of him was skeptical and he feared this whole thing might be like waking up from the baseball dream—depressed because it didn't come true. Maybe Biff Goolson hired this guy to deal him the ultimate tease. He expected someone to jump out of the closet and yell "Gotcha!" or, even more fittingly, "Game over!" If this was the case, he'd be even more depressed than before.

He could barely contain himself at the thought of not being the sick kid with CF anymore. Ever since he was little, he'd wanted to feel the satisfaction of helping somebody rather than always having people help him. As a superhero, he'd have no more awful coughing fits and he would never be out of breath. It also dawned on him that he wouldn't need medications anymore, do therapy or worry about life expectancy.

The minutes ticked by...11:40...11:45...11:50. Soon, he would be a superhero helping people. He would be The Solution! Finally, it was midnight. It was time.

Nothing dramatic happened, though. He looked over to the nightstand next to his bed and saw that a red and blue shirt-box had materialized there. Next to it was an envelope with "Open at midnight" scrawled across its face. He opened the note and read:

You are a bold hero to me. I pull for you. Gregory Vern Hartman.

Inside the box he found a blue cape, red shirt and tights and blue boots. The contrasting logo on the back of the cape and the front of the shirt was shaped like a baseball glove with an "S" for the Solution stitched on it. Suddenly he heard a rustling sound and, out of nowhere, Gregory appeared before him.

"So," Gregory said softly, "are you ready to be transformed from a sick kid to a superhero?"

"Gregory, how did you know about how much I loved baseball and dreamed of being a professional baseball player?" he asked. "How did you know to include a glove on my symbol?"

"My friend," Gregory said, "it was obvious. I saw that interesting pendant around your neck, the one shaped like a baseball."

He reminisced to the time when Garey had given the pendant to him more than a year ago, on his first anniversary of being in the hospital. Tears flowed when he realized that now he'd give Garey a real reason to be proud of him. He'd really be a superhero, just like he and his brother dreamed.

"Paul." Gregory's voice snapped him out of his memories. The dream-giver looked stern. "Listen carefully. I'm going to come back to you in three months and give you the choice to either remain a superhero and venture on to heaven or return to your old existence as Paul Morgan and battle cystic fibrosis."

"You must be kidding," he chuckled. "I'll save you the trip. There is no way I am going to change my mind."

But he was already gone, as quickly and mysteriously as he'd come. At that moment, his wheelchair suddenly re-appeared next to his bed. Paul glanced back toward the box on his bed and realized there was another letter in it, listing the rules. He read it carefully.

1) You cannot have any encounters with any person who knew you as Paul Morgan, the sick kid. If you are recognized, you will turn into Paul Morgan again, and instantly return to your old life.

2) You cannot tell people how you became The Solution. If you mention that your real name is Paul, or if you mention Gregory, you will lose your super powers.

3) Remember the words in your card from Gregory: "You are a bold hero to me. I pull for you. Gregory Vern Hartman."

Paul looked down at himself and realized he still looked the same. It was time to test these superpowers. He easily moved from his bed to his wheelchair and rolled into the elevator, calling out to the nurses' station that he was going to get a breath of fresh air. It was a couple of minutes after midnight when he wheeled himself outside into the late night quiet. It was spring, and the delicious light, cool breeze blowing against his face was the most glorious feeling he'd experienced in a long time. He had been too depressed to come outside at all, let alone at night. Months had passed since he'd gazed at the moon with his naked eyes. He'd almost forgotten how bright and brilliant a full moon could be.

He pulled himself off of his wheelchair and lowered his body onto the sidewalk. He felt better, lighter, more at peace, already. He realized he wasn't coughing or wheezing anymore, either. Pulling himself up onto his arms, he began to crawl toward the deserted parking lot next to the hospital to change into his superhero costume.

"Hang on here," he said to himself. If he was indeed a superhero, then he could walk! "What am I doing?" he wondered. He pushed off on the ground and in a split-second, had sprung to his feet. He couldn't believe it. He was standing for the first time in five years. He looked around from this unfamiliar vantage point, where everything looked different—bigger, brighter, more beautiful. He started moving his legs and suddenly he was walking! He took several steps, spun around and then, to test his strength even more, he began jumping up and down. He'd never felt more elated in his life!

He sprinted into the middle of the parking lot, then ducked behind a dumpster to put on his outfit. Then it was time to fly. He flapped his arms like Gregory had instructed, but nothing happened. Oh boy, he thought...maybe this *was* all a joke, or a dream. He tried again, but, alas, no liftoff.

"Gregory!" he whispered loudly into the dark. "Gregory! Can you hear me? Help! I can't fly!"

He heard Gregory's footsteps come out of the darkness behind the dumpster where Paul had just changed. He looked Paul up and down and then put his hand on the fledgling superhero's shoulder.

"Paul, if you want to fly, you must visualize yourself flying. If you can't see yourself doing it, then you'll never be able to accomplish it. Do you understand?"

Paul nodded. Gregory smiled and disappeared again behind the dumpster. Paul closed his eyes and pictured himself flying effortlessly among the stars. As he visualized he flapped his arms again. Suddenly, he had that roller-coaster feeling, like his stomach was in his shoes. His legs felt light and dangly. He opened his eyes, looked down and realized he was quickly rising from the earth. He felt the wind gather in his cape and soon he was flying swiftly through the air, above the hospital, the houses, the highway. In less than a minute, he was not only walking again, but flying. He was The Solution!

Was this really happening to him? He gazed at the glittering Atlanta skyline below and the white, stringy clouds above. He was feeling his body grow stronger every second and his brain was now flying along with these incredibly positive, happy thoughts of what could be. Soaring into the thick night air, he yelled goodbye to the sick kid who felt sorry for himself; goodbye to all of the pain he had endured and goodbye to Dr. Knotts' death sentence. He bid farewell to Paul "The Puzzle" Morgan and hello to the newest superhero! The Solution had arrived!

Chapter 12
Time to Say Goodbye?

While Paul's spirit sailed above the clouds, preparing to battle villains and rescue heroines, his body lie on his bed in room 205. With his new attitude that he no longer cared about his old existence, his real body was continuing to wither away.

Paul's mom cried as her left hand grasped Paul's left wrist.

"Paul, wake up!" she demanded. "I love you."

Paul's pale body lay motionless on top of the bed. In order to help him breathe, a long white tube ran from a life support machine through his mouth and into his trachea. White tape stretched across Paul's bare chest to hold the tubes in place. A large plastic tube was stuck in his neck to keep him intravenously nourished. Paul's gaunt face pointed towards the beige stucco ceiling—his eyes shut and his lips virtually colorless.

Paul's father stood there with a blank look on his face, visualizing the bed as actually the coffin that Paul would be buried in. He'd already buried his oldest son. Now, he was losing his baby.

Other solemn thoughts crept into his father's mind. He would never have grandchildren. His children would both go before him—a nightmare for any parent. Neither of his children would see his dreams come true. He tried to brush those thoughts away, but his mind was polluted with negativity at that moment that just wouldn't leave.

"Paul, come back to us," his mother insisted. "You can't give up. I won't let you die!"

"Lilian," Paul's father begged. "Stay calm. We need to think positively. He's going to get better."

"That sure worked for Garey, didn't it, Sam?" she sarcastically replied. "Sam, I'm sorry, but I don't want to lose our little boy. I can't go on if I have to lose another child."

He grabbed his wife and held her tight as her tears soaked his white-collared Polo shirt. "We can't give up, Lilian. We can't give up!" Outwardly, his father pushed optimism, but deep down he was doubtful that his youngest son's eyes would open again.

Paul's vital signs continued to dwindle. His heart rate worsened, his lung function deteriorated even further, and his X-rays confirmed the worst. His lung function had decreased more than fifteen percent since he went into the coma—the kind of numbers that frequently ended the hopes of many other cystic fibrosis patients. The clog of gunk in both his left and right lungs looked like dark storm clouds on the X-ray. His airways were now almost completely obstructed.

Dr. Knotts walked into Room 205 and initiated the conversation he always dreaded with his patients' family members.

"Lilian, Sam, I'm sorry to tell you this, but we're going to have to consider the fact that your son may never get off the ventilator. It's been about a month now. All of his numbers continue to drop. It's my job to make sure your son does not suffer. It is my job to be realistic and…"

"No," Paul's mother sharply interrupted. "While it's your job to be realistic, it's my job to be his mother. What would you do if this was your child? Would you give up? Or would you pray for a successful outcome? I am not giving up on my little boy. Dr. Knotts, he needs more time to get better. He is going to be okay. God would not do this to both of our boys."

Paul's father quickly jumped on Lilian's bandwagon. "Give him some more time, doctor. We are not ready to say goodbye to another son."

Paul's mom looked at Paul again, staring at the tubes in his veins. More tears fell from her eyes as she couldn't bear to see her little boy in so much pain. Sam was always good at masking his feelings, while Lilian was not afraid to wear her emotions on her sleeves.

Dr. Knotts stood there, Nurse Johanson by his side. He looked at Paul's father.

"Sam, we'll give him some more time and hope for the best but I must tell you, as a doctor who has done this for many years, the odds are not on his side. I completely understand and respect your decision."

Sam and Lilian each took a deep breath and stared at one another, trying to stay strong for their little boy. A tear fell to the floor but not from either of Paul's parents. It was Paul's favorite Swedish sensation who needed a tissue.

As many patients as Nurse Johanson assisted, she didn't like to pick favorites, however, Paul was always special to her. He was so sweet to her and the Morgans treated her as if she was a family member. She remembered when she first met Paul, wearing his Braves jersey and hat and waving his red foam tomahawk at the television. She recognized the same smirk on his face every time The Jet took the mound. No matter how much pain he had to endure, it seemed like the only successful treatment was a victory from his beloved Braves.

Paul was so kind to her and so fun to hang around with that he grew to be her favorite patient. They used to play checkers or watch television shows some nights when her shift was over. Of course, she waited for the final out of the Braves game before she came in. She always knew that he had a crush on her. Nurse Johanson didn't have any children, but Paul was the closest thing she had to a son.

She knew she had to get herself together. She did not want to upset the family any further. "Sam, Lilian, if there's anything I can do, please let me know," she pleaded. "I will continue to check on Paul every hour and make sure that he is as comfortable as possible."

She stared at Paul, hoping that his eyes would open one day soon. Unfortunately, she, like everyone else in that room, was beginning to have her doubts.

Chapter 13
The Solution Begins

As Paul flew through the air—actually flew!—he felt invincible. His blue cape flapped in the wind behind him. His skinny arms had transformed into pumped pistons of power. He didn't cough anymore. His chest didn't hurt. Garey was right—he was a superhero. He only wished his big brother could see him now, flying high!

High above the clouds, looking down on his sleeping city, Paul made a list in his head of all the things The Solution stood for. He solved problems. The Solution saved people from dire circumstances. The Solution would be the greatest superhero ever. The Solution would meet girls, go on dates and have lots of friends. The Solution was going to have all of the things Paul Morgan never had. He admitted to himself that some of the things were superficial, but he didn't just want to be a superhero. He wanted to have a life. Surely he deserved that much, he told himself as he cruised the sky over Atlanta.

He dropped down a bit so he could see the few people walking on the street at this hour. He saw two girls, maybe a little older than him, coming out of a restaurant in Midtown and heading toward a car. Suddenly, out of nowhere, a man in black grabbed one of their purses and took off down the street. This was his first chance to be a superhero, to be The Solution! He began humming the Superman theme song and swooped down like a hunting hawk to confront the mugger. His blue boots landed directly in the robber's path. The imposing, muscular thief wore a ski mask and towered over Paul, but the young superhero stood his ground.

"Get out of my way, kid, in that crazy get-up!" the thief yelled as he tried to push past him.

"Give me the purse," Paul said calmly, even though inside he was still a tiny bit worried this was all a dream and he really *didn't* have the strength to take on such a hulking criminal. He swallowed hard and told himself, "Believe. Believe and you can do anything."

The mugger let loose a menacing laugh, shoved his adversary out of the way with a stiff arm and tore off down the street again. The Solution ran after him and, with superhero speed, easily overtook the assailant. The thief cocked his fist back and drove it into Paul's stomach, just below the symbol on his chest. The Solution didn't as much as flinch. He nonchalantly grabbed the thief's wrist and lifted him a foot above the ground. Paul didn't think he was squeezing that hard, but apparently he was, as the man in the ski mask cried out in pain, dropped the purse and fell to the ground.

"Who are you?" the thief asked.

"I'm the greatest superhero of them all. I am The Solution!"

The thief turned like he'd just seen a ghost and scampered away. When Paul turned around, the two girls were standing on the corner, gaping at their new hero, holding each other and shaking. He walked slowly over to them and held the purse out to them.

"Here you go. You girls okay?" he said softly, so as not to add to their frightful evening. "You really should not be walking around this late at night. There are a lot of dangerous people running around. What's your name?" he asked the girl closest to him.

Her name was Andrea. She was beautiful, with auburn hair and emerald green eyes. She and her friend had just come from a concert that had gone late into the night. On a whim, he asked her if she would like to go out some time. She looked at her friend, who shrugged her shoulders and smiled at him.

"Sure," Andrea said brightly, her fright having disappeared as fast as her attacker.

He'd never asked for a girl's number before but suddenly he had this new confidence, and he knew it didn't have to do with his tights. In a span of one night, he had learned to fly, foiled a robbery and scored a date. It was already a good day's work for The Solution. Paul chuckled, thinking of Gregory coming to him in three months asking if he wanted to give this up and go back to being Paul Morgan the sick kid—The Puzzle.

"Never!" he thought. "Never would I give up this gig."

It was almost 2 a.m. by then and Paul decided to fly home to his parents.

He swooped down on the front lawn before he realized something. He couldn't go in. His parents could never know he had become a superhero. That was one of the rules: he couldn't have contact with anyone who knew him as Paul Morgan.

Instead, he flew about five miles north into a secluded forest. He used a dozen oak trees to build a one story, log cabin that night. For most people, this might take months, but in less than an hour, he had cozy sleeping quarters. He lay down on the cushy leaves he had gathered and realized that while he did miss his parents, Dr. Knotts, Nurse Johanson and especially Garey, he was a superhero now. He was making his dreams come true and now he had much more than the four months to live that the doctors had given him.

Weeks passed, and he continued his good deeds. He rescued a school teacher from a burning building, saved a boy from drowning in the river, and even prevented a train-wreck by fixing part of the railroad track. When he wasn't performing heroic feats, he was dating. Andrea was a nice girl and seemed to really like him. The only problem was that he couldn't tell her much about the real him. Now he knew how Clark Kent, Superman's alter ego, must have felt.

He had moments where he thought he forgot to take his antibiotics or do his therapy, until he realized that he didn't need to worry about those things anymore. He missed his family more every day, though. He wondered if they were sad, if they wondered where he was or if he had left Paul Morgan's body behind in that hospital bed. Having already lost one son, he couldn't imagine how that must make his parents feel. But he shook off those feelings. He finally had a chance to live his life. The pros of this life far outweighed the cons.

Some days, he would pinch himself to make sure it still was real. He was really a superhero. He was really not sick anymore. He was making a difference in the world. When he was sick all of his life, he didn't have many chances to positively reflect on things. It was a nice feeling that he could surely get used to. As far as he was concerned, Paul Morgan would only live on in people's memories.

The Solution's flight would last forever.

Chapter 14
Losing Faith

Paul's vital numbers were at an all-time low. His spirit, now transformed into The Solution, had totally forgotten about his old existence. Therefore, his bed-bound body continued to shrivel. His lung function declined another five percent. His chest continued to be clouded with obstructions. His face was now milky pale. It had been two-and-a-half months now since he'd fallen into a coma and he was getting considerably worse by the day.

Dr. Knotts was constantly monitoring Paul's statistics. As Paul grew worse, the doctor discussed the possibility with Paul's parents of signing the papers to take him off the life support system and let him go. Dr. Knotts didn't want Paul to die. Paul was his patient and a friend, and he cared for him very much. He felt responsible for his decline and wanted more than anything for Paul to make a full recovery. Though he wanted his patient to get better, his job was to be realistic about the prognosis. That's what he swore an oath to do when he became a doctor in the first place. A person with cystic fibrosis who was on a ventilator for two-and-a-half months did not stand much of a chance of survival even if he did wake up.

Paul's mother battled every day to stay strong, spending all her time at the hospital. His father would join her after work in the evenings. They would pray out loud and lay their heads on his chest. They began reading some of Garey's old letters to their youngest son as they knew the letters motivated him when he was conscious. His mom began reading one dated three months before Garey died.

Paul,

How are you doing, bro? I'm thinking about you. I know you're having good days and bad, but you have to enjoy the good days and work hard to make sure that the bad days are few and far between. When you wake up in the mornings, you have a choice. You can have a wonderful day or you can sulk about the bad things happening to you. I hope that you take the first option.

I read that Killer Creek finally won a basketball game. I never thought I'd see that in my lifetime. More proof, though, that if Killer Creek can be victorious so can you, Paul. I'm thinking about you often.

Right now, I'm in Phoenix working out for the Diamondbacks. Phoenix is a great city. It never gets cold here and there is so much to do. The problem is that it's not in your same time zone and we probably wouldn't be able to talk as much over the phone. I'll still send you letters though. I think they're picking too late in the draft to pick me, anyway. I guess they just wanted to see how I'd fit into their system if I slip down to the 24th pick.

Don't forget to read the May issue of Pro Bodybuilding Magazine. They have a great article on curls. If you can have mom or dad buy you some ten pound weights, you can really increase the muscles in your biceps and triceps just by doing three sets of exercises every other day. Talk to you soon.

I love you, Paul.

From your older brother,

Garey Ethan Morgan

Lilian and Sam looked at their son. His breathing seemed to grow weaker by the day. Paul wasn't getting any better and they both knew the day would come that they may have to do the inevitable—allow their youngest son to die. Almost three months to the day after Paul became comatose Dr. Knotts approached Paul's family yet again.

"Sam, I know that you both must be going through so much, but my job is to make sure that your son does not have to suffer. I'm afraid if he's under for much longer, he may not be pain-free."

Paul's parents looked at each other at that moment.

"Lilian, what do you think?" Sam asked, the sound of defeat creeping into his tone. He hadn't slept in days and was no longer capable of making life or death decisions regarding his son. Lilian, now the stronger of the two, was quiet for a few moments. Her hands were trembling. She loved her son very much but she didn't want him to suffer. She grabbed a tissue out of the blue Kleenex box by his bed as she slowly spoke.

"Sam, I love him so much. He did not deserve this. I hate that he is enduring so much pain. I don't want him to die…"

"None of us do, Lilian, but I don't want our boy to suffer."

His mom shed new tears—her hopes were pretty much shattered.

"I guess that it's time to…"

Suddenly, from the corner of her eye, she saw something shining underneath Paul's bed. She rubbed her eyes and moved a little closer but still could not tell what it was. She reached under his mattress and snagged it. Lo and behold, it was Paul's silver chain and pendant, a gift from Garey—the same pendant that he ripped from his neck before he went in the coma. She held it in her left hand and then clinched her hand tightly around it. She remembered the special relationship that her sons had and how Garey always pushed Paul to fight even when he was in pain. She knew what Garey would want her to do in this situation.

"Dr. Knotts, Sam, I need another couple of weeks. Please, grant me that. I'm sorry to sound selfish, but I'm just not ready yet. If he's not better in a couple of weeks, well…we'll cross that bridge when we come to it."

"Lilian, that's fine," said Dr. Knotts, "But please know your insurance may run out at that time."

"Then we'll pay with our own money. I can't give up on my son."

His spirits raised by Lilian's strength, Sam joined in.

"We won't give up on our son."

Chapter 15
Second Thoughts

The Solution continued his noble work, flying back and forth from his cozy cabin to do good deeds throughout the community. The comatose Paul Morgan wasn't even a blip on his radar. One day, he flew above his old school and saw a kid in a wheelchair being harassed. Another boy had pushed him to the ground, and a crowd had gathered around him, laughing and pointing. With flashbacks of Biff Goolson popping in his head, he immediately swooped down and pulled the bully off the kid.

The Biff wannabe, no longer in charge of the scene, screamed and ran away with the other kids close behind. The Solution looked down at the boy on the ground, ready to accept his thanks, but the boy looked indignantly up at the unwanted intruder. He started to crawl toward his wheelchair and shrugged off The Solution's arm trying to help him.

"What are you doing?" the boy snapped at him. "I'm not afraid of him. I was going to push him back!"

"But, you're in a wheelchair," Paul said, confused. "You can't fight back. You needed my help." "Oh, please, I can take that guy," the boy said angrily. "Don't assume that just because I have a wheelchair, I'm weak."

As the boy wheeled off in a huff, Paul watched his back and started to visualize the boy in the wheelchair as himself. The regrets and questions of his own life suddenly struck him.

Why didn't I ever think of that? Why didn't I fight back? Why was I so weak?

He longed to face Biff as The Solution, not The Puzzle. But he knew he would revert to the old Paul Morgan if he ever came face to face with his old nemesis while wearing his superhero outfit. And if he was Paul Morgan, he'd be too weak to confront him.

"Or would I be?" he wondered. That was one sacrifice he made when he became The Solution—he might never know. There would be no second chances to solve problems from his past.

One night a few days later, he flew to the aid of a little boy who was crying for help outside of a shopping mall. "I can't find my parents," he sobbed. He looked about eight or nine years old. "I don't feel very well and my mom has my medicine."

"What's your name?" The Solution asked.

"Tommy Stevenson," he said, wiping his eyes and looking up at the superhero with a forlorn gaze. The boy was chalk white and his lips were starting to turn slightly blue. "Can you please help me?"

"Tommy, I'll take you to the hospital and then I'll find your mom and bring her to you, okay?" he said as he scooped him up and they took off to St. Luke's, Paul's old stomping ground.

As they flew through the clouds, Tommy, holding tightly around his neck, told The Solution his story. As he spoke, Paul realized they had very similar childhoods: They both had over-protective mothers, they both grew up in Atlanta hospitals and when he looked at Tommy's medical ID bracelet after hearing him cough, he realized another similarity—Tommy had CF. Thankfully, since he was The Solution, Paul no longer had the disease but knowing that this little boy was like him when he had been that age made the superhero's heart pound a little harder.

The Solution dropped him at the entrance to the emergency room and watched from above as the nurses ran to check on him. Then The Solution went to retrieve the boy's mother. Later that night, he went back to the hospital. He wanted to see how his young friend was doing. When he finally found him, he was in Paul's old room, 205. He felt a little strange entering the room as a visitor, much less a superhero, but once he made sure there were no doctors or nurses around, he snuck in the window and saw Tommy sitting on the bed, flipping TV channels like he used to do.

"Hey, Tommy, how are you feeling?" he asked as he approached the bed.

"Hey!" he looked up, his eyes as bright and wide as his smile. The Solution surveyed the scene: like Paul, he had IV's in his arm and a bottle of pills on the table. He opened the doctor's folder next to Tommy's bed and began reading his chart, learning he was in worse shape than Paul had ever been. The Solution tried not to let Tommy see his face fall. This must be how people felt when they saw him lying in that same bed, looking for encouraging words to keep the patient's hopes up. Tommy noticed The Solution wasn't as happy as he had been when he first walked in.

"Don't worry about me," he said, sounding wiser than someone his age should. "I'll be okay. I'm a fighter."

"Why aren't you scared?"

"Because I can only win," Tommy said with certainty.

"I don't understand."

"The doctors don't think I can beat my disease. My parents don't think I can beat my disease. Every TV show I watch about my disease says I will not live. So there's no pressure on me," he explained. "I could win and I would be a hero. I could lose and I'm still a hero. Do you understand what I'm saying?"

Paul not only understood completely, he suddenly felt bad for giving up his own fight so easily. His superhero lifestyle was just a way out of fighting the disease, yet he never even tried to fight. Doctors had told him if he exercised and was more motivated, then there was a chance for him. Had he given up on himself too early? Could he have beaten CF? He remembered what the kid in the wheelchair told him in the schoolyard, that he was stronger than the bully and he could've fought him. He shouldn't have thought the kid was weak just because he used a wheelchair to get around.

Paul was the superhero, but these kids were stronger than he was. He asked Tommy if he wished he was a superhero.

"My mom tells me I am a superhero," Tommy told him. "I don't have a cape and I can't fly like you, but she told me that a superhero needs no cape. He just needs to have a big heart and a positive attitude.

"How did you get to be a superhero?" he asked Paul, seeming genuinely interested. Paul looked down at his outfit and realized there was another answer to his question.

"*You* are the superhero," Paul said. "You're helping people because you're inspiring them. You're fighting. You have a positive attitude and a big heart. I never had any of that. I'm just a guy with a cape."

The Solution flew back to his cabin that night thinking the decision whether to stay a superhero was no longer the easiest decision of his life. In fact, it had turned into the toughest.

Chapter 16
Sad Times

Paul's parents would face their most agonizing decision over the next two weeks. Do they keep him on the ventilator and risk his suffering or take him off life support and lose their youngest son?

Paul's mom began spending less time in the hospital and more time at home staring at pictures of her little boy, remembering the good times they had together. She watched two videos one afternoon. One was a video she took of him taking his first steps in the living room of their house. She watched as her eleven-month old son, wearing a red and blue Braves shirt and some navy blue corduroys tried to get up. When he struggled, his older brother grabbed his waist and helped him walk across the room. When Paul got to the end of the room, he smiled, clapped, and gave his big brother a high five. Typical of Garey; he was always looking to help his little brother. She still had a tight grip on Paul's pendant as she watched the video, tears streaming down her face.

The second video was taken at Paul's ninth birthday, of him playing with his new puppy, Delta. She could have noticed how happy he was with his little dog but now all she saw were the coughing spasms that erupted from her nine-year-old.

"Damn cystic fibrosis!" she screamed in an empty living room. "Damn you for taking my baby! What did he do? Why my Paul?"

She wasn't ready to let go. What parent would be ready to face such a difficult decision?

Sam only cried at work, sometimes as long as five minutes. He would shut his door and allow the tears to gush from his eyes. Pictures of Paul and Garey surrounding his office just destroyed him inside. He didn't want his wife to see him cry but it wasn't a pride thing. He just knew that his wife was going through hell. When he cried at Garey's funeral, it triggered Lilian's collapse as she fell to the ground and lost all control of her emotions. He did not want to see that sight ever again. The ironic thing was that Lilian wanted to see her husband cry. She wanted to know that both of them were going through this war of emotions together.

Both of them became very depressed. They observed things they never noticed before. They noticed their friends' children and how well they were doing. Debbie Adams, Paul's childhood crush, was now a high school soccer star who had made the local papers. Kevin Oates, Paul's brilliant grammar school friend, had graduated early and was on his way to Yale. They were jealous. Why couldn't their boys have had the same "easy" road? Why did their kids have to suffer? What did they do wrong?

Little things aggravated them more than usual. Before, they laughed off a parking ticket. Now, Paul's dad ripped the ticket off his car and yelled at the police officer, leading to a second, more expensive citation. Paul's mom tried to return a pair of shoes. When the clerk denied her request, she screamed at him and demanded to speak to the manager. When the manager wouldn't budge, she disgustedly flung the shoes into aisle three and stormed out. That wasn't like Lilian. And it certainly wasn't like Sam. But they were dying inside. Their oldest son was dead and their youngest son was on the verge of passing away. There was no way to prepare for that set of life's trials.

Everyday, Lilian and Sam would drive to St. Luke's and the results were the same. Paul wasn't getting any better, Dr. Knotts was less optimistic, and the number of days their son had left was dwindling. Lilian looked at the calendar. Tomorrow was the deadline in her mind that she could keep her son alive. She didn't want him to suffer anymore. Little did she know that he was flying in the clouds as a crime-fighting superhero.

Lilian and Sam looked at each other all night for answers neither one had. They couldn't sleep. The whole ordeal had taken a toll on the tormented couple. Their marriage had even been affected as they hardly talked about anything other than the certain death of their second son. They couldn't even look at each other when they lay in bed.

The following morning, Lilian got out of bed and put on her son's "Special K" pendant. She rubbed it and hoped it would bring her luck but it was going to take a lot more than luck for Paul to make it another day.

The same morning, with another disappointing trip to the hospital looming, Sam pulled over at an abandoned field, flung open his door and jumped out of the car. Lilian watched helplessly as he ran over to a thick cornfield, raised his arms and screamed as loud as he could.

"Why are you doing this to us? Why? What did we do? I can't lose another son. I want my boys back! I hate you cystic fibrosis! I hate you!"

He fell to his knees as Lilian, with tears in her eyes, rushed over to embrace her husband.

"I'm sorry, honey. I'm so sorry that I've lost control. I have all this rage and sadness inside of me," Sam said, apologizing for his long-overdue outburst. "I tried to collect myself. I really did. My heart is empty. How are we expected to go on without our children?"

"It's okay, Sam. It's okay. I feel the same way. Let it all go. Let it out. I love you! We will get through this."

The two of them embraced in the field for nearly a half hour while communicating every emotion that they were feeling. It was the first time in so long that they talked about their feelings. It was as if the cornfield was a therapist that helped save their marriage.

They returned to the car hand-in-hand knowing full well that their journey was not over. A trip to St. Luke's still lie ahead. Would it be the last trip they'd take to room 205? Was there any hope left for Paul? Was there one miracle left?

Chapter 17
Time to Fly

The Solution flew to the hospital and snuck in to see Tommy every night for the next three months. Though his condition worsened, Tommy always had time to talk to Paul. He always stayed positive, telling him he was a fighter. He inspired Paul. One day, Tommy told him he had a brother named Denny and asked if Paul had a brother.

"I did," The Solution said. "He loved me so much. He was always afraid that I'd forget about him when I became a superhero." Nothing could be further from the truth. He reached down to rub the baseball pendant. Suddenly, he realized with horror that before he became a superhero, he ripped it off and threw it to the ground. Now it was gone. He thought of all the letters Garey had written him and how he had ended each one.

I love you Paul.

From your older brother,

Garey Ethan Morgan.

Paul used to think Garey was the lucky one, but it was Paul who still had the chance to live. No matter how short his life expectancy was, he was the lucky one. Maybe Garey never wanted him to be a superhero after all. Maybe he just wanted him to fight. He thought back to Tommy's mother's words, "A superhero needs no cape."

Two weeks later, Tommy passed away. Paul went to the funeral but hung back behind a tree so no one would see him. He cried, realizing that Tommy was right. He may have lost the battle, but he was still a hero. His tombstone fittingly read, "A superhero needs no cape." As Garey would have said, "He wasn't special because of his illness. He was special because of the way he fought his illness."

After the funeral, he walked to his cabin in the woods instead of flying. Losing Tommy really made him long to see his family. He wished he had someone to talk to about it but he knew that was impossible. He thought about the things Tommy told him, and about how he had lived his life when he had CF. He wondered if there was a reason he and Tommy met. He wondered if Gregory had something to do with it. He thought about the old saying, "Life is a gift. Just because you're breathing doesn't mean you're living." He was just breathing, but that wasn't because of cystic fibrosis. It was because of his poor, defeatist attitude and his failure to appreciate what he did have.

His three months as a superhero were almost up. Should he ask Gregory to turn him into Paul Morgan again? Should he risk his health and depend on a new attitude to get him through it? His mind was full of questions as he began to drift off to sleep. A few hours later, he heard a knock at his door. It was Gregory.

"Hello, Paul," he said as he breezed into the cabin and sat down on the couch Paul had built with wood from the forest and his own two hands. "I hope you've enjoyed your time as The Solution. Now, you must decide if this is what you want to do forever. If so, you will continue to be The Solution, and you will be The Solution from heaven. However, know that if you decide to stay like this, the past of Paul Morgan will disappear. In other words, no one will ever know you existed."

"So, you're saying no one will remember Paul Morgan?" he asked, surprised.

"There are consequences to becoming a different person, and that's one of them," Gregory said without a trace of sympathy in his voice. "I would think you'd be okay with the loss of your past since you wouldn't have to worry about your health in the future. Paul Morgan won't be a memory for anyone, and that includes you. As The Solution, you will lose the memory of your parents and your brother. You will forget that you were ever Paul Morgan."

Paul hadn't considered such terms when weighing his decision. He never wanted to let go of Garey's memory and he never wanted to quit on all the dreams that Garey had had for him. He had a lot of things he still wanted to do on earth. He had a lot of things he wanted to accomplish and had a lot of people he wanted to prove wrong about him—one person in particular.

"So what's your decision, Paul?" Gregory's question pulled him back to the present. "Do you want to be Paul Morgan again or do you want to be The Solution?"

He didn't want to go back to the pain and depression. But if he didn't go back, he'd feel guilty for taking the title "superhero." He didn't deserve it and he knew it. He'd be letting Garey and Tommy down. He also didn't want to forget about his past. As bad as it was, his past made him who he was. So what was he to do?

"I see this is difficult for you," Gregory said softly. "I will come back in three days and you can tell me your decision then." With that, he vanished back into the forest.

It would be a long three days!

Paul brooded over what to do. Selfishly, the most important things to him about being a superhero were that he didn't have pain in his chest anymore and he didn't have a life expectancy of four months. Should he just go on to heaven and be The Solution forever? But, would he ever truly respect himself? Maybe he really *could* be the first person ever with CF to make it to the big leagues. But how could he give up being a superhero? Why did he even want to be a superhero in the first place? Was it because he wanted to help people? Was it to see that Garey's prophecy came true? Was it because he didn't want to be sick anymore? The last thing he had done as Paul Morgan was try to kill himself. Would anyone want him back? Would his parents be angry at him for trying to kill himself? How much rehabilitation would it take to have a normal life? Was he willing to put in the time? Would it matter?

He didn't truly understand the options available until he met Tommy. "Imagine if I had actually said something positive while lying in that hospital bed," he thought. Three days passed and Gregory returned.

"Have you reached your decision?" he asked.

Paul had. As he stood there, he took off his cape, folded it neatly and slowly handed it over to Gregory. Though he no longer had the heart to be The Solution, he realized the strength of his heart *was* the solution.

"Gregory, a wise little boy told me a superhero needs no cape," he explained. "This may surprise you, but I've decided to delay my trip to heaven and my life as The Solution forever, and return to my old life."

Gregory smiled. "I'm not surprised at all," he said, his voice swelling with pride. "I'll always be proud of you, and I'll always be looking after you, even though you won't see me anymore."

"I'll never see you again?" Paul asked, his voice breaking.

"You won't see me but you'll know I'm there," he said, his voice breaking slightly, too. "Trust me. Good luck with everything…and remember that if you have a dream, no matter how far-fetched it is, believe! I bet you never thought you'd get a chance to be a superhero. I'm sure you have other dreams you'd like to accomplish. Don't let anyone or anything prevent you from reaching your goals."

"So Gregory, why did you choose me?" he asked him.

"Remember that note I gave you when you first got your uniform?" he reminded Paul, and handed him the crumpled piece of paper he had had lying on a table. Paul read the words again: *"You are a bold hero to me. I pull for you. Gregory Vern Hartman."*

"This will tell you why you were chosen for the wish," he said. At midnight, he explained, The Solution would become Paul Morgan again. With that, he hugged Paul tightly and quickly turned to go.

Paul stood there taking in the sights of all the pieces of this cabin he had created by himself. He knew deep in his soul he had made the right choice. He felt for the first time he could beat cystic fibrosis, that it didn't matter what the doctors or statistics said. Garey would be proud of him for fighting. Garey would have been ashamed if his little brother had called himself a superhero when he wasn't. Now, standing in the middle of the room with regular jeans and a T-shirt on, he felt more like a superhero than ever before. He was smiling like a person who realized he had a second chance. He was going to inspire someone who hadn't been inspired in a very long time—Paul Morgan.

Not knowing why he was granted a wish reminded him of the recurring dream of his first Major League Baseball game. It reminded him that he couldn't figure out who was helping him to get a base hit. Were these two mysteries related? He'd solve that soon enough. Now it was time to focus. He had a tough comeback to make.

He took apart his cabin piece by piece and then tossed his uniform tights and boots in the middle of the wood and lit the pile ablaze. As soon as the fire burned itself out, he left the forest and took a taxi to the hospital where he had lived for so long. He could've flown one last time, but he wanted to be Paul Morgan again. When he got to the hospital, he waited till no one was around, and then, in his final use of superpowers, flew up to the room. Tommy had passed away days earlier, and they still hadn't put anyone else in Room 205.

He put on his old blue-checkered hospital gown and plugged the IV's back into his arms. He tucked himself into bed. Everything had to be in its original place so none of the doctors would suspect he had lived the life of a superhero for the last three months. He turned the TV on to his favorite sports channel and assessed his new/old life.

Physically, he'd still be the same Paul Morgan, a teenager with CF. But mentally, he was a new person with a new attitude. Nothing was going to stop him from living a successful life. Nobody could tell him he would be a failure. His biggest critic was now a support by his side, Paul Morgan. As he nestled his head into the pillow, he glanced at the clock. He didn't remember exactly what time it said, but he knew that *his* time was now.

Chapter 18
Do You Believe in Miracles?

Paul's attitude had changed, but was it too late? Could he still make a comeback? What was in store for the former superhero?

Lilian and Sam drove down to St. Luke's for a final goodbye to their little boy. Both were drained after Sam's cornfield outburst. Sam saw a digital advertisement for the Atlanta Braves on a billboard downtown. Realizing the irony of seeing the one team that kept Paul's spirit alive, he glanced at his wife and smiled. She too noticed the sign, smiled back at Sam, and rubbed Paul's silver pendant.

Sam couldn't help but remember many years before when he was on his way to St. Luke's for far different reasons. Little Paul was about to be born. He recalled the dreams of an expectant father about the endless opportunities that his son would have. He now realized that those opportunities were all but gone.

Lilian thought about the day she brought Paul home from the hospital and he began to cough incessantly and would hardly eat. She didn't know what was wrong with him. The doctors diagnosed him later that night with cystic fibrosis. Lilian remembered the helpless feeling she had when the doctors told her that her son might not live ten years. She believed that if she protected her son twenty-four hours a day that she could change their prognosis of doom. Now she couldn't help but blame herself for being so naïve.

When they arrived, Nurse Johanson greeted each of them with long embraces. "I loved him so much, Lilian. He was my favorite."

"Thanks Ingrid. Paul loved you very much," his mom dejectedly replied. Though her son was still breathing, she felt like she was at his funeral.

They walked up to 205. There was their son, tubes coming out of his arms, neck and mouth. "Such a sad sight to see anyone looking like that, but especially someone so young," Lilian thought. "My poor baby boy. He never had a chance to live his life."

"Sam," she cried, "I could have done more for him. I should have never put him on that medication that caused him to stop walking. I destroyed his confidence. I'm the reason he is lying here. I should have…"

"Lilian," he interrupted. "Don't blame yourself. You did nothing wrong. You loved your son, as did I. We did all we could for him. We thought the drug would help him. We were blessed to have him in our lives all these years. When he was born, doctors told us we might not have him ten years, and he far surpassed that."

"I know," she said. "I always thought it would be tough to say goodbye to Paul when he went to college or got married. That's nothing compared to how difficult it will be to say goodbye to him today."

The two of them hugged each other, not wanting to let go. They were holding more than just each other, they were trying to hold on to all the precious memories of having been blessed with two sons. Garey was already gone and soon Paul would be gone, too.

Dr. Knotts walked in, his ever-present smile noticeably absent. "Sam, Lilian, I wish we were meeting under different circumstances. I need you to fill out some forms, and we'll take care of everything for you."

Lilian pleaded her closing argument as if she was trying to win her son's innocence in a big court case.

"Dr. Knotts, I really believe that he'll come out of this. I know that Paul can fight. I just don't want to say goodbye, but I also want to do what's best for him. He is my baby boy. No one has given him a chance his whole life. I know everything seems lost right now, but…

"Wait a minute, Lilian!" Dr. Knotts erupted. He turned up the volume on the ventilator. "Beep…beep…beep…beep." Sam didn't understand what the big deal was but Lilian immediately picked up on it. She had researched ventilators ever since Paul was put on the device.

"His heart rate is improving, isn't it Dr. Knotts?" she asked, expectantly. Sam grabbed her hand and motioned towards Dr. Knotts.

"Doctor, is he getting better? Well, is he?"

Dr. Knotts bolted to the intercom. "I need some doctors in here now! Right now!" Moments later, several men in light blue scrubs rushed in. Paul's parents scurried to the back of the room, straining to eavesdrop on what the men were discussing.

"What do you guys think?" Dr. Knotts asked.

A balding doctor with a slick brown mustache and wide-framed glasses responded, "Isn't this the Morgan kid? The one with CF?"

"That's him," another doctor interjected. "Look at his oxygen saturation numbers. Check out his heart rate. It appears that he's stabilizing…"

Paul's parents looked at each other. They weren't sure how to react. Was he really getting better or was this just a moment of glory preceding more heartbreak? Still, it was the first bit of good news they'd had concerning their children in nearly six months, so they weren't about to ruin it with pessimism.

Beep…Beep…Beep…Beep. Paul's heartbeat continued to stabilize. *Beep…Beep…Beep*

Lilian began to cry again but this time, they were tears of joy and optimism.

"I thought my son was lost. I thought my son was lost. I thought my son was…"

Dr. Knotts interrupted her with news they'd prayed to hear for months: "Lilian, Sam, I think we found your son."

Chapter 19
Awakened

The next time Paul opened his eyes, he saw before him a face he had sorely missed.

"Mom," he said hoarsely, his eyelids fighting to stay open.

"Paul," she whispered. "Oh, Paul, you're awake." Lilian's hands were shaking as she leaned over him and the huge smile on her face belied her tired eyes. She pressed the nurse call button and when the crackled voice said, "Yes?" His mother's voice changed.

She became all business. "He's awake!" she yelled. "Get Dr. Knotts immediately!" Her attention returned to her conscious son. "Paul, I knew you would survive," she said. "I just knew it. The doctors doubted you, but I never did."

The door flew open and Dr. Knotts rushed in, several nurses in tow. He took one look at Paul and he, too, broke into a wide grin. "Paul, son, we are so happy to see you're awake. How do you feel?"

"Okay, I guess," he said, looking around. It looked like he'd never left the hospital room. He must have done a good job of putting everything the way it was when he'd left. "I'm just a little tired."

Nurse Johanson hurried in. "Paul," she said in her sweetest Swedish accent, "You're back. I'm so happy to see you. I wasn't sure I'd see that welcoming smile again. We all missed you."

Dr. Knotts checked his pulse and took his temperature. He checked his oxygen saturation numbers and then brought a portable lung function machine in to test his lung function. While his mother beamed at him, the doctor took some notes in his notebook and left them alone.

"Mom, how long have I been asleep?" he asked softly. He knew he was talking, but he couldn't feel his lips moving.

"Three months, dear," she said, her voice breaking with emotion. "You were in a coma. We were so worried that we'd never see your smiling face again."

Three months, he thought. He remembered hearing he only had four to six months left to live. Suddenly, he panicked. "Does that mean I only have a month or so to live?" he asked.

"That's the crazy thing, Paul," she started to explain. "About a month after you went into a coma, the doctors asked if we wanted to turn off the ventilator that was keeping you alive. Your lung function, oxygen levels, and heart rate were so low at that point that the doctors thought it was the sensible thing to do. At best, they said your chances of survival were maybe ten percent. But your father and I wouldn't let them turn it off. We believed in you."

Her eyes got moist as she continued. "After losing Garey, we couldn't see our other child lose his life, too."

She told him about how, two months into his coma, his numbers continued to dwindle. Dr. Knotts asked them again what they wanted to do.

"We told him to please give you a little more time," his mother said. "But I have to admit that we were beginning to worry that you would never wake up. A month later, just when it looked like your body had shut down, the doctors saw an immediate improvement one day. We were in the room when it happened. According to the blood tests and chest X-rays, you continued to get stronger every day, stronger than you had been in a long time."

His mother showed him a copy of the tests the doctors had done while he was in a coma. His numbers had climbed from life-threatening over the first two months to stable over the last couple of weeks. But for someone who has been in a hospital room for much of the last couple of years, the numbers seemed to reflect that Paul was doing pretty well.

Dr. Knotts knocked softly on the door and came back in to report the results of the lung function test he'd just given Paul. "Paul, your pulmonary function scores are in the sixty percent range, which is about twenty-five percent higher than when you went into the coma," he said with disbelief in his voice. He shook his head, not comprehending how this could have happened. "I even had the machine checked to make sure it was calibrated correctly. I don't understand how you grew so strong so fast, but I'm not complaining. This is miraculous news."

According to Dr. Knotts, Paul was in critical condition when he went into the coma but he was now upgrading him to stable. Dr. Knotts grinned as if he'd written a eulogy he could now throw away.

His mother was still beaming. "It's as if you started fighting back against the disease," she said happily. "You heard Dr. Knotts. He says you're a lot stronger. He thinks you may have a chance now to beat this. You still have to work hard so you don't regress, but there is hope. It's a miracle, Paul."

She leaned over and hugged him hard. He hugged her back with what little strength he had regained and grinned. It wasn't a miracle, though. He knew it was something far different. It was his attitude. It wasn't a coincidence that the moment he gave the cape back to Gregory his vital signs improved significantly. He was not scared anymore. As he lay there conscious for the first time in months, he realized everything looked different. It was as if he was seeing his surroundings—the stark, fluorescent-lit hospital room, the dim hallways, even his beloved Turner Field through the window of Room 205—with new eyes.

"Mom, I'm not worried about regressing," he smiled at her. "I'm more concerned with progressing. Cystic fibrosis has a fight on its hands, Mom. I promise."

"Wow, Paul, your attitude is so different now," she said, surprised but pleased. "What's changed?"

"I realize I can do anything I want. I'm not going to give up. I'm going to stand up for myself and inspire others, and I'm going to appreciate my second chance," he told her. And it was all true. "I learned from Gregory that my goals are limitless. He told me I could beat this."

"Who is Gregory?" she asked, bewildered. "An old roommate?"

"Gregory Vern Hartman, Mom, from the Make-A-Wish Foundation," he said, as if she should have known, "He was the guy you asked to see me after Dr. Knotts discussed my poor test results with me. Thanks for asking him to talk to me. He really helped me." Paul winked at his mother, hoping that maybe she knew how special Gregory was.

His mom looked concerned. "Paul," she said, "we turned the Make-A-Wish representative away when you went into a coma. We thought it was too late."

Paul, too, was baffled. Was all of it just a dream? It felt so real. And it *was* three months. He was a little disappointed but still more motivated than he'd ever been. He prattled on about Gregory and what he'd learned from him but soon his voice grew hoarse again, drawing a warning from his mom.

"Just slow down, dear, that's enough. You're going to hurt your throat. Here," she said, handing him his magnetic board that Garey had given him. Using it, he spelled out the note he had received from Gregory.

You are a bold hero to me. I pull for you. Gregory Vern Hartman.

She read the message and furrowed her brow. "He sure isn't the guy from the Make-A-Wish Foundation, but that's a nice note," she said, slightly patronizing. "The important thing is you know people believe in you, Paul. We believe in you. Garey always believed in you. We love you very much."

He decided to tell his mother the fantastic, true story of the past three months, everything from meeting Gregory to becoming The Solution to meeting and being inspired by Tommy to finally waking up. His mother wiped away her tears and smiled at him as if her son had completely lost his mind. Then she reached around her neck and removed the silver baseball pendant.

"Thought you might want this," she said as she returned it to its rightful place around his neck. He looked down and rubbed it, and smiled through his own tears. The touching moment was shattered when the door burst open and Paul saw his dad, who had heard the great news from his mom and rushed out of work to see his son.

"Paul, you look great," he said excitedly, running over to grab him in a huge bear hug. He told Paul he prayed every day and night for him, and had everyone at work do the same. As his parents celebrated, he glanced out the window and saw a rainbow.

"See, that's good luck," said his dad, pointing outside. "Things are only going to get better." Paul didn't need a rainbow to tell him things were going to get better. He had a new attitude that was doing just fine.

"Mom, Dad, are you upset with me that I tried to kill myself?" he asked tentatively.

They looked at each other, and his mom spoke first. "We were disappointed and scared but we knew that you were going through a really tough time. But, that's no excuse to try to take your life—you need to learn to talk about how you're feeling rather than explode."

Then it was his dad's turn. "Paul, we can't lose you, too. It was so hard for us to lose Garey. We grieve every day. But we also pray every day that good things will happen to you. We're so happy to see you again."

Paul, too, was elated to see his family. He couldn't believe that he'd become so desperate that he was willing to end it all.

When they left him alone, he sat up in bed and pondered how something that felt so real could have been just a dream. Was his experience as The

Solution like his baseball dream? Regardless, he was ready to change. He had learned something very important—that he couldn't get mad at people because he was sick. He was the only one who could make himself better. He had to take better care of himself and assume responsibility for taking his medications and doing his treatments. He'd learned something else, too. His dreams weren't meant to tease him about things he couldn't do, but rather to inspire him to strive for things he *could* do.

He also realized that his sixteenth birthday was in eight months. He never thought he'd see another birthday. He was saddened that this would be his first birthday without his big brother and he knew that would be difficult. Still, he now had plenty to be thankful for.

He looked at the magnetic board once again and read the words he had spelled out for his mother:

You are a bold hero to me. I pull for you. Gregory Vern Hartman.

He lifted the board above his head in triumph and pronounced to himself that his glory days lay ahead. When he went to lower the board back onto the bed, he accidentally dropped it on the floor. There was a loud crash as the letters spread all over the floor.

His mother rushed in, afraid he'd fallen or something else had happened. When she saw he was just sitting there, she relaxed.

"Mom, I dropped my magnetic board is all. Can you pick it up for me?"

She looked down at the board on the floor and froze. A heavy silence filled the room. Paul suddenly became afraid to speak. She quickly gathered her composure.

"What's wrong?" he asked as the moment passed.

"Nothing, dear," she said quickly. "I'll pick up all the letters for you and put them away, but the board is broken. I'll get you a new one tomorrow."

She kissed him goodbye and left. As he lay back down, he started thinking about how he was going to change his life. He would have to combat CF with a tough attitude, much tougher than before. He would to have to be willing to deal with disappointments and not be satisfied with small accomplishments. He made a list of the top-five things he wanted to accomplish:

5. I will walk again. I will take rehabilitation seriously and get back on my feet.

4. I will tell my story to kids and adults afraid of having an illness. Tell them how I learned to cope with it and how I used my attitude to defeat it. Inspire others to succeed, like Tommy did for me.

3. I will never take life for granted again and I will appreciate my family, who remained by my side holding my hand and talking to me while I was in a coma.

2. I will find that horrible bully Biff Goolson one day and show him what Paul Morgan is all about, that Paul Morgan can stand up for himself.

1. I will go after my life-long dream to be a Major League Baseball player.

Just then, he saw the rainbow again, but this time he noticed something peculiar about it. He couldn't help but smile at the fortuitous sight—the rainbow, fittingly, was cast over Turner Field.

Chapter 20
An Emotional Rehab

Paul had a lot of work to do, so he wasted no time. First up: strengthening his lungs. To do that, he had to exercise and be diligent about taking his meds. Suddenly, he remembered some literature in the nightstand drawer that could help, if it was still there. He leaned over and opened the drawer underneath the phone, anxious to find his stash. Sure enough, there they were—about forty body-builder magazines his brother had ordered for him. He hadn't cracked opened any of them but that was going to change.

But to truly feel good about himself, he thought, he needed to get out of the hospital. He vowed to *walk* out, not wheel out. For some accountability, he shared his goal with Nurse Johanson.

"Paul, I'm so proud of you," she said. His heart soared when she asked if there was anything she could do to help.

"Well," he said, "do you know anyone who could help me walk, like a personal trainer or something?"

"Actually, I have a friend who works downstairs in rehab, and I'm sure he'd love to work with you," she smiled. "I'll call him as soon as I finish my shift." She winked at him as she backed out of the room and he now had another motivation to succeed—to continue to make her proud.

Paul met Nurse Johanson's friend, Larry, a physical therapist, toward the end of January. He was short, probably in his mid-fifties, had a slender build and was balding on top. This wasn't exactly what Paul envisioned in a personal trainer. Early on, during their first meeting in 205, Larry told him he used to train a women's professional softball team in Phoenix.

"These women were amazing athletes," he said as he paced around the room, unable to sit still for a second. "I was there for almost 20 years, and now I train athletes individually. I work a lot with athletes with disabilities, which is why Nurse Johanson thought I could help you."

Athletes with disabilities. Paul wondered if that was what *he'd* be some day soon—a real athlete who just happened to have CF.

"I've spent a really long time in this hospital room," Paul said, trying to keep his voice bright but wanting to tell Larry there was so much work ahead of him. "Actually, that's kind of an understatement—I've spent most of my life here." He began coughing and couldn't stop, as if presenting evidence of how long a road to recovery this might be.

"That doesn't matter," Larry said, literally brushing away Paul's comment as trivial. "Paul," he said, locking eyes with his expectant patient. "You can do this. You can walk again. Push yourself. Believe in yourself. *Know* you can do it."

Where had Paul heard that before? He swallowed hard and remembered. Garey. He realized, yes, Garey had been right all along. He could do this. And he would, with Larry's help.

"I did some research on your case," Larry continued, still pacing. "It seems you have a very rare condition but it's not hopeless. My feeling is you won't be able to walk right away, and it might take months or even years."

Paul nodded. He knew there was a lot of work ahead. He just had to keep his eyes on the prize—walking out of St. Luke's under his own power. Truthfully, he wanted it to be months, though. It was hard to hear that it could take years. He was impatient. He wanted immediate results but talking to Larry confirmed that a quick recovery was not in the cards. Accepting the fact that success would take time was an accomplishment in itself.

"Paul, you also must know that there's a possibility that no matter how hard we work, you still may not be able to walk. I know I'm supposed to motivate you and I really do believe that you will walk again, but I also want to be upfront with you."

As much as he hated hearing that he might never walk again, he knew deep-down it was a real possibility. He understood that Larry had to tell him the worst-case scenario, but if he wanted to succeed he had to put the negative thoughts behind him.

"Larry, I understand. I've learned to live with a wheelchair and I'm prepared to use it the rest of my life if I need to. However, I never want to say 'What if I'd just worked harder or listened to my brother?' I never want to say that I could have done more to reach my dream. This is as much mental as it is physical for me, Larry."

"That brings me to my next point. Before we get started with the physical work, I want to make sure you're prepared for this, emotionally," Larry said, coming back around the side of Paul's bed and staring intently at him again. "I want you to speak to another friend of mine, a psychologist. Her name is Dr. Sarah Billingsley and she's worked here at St. Luke's with several patients. My recommendation is that you see her for several weeks and then we'll talk after she assesses you," Larry explained. "How's that sound?"

Paul pondered for a moment. He was so eager to get up and start moving right away but he recognized that he had spent so much time hating himself and his life, being depressed and unmotivated. It would do him good to really talk to someone about what he wanted for his life, now that he was taking control of it again.

"Yes, that's fine," he said to Larry. "Thank you—this means a lot to me."

"Okay, kid," he said as he crossed the room in long strides toward the door. "We'll be in touch."

Paul saw Dr. Billingsley almost a month later. They met in her small, cozy office next door to the hospital. She looked to be in her early forties, had light brown curly hair, and kind brown eyes. Her voice was very soothing and soft. She smiled a lot and if she wasn't about the same age as his mom, he might have had a crush on her, too.

"I know this won't be easy for you," she said, as they both settled on overstuffed green couches across from each other. "But I just want you to take me through your life, bring me up to this point. What led you here, Paul?"

Over the next several weeks, he told Dr. Billingsley everything. It was actually very easy to talk about, his feelings spewing forth like a shaken soda after the cap is removed. He told her how he didn't have many friends growing up and how Biff Goolson tormented him. He explained to her about CF and how painful it was and how he was not supposed to live much longer. He told her how he felt he had accomplished very little in his life, having spent most of it in hospitals. He talked to her about Garey's death and his dream to get a base hit to win a Major League baseball game. He even told her about the masked man in the recurring dream.

102

For the next six months, he let all his bottled-up emotions spill out. During most sessions he would be on the verge of tears—sometimes they were happy tears but most of the time they weren't. Dr. Billingsley was very patient with him and asked him a lot of questions to help him understand his feelings about all the events in his life. He realized he had a lot of frustration trapped inside. For a long time, he had felt like he'd been treated unfairly by God.

"I want you to work on using your anger, your frustration, as energy," Dr. Billingsley explained. "Use it as a way to push yourself to do great things. Let's work the next few weeks on taking that negative energy and making it positive."

Toward the end of their final session, she offered a pep talk. "You've told me for several weeks that no one but your brother truly believed in you," she said. "That your parents do, but that Garey believed in you so much he told you you'd be a superhero. He really believed that. Do you have faith in yourself?"

He hadn't really thought of that. "I guess I do," he answered. He flashed back to when he was a superhero and all of the good deeds he did. He thought about how Tommy fought hard to live. He remembered how Tommy said that superheroes didn't need capes. If that's true, then he did believe. "Yeah," he answered a bit more forcefully. "I can accomplish my goals."

"And why are you here right now, Paul?" Dr. Billingsley asked him.

"Because I want to walk again. I want to accomplish that goal. I want to be a stronger person," he said confidently.

"Well, you've already accomplished a lot toward that goal," she said, smiling. "You've already made up your mind that you're going to walk again and be a stronger person. You've already talked about your life and relieved yourself of some of those negative feelings you've been carrying around."

That didn't seem to compare with jumping out of his wheelchair and running around the bases at Turner Field. He rolled his eyes.

"Dr. B., those don't sound like big accomplishments," he said. "I mean, the big accomplishment would be to walk again, right?"

"An accomplishment is an accomplishment—there are no big or little accomplishments," Dr. B. answered. She let him stew on that for a minute before asking, "Do you think you will become a Major League baseball player?"

No one had ever asked him that directly. He thought about it. "Well, sure," he said. "I guess so."

"You *know* so," she said sternly. "That's your goal. So shoot for the moon, Paul. There's a saying I like: 'Shoot for the moon. Even if you miss, you'll still be amongst the stars.'"

He liked that! After talking to her, he became even more focused on the task at hand: to walk again.

And so the journey began...

Chapter 21
Time to Get Moving

On the morning of his sixteenth birthday, August 12, he took the elevator and rode his wheelchair over to Larry's third-floor hospital office for the first time. The first thing he noticed in the sparse office was that the walls were whiter than the clouds—there was not a picture in sight.

"Why so barren?" Paul asked with a laugh.

"I'm not much of an interior decorator," he mumbled and looked away.

Paul shrugged as they started with some chest exercises.

Later, he asked Nurse Johanson about Larry's blank office walls. She told him that several years ago, on his first day working as a physical therapist for St. Luke's, Larry was assigned to work with a patient named Joey Sakes, a twelve-year-old boy with CF. Joey had had a lung transplant a few months earlier but was told his chances of living a normal life were slim. Larry wouldn't hear of it. Joey was able to walk and even run but his weakness was his endurance, so Larry vowed to make him stronger. He and Joey worked intensely for several months. Joey pushed himself to be a big success, and Larry was so proud that he put a twelve-inch by twelve-inch, wooden-framed photograph of Joey on his wall. It was the first decoration in his new office.

"I didn't see that picture," he interrupted.

"Well, he took it down," she continued. "Apparently, during one of their workouts, Joey started to gasp for air. Larry thought he was faking, since he'd done that before as a practical joke, so Larry urged him to work harder instead of fooling around. But ten minutes later, Joey collapsed and passed out. The new lung had rejected his body. Joey died later that afternoon."

Paul was quiet as he listened to the rest of her story. "Larry took it the hardest of anyone at the hospital. It took several doctors at St. Luke's to convince him not to quit his job. But to remind himself of what happened, he removed Joey's picture from his wall and left it bare. He's never put another picture up because no one has inspired him like Joey Sakes did."

Nurse Johanson paused, "And quite frankly I don't think anyone ever will."

Paul saw the irony right away. Larry had tried to inspire everyone he worked with but the truth was, nothing had inspired him in a very long time.

He and Larry began their training that August by working with dumbbells. A month later, on September 15, Paul had an especially difficult day. It was the one-year anniversary of Garey's death. He cried a lot that day and didn't feel like going to rehab. His parents came to his room and they just sat together for several hours, occasionally sharing memories of Garey. Though it was a depressing day, he found some motivation in it. He remembered all the times Garey pushed him to be stronger. He wouldn't allow Paul to quit. So the next day, he took that advice and used it to inspire him when he worked out with Larry. Three months later, he had gone from lifting 5-pound dumbbells to 25-pound weights. Soon, he was seeing results in the mirror. His biceps—he actually had biceps now—curved upward when he flexed them. But something else was growing along with those muscles— his spirit. You wouldn't know how sore his body was by seeing his clown-shaped smile when he looked into the mirror. He still had no leg strength, but Larry said they would eventually get to that.

"If you can strengthen your upper body, there's no reason why you can't strengthen your lower body," Larry would say.

On his days off from Larry's regimen, Paul still worked out. He lifted dumbbells in his room. The nurses didn't look too kindly on that, thinking he could get hurt, but as long as someone else was in the room with him, they relented. Paul thought they were silently pleased that he was motivated by something and occasionally he'd see a smile from one of them as he pumped dumbbells in front of them. To Paul, a day without working out meant waiting a day longer to capture his dream. And he wanted those nurses to know that having CF didn't mean he was incapable of getting stronger.

A week or so later, a doctor came strutting in with four of his residents in tow. Paul was sitting up in bed with three pillows stuffed behind him, watching the Braves-Astros game. The Jet was pitching a two-hitter into the eighth inning. It annoyed Paul when anyone interrupted a Braves game, especially a doctor he didn't even know. He knew the routine though. He was supposed to lie there and let the doctor talk about him as if he was just a statistic. The only thing Paul liked about this guy was his beard, which resembled Dr. Knotts' facial fur.

"The patient suffers from cystic fibrosis, cannot use his legs, and..." Before he could say another word, Paul suddenly interrupted.

"And I'm going to live a long life because I have a strong attitude." The doctor grimaced but Paul was more concerned about his students who wanted to learn about cystic fibrosis.

He'd always wanted to hear a doctor tell his residents that CF wasn't a death sentence and if the doctor wasn't going to do it, then Paul would. When someone has an illness, that person doesn't want a doctor to tell him repeatedly what he has and what his chances are. He wants his physician to treat him like a person. That someone wants a doctor to support him the way that Dr. Knotts supported Paul. A doctor needs to mix in personal questions like asking the person what he watches on television or what his favorite food is. When a doctor can become a friend, he gives the greatest gift any patient could ask for. A patient with a life-threatening disease knows what he has and there's no need to repeatedly remind that person of the obstacles that lay ahead. Paul looked at the two students standing to the left of his bed and in front of the window.

"My pulmonary function scores have been increasing monthly. I work out daily. Did you know it's possible for CF patients to improve and live normal lives?"

The students looked somewhat dumfounded, as if they weren't sure if they were allowed to talk to him. He noticed a tall, skinny woman with curly brown hair and a dark complexion towards the back of the room. He saw that her name tag hung a little crooked on her sweater as she stepped forward.

"I didn't know a person with CF could get better. I thought lung disease got worse everyday. How do you get stronger?" she said, raising her hand to her face with a contemplative look, intrigued how he could disprove a theory she'd studied for years.

"Good question," he said. "Doing treatments. Taking my pills when I'm supposed to. Treating infections when they start. Getting exercise by working out. But most importantly, by having faith in myself. You'd be surprised how far a strong will can take you."

She smiled, nodded and then jotted some notes down on her small notepad. A young man with short blonde hair and brown eyes, wearing a red and white striped shirt and a navy blue tie, posed the next question.

"Do you worry about your life expectancy?"

This probing personal quiz prompted the doctor to smack his hands together suddenly.

"Why don't we let the patient rest? Sorry, son. We'll be leaving. You probably don't want to answer these questions." He adjusted his white coat but before he could turn around, Paul stopped him.

"No, it's okay," he said calmly. "Your resident has a good question. Of course I worry about my life expectancy. There's not much I can do though. I just have to keep fighting. The median life expectancy of CF patients goes up a year each year that they survive. So, last year it was twenty-eight and this year it's twenty-nine. New treatments and research have led to this. I hope that some day there's actually a cure."

He'd always hoped that CF would have a cure, but honestly, he'd learned to put that out of his mind. When he was a lot younger, doctors said a cure was seven to ten years away. Since gene therapy and other methods had failed or taken a lot longer to get approval, doctors continued to say seven to ten years. There was no certainty that there would be a cure in his lifetime so he didn't spend a lot of time thinking about it. Paul knew that if he did, it would just bring him down, knowing that the cure was still years away. So, as far as he was concerned, there would never be a cure for cystic fibrosis and he would have to be okay with that.

The six-foot tall Asian student, wearing a navy blue collared shirt, chimed in. "I'm sorry that you have to suffer so much. It must be really tough emotionally, not to mention physically." He lowered his head with a glum look on his face.

"I have cystic fibrosis but I don't suffer from it. I thrive despite it. Don't feel sorry for me. Like I said before, I'm going to live a long life." The student lifted his head, adjusted his wide-framed glasses and smiled.

The other resident, a short young man with a pale complexion and a small patch of gray hair near his right temple, appeared timid.

"Will, anything you'd like to ask?" the doctor said.

"Yes, sir," he replied. "As a doctor, what role can I play to better serve my patient?"

That might have been the best question of all, Paul thought.

"I think the best thing a doctor can do is have faith in his or her patient. My doctor is very supportive of me. Treat your patient like a person. Don't be afraid to joke with your patient or ask that person what his or her favorite musical group is. Being in a hospital is very scary. Whatever you can do to alleviate some of that fear will do wonders for your patient."

Paul had noticed something in the twenty minutes he talked to these residents. They seemed more interested in the patient's point of view rather than the numbers and percentages on a chart. He couldn't help but think he'd helped them to become better physicians. The doctor gathered the students around him and walked toward the door. After the residents had filed out, the doctor looked back at Paul before leaving.

"Thank you, Mr. Morgan. I can safely say that we learned a lot today."

Paul didn't want to inspire people by lying in a hospital bed anymore. He'd done that far too long. If he was going to inspire anyone, it would be because he wouldn't need to lie in a hospital bed much longer.

His seventeenth birthday marked the first anniversary of training with Larry. Paul celebrated by lifting fifty pounds with his arms. Doctors and nurses around the hospital were starting to notice. Nurse Johanson asked if she could feel his muscles. He blushed but obliged, of course. Larry didn't want him to get complacent, though. He walked into the room the following day with the next step to his recovery.

"Buddy," Larry said, "it's time to start your lower body training."

Lifting his legs was extremely difficult. It was as if his feet, as well as his legs, were asleep and anytime he tried to move them, he felt a tingly sensation. He could not hold them still for a very long time and he certainly couldn't move them in any sort of rhythm. Larry sat Paul in a chair and would have him hold his legs in the air as high as he could. The tingling sensation would take over and it would be difficult to keep his legs up. He was able to lift his legs only about three inches. Larry would put his arm behind Paul's legs and help him hold them up. After three weeks, he was still stuck at three inches and starting to get frustrated again.

"It's going to take time," Larry kept reminding him. "Just remember that this might hurt, but the day you walk, it will make the struggle worth it."

As much as Paul knew that he would not walk immediately, part of him hoped for the same type of miraculous recovery he'd made with his lungs— how he'd gone from near death to doing relatively well. Though he was having some success, he was disappointed that he wasn't having more. Two weeks later, on the second anniversary of his brother's death, he told Larry he wanted to try and walk on crutches for the first time.

"Just let me try it, for my brother," he pleaded when Larry told him it was too early. "Garey always pushed me to persevere regardless of the odds."

Shaking his head but relenting without further protest, Larry got all of the equipment together and wheeled him to a different room, which had two beams sitting side by side.

"Ok, hold each of these beams and try to take a step," he instructed.

Paul realized that these could be the first steps toward his dream. He took a deep breath and tried to put all his weight on his legs. Suddenly, they buckled under him and he fell on the mat below. He failed to hold himself up in his next two attempts, so they stopped for the day. Paul was a little disappointed but he knew Garey would have been proud of his attempt.

A week later, Dr. Knotts said he didn't have to stay in the hospital for three weeks of the month anymore. Since his pulmonary scores had risen so high over the last couple of years, he only needed to be at the hospital ten days per month. He was elated, but he knew that was just a small step toward progress. He tried to keep Dr. B.'s statement in his mind—that any accomplishment, regardless of whether it was small or big, was still an accomplishment.

During the third month of leg-lifting, Larry asked him to try to lift his legs up without any support. Paul took a few deep breaths, and then slowly pushed with all of his might. Everyone living on that floor could hear him groaning.

"Come on! Come on!" Larry prodded. Paul could feel his shaking legs slowly climbing until finally, he'd had enough and dropped his legs to the ground.

"How much was that?" he asked, out of breath.

"Nine inches," Larry said proudly.

They continued to train through the winter. His pulmonary function scores kept climbing. A good score for someone with cystic fibrosis was in the mid-seventy percent range. He was now in the mid-eighty percent range and he could lift seventy-five pounds with each arm and could hold his legs two feet off the ground. He was making true progress.

As he worked with the weights, he continued to focus on his studies. He'd had a tutor for several years and hadn't paid much attention but since he'd started working with Dr. B. and Larry, he pushed himself with schoolwork too. He graduated from tenth grade work in June and had progressed to eleventh grade on many subjects, finally catching up to where he should be. He was a few weeks shy of his 18th birthday, and just a few months shy of another chance on crutches. A few steps would be progress, but he wouldn't be satisfied until he finished the course.

On his birthday, his mom, dad and Larry presented him with a gift. The card read, *Never lose focus on your goals. You're making all of us believers.* Paul grinned widely when he saw what was inside the box: baseball videotapes. The three of them sat around his bed and watched as Paul's dream came to life on screen in one video, "How to Become a Better Baseball Player," which featured Ricky "The Jet" Kilmer. He thought as he sat there staring happily at the screen that maybe everyone else was beginning to believe in his goal as much as he did. Maybe he was inspiring them the way Tommy Stevenson, during his superhero days, inspired him.

The first thing the tapes taught him was to practice every day by just taking the ball out of the glove and throwing it back in. His dad bought him a new Mizuno baseball glove and the first thing he did was oil it so he could squeeze it. Day after day, he took the ball out of his glove and threw it back in, adding that exercise to Larry's regimen. Soon he was bouncing the ball off the wall behind his bed back into his glove.

By the third anniversary of his brother's death, he was ready to show Larry that he could do the beams now. He just knew he was ready. Larry positioned him between the two bars and Paul grabbed each one and hoisted himself up. He took one step, then another. He was walking! With confidence, he took a third step but suddenly, his legs just gave way under him and he tumbled to the ground. He cut his lip when he hit the mat, and broke his thumb trying to catch himself. Larry needed the assistance of two doctors to get him back to the room and get him fixed up.

Paul was so angry with himself. Even with his brother's spirit to motivate him, he still couldn't walk. Negative thoughts began to creep back into his psyche. Will I ever be able to walk? Was this goal inconceivable and unrealistic? Maybe I *am* just a puzzle like Biff Goolson always said. Who was I kidding with this new attitude?

After the doctors finished wrapping his thumb and bandaging his lip, he sat in bed wondering if he had done the wrong thing by not staying a superhero and going to heaven. Negative thoughts continued to occupy his head. Should I have just kept being The Solution? Why do only bad things seem to happen to me? He grabbed all of the Jet's videos and shoved them in the garbage. He called Larry, ordering him to come to his room. When he arrived, Paul pointed to the garbage can and started yelling at him.

"I'm never going to walk! Why are you encouraging me anyway? You know that! I'm sick of you telling me that I'm going to reach all of my goals when the truth is I'll be stuck in a wheelchair for the rest of my life. So from now on, just leave me alone."

Larry stood there looking at his angry patient, having taken the outburst with no expression at all.

"You know what, kid," he replied, calmly. "I think you need a break. You've been working too hard the last couple of years. Take some time off. I predict when we resume rehabilitation you'll be much more motivated."

After having his say, Larry walked out. Paul threw a pillow at the door as it closed behind Larry, still enraged and feeling defeated. His mind began to wander.

Did Larry not hear a word that I was saying? What was he talking about? What in the world was left to motivate me?

Chapter 22
Field of Dreams

Two weeks later, Paul had been asleep most of the day when someone knocked on his door.

"Come in!" he yelled. "Oh. Hi Dr. Knotts."

"Someone outside has a gift for you," Dr. Knotts said, a twinkle in his eye. "Can he bring it in?"

Not one to decline a present, Paul agreed. Dr. Knotts turned to whisper to someone standing next to the door. Paul figured that it was Larry trying to make amends after their little falling out. Then Dr. Knotts stepped out and in his place loomed a man, six-foot, three-inches tall with short brown hair and brown eyes, wearing an olive green suit and a Braves baseball cap that Paul had seen him wear 162 times a year.

"Whoa," Paul said, perked up by who had just walked in 205. "Are you really…are you?"

"Hi, Paul," Ricky "The Jet" Kilmer said cheerfully. "I have something for you."

He just stared at The Jet as he handed over a large color photo of himself on the mound. It was an action shot of him throwing one of his 101-mile-per-hour fastballs. It was signed, *Dear Paul, Good luck on your dream. The Jet.*

"How…? Why…?" Paul could barely speak he was so shocked. Here was his hero standing right in his hospital room! Ricky laughed and told him he had gotten a call from Larry, who had helped Ricky recover from a ligament injury several years before. Larry had told The Jet his patient watched every game he pitched. The Jet was so moved that he wanted to come visit Paul on his day off.

Rather than just stopping by, though, The Jet stayed a while. They spent a few hours talking—once Paul was able to get his jaw back in place. He told him about Garey and Ricky actually remembered facing him a few spring trainings ago. Ricky told Paul if he ever wanted a shot in the Braves organization to let him know. Paul didn't know if he was just being nice but he hoped that he was being sincere.

"I will definitely take you up on that offer someday," Paul said, unable to stop grinning. He still couldn't believe it. He was sitting here talking face to face with his idol, probably the best southpaw of all time. How many people got this opportunity? He was so happy that his eyes got misty. Embarrassed, he grabbed a tissue from his dresser and quickly wiped away the tears before they could fully form.

"So," Ricky said, "do you have any plans for the rest of the day?"

"Well, I have to be here for red Jell-O at 5 p.m.," he quipped, "but other than that, I'm free."

"Well, Paul, put on your jacket," he said as he retrieved his wheelchair from the other side of the room. "We're going out."

Ricky wheeled Paul downstairs and got him into a blue minivan parked in front of the hospital. Who should poke his head out of the van but Larry, with a huge grin on his face. As soon as they got onto the highway headed downtown, Paul realized where they were headed: his favorite baseball stadium, Turner Field. When they arrived they went through all these underground tunnels and finally emerged at the place he'd been dreaming about for so long. He stared in awe at the immense green field, the huge billboards on the side that he had only seen on TV, the enormous stadium surrounding the field itself. It was a good thing someone was pushing his wheelchair or he'd have just stayed in one place, awestruck. The Jet pushed him out to home plate.

"I brought you here because Larry told me about the dream that you keep having," he said quietly. "The one where you get to home plate in this stadium, and you get a chance at your first Major League hit to win the game."

"Uh-huh," he answered, staring out at the stadium and the field, barely hearing Ricky's words.

"Paul, it doesn't always have to end with you waking up. Do you understand what I mean?"

He most definitely understood. Paul knew it was up to him to make the dream into reality. He was frustrated at himself for giving up on his dream. The Jet steered him around the bases and as they passed second, he asked Paul to visualize running around the bases. When they crossed home plate, he had a new message for his young friend.

"The next time you do this," he said, looking into Paul's eyes, "I want you wearing a Major League uniform and I want you running."

Yet another motivation to get up and walking—so he could fulfill this part of his dream. Reach for the moon, Dr. B. continued to tell him. And now his new friend, Ricky "The Jet" Kilmer, was telling him too.

Once Paul came down from his high and realized that he was, in fact, talking to his idol, he and Ricky became good friends. Paul charted his statistics like he did his brother's. The Jet kept up with Paul's "stats" too, his pulmonary function scores. Once, he told Paul that he only had one goal left in baseball: to throw a no-hitter. It was amazing to Paul that someone who had accomplished so much still had goals, but Ricky told him that the key to being successful was to always establish goals. Ricky was very passionate about getting that no-hitter and nothing was more important to him. Ricky was still his idol but, in time, he also became his best friend, the closest thing he had to Garey.

During his fourth year of working with Larry, Paul grew so strong that his pulmonary function scores rocketed into the mid-nineties. One afternoon while his parents were visiting, Dr. Knotts came by to tell them that he didn't have to be on IV antibiotics or some of his other medicines anymore. And, Dr. Knotts said, there was more.

"I've talked it over with your parents," he said, "and we've decided that you don't need to stay here anymore. You're doing so well."

"This isn't one of your jokes, is it?" Paul asked, skeptically.

"No, Paul," he sighed. "I'm thrilled to say you're free to go. You don't even need Nurse Johanson to come by while you're at home. I still want you at the hospital one day a month so we can track your progress, but that's it."

"Yes!" he shouted, pumping his fist in the air. "One huge hurdle overcome!" Of course, he was slightly disappointed that Nurse Johanson wouldn't be showing her beautiful face at the Morgan house anymore.

"We're so proud of you, son," his dad said, slapping him on the back. "Let's get you packed and ready to come home tomorrow."

Paul thought about the friends he'd lost at St. Luke's, like Stan Blue. He thought about the time Dr. Knotts told him he had four months to live. He thought about all of the doubters whom, through sheer force of will, he'd turned into believers. He proved that escape from St. Luke's was possible. He was going home.

The next day was his homecoming. The first time he'd been home in a couple of weeks. He wheeled himself into the house and took a big breath of home air. Delta was sitting there, then barked a few times, and slowly came over to lick his hands. He turned toward his mom, who was all fidgety with glee.

"Mom," he laughed, "you haven't stopped smiling since we left the hospital."

"I'm just so happy," she said, pushing him over to the wheelchair lift next to the staircase. "Why don't you go to your room so you can take a nap?"

"Yeah, I am a bit tired," he said, not realizing that she wanted him upstairs for a reason. He rounded the corner to his bedroom, which was just to the left of the stairs. He noticed that though the door was usually ajar, this time it was conspicuously closed. When he opened the door, he gasped in amazement. His parents, the people whom he thought were just humoring him when it came to his dream of playing Major League baseball, had his room painted and decorated to look like Turner Field. The floor was covered in green carpet. The walls were painted to look like a stadium, complete with seats and cartoon-like fans cheering. Along one wall was a replica of a peanut stand and another wall had what looked like a dugout painted at the foot of the stands. Everything looked exactly like a real baseball stadium. Next to his bed on the floor was a replica of a home plate with an inscription:

A superhero needs no cape.

His mother had remembered the story he told her when he came out of his coma, about what Tommy had said to him just before he died. She knew his dream was to get his first base hit to win a game at Turner Field. *They believed in me*, he thought. *They really did.*

"We want you to be comfortable when you get to bat at Turner Field, so we thought we'd get you a bit more familiar with it," his mother said softly behind him.

"Hey Paul," his father uttered, "How's that for a home field advantage?" His parents had followed him up the stairs and stood quietly as he took it all in. He turned toward them, his eyes watering, and reached out and gave them each a big bear hug.

"I'm just amazed," he said, choking back tears. "I can't thank you enough."

"We should be thanking you," his father said. "You've given us reason to hope and believe, and we know now that you are truly going to get well."

As he lay in bed that night, he kept looking at cartoon fans on the wall. It made him smile, but he couldn't help thinking that his brother would never be one of them. He started to tear up but then realized that this was not the time. He still had a lot of work to do.

Chapter 23
A Significant Move

The next day, he could think of nothing else but walking by himself. His mother dropped him off at the hospital to meet with Larry for an hour or so each day and sometimes he spent an extra hour working on the beams. He was able to walk six steps, about ten steps short of completing the course. He also was working hard on the hand weights, and now could do three sets of ten repetitions lifting eighty-five-pound dumbbells with each hand. Nurse Johanson joked that his muscles looked like the bulging arms you'd see on an action figure. He was nineteen now and his attitude hardly resembled the young teenager who had given up on life.

In early fall, he was able to take thirteen steps, so close to the full course. When he was with Larry, Paul always used crutches instead of his wheelchair. Larry would spot Paul while he practiced walking with them. It wasn't easy and he fell a few times, once even breaking his finger. But this time, he didn't let it distract him. He thought back to what The Jet said to him—that he wanted to see Paul running around those bases at Turner Field some day.

Larry now had him working with heavier leg weights. It was painful but his quads were responding, growing stronger and larger. He also wanted his chest to get broader, so Larry taught him how to do bench presses.

"You're ahead of schedule," Larry told him proudly one day. It felt so good to actually over-achieve, he thought.

Five years to the day after he chose to give up being a superhero, something miraculous happened that reminded him about superheroes having no cape. He and Larry entered the physical therapy room to work the beams, just like they had almost every day the past several years.

But something just felt different on that fifth anniversary. Steps one through ten had become relatively easy for him. Eleven, twelve and thirteen were a little more of a struggle. Fourteen was tough. Fifteen was excruciating. As he took his left leg and pushed it with all he had, he could feel himself losing balance. But he was close, so close to the finish. Just one more step. He pushed his right leg to his left and landed on the sixteenth and final step. Now, all he had to do was step off into Larry's arms. He used his pumped arms to push off the beams and fell into his trainer's arms. Larry let out a loud whoop as he caught Paul.

"Paul, you did it! You did it!" he yelled, slapping Paul's back in celebration. "Do you want me to call your parents or do you? They have to see this! How does it feel to walk again my friend?"

Paul, too, was excited, but the goal did not feel complete. "I wouldn't call what I did 'walking.' I want to wait until I can walk without the beams," he said firmly.

"That might take another couple of months," Larry explained. "But that's just fine—let's get to work, then!"

All he had to do was picture his parents' faces when they saw him walk across the room with no help at all and that was all the motivation he needed. For the next four months, he and Larry worked with the crutches every day. Every day, he limped a little further. In May, just three months shy of his twenty-first birthday, he called his parents and asked them to come to the hospital. He had a surprise for them. He said that the only thing that they needed to bring was a video camera.

When Sam and Lilian entered the physical therapy room, they saw Paul in his wheelchair, as usual.

"I have something to show you," their son said from across the room.

His parents had no idea of what to expect.

Paul smiled and said, "Dad, turn on the camera."

Paul then rose out of his wheelchair, leaving his crutches beside him on the floor. His father's hands began trembling as he fought to steady the camera. He hadn't seen his son walk in many years. Slowly, Paul limped about twenty feet toward them, touched the wall, and went back to the wheelchair, all on his own. Larry stood beside him the entire time, ready to help him if he lost his balance or got tired but Paul made it without assistance. He actually walked! It was more limping than walking but to his parents, he was flying. His mother wept with joy.

"I'm so proud of you," she said, running over and grabbing him into a hug. She kissed him so many times that he had red lip marks all over the side of his face. His dad put down the camera and jumped up and down, pumping his fist. Paul imagined this was more dramatic than his first steps as a baby.

"You did it," Sam kept shouting, "You did it!" He didn't see his dad cry often but he noticed a few tears sliding down his cheeks at that moment.

Other than when he was The Solution, he hadn't walked in more than ten years. He'd forgotten what it was like to put one foot in front of the other. Larry winked at him and grabbed him into a hug.

"Thatta boy," he said. "You did it!"

Sam, Lilian, and Larry left the room an hour later to take care of some paperwork and that's when Paul lost it. He sunk to the floor and sobbed, for once, because he was happy. All the things that had gone wrong in his life would no longer make him cry; they would fuel him. He was going to be the best he could be. He had a dream to fulfill. Wiping away tears, he pushed himself into an upright position, and practiced limping from one side of the room to the other. The Puzzle was officially put back together.

For the next six weeks, he practiced walking from his bed at home to his television and back to his bed—a total distance of about fifteen feet. He and Larry kept working with the weights at the hospital and with the crutches, too, until finally he wasn't limping anymore. Soon, it was impossible to tell that he had ever been in a wheelchair, let alone for a decade. Now that he trusted his legs, the sky was the limit.

One night that summer, Paul had the dream again. He came up for his first Major League at-bat with a chance to win the game and the guy with the mask gave him advice on how to get a hit. Maybe it was his dad, who was now so proud of him. Maybe it was Larry, he thought. He tried harder than ever to get a look at his face but the dreaded alarm clock ruined it, again. This time, however, he wasn't disappointed when he awoke. Now he was inspired to make it come true. He'd never awakened from the dream with the ability to jump out of bed and walk, but he could now.

He continued to work at home every day with Larry. Soon he was not only walking, but jogging at the hospital. Yes, at St. Luke's. He now went there not for treatment or medication, but to inspire people. He'd gone from riding around in a wheelchair to becoming a pretty good runner. Some patients were so impressed with his speed that they told him he was lightning-quick. Nurse Johanson shortened it to "Lightning," and started calling him "Lightning" when he ran from floor to floor. That nickname sure sounded better than "The Puzzle," Paul thought.

He got stronger every day, physically and mentally. He was even out-running his black lab now; the dog that had run circles around him when he was a kid. Paul had mixed emotions about that. While he was happy that he was getting faster, it was kind of sad that Delta was now slowing down. Like his dog once did for him, Paul sat by his dog and consoled her as she grew older. Delta was nearly eighty in dog years and had certainly lost a few steps. She died six months later from old age but her unconditional love was forever etched in Paul's memory.

Paul and The Jet were still friends and he would bring his baseball videotapes for Paul to watch. A local journalist got word of Paul's story and it made the front page of a small local newspaper. The morning it came out his mom bought one-hundred copies and sent them out to family and friends. The article, titled "A Dream to Play Baseball," mentioned the difficulties one faces with CF but how a positive attitude can help an individual win the battle against the disease.

In early April Paul went to the hospital for his final monthly check-up. If it went well he would only have to go to the doctor twice a year from then on, Dr. Knotts promised. He looked at his pulmonary function scores and said they were in the low hundreds, twice as high as when Paul had first entered the hospital more than a decade ago. He now had the stamina to play a nine-inning baseball game.

"Good luck, Paul," Dr. Knotts said. They embraced as he added, "I look forward to seeing you in the Majors some day."

"Our little Paul is all grown up," said Nurse Johanson, wiping a tear from her eye. "We're so proud of you." As Paul left, she gave him a T-shirt she'd made for him. It was gray and was stitched with green text that read, "Paul 'Lightning' Morgan: The Pride of St. Luke's."

"Wear it for good luck at your first baseball tryout," she said as she hugged him. She passed the same shirt out to all the patients on the second floor. She told him Dr. Knotts had bought season tickets for the Braves, and was not going to use them until he could see Paul at Turner Field.

Paul didn't need to work with Larry anymore, so after his last appointment with Dr. Knotts he went up to Larry's office to say goodbye. He told Larry he wanted to do something for him, really thank him for pushing him and bringing him to where he was.

"How about we make a bet based on your first at-bat at Turner Field?" Larry suggested. "If you get a base hit, you have to do me a favor. If I get another patient who needs motivating like you did, I can call you at any time, and you will come and help my patient—the way The Jet helped you."

"That sounds fair," Paul smiled. "What if I get an out?"

"Then you don't owe me anything," he answered.

"What if I walk or reach on an error?" he teased.

"You still don't owe me anything," Larry laughed. "You only owe me if you get a hit."

"You've got a deal," Paul agreed, "but I have to tell you that the odds of me getting a hit in my first Major League at-bat are pretty slim."

"Yeah," said Larry, "Didn't they also tell you that you had four months to live and that you might never walk again?"

Paul smiled, "You have a point." They shook hands to make the bet official.

Paul met his parents in the lobby. His mom said she couldn't wait to see him in a big league uniform some day. That led him to the next part of his plan.

Chapter 24
Play Ball!

If he wanted to make it to the Majors some day, Paul had to start somewhere. His dad read about a beginner's baseball camp near his house. It was a good opportunity for him to start playing the game.

When he arrived at the camp, the director asked him if he was one of the campers' older brothers. He laughed and said, "Nope, I'm here to play baseball."

That's when it dawned on Paul that he could have been every other camper's big brother. Everyone at the camp was between ten and fourteen, except Paul, who was twenty-one. But he didn't care. Every day for the next six weeks, the coaches taught them the art of hitting, base running, catching and throwing.

The kids were a little in awe of him since he was so large and much older, but he was used to being different from the crowd. What he wasn't accustomed to was throwing and catching a baseball but each day he got more adept at it. The first week, his aim was so bad he actually hit one of the kids in the stomach by accident. It was then that the camp director realized that Paul should be on his own, so the director assigned him a private instructor, Coach Gavin Alexander.

The coach was almost six feet tall, with big muscles and he was a two-time All-American shortstop at the University of Miami. First, he taught Paul how to hold his glove and catch the ball. He also worked on his aim and had him throwing a pretty good fifty-to-sixty-mile-an-hour fastball by the end of camp.

The coach threw about twenty pitches of batting practice to Paul a day. Over the first few weeks, Paul only hit about three or four per session. But with a little practice and a few tips on holding the bat and how he spaced his feet in his stance, Paul was solidly smacking seventeen or eighteen out of twenty by the last week of camp. His God-given talent was obvious.

"You've picked up this game faster than anyone I've ever taught," the coach told him. "And you have a very easy hitting stroke. You are a natural." Paul didn't know if it was because he'd watched the game all his life or because he had the athletic talent that his father and brother possessed. Regardless, it made him proud to hear that he had the potential to succeed at the sport he loved.

After hitting and catching, he practiced sliding in the backyard. He put a big, red stadium seat cushion—the closest thing he could find to a base—on the lawn and ran as fast as he could and slid feet-first into the cushion. The scrapes and bruises from sliding over sticks and rocks were well worth the pain because he was improving. The neighbors probably thought he was crazy but he was having so much fun he didn't even notice.

Coach Alexander was the perfect teacher for those six weeks. By the end of camp, Paul had the skills of a good high school baseball player. The problem was that if he wanted to reach his dream of playing Major League Baseball, his play would have to improve ten-fold.

Paul looked in the newspaper and on the Internet for an advanced baseball camp but the problem was that all of the camps were for kids. All of a sudden, a light bulb flickered in his head. He called The Jet and asked him if he would be his coach and throw with him when the season ended.

"Well, my wife and I usually go back to Cincinnati when the season ends, but we'd been talking about staying in Atlanta this off-season to go house-hunting so you just made our decision a whole lot easier. It would be worth it."

That sure beat staring at a baseball video for an hour or two a day, Paul thought. The chance to throw with a Major Leaguer was an incredible opportunity he couldn't miss. He had about fourteen weeks to get into shape to play with his idol, so he had his father throw with him every day. It took Paul a while to catch up to the speed of his pitches, but he did it. Sam also helped Paul with catching and had a trick to motivate him—he would take out the aluminum bat and hit the ball as high as he could and yell, "You won't catch this one!" Being that he loved to prove people wrong, that was all the incentive Paul needed to catch it.

Not only was he becoming a better baseball player, but for the first time he was also bonding with his father. They never really had the chance to spend quality time together when he was younger because he was always so sick. Back then, his dad spent most of his time traveling with Garey to baseball tournaments around the southeast. They were finally having traditional "father-son experiences," playing catch, laughing and joking around. Every night, they would talk about the fundamentals of baseball over dinner.

On his twenty-second birthday, Paul came home from a five-hour practice with a couple of his neighbors. He noticed a huge yellow Ryder truck parked at the top of the driveway. His dad summoned him into the backyard with a grin from ear to ear. It was the same smile his dad had when he brought home little Delta the first time.

Paul peeked into the backyard, and there stood a giant fifty-foot-long batting cage equipped with an automatic pitching machine and surrounded by white netting. His father pleaded, "Read the inscription on the front, Paul."

You are a bold hero to me. I pull for you. Gregory Vern Hartman.

Amazingly, his mother had remembered the words from the magnetic board and told his dad how much they meant to him.

"Son, I understand your dream," his dad said. "Your mother and I are so proud of you and we believe in you. Go for it!" With his mom watching tearfully from inside, Paul and his dad embraced.

Things were finally looking up for Paul. He hoped his achievements on the playing field could translate into success off the field as well.

Chapter 25
Getting On with Life

In late August, after all the studying and tutoring he did, in addition to his rehab work with Larry, Paul officially graduated from high school. They had a private ceremony in his backyard, where his teacher presented him with his diploma. The guests included Larry, Nurse Johanson and Dr. Knotts—The Jet was unable to attend but he did call to congratulate him. Earning that diploma gave him another sense of accomplishment, which spurred him on even more.

A week later, his father took him to take his driver's test. He passed and considered his license the first step toward independence.

"Son, if you want a car, you're going to have to work for it," his father said on the way home. "I'll match dollar for dollar whatever money you make, though."

What can I do to earn any money, Paul wondered? His only skills were lying in a hospital bed and eating Jell-O. He was 22 years old and had never been employed. First, he interviewed for jobs waiting tables but most managers didn't want to hire him since he didn't have any experience. He found that ironic because he couldn't gain experience unless someone hired him. Then he applied at a rental car company but they said he had to be twenty-five years old. He was getting frustrated when he got a call from The Jet in mid-September that brought him one step closer to his dream.

"How would you like to be one of the Braves' batboys during tonight's game, and also for the last fifteen home games of the season?" Ricky asked excitedly, explaining that Paul would be paid $15 per hour and work about six hours a night. "You'd also get to warm up with some of the players, so that would give you some good practice."

"Gee, let me think about it," he joked. "Wow, man, thanks! I'll do it!"

Paul was elated. He'd get to see all of his favorite players in person and he'd get to go to Turner Field for the second time in his life, this time without a wheelchair. It sure beat working as a waiter.

For his first game on September 20, The Jet met him at the players entrance four hours before the game and escorted him into the Braves clubhouse. It took Paul a minute to realize he was standing face to face with all of his revered Atlanta Braves. Some of the players were playing cards; others were practicing their putts on a small putting green in the locker room. Some were looking at game film. A couple of them were playing video games. He immediately recognized All-Star pitchers Tom Glavine, John Smoltz and Greg Maddux, who were eating their pre-game meals. The Jet introduced him to everyone. Scott Milford, the second baseman, told Paul he had read his story in the paper and was very inspired, especially since he had two children with CF. He pulled his newspaper article from his locker and said, "Can you autograph this?"

Was he kidding? A Major League baseball player wanted *my* autograph, Paul wondered? He'd never given an autograph before, so his hand was shaking as he wrote. But he even scribbled his new credo above his name: *A superhero needs no cape.*

The Jet introduced him to the other two batboys, Dan and Tim, who worked all of the Braves games. Dan had been a batboy for six years and was eighteen years old. Tim was fifteen and in his third year. They didn't seem overjoyed to see Paul—he figured they got tired of showing people the ropes. They gave him a uniform and told him to meet them on the field. After he suited up, he took a second to check out his new look in the mirror. He looked like an actual Major League baseball player! On the field, Dan and Tim told him to remember three things: grab the bats after each at-bat, grab any foul balls hit near him and warm up the outfielders before each inning.

"You know," Paul told them, "this isn't the only time I'll be wearing a Major League uniform. One day, I'm going to get to the big leagues, and get a hit to win a game in this stadium."

Dan busted out laughing as if he'd heard the funniest joke in the world. "Right, Paul!" he said sarcastically. "Come on! Only the best players make it to the big leagues."

"Besides," Tim chimed in, "Didn't you just get out of a hospital? Don't you have some disease? I read about you in that newspaper article that Scott brought in. It said that a lot of people who have your disease are very sick. So dream on, Paul."

"The day you make it to the big leagues," Dan said patronizingly, putting his hand on Paul's shoulder, "is the day I walk on the moon." Then he and Tim joined together for a good laugh, all at Paul's expense. But he didn't see any humor in their remarks.

"It's not funny!" he shouted at these snot-nosed punks. "Really, I'm serious. I'm going to make it. I'll show you guys."

"Whatever!" Dan said, rolling his eyes and walking away with Tim at his side, snickering and smacking him a high five. "Just don't screw up or you'll be giving back that uniform faster than it took you to put it on."

Paul shouldn't have said anything. He suddenly felt humiliated, almost like he had when he was back in school and Biff Goolson was tormenting him. But just the same, he worked the game with Dan and Tim. He picked up the bats and balls for the players. He brought the umpire a towel and water every three innings. He warmed up the outfielders between innings. He took the players' uniforms to the laundry room after the game. It was a full day's work. Being a Braves' batboy should have been the greatest job in the world but Dan and Tim tried to ruin it for him with their snide comments. Dan's comment about him setting foot on the moon the day Paul makes it to the majors really ticked him off. Years ago, he would have believed them and blamed the world for his problems. But now, they just added fuel to his already burning desire to reach his goal of making it to the bigs.

He worked all fifteen of the remaining home games for the Braves. The job was thrilling each game. He got to talk to a lot of the players, both from the Braves and the visiting teams. He learned a lot about the sport. Tom Albertson, a catcher for the Montreal Expos, taught him to take a plastic bat and swing it under water in a swimming pool to strengthen his arms. None of the coaches in his baseball camp taught him that trick. Nick Green of the Tampa Bay Devil Rays taught him to develop a routine at the plate. He said the routine would be Paul's checklist to prevent him from developing any bad habits, like not keeping his head up or not bringing his bat back far enough. Paul knew he'd learn even more when he and The Jet began their practice sessions in about four weeks.

By the end of the season he'd earned about $2,000. He took that and his dad's matching funds and bought a ten-year-old Honda Accord he'd spotted in the newspaper classifieds. He had a CD player installed with the little bit of money he had left over. The CD player, he thought, would help him in his next endeavor—dating!

He even let his mother set him up on a blind date with her tennis partner's daughter, Winnie. She was nineteen with beautiful blue eyes and long blonde hair. He hoped she was unaware that this was his first date. He had enough jitters for both of them. They went out to dinner and the conversation was going well until he began coughing and couldn't stop. Concerned, she asked what was wrong. He could have said he had a cold but he realized sooner or later, he'd need to get comfortable talking with women about his condition.

"Actually, I have cystic fibrosis and it makes me cough a lot," he matter-of-factly explained.

"Oh," she stared at him, mouth hanging open, not knowing how to respond. Her eyes told him she had more questions but instead they finished the meal in silence and he took her home. He realized that bringing up cystic fibrosis on the first date was perhaps not the best idea but he was relieved his first date was over and he never had to go through that experience again.

The next day, he logged onto an online dating service. A week after that, he met Emily online. They e-mailed back and forth a bit and met in person a few days later. She had pretty hazel eyes and long brown hair. They went out for dinner and a movie and then he took her back to his house. He was a bit embarrassed that he didn't have a place of his own, but, since his parents were also out, they hung out and talked for a long time. About thirty minutes after they started talking about their future goals, he summoned enough courage to go in for the kiss. His stomach was doing cartwheels by the time their lips separated at the end of the kiss. She was smiling, too. Maybe Emily was the girl for him. But then when he showed her his bedroom, she saw the mechanical monstrosity on the left side of his bed.

"What is that?" she asked, her eyes wide.

"It's a therapy machine," he said, trying to sound like everyone should have one. "I suffer from cystic fibrosis, which means I have a life expectancy of close to thirty years but I'm doing pretty well so far."

He sensed a major shift in mood after that statement, so he reluctantly took her home. What was I doing wrong, he wondered? After thinking about it for a while, he finally figured it out. One, he had to stop talking about life expectancy. Two, he shouldn't use the word "suffer" when he referred to CF. After all, he had CF but he wasn't suffering anymore—he was thriving. If he seemed more confident about his condition, then so would the women he dated. His father gave him some good advice: he said CF would actually give Paul an advantage when he was dating.

"Most people don't know how to find a special person who can deal with anything," his father explained. "You'll have no choice but to find that person, because she will have a lot to deal with. But when you do find her and know she is the one, you'll be a very lucky man."

His father was right, of course. CF might limit the number of candidates but the ones who stuck around would be pretty amazing, he figured. He decided he had to look at dating in a positive way, just as he had learned to do with everything else in his life. He continued to go on dates until mid-November, when his focus turned exclusively to baseball.

It was time to step up to the plate.

Chapter 26
Idol Chat

Early that morning, The Jet picked him up in his 1996 black Ford Explorer. The line of dirt down both sides revealed The Jet was not opposed to four-wheeling from time to time. They talked about the charity work The Jet did in his hometown of Cincinnati, much of it for the Cystic Fibrosis Foundation.

"When you told me your wish, I thought, 'What better way to do something for CF than to help someone with the disease make it to the big leagues,'" he explained. "That would show kids with the disease that they should have hope and there's nothing better than giving kids hope. It didn't hurt that you've become such a close friend."

From the time baseball camp ended until that day when he started practice with The Jet, Paul had practiced almost every day with his father. But, as he suspected, it was only a warm-up compared to the demanding practices with The Jet. When they began to throw in the park, Paul dropped most of the balls, since The Jet threw a lot harder, further, and with a lot more action than his father or Coach Alexander. Even when Paul threw with the Braves players as a batboy, they just lobbed the ball back to him. He was also a little intimidated throwing with a future Hall of Fame pitcher.

"Be patient. You'll get good, it just takes time," Ricky would tell him. "Nothing worthwhile comes easy." To help Paul, he showed him how to wind his arm and throw the ball with an easy motion. He then showed him how to position his glove to catch the ball easier. He taught him how to side-step back for a ball instead of back-pedaling and falling. Ricky told him he'd make a great outfielder, but Paul told him he preferred to be a catcher. The Jet said his speed was too good to be a catcher.

How ironic, Paul thought! He couldn't even get out of his wheelchair two years ago and now his "speed was too good." His daily jogging at St. Luke's had really paid dividends. Paul learned so much more in just that first day than he did in several weeks at camp.

The Jet then turned his attention to Paul's batting stance. Most Major League starting pitchers were poor hitters because they only hit every fifth day, sometimes only getting two or three at-bats per game. The Jet constantly downplayed his hitting but he was no slouch at the plate. For a pitcher, a .200 batting average was pretty solid. His lifetime batting average was an extraordinary .275. He threw Paul a few batting-practice pitches to check his swing out. He didn't break out the 101-mile-per-hour fastball, thank goodness for Paul, but served up some pretty fast ones. Paul swung and missed all of them, and started to get discouraged.

"Watch the ball, make contact with the bat and swing through," Ricky advised. So he did just that. Sure enough, on the fifteenth pitch, he lined a rope to centerfield.

"Not bad," said Ricky, running out to fetch it. "You might just make it to the big leagues after all."

Each day, they would throw about fifty tosses to each other and Paul would take fifty pitches of batting practice. He was getting better and better.

Ricky also taught him about the mental aspects of the game such as how to read a pitcher's eyes so he knew when to steal. He taught Paul the importance of always hitting the cutoff man. In fact, The Jet would lay a barrel on its side at second base and Paul had to catch the ball from the outfield and throw it into the barrel six out of ten times, otherwise he'd have to start over. By the final days of their practices, he filled the barrel up every time.

Paul also learned how to switch-hit, that is, be able to bat from the right side or the left side. Switch-hitters were a more valuable commodity, The Jet explained, because it's easier to hit from the left side when facing a tough right-handed pitcher and vice versa. He would throw Paul twenty-five pitches while he batted left-handed, and twenty-five more from the right side. He hit most of the balls from the right side, being that was his natural stance, but only a couple of balls from the left. When he'd get frustrated, Ricky would remind him this was no cakewalk and he'd have to earn the hits now just as he would in the Majors.

132

Paul's favorite part of their practices was talking about The Jet's playing career. Paul grilled him incessantly, and loved hearing his answers.

"Who was the best pitcher you've ever seen?"

"Nolan Ryan," he answered. "He had seven no-hitters in his career."

"Name something besides a no-hitter that you have yet to accomplish in baseball."

"Honestly Paul," he answered as he threw him a pitch, "the no-hitter is my only goal left."

"What's the one thing you would never do on the baseball diamond?"

"I would never tip pitches," The Jet said firmly, explaining how tipping pitches is when a pitcher tells a batter which pitch he is going to throw, either through hand signals or in conference before a game. "I knew one pitcher who did that and his team lost a division because of him."

The Jet's answer reminded Paul of that kickball game when he was ten, when he was tipped off to Josh Wilson's pitch. He thought that had been the lone highlight of his athletic life so far. During those days, he would have done anything to be a hero.

"What's a ritual you have?" Paul asked as they continued to practice.

The Jet told him about his three pitches. "I tell myself in my head which I'm going to throw by giving them nicknames," he explained. "I call the curve ball 'the snake' because of the way it slithers from side to side. I call the 101-mile-per-hour fastball 'The Jet' because, well, that's what I'm known for. And I call the 80-mile-per-hour fastball, the one I use to ruin the batter's rhythm, 'taking the batter out to the ballgame.'"

"Why?" Paul asked, chuckling.

"Well, there's this ritual at Turner Field, and in most ballparks in fact, that during the seventh-inning stretch when fans are half asleep, they play the song, 'Take Me Out to the Ballgame' to get everyone revved up," he grinned as he got to his punch line. "So I figure the batter is tired, too, and this is a way to shake him up a little."

They practiced four days a week for two-and-a-half months until The Jet had to report to spring training in Orlando. He spent the last day throwing eighty-mile-per-hour pitches, most of which Paul sent into the outfield for base hits. He even launched two balls over the fence on their last day of practice. Hitting a homerun was the most amazing feeling. He couldn't even feel the ball hit his bat. He just swung, heard the pop, and watched the ball sail over the fence. Ricky never threw him "The Jet." Paul begged him to throw one but Ricky said Paul would lose confidence if he ever did. He said if his young apprentice could hit eighty and ninety-mile per hour fastballs with consistency, he'd be able to hit decent Major League pitchers. Paul was doing just that. He was so thankful for his training—he wanted to return Ricky's favor just as he'd promised to return the favor to Larry. Then, Ricky shocked him.

"I am retiring after this season," he said as they drove back to his house.

He hadn't told anyone. "That means this season will be my last shot to get a no-hitter. So, when you see the no-hitter getting close, I want you pulling for me. That's one important favor that I ask of you."

He had two other requests of his pupil. One was that no matter how many years it took, Paul make it to the big leagues and get that base hit he'd always wanted.

"You bring hope to so many kids with cystic fibrosis," Ricky told him. "I hope you remember that. I don't know if you truly understand the magnitude of what accomplishing your goals can do for others. You're not just living your dream; you're helping other kids believe in theirs."

That really touched Paul. "So what's the other thing you want me to do?" he asked as they pulled up to his driveway.

"Be ready at seven tomorrow morning," The Jet said shortly. "I want to take you somewhere."

He wondered where Ricky was going to take him. Maybe to Turner Field for their final practice? Paul woke up at six the next morning and did his therapy. An hour later, Ricky picked him up in his Explorer but wouldn't tell him where they were going.

About fifteen minutes later, they arrived at Hammond Park, a public park with a basketball court, tennis courts and a softball field. The two of them walked up to the softball field and suddenly, Paul knew where they were going. He saw a sign that read, "Major League Baseball Tryout Camp." He noticed a few guys filling out some paperwork. A couple of men, one much older than the other but both wearing Braves caps were issuing the forms and putting the completed paperwork in stacks on a big brown table.

The Jet walked up to one of the men and said, "This is Paul Morgan. I think he's a pretty good prospect. You think you can sign him up?"

"Sure," he said, pulling a blank form out of a pile. "Where did he play minor league ball?"

"He didn't," Ricky said. Paul gulped and stood behind him.

The guy started looking Paul up and down. "Ok, how about high school or college ball?" he asked.

"Nope," Ricky said, "he's never played organized ball."

Hearing that, the other man started snickering and turned to Ricky.

"Sorry, Jet," he said, with a patronizing grin. "Our policy states that we can only select players who have some type of organized baseball experience."

"Besides," the other guy interrupted, "we don't want to be laughed at for trying out some kid who can't even hit a major league fastball."

Paul had no idea where the conversation was going but he was so disappointed that he lowered his head, tucked-tail and quickly headed back to the car.

"Wait, Paul!" Ricky shouted, running after him. When he caught up, he was quiet for a moment. He put his arm out to get him to stop, and then turned his student around. "I have an idea. Come with me," he said.

They went back to the two men, who had moved on to hassling someone else. Ricky got the older one's attention.

"How about I throw Paul here ten ninety-mile-per-hour fastballs right now, and if he hits one of them over the fence, you let him try out."

The man who wore a navy blue collared Braves shirt and sported a long wavy mustache looked at Ricky. He put his hand on his chin as if to think. Then he took another long look at Paul, much longer than when he sized him up the first time. He was taking stock of an inexperienced kid, trying to determine if it was worth the risk. And he took his time about it before giving Ricky his answer.

"Jet, I'm sorry. Rules are rules. I have to be honest. I don't think he can hit your fastball anyway."

Ricky stretched his hands on the table and leaned in close to both men, continuing to plead on Paul's behalf.

"Guys, this kid is going to be the next good young player in the Braves' organization. How about five ninety mile-per-hour heaters? That won't take but five minutes. Just give the kid a chance. If it doesn't work out, you're only wasting five minutes. If he's half the player I think he is, you guys will be famous for finding him. I know one thing is for certain. If you let a young star player from Atlanta go and he catches on with the Mets or Phillies, you'll have to answer a lot of questions from the Braves upper management."

The man looked at his sidekick, who shrugged. "Okay," the older one finally relented. "Normally, we wouldn't do this, but Jet, I have to believe you have an eye for talent. Let's see what the kid's got."

Paul couldn't believe that Ricky had convinced them to give him a shot.

He didn't want to let him down. Ricky took out a wooden bat and some balls and led them both onto the field. Paul was terrified that he wouldn't be able to hit a ball over the fence, although Hammond Park's field dimensions were much smaller than a Major League park. However, the added pressure weighing on Paul's shoulders seemed to add another hundred feet from home plate to the fence. Ricky gave him a quick pep talk at home plate and scooted out towards the mound.

"Are you ready?" he yelled.

With butterflies the size of B-52's dancing in his stomach, Paul didn't trust his own voice so he just raised his hand to signal that he was as ready as he could be under the circumstances. He took a deep breath and took his right-handed stance in the batter's box. Ricky threw a fastball right down the middle. Paul swung with all his might but only managed to foul it back. At least he got a piece of it, he thought, trying to reassure himself. Only four more pitches. Come on, concentrate, he demanded.

He missed the second fastball entirely. He looked over at the two men, who were shaking their heads and smirking at him.

"Come on. Focus, Paul," The Jet shouted. "Don't worry about those guys." Paul turned away, not wanting their doubtful demeanors to rattle him.

He hit a line drive on the third pitch but it didn't reach the outfield until the second hop. He was starting to get frustrated and he felt like he was letting his teacher down. Ricky was risking his reputation by insisting that Paul had major league skills. Paul wasn't doing much to prove him right. Ricky had thrown him several of these ninety-mile-per-hour pitches during practice but he'd only hit a couple, and he had maybe hit one out of the ballpark. He wondered what made Ricky think he could hit one out in only five chances today, especially with all of this added pressure.

Come on, you can do this, Paul mumbled to himself. Ricky's fourth pitch was right down the middle. He swung hard again but got under the ball, flying it to the middle of the outfield where it dropped about fifty feet shy of the fence. He had one more chance to prove himself to these guys.

He needed a minute to gather himself. He walked away from home plate and took some deep breaths. He tightened his batting gloves and pushed his elbows up. He took his bat and positioned it behind his head. Just then, Garey's words rang inside his head.

"You can be a superhero, Paul."

He looked toward The Jet and signaled to him he was ready for the pitch. He threw it right down the middle and this time Paul put a pretty good charge into it. The ball sailed toward left field but didn't have much height.

"Get out of here, ball," he whispered. It clipped the top of the fence and bounced over. Relieved, he shouted, "Yes!"

The Jet ran over and grabbed him in a bear hug. "You did it," he said, grinning. The Jet strode over to the two men and shot them a satisfied smirk. "Paperwork please, gentlemen," he said.

Paul practiced three hours a day for the next few weeks in his new batting cage. Each day, he'd hit fifty fastballs in the eighty to ninety mile per hour range from the left side and fifty more from the right. The Jet was at spring training by then but checked up on him daily. Ricky kept reminding him that if he could hit pitches of those speeds consistently, he would be Major League caliber. Paul kept watching The Jet's videos for more hitting tips and he continued to lift weights. He was running five miles a week and eating a good diet. He was in the best shape of his life, better than most people who didn't have cystic fibrosis. He was coughing less and less.

He still hadn't met his special woman but he was having fun trying. When he mentioned CF on dates, it was with confidence now. He realized what a tremendous time he was having—working his first job, driving his first car, graduating from high school, dating and playing with the best baseball player in the country. He couldn't have asked for more.

Then he had the dream again. You'd think after twelve years he would have figured out at least some part of this dream but he was still clueless. He was tired of dreaming of playing at Turner Field. He was ready to really play there. He was ready for the next stop on the way to the dream—a Major League Baseball Tryout Camp.

Chapter 27
Baseball Season Begins

Paul walked into tryout camp at Blackburn Park in Atlanta that first morning like a new kid on the first day of school. The grass glistened from the early morning rain. A light mist hung over the two-field baseball complex. A hundred baseball players were present, most carrying a bat case and wearing baseball pants with shirts boasting tournaments won or alma maters. Paul, on the other hand, brandished his ten-year old brown Louisville Slugger bat without a case, Adidas shorts and, as he promised Nurse Johanson, the gray T-shirt she made for him. He hoped the scouts wouldn't judge the players on appearance or he'd be the first contestant to be eliminated. Looking around, he just hoped he wasn't in over his head.

Some of the guys were there because they'd had injuries in college or in the minor leagues. Some were there just to say they were there. Others were undrafted free agents looking to prove themselves. Everyone was there to make a great impression on the Major League scouts.

Paul had no concept of how he compared to these guys but he knew that being better than most wouldn't be enough. If he wanted scouts to notice him, he had to be the best. He had some of the Morgan family's athletic talent and had worked with the best pitcher in Braves history, so he felt prepared but anxious at the same time.

The head of the camp, Rick Johnson, told the players this wouldn't be a normal tryout camp. Instead of judging the players' talent on throwing, catching and hitting, this season the staff was trying something different, he explained. He divided the players into four teams and said they would scrimmage each week. The scouts would choose one player they felt had the intangibles necessary to succeed in the Major Leagues—qualities such as playing under pressure, showing a positive attitude and being a team player. The season would last only four weeks, since the scouts would need to submit the top player's name by the beginning of April.

The Jet had mentioned that participating in a tryout camp was the best way for a Major League team to sign a player to a minor league contract. Paul was so excited to play in front of scouts. Atlanta Braves scouts at that. It was time to lace up his cleats and show these guys what he could do. He was kind of curious himself.

The four managers, each a hitting or base coach in the Braves minor league system, drafted players that first day. None of the coaches knew Paul nor did they have any idea what kind of ability he had, so he wasn't drafted in the early rounds. Instead, only players wearing tournament or college shirts were taken. By the fifteenth round, he still hadn't been drafted. He got a bit antsy. Now players with bat cases were being chosen. He felt like the last kid picked in gym class. Finally, in the twenty-fourth round, the next to last one, his name was finally called. Coach Tomlinson of the Acid Rain team picked him. The only ones drafted after him, it seemed, were the squirrel and chipmunk playing in the oak tree behind him. The draft may not have been the start he was hoping for, but it provided him with that much more motivation. A week from now, he would show these guys what Paul Morgan could do.

Game 1, March 8th

Paul suited up for his first true baseball game and it just happened to be Garey's birthday. He was both sad realizing that Garey wasn't around to see this day, but also proud that here he was, fulfilling his dream. Garey would have been proud, too. His uniform was cool: the shirt was mustard yellow with *Acid Rain* in white lettering and he wore a yellow cap with a white *A* in front and a pair of white baseball pants held up by a yellow belt. He threw on his white socks and then tucked his yellow stirrups tightly into his cleats.

Coach Tomlinson benched him for the first game, as he, like everyone else, had never heard of Paul Morgan. Paul was the team's backup centerfielder. Their first opponent was a team called Tragic Magic. When the game started, he deposited a large wad of chewing gum in his mouth.

Something about the Tragic Magic's pitcher looked all too familiar as

Paul watched him warm up. He was about six-feet, six-inches tall, weighed in at three-hundred pounds of muscle and had a face you would expect to see in a police lineup rather than a baseball lineup card. Then it clicked. It was none other than the boy who ruined his childhood, Biff Goolson—the one who threw eggs at him, the one who put pudding in his hair and, most notably, the one who made him cry through much of his childhood. His last encounter with Biff was the time the ogre beat him up, threw him in a trash can like garbage and left him for dead.

Paul's emotions went into overdrive. Biff was one of the driving forces behind his choice of living as Paul Morgan rather than The Solution. He could think of nothing sweeter than getting a little revenge; he just never imagined that it would be on the baseball field. The problem was that he'd have to crack the lineup at some point in the game and Coach Tomlinson wasn't going to be so easy to convince.

He was so ready to hit the baseball right between Biff's eyes. He had fought for years to raise his self-esteem, which Biff had stripped away with his constant school-yard torture. Paul thought about what it would be like to take Biff deep. He would casually prance around the bases until Biff remembered him. Biff didn't recognize him, yet, since he sat in the corner of the dugout and bore no resemblance to the wheelchair-bound punching bag of their youth. The game was pretty boring until Tyler Whaley hit a three-run homer to give the Tragic Magic a 3-0 lead. Biff had chalked up twelve strikeouts and only allowed one hit—an infield single. In the bottom of the seventh inning, Coach Tomlinson asked Paul if he was ready to go in. Paul exploded with readiness.

"Sure, born ready, Coach!" he yelled as he jumped off the bench. He could feel his heart trying to pound its way out of his chest. This was his chance to shine. He put on his batting gloves and helmet, grabbed his bat, and stepped out to the on-deck circle. Biff Goolson would never question Paul Morgan's ability again. He pictured the greatest birthday present he could ever give to Garey, a homerun off the bully who made his childhood miserable.

Suddenly, out of nowhere, the biggest bolt of lightning he had ever seen shot out of the sky into the outfield. Rain followed. After an hour-long rain delay, the umpires called the game. His team lost, 3-0, and he wasn't even a part of the box score. He was disappointed and a little humiliated. After all, everyone else left with game experience. The only experience he got from the evening was counting the number of smashed Gatorade cups on the dugout floor.

But by now, he was determined to face his childhood bully on or off the diamond. He ran over to Biff, who was about to climb into his beat-up, black Jeep Wrangler.

"Biff," he shouted, "do you remember me?" Biff looked him up and down until finally the spark of recognition lit up his face.

"Yeah, I remember you. Morgan, right? Puzzle? I thought you died years ago. You played on that pathetic team? I didn't even see you bat."

"I didn't." he said, kind of embarrassed. "But I could hit your best pitch." That drew a sarcastic laugh from the egotistical brute.

"Puzzle, you couldn't hit a basketball if I threw it over the plate. I don't care if you look stronger or that you don't need that stupid wheelchair anymore. You will always be Puzzle to me. Always! You got it? Now, get out of my way, punk!"

He swiped Paul away with his tree-trunk sized left arm. Part of Paul wanted to walk away and just say that Biff got the best of him again but there was another part of him who'd built up so much resentment from those years as Biff's target. Though it would have been nice if Biff's attitude had changed, Paul kind of looked forward to facing the bully. The rain continued to pour down but Paul wasn't ready to let his chance to face Biff get away just yet.

"Goolson," he yelled, "I'm not finished talking to you." Paul couldn't believe what he was saying. The thought of writing his last will and testament flashed through his mind.

"That's it," Biff groaned, as he turned around. A bolt of lightning flashed across the sky. Paul thought of his hospital nickname and maybe that was a sign of good luck. Biff walked up to him, gave him a stare and threw a wicked right hand right at Paul's face. He tried to duck, but Biff's punch caught him square on the forehead. He fell to the ground like a sack of potatoes. He immediately flashed back to middle school, where Biff laid him out and threw him in a garbage can. His eyes squinted as he looked up but he was in too much pain to actually get off the ground.

"How fitting," Biff laughed. "Puzzle can't get up. Game over, Puzzle. Game over!" Biff kicked Paul in the ribs for good measure, jumped in his Jeep and sped off. The exhaust must have triggered a coughing spasm as Paul coughed up some phlegm. It was mostly yellow, so at least that wasn't a huge concern.

The rain continued to fall as puddles were forming along the street. Paul shrieked in pain. One of his teammates helped pick him up and drove him to an emergency room nearby. He didn't need stitches and no ribs were broken.

He had some ice applied to his head and a bandage put on his swollen ribs. Paul's teammate told him to press charges against Biff but he decided otherwise. He knew his team would play Biff's team one more time before camp ended and he intended to be in the starting lineup for that game. He was upset that Biff had beaten him again but he vowed that it wasn't over, yet.

"Well, how did you do?" his mom asked from the couch as he slunk in the door after midnight. He was surprised they were still awake but he knew they were excited to hear about his experiences.

"I didn't get to play. I rode the bench," he said dejectedly.

"Paul! What happened to your head? It's black and blue!" his mom demanded.

"Just a baseball injury, mom. Got hit by a foul ball in the dugout," he mumbled.

"Oh Paul, baseball is so dangerous." Suddenly, his mom stopped. "But I guess there are injuries along the way." His mom used to be so over-protective, but ever since he recovered from his coma, her attitude had changed. Why? He had no idea.

"You'll get your chance, son," his father said. "Your mom and I believe in you. Now, let's put a cold steak on your forehead."

Paul enjoyed receiving positive reinforcement from his parents but he was still frustrated. The scouts didn't even get a chance to evaluate him. He didn't want to bore his parents with his frustrations. After all, it was Garey's birthday and he was sure that they had bigger concerns than his playing time. After Paul grabbed a cold steak from the freezer, he headed up to his room.

There would be other games and he knew of one in particular he was now looking forward to. That night, he called The Jet. He told him everything that happened including the fight afterwards—if you want to call a one-punch knockdown a fight.

"Paul, you'll get another shot at that guy on the baseball field. And when you do, I'll be there to see it. I'm proud of you for standing up for yourself, but don't burn your anger out with your fists. Turn it into positive energy when you step to the plate. Let the counter-punch come from your bat."

The Jet's pep talks inspired Paul but he checked the schedule and Ricky had a game at Turner Field against the Reds the next time he would face the Tragic Magic, so Paul knew he probably wouldn't make it. Nevertheless, he looked forward to seeing Biff again.

Game 2, March 15th

The coach couldn't justify benching me again, could he, Paul wondered? He looked up and down the lineup card for the game against the Zephyrs and his name was absent. He was supposed to play centerfield but for the second consecutive week, it was another player, one who went 0-for-3 in the first game. Certainly the coach didn't think he could do worse. His impatience got the best of him in the third inning and he had to ask.

"Coach Tomlinson, why am I not in the lineup?" he asked.

"I'm using the same starting lineup as last week," Coach Tomlinson said flatly. In the ninth inning, though, the coach said he would pinch-hit Paul if one more runner got on. Paul darted to the on-deck circle. Would he finally get his chance or would an earthquake hit the field this time? He saw his parents sitting on the edge of the bleachers waving and smiling at him. He wanted to make them proud.

The batter in front of him lined a screamer up the middle for a hit. Paul walked toward the plate as the tying run. Hugh Pelter, the Zephyrs' pitcher, stared at him. This was it, his first at-bat in organized ball. He could not have been more excited. He took a deep breath to calm down before taking his stance in the batter's box. He put his hands back and his elbows up.

The first pitch was a high and tight fastball. He couldn't stop his swing.

"Strike one!" the umpire shouted loud enough that Paul was sure people in Australia must have heard. He stepped out of the box to adjust his batting gloves and then strolled back in. He knew he swung at a bad pitch. He chalked it up to nerves. He had to be more selective. Pelter had been dominating all day, striking out twelve and allowing only a few hits. He took the second pitch, a curveball on the outside corner.

"Strike two!"

Paul thought it was too far outside but his opinion didn't matter. Come on, he mumbled to himself. From the corner of his eye, he caught a glimpse of Biff Goolson in the stands, wearing a brown leather jacket and blue jeans. Was he scouting our team or just one particular player, Paul wondered? Now he was really pumped up to jack the ball over the fence.

The pitcher came set and threw him a fastball—which is exactly what Paul was looking for. He swung with everything he had.

Bam!

The ball jumped off his bat like a bullet shot deep into centerfield. The only question in his mind was which row of bleachers it would land in. This game was going to be tied, he told himself, as he rounded first and went into his homerun trot. He watched as the centerfielder jumped, stretching his glove above the centerfield wall. No way he'd catch it, Paul thought. As he confidently stepped on second base he saw the centerfielder pull the ball out of his glove and show the umpire that he had in fact robbed Paul of a homerun.

"Out number three!" shouted the second base umpire. "Game over!" It was as if the umpire was quoting Biff Goolson. "Game over!" once again. Paul couldn't believe it. How did that outfielder make that catch, he wondered? The guy had made two errors in the first three innings. Paul flung his helmet, totally dejected. He looked back in the stands to see Biff brushing off his jeans, smiling, and walking away. Paul could read his mind.

"You'll always be The Puzzle to me. Game over!"

"Darn it!" Paul screamed.

His parents consoled him after the game. Following their chat, he caught up with Coach Tomlinson at his car. He wanted him to know how he felt.

"Coach, we've lost two games and you have only given me one chance to bat and I came within inches of tying the game for us," he said boldly.

Coach Tomlinson grunted, barely looking at him. "What makes you think you can make a difference? Didn't you just line out?" he said. "You've never even played high school baseball before."

"I'm here for a reason," he said firmly. "And you'll never know that reason unless you give me a chance. Let me start one game. Please."

While Paul thought it was a good speech, Coach Tomlinson just stared coolly at him for a moment and then said, "See you next week, Pete."

"It's Paul!" he shouted, as the coach drove off.

Game 3, March 22nd

Paul was sure he had riled Coach Tomlinson to the point that he would never give him an opportunity to display his skills. He didn't have to look very far in the batting order to see he was wrong. Just to see "Paul Morgan" on a lineup card was so exciting to him that he wanted to grab it and frame it. He ran up to the bleachers and yelled to his parents, "I'm starting!" Today, they were playing a team called Balls to the Wall, which had won a game and lost a game thus far. Coach Tomlinson let the team know that two scouts were in attendance, both from the Atlanta Braves.

Paul batted second and after the leadoff hitter popped out to third base, he strolled to the plate. He gripped his Louisville Slugger, adjusted his helmet, then his batting gloves. He batted left-handed since the Balls to the Wall pitcher was a righty. He dug his cleats into the dirt and stood tall for the first pitch. Again, he was a little impatient and swung at the first pitch. He felt the ball leap off his bat and watched it land safely between the second baseman and right fielder for a bloop single. He looked into the stands to see his parents clapping. The Jet couldn't make it since the regular season had just opened but he had called to wish him good luck before the game. Paul hit a ground-rule double in his next plate appearance, singled in his third at-bat and stretched a double into a triple in his final at-bat. He went 4-for-4, and stole two bases. After his team's 3-2 victory, one of the scouts approached him.

"Paul, outstanding game," he said.

"Thank you," Paul said humbly.

"I'll be here next week. Can't wait to see how you do against that Goolson kid. He's been pitching really well."

Can't wait myself, Paul thought.

Chapter 28
Game Over!

Game 4, March 29th

Paul was 4-for-5 in tryout camp games, with two runs-batted-in and two stolen bases heading into the grudge match with Tragic Magic. Biff would be on the mound.

Paul checked the lineup card and was happy to see that he'd cracked the starting lineup yet again. He'd finally get to face his nemesis. He looked towards the mound in the bottom of the first and watched Biff warming up. His fastballs looked like they had more velocity than the last time his team faced him. The huge hurler mowed down the leadoff hitter on three straight pitches.

Paul left the on-deck circle and looked into the stands as he walked towards the plate. The scouts were there with notebooks open and pens at the ready. His parents were there smiling and cheering, of course. He was not sure they totally understood the significance of what was about to happen. The Jet couldn't be there, he was playing at Turner Field.

Paul wrapped his fingers around the familiar wood handle of his Louisville Slugger. He adjusted his helmet, then his batting gloves. He batted left-handed since Biff was a righty. He lifted his head, the black and blue spots on his forehead still showing the signs of Biff's most recent handiwork, to look out at the mound. Biff stared right back at Paul, pausing a moment as if to acknowledge the moment of truth that was at hand for both men. Finally, after nodding agreement to the catcher's sign, he went into his wind up. When he uncoiled he fired some chin music with all his might that came within about three inches of re-arranging Paul's face. In self-defense, Paul ducked and swung feebly all in one motion to avoid being beaned.

Biff smiled, proud that he came within inches of ending Paul's career before it got started. He followed the high-and-tight heater with a curve ball that Paul took for a called strike on the outside corner. Finally, he threw a fastball right down the middle and Paul swung for the fences. But, rather than seeing it flying over the fence, Paul whiffed.

"Strike three!" bellowed the umpire. "You're out!"

Paul looked back at Biff and again, Biff glared back with his evil smile. Paul's dislike for the guy on the mound was eating him up inside.

Paul couldn't believe he struck out but it only got worse, since he did it again in his next two at-bats. After the third one, Biff mouthed the three words that always caused Paul's blood to boil—"Game Over, Puzzle!"

Paul flung his helmet and bat into the dugout and sunk down on the bench to sulk. Would Biff Goolson always get the better of him? He told Coach Tomlinson to take him out of the game. He was sure the coach was itching to anyway. He'd rather quit than see that gloating grin from Biff the bully if he struck out again.

Coach Tomlinson began scratching his name off the card when Paul heard a commotion among his teammates. He couldn't figure out what they were talking about but then he saw Manny Martin, their catcher, point towards the stands. He looked over and saw The Jet sitting in the bleachers next to his parents. He'd never seen Paul play in a league game before, and since he wasn't scheduled to pitch that night, he had left his game to watch his young friend.

"Coach Tomlinson, wait," Paul pleaded quickly. "I want one more chance."

The completely befuddled coach shook his head but left his name in the lineup. The next inning, as Paul took his position in the outfield, he saw Ricky smiling at him. The Jet motioned like he was swinging a bat and uttered the words "Swing away." That was his way of telling Paul to relax and just hit the ball. He was so excited The Jet made it to his game. Paul smacked his Mizuno mitt with his fist. Not a single ball was hit his way in the outfield. Two innings later, he got his chance to bat one more time against Biff.

In the bottom of the 9th, Paul's team trailed by two runs, with a runner at first base. He was on deck and one of his teammates, Darius Stone, came to bat with two away. He swung and missed the first pitch. Could Biff pitch any better? Darius took the next pitch for a ball. Biff threw another ball to Darius, and then another, for a count of three balls and one strike. One more ball and Paul would get one last chance to redeem himself. He did not want to be stranded in the on-deck circle again. Biff threw a curve ball that just missed the outside corner.

"Ball four. Take your base!" shouted the umpire. Paul walked up to the plate as the winning run. As he ambled up to the plate trying to act cool, his parents and The Jet stood in the bleachers clapping in unison. He was sweating as Biff dug in on the mound. Relax, he kept repeating to himself. He adjusted his batting gloves. He took his helmet off, and then put it back on. He dug his cleats into the dirt. He had come up with some crazy habits. He pulled his bat back behind his head. Biff threw a strike right down the middle, and he got nothing but air. Biff pumped his right fist, knowing he was two strikes away from slamming the door on this game; two strikes away from destroying Paul's self esteem yet again.

Paul had seen ten pitches from Biff and had yet to even foul one off. He took the next pitch on the outside corner for strike two. This was getting ridiculous, he thought. He stepped out of the batter's box for a minute to take a deep breath and reminded himself he could do this. He stepped back in and got into his relaxed stance. Biff had thrown him two heaters in each of his four at-bats. The only other pitch he threw him was his curveball. The Jet taught him to use deductive reasoning to figure out which pitch was coming next, so he prepared himself for the curveball. It was dangerous to look for only one pitch. If Biff threw him another fastball, he'd surely swing late and strike out.

Biff came set on the mound. Paul was going to hit this pitch—he had no doubt in his mind. Again, he adjusted his batting gloves, took off his helmet and put it back on, dug his cleats into the ground and pulled his bat back. Biff sneered at Paul, went through with his motion, and released the pitch. Sure enough, Paul spotted the rotation of a curveball headed for the inside corner. He swung with everything he had and hit the ball right on the sweet spot of the bat.

Bang!

The sound of contact was like a cannon shot, which seemed appropriate, given that the ball jumped off the bat as if it had been shot from a cannon. It sailed majestically through the air, rising and arcing toward the right field wall. Paul dropped his bat and started running as the ball kept carrying. He rounded first as fast as he could. If the ball hit the wall, he could get in scoring position to win the game. "Come on, ball!" he shouted to himself. The ball kept carrying. It soared through the air for what seemed like an eternity. This ball wasn't going to hit the wall! Paul looked up to see the right fielder's back as he watched the ball clear the fence by fifteen feet. No outfielder was coming up with this ball. His running immediately turned into trotting.

HOMERUN!

He did it! The Jet jumped from his seat in the bleachers. His parents hugged each other. Paul pumped his fists as he rounded the bases. All he could think about were the days Biff bullied him around the schoolyard. He remembered the kid who refused The Solution's help because he could fight his own battles. He'd fought back against Biff Goolson, and he won. He finally stepped on home plate and celebrated with his teammates and Coach Tomlinson. One of his teammates grabbed him and put him on his shoulders as they all carted him to the dugout. Coach Tomlinson had one of his base coaches retrieve the ball as a keepsake for his new star. Paul looked over at Biff. This time, the scrawny CF kid was the one who landed the pride-stinging haymaker.

One of the scouts came up to Paul and told him how impressed he was with his hitting. This was the second scout in two weeks that had complimented him. When he left the field, his parents each gave him a long embrace. Paul's mother was fighting back tears of joy. Sam was radiant with a father's pride. Ricky gave him a hug, too.

"Way to go, Paul!" The Jet shouted. "The scouts are interested in you. You have a chance now." Though it was great to know that he'd caught the scout's eye, it was more important to him that he caught someone else's attention.

Later, he caught up with Biff outside the park. "Good game," Paul said flatly. Obviously, he'd wanted to say that he kicked his sorry butt and that revenge was finally his, but he felt like he'd done his talking on the baseball diamond.

"You were lucky," he answered, with an edgy tone. "Anyone can have one lucky swing. Anyway, I struck you out three times. As far as I'm concerned, I won this battle."

Paul looked at the playground about a hundred feet from them. He knew he could have left it there and walked away with the last and best laugh but he wanted to make sure that Biff understood who the true winner was that day. After all, there was something he'd been meaning to do since he was thirteen.

"I have an idea," Paul said.

"Want to get your butt kicked again?" Biff snickered.

"Nope, I have a more peaceful way to resolve our issues, once and for all." Paul knew if Biff punched him again, he might have suffered brain damage. He told Biff to come with him. They stopped at the monkey bars.

"All my life, you made fun of the fact that I couldn't do ten pull-ups. Well, let's go. You and me. Let's see who can do the most pull-ups."

"Are you kidding, Puzzle? You have no chance!"

"Are you up for it or not?" Paul shouted.

"I'm in," Biff replied. "You are going to fall to pieces just like the puzzle you are."

"Okay," Paul said. "But there's one thing."

"What!" Biff shouted impatiently.

"If I win, you can never call me Puzzle again."

Biff thought about it for a few seconds before putting Paul on the hot seat. "Okay, and if I win, you quit the tryout camp and take yourself out of contention for the major leagues."

Wow, that was a tough bet. Playing Major League Baseball was his dream. Was he willing to quit on his dream just for a little redemption? You're darn right he was. He had a thirteen year old kid's honor to defend.

"You got a deal, Biff. I'll go to one end and you go to the other so that we can face each other and see who falls first."

"Wait!" shouted Biff, still surprised that Paul was willing to take the bet. "How do I know that you will accurately count my pull-ups? You'll be doing pull-ups at the same time. You're not going to be able to count mine, too."

"Why don't we count them aloud?" Paul said.

"No way," Biff replied. "That will cause me to expend more energy than I need to. Since no one will be able to count for us," Biff said, "we're just going to have to cancel…"

"We'll count them for you," a voice interrupted. Turning around, Biff and Paul saw The Jet walking onto the playground.

"*We'll* count them?" Biff asked puzzled. "I only see one of you." Suddenly, behind him walked Paul's father.

"Yeah, we'll count them. I'll count yours Paul and The Jet will count Biff's. The Jet and I will shout out each time one of you does one." Paul smiled at his two allies, who would have to be unbiased for this competition.

"Fine," said Biff, sounding agitated that he was running out of excuses to get out of a potentially embarrassing situation.

They set themselves at opposite sides of the jungle gym, facing each other, and grasped tightly to the pull-up bars.

"You ready?" Sam asked both competitors.

"Born ready," said the always cocky Biff.

"Go!" The Jet shouted.

Paul and Biff kept pace with each other for the first few pull-ups but then Biff got faster. Paul figured that he'd save his energy for the end but he caught up to Biff by the tenth pull-up. Paul still felt pretty good. At fifteen, both of them were starting to get tired but Paul was now going at a better pace than Biff. When Paul reached twenty, he looked into Biff's eyes and, for the first time, he saw concern. Biff was still at eighteen. His brow was sweating. His muscles were clearly straining. His body was shaking. At twenty-two, Paul barely got his chin over the bar. He was starting to shake, too, and the sweat started pouring down his forehead as well but what kept him motivated was imagining all the kids who saw him fail to do pull-ups back in school.

"Twenty-three," his dad shouted, as Paul edged his chin over the bar one more time. The Jet was waiting for Biff to hit twenty-two. Biff pulled with all his might but then his arms relaxed as he lowered his body back down. His hands were still clinging to the pull-up bar. He tried one more time, his face contorted from the strain. "Come on!" he screamed at himself. Finally, unable to lift his heavy carcass again, his blistered and bloody hands slipped off the bar and he tumbled to the ground.

"I won!" Paul shouted, as he dropped to his feet.

His dad and The Jet smiled, still trying to look impartial. He knew that they both wanted to bust loose with jubilation but they held it in and walked back to the parking lot so Paul could have his moment of closure.

Biff, still huffing and puffing to catch his breath, asked, "Who do you think you are?"

Paul paused to ponder that one. He thought about all those times Biff said he'd never do ten pull-ups. He remembered how Biff said that even the girls could do ten pull-ups. He remembered all the anger that burned inside of him and how humiliated he'd felt those days. The answer was simple.

"Who am I? I'm the guy who can do twenty-three pull-ups. You'll never do twenty-three pull-ups."

Biff glared back at him, stung by his own words.

"Game over, Biff," Paul yelled into his face. "GAME...OVER!"

Paul walked away that day with blisters all over his hands, a forehead that still ached, and a newfound confidence in his abilities. Best of all, he walked away with his pride still intact for the first time in his life after a confrontation with Biff Goolson. He was not only becoming a very good baseball player, but he was also becoming the strong person he'd always wanted to be. He was "building character," as they say. And, though Dr. B convinced him that there were no big or small accomplishments, he chalked this one up as his biggest accomplishment to date.

Chapter 29
And the Winner Is...

The head of the camp announced that there would be a season-ending banquet, at which the Braves scouts would announce which player would get an Atlanta Braves minor league contract. Paul noticed the scouts talking to Hugh Pelter, the Zephyrs' pitcher, after his last game. He gave up only five hits and struck out twenty-two batters in three games. Hugh would have played minor league baseball two seasons ago for the Cubs but a knee injury in high school set him back. Paul knew that he came within inches of hitting a towering homerun against Pelter which probably would have ensured him a minor league contract. He was getting worried that he would be passed over, and that he would have to try out at another camp.

Paul's parents escorted him to the league banquet at a beautiful theater downtown. All the players and their families mingled before the awards were handed out. Coach Tomlinson was named Best Coach. In his acceptance speech, he said if Paul hadn't pushed him to get in the lineup, he wouldn't have won the award. Paul appreciated hearing that but he was still getting nervous. Had he earned that minor league contract or not? Would his journey begin today, or would he face yet another setback?

During the dinner, his dad had bragged to all the other parents in attendance how his son was able to do more pull-ups than the dominating pitcher from the Tragic Magic. He told the story of his dramatic homerun off of Biff about ten times before Lilian told him to quiet down. Though it was a bit embarrassing, Paul enjoyed hearing his dad brag about his accomplishments.

When he was younger, he always heard him brag about Garey. While he loved Garey, he longed for the day that his father would boast about him, too.

His mom, who Paul finally told the truth about his fight with Biff, didn't condone violence or dishonesty but she knew he was a grown man and understood that he did what he had to do. She continued to be less over-protective of her son and more accepting of his fighter's mentality.

Paul noticed that Biff was conspicuously absent from the banquet. Paul was pretty sure that Biff was too embarrassed to attend after getting lit up on an 0-2 curveball to lose his final tryout game. Finally, the head scout for the Atlanta Braves walked up to the podium.

"It is tough deciding which players deserve a shot in our farm system," he began. "We saw many great baseball players over the past few weeks. Unfortunately, we can't choose all of them. So let's get down to business."

Paul held his breath.

"The Atlanta Braves would like to present a minor league contract to…"

Paul was ready to bite off all of his fingernails by now.

"Hugh Pelter!"

The crowd cheered. Paul clapped, knowing Hugh deserved the promotion. He had pitched well for the Zephyrs. Still, Paul wondered how close he came to making it. Was his near-miss against Pelter the difference-maker? Was it the three strikeouts against Biff that kept him from the next step? Had his bully gotten the best of him, again? His parents each gave him a quick embrace—their way of telling him that everything would be okay. Sure, he was disappointed but he decided right then and there he would just try out again until he made it. There was another tryout camp in North Carolina next month. He'd never been to Charlotte so he figured he'd make the most of it. Hey, maybe he and Biff would face off again. The only thing better than hitting one homerun off of Biff was hitting two. He would never give up on his dream.

But the head scout wasn't finished yet. He was given a second piece of paper from one of the scouts.

"We'd also like to extend a contract to the best hitter at our tryout camp. I believe Coach Tomlinson has already told you what role he played on his team. Ladies and Gentlemen, Paul Morgan!"

Was he kidding, Paul wondered? Was this another dream? He looked around for a masked man just in case. Shocked, he hugged his parents. The crowd began to cheer; Paul was so nervous he was shaking as he walked to the podium.

After he and Hugh had their pictures taken signing their minor league contracts, the scout told Paul he'd be going to Rome, Georgia, to play for the Braves' Single-A affiliate, the Rome Braves. To get back home to Atlanta and play at Turner Field, he'd have to prove himself at Single-A Rome, Double-A Greenville, and then Triple-A Richmond. The journey was about to begin.

"Most players who play minor league baseball don't make it to the Major Leagues," the scout explained to him later that evening. "And coming out of a tryout camp, the odds are even longer."

"Yes sir, I know the odds and I'm looking forward to the opportunity to show what I can do on the field."

"To my knowledge, not one person with cystic fibrosis has ever made it to the Major Leagues," the scout continued. "I'm sure by getting this far you've inspired many people already. Whatever you do now is just gravy, right? Good luck, Mr. Morgan. I wish you well."

He patted Paul on the back, shook his hand and began to walk off when the young man with CF stopped him.

"Wait!" he called. The scout whirled around as Paul continued. "You don't understand, sir. There was a one-in-four chance I'd have cystic fibrosis. When I was born, doctors told my parents I'd be lucky to live into my late teens. There were one hundred players here, and I was one of two players who made it. Statistics mean nothing to me. What matters is that I get to the Major Leagues, and some day I will."

The scout smiled and continued on his way. Paul realized for once, he wasn't lacking in confidence. He had faith in himself, and he was going to need it.

Chapter 30
A Minor Struggle

Paul awoke on the morning of April 13 packed to leave for Rome, where he would be playing for the Rome Braves. He had the dream again: he was up at bat in a Major League Baseball game when someone with a mask came out to the plate to give him pointers on how to get a hit to win the game. He got set at the plate, and the pitcher was smiling at him. Why was he smiling, he wondered? Paul used to be disappointed when he woke up but this time he was psyched. He was closer to the Major Leagues than ever before, though he wasn't any closer to figuring out who the masked man was.

He packed clothes, baseball equipment, medications and his therapy machine into his car. He brushed his teeth, showered and ate breakfast. He read the morning sports section, then loaded the rest of his luggage into the car. At 9:15 he touched his pendant and thought about Garey. Anytime he saw the sequence nine-one-five, he thought of the date his brother passed away. He was going to get to the big leagues for both of them. He hugged Sam and Lilian goodbye.

"Go get 'em, Paul!" his dad said proudly.

"Don't slide and hurt yourself, unless you're trying to break up a double-play," his mom said with a wink. She had been trying to learn baseball lingo to show her support.

As he pulled out of the driveway, he turned on the radio. He could not find a good station until he heard "Centerfield," a classic baseball song they played before every Braves game.

Oddly, he found the song on the frequency 91.5. He tapped his pendant again and headed north for the ninety-minute trip to Rome. During the trip, he remembered the phrase that Gregory said would help him to figure out why he was given a chance to be a superhero.

You are a bold hero to me. I pull for you. Gregory Vern Hartman

Was the phrase supposed to tell him that he was already a hero and that being The Solution was supposed to convince him of that? Was he chosen because he could come back to earth and help people by showing them that nothing is impossible if you work hard? Was there a chance that the phrase meant nothing at all and was just a way to mess with his head? Much like with his dream of Turner Field, he had no answers.

He arrived in Rome around noon, and met the manager, Mack Thatcher, at the stadium. Mack had pitched for the Yankees and Cubs in his brief career. He was one of those players who hustled on every play and he demanded the same effort from his players. He was only thirty-two years old, the youngest manager in the Braves' farm system. An elbow injury had shortened his career. He congratulated Paul and told him that he remembered his brother. Paul heard that quite often. A few guys from his tryout camp had even asked him if he was Garey's brother. He had gotten so much bigger and resembled Garey quite a bit now. Garey was a legend to many people in the southeast who saw him pitch. The rest of the world was robbed not to see him play. The mention of Garey's name made him tear up a little, but hearing his name also made him realize that people had not forgotten him, and that made him happy.

Coach Thatcher gave him an envelope with his weekly pay and a key to his new apartment. He explained the players got paid enough money to get some food for the week, but not much more than that. First year minor league ballplayers made about two-hundred dollars a week. Still, someone paying Paul to play baseball was like giving a millionaire a lottery ticket. Hopefully, he'd make it to the Majors so he didn't have to go to restaurants that featured combo meals every night.

The apartment was a quick trip, about two miles from the stadium. Upon his arrival, he was greeted by his new roommate, Terry Myers, the team's right-fielder. Terry was twenty-one years old and in his second year of Single-A ball. They became fast friends and in the gym, Terry motivated him to lift more. Paul was pressing about two-hundred-seventy-five pounds on the flat bench now but Terry continued to push him. They would chat while lifting. Paul told him his story and the dream he kept having.

"Hey, maybe I'm your masked man," he'd joke between reps. "I *am* giving you pointers, aren't I?"

Terry was quite the clubhouse prankster. Before Paul's first minor league game, Terry snuck into a player's apartment, with the roommate's help, and put shaving cream on a teammate's hand while he was sleeping. Then Terry tickled the guy's face with a feather so when the guy brushed his face, he spread the shaving cream all over it. It was juvenile stuff but they all got a kick out of it. Terry also told jokes around the clubhouse. He once joked that, due to low attendance at their games, they took attendance by taking roll of the team!

The next day, Paul arrived at Rome's State Mutual Stadium for his first game against the Augusta Green Jackets, the Single-A team for the Boston Red Sox. Hanging in his locker was the red and navy-blue home uniform with MORGAN stitched on the back. It was pretty exciting to see his name sewn on a uniform for the very first time. The cap had a red bill with a navy-blue top, just like an official Atlanta Braves cap, except it had a white R for Rome. After he put on his uniform and cleats, he grabbed his glove and bat and headed onto the field to warm up.

It was a beautiful, sunny day in Rome, about eighty degrees. The field had just been manicured by the grounds crew and had to be the prettiest Paul had ever set foot on. The outfield wall was green, with bright yellow distance marks of 335 down the left-field line, 401 to center and 330 to right. He remembered from his batboy days that the dimensions at Turner Field were exactly the same, so this would be a nice gauge to see if he was strong enough to hit homeruns in a big league park. The sponsors were listed behind home plate. In the dugout, the organization provided players with a choice of sunflower seeds or bubble gum. The public address announcer played a Rolling Stones tune to get everyone in the mood for the game. Paul started warming up with Terry by playing catch in foul territory. After about twenty-five tosses, the manager called them into the dugout. He looked at the lineup card and was pleased to see that Coach Thatcher had him batting seventh and playing centerfield.

When he walked to the plate for his first professional at-bat, the public address announcer gave the total attendance at 2,456—not exactly a packed house but still it was the most people he'd ever played in front of. When Paul heard his name announced on the loudspeaker, it didn't matter how many people were there. He had to suppress a schoolboy grin. He wanted to keep a poker face so the pitcher wouldn't know this was his first minor league at-bat. Unfortunately, his teammates knew this was his debut. The tradition in Rome for a first-timer was for the veteran players to put itching powder in a rookie's socks. Much to their amusement, Paul was scratching his feet at every opportunity.

He adjusted his batting gloves and helmet. He focused on the pitcher, dug his cleats into the dirt and pulled his bat back as he awaited his first minor league pitch. He had a gut feeling it would be a great day.

He was wrong. In fact, he couldn't have been *more* wrong. He struck out in his first at-bat, popped up in his second and grounded out in his third. With two outs in the ninth inning, he stood in the on-deck circle taking practice swings. His team trailed, 1-0, and the second baseman, LeMarcus Baskin, was batting with a count of two balls and two strikes. The Green Jackets' pitcher tried a fastball but missed low and outside for ball three. After a less than stellar 0-for-3, he still had a chance to be the hero. One in the seats would win the game.

"Come on, LeMarcus," he whispered. "Get on base. Give me one more chance." The pitcher threw the payoff pitch to LeMarcus. Ball four was low.

Paul strutted to the plate like he was Hank Aaron. He figured he was due to get a hit. He had gotten pretty confident since making it to the minor leagues. He took ball one outside. Then he took a curveball low and inside. Another fastball missed low and outside. The count was now three balls and no strikes. There was no better pitch count for a hitter. He adjusted his gloves and helmet, dug his cleats into the ground and pulled his bat back. He knew that since he was the winning run the pitcher didn't want to walk him, so he expected he would get a pitch to hit. His new teammates were chanting his name.

The pitcher tossed a knee-high curve ball that he swung right through, expecting something harder. No one in the Braves tryout camp had that kind of curveball. Three balls and one strike. The pitcher released the ball again and Paul swung with everything he had.

Bang!

He gave it a ride. "Get out!" he shouted. "Stay fair!" Going, going…foul! It was only three feet to the left of the foul pole. Now the count was full but he had the pitcher's best fastball timed. He was ready. He adjusted his gloves and helmet. He dug in again and pulled his bat back. The fastball blew right by his flailing bat.

"Strike three! You're out!"

Three chances to be a hero and he came up empty. Going 0-for-4 was bad enough but waving at a pitch with a chance to win his first minor league game was salt rubbed in the wound. Plus, going 0-for-4 would not get him sent up to Double-A. He sulked into their clubhouse and threw his glove in the locker. He sat there in silence until Terry asked him to go get a bite to eat.

"Listen, bud," he said, his mouth full of pizza, sitting with two other teammates at the local Pizza Hut that night. "It takes time to become a good hitter. Listen, I had gone 0-for-4 with three strikeouts in my first minor league game last year, so you didn't do that badly."

That night on a TV sports show, they watched the highlights of The Jet's pitching performance. He struck out twelve that day and shut out the Dodgers. Paul called to congratulate him.

"I stunk today," Paul said in the next breath, telling him about his last strikeout.

"Don't worry—it was your first time," he consoled him. Then The Jet reminded him of his last goal for the Major Leagues, before he retired. "I came so close to throwing a no-hitter tonight, man," he told him. "I still can't believe this is my last season. But remember, don't tell anyone. I don't want to make it a big deal during the season so I'm going to make the announcement public after our last game."

"No problem, Jet," he said. "You know your secret is safe with me. You know my family and I will be in attendance to celebrate your last game."

The next day, Paul struck out in his first at-bat. The next time up, the Green Jackets' pitcher threw him a hanging slider that he ripped down the right field line. He sprinted to second base and slid in with his first professional hit, a two-out double that drove in a run. Unfortunately, that was his last successful at-bat of the day. He went 1-for-5 with two strikeouts, yet the Braves somehow won in twelve innings.

After the game he had mixed feelings. He was happy that they won but he was very disappointed about his play. He had the lowest batting average on the team and this was only Single-A. He was really concerned that he wasn't going to make it through the Braves' system.

"Hey, man, quit moping," Terry said. "Why don't you come to my parents' house for dinner? They live a few miles from here and it would mean a lot to them—they've met all my other teammates and I'd love for them to meet my new roommate. So what do you say?"

"I dunno, Terry," he said glumly, slumped on the couch. "I really ought to stay home and analyze my swing. I must be doing something wrong!"

"Come on, Paul," Terry cajoled. "My mom is an amazing cook. And if you want, we can analyze your swing over dessert."

Food and a free lesson? How could Paul resist?

Chapter 31
Rome Is Where the Heart Is

Paul relented, and they drove to Terry's family's house in Rome. He met his parents, his brother Jake, and the best looking girl he'd ever laid eyes on. Sally was Terry's younger sister. She had long blonde hair down just below her shoulders, sparkling blue eyes and a petite figure. He had trouble introducing himself because he was so nervous, but once he had the guts to talk to her, it felt as if they'd known each other forever. He and Sally connected immediately, and they practically ignored everyone else. He told her about his struggles at the plate. She predicted that would soon change. As he was leaving, he asked her if he could take her out some time. She smiled and said, "That's sweet, but I don't date ballplayers."

"Why not?" he asked, surprised. She seemed so friendly.

"Ballplayers are always moving on to different teams in different cities," she explained gently. "I like where I live, and I don't want a long-distance relationship."

He understood her apprehension but he was so taken by this woman that he had to find a way to get her to go out with him. His brain started churning, so he said, "How about when I hit my first home run, you will go to dinner to celebrate with me?"

She hesitated. "I don't know," she mumbled.

"Look, it doesn't even have to be a date place," he said, a begging tone emerging. "I'll make sure each meal has a number next to it and that they allow super-sizing there. That's all I can afford anyway. What do you think?"

Sally laughed and poked him in the arm. "Paul, you are tough to say no to," she said and handed him her phone number. "I guess I don't see the harm in going out one time."

Unfortunately, he wasn't going to be calling her anytime soon. He went 2-for-10 in his next three games with no homeruns. He kept working hard, though. One week later, he got a two-and-one fastball from Tim Bolen, the Hickory Crawdads starting pitcher, and cranked it over the centerfield wall. He hit two homers that day but the only thing on his mind as he left the ballpark was calling Sally.

The next night he and Sally went to a quaint, Italian restaurant called Giovanni's near her apartment. He kept to his promise as every meal did have a number by it. They talked about their lives over dinner. He told her his story, which moved her to tears. He must have talked for hours about Garey but she really seemed to listen and be interested. After dinner, they went back to his place and talked until sunrise. Thank goodness Terry stayed at his girlfriend's house that night—he realized it would have been a little awkward bringing his sister back to their place with her brother sleeping just a few feet away.

He told Sally his goal was to make it to the big leagues, then get a hit in his first Major League game. He explained to her about the masked man in his dream. He told her about the three people who affected his life the most—his brother; Biff Goolson and Ricky "The Jet" Kilmer. He let her know he had CF and that it was incurable, but that the statistics no longer bothered him. Despite his rule about bringing up cystic fibrosis on first dates, he felt comfortable telling this kind woman.

She told him about herself, too. Sally grew up in Rome. She'd never really traveled anywhere outside of Georgia, which they had in common since Paul was always too sick to travel. She loved animals and had a tiny gray kitten named Mister Wrinkles. What he immediately noticed about Sally was her wonderful heart. Sally had an aunt she was very close to who had succumbed to bone cancer, so in her spare time, Sally did a lot of charity work for the American Cancer Society. What really drew him to Sally was the immediate comfort level he felt in talking with her. He felt like he could tell her things that he couldn't tell anyone else. She was a great listener and she gave him some pretty insightful feedback in return. He told her there was a tremendous probability that he wouldn't make the big league squad. She told him that he was looking at it the wrong way.

"How many people have the talent to pursue their dreams?" she said. "You're closer to your dream than most people ever get to theirs. You should relish every moment rather than pre-occupy yourself with the notion that you won't fulfill your goal."

Sally told him that her professional goal in life was to become an award-winning journalist and, at age 20, she already was writing for a local newspaper. She even asked if she could do a story on him.

"Sure," he agreed, "but only if you go on a second date with me."

"Paul, I told you, I don't date ballplayers," she said, starting to get nervous. "I should leave."

"But, Sally," he said, the begging tone coming back, "How do you know it's going to be a disaster dating a ballplayer unless you do it? Haven't you had a good time tonight?"

"I have dated ballplayers and the result is always the same," she answered, a slight edge to her voice. "Please just take me home."

The car ride back to her apartment was quiet. He didn't know what to say, or how to convince her that he wasn't the average ballplayer. He walked her to her door and said an awkward goodbye. Part of him knew that her refusal to date him wasn't just because he was a ballplayer—he knew that CF played a part. He knew that considering a relationship with someone with cystic fibrosis was a big decision for anyone. He couldn't hold that against her.

The next day he spoke to Terry about his sister's baseball-player phobia. Terry told him that she had once dated a shortstop for the Rome Braves. She and Russ developed an intense relationship that lasted more than a year. Sally came to all his games. She thought he was "The One," but then he was moved up to Greenville, South Carolina, where he met another woman and dumped Sally. Since then, Sally refused to date ballplayers. Paul understood Sally's concerns and decided that he would stop pursuing the relationship. If she was that much against it, it obviously wouldn't work.

Though Sally was often on his mind, she was not a distraction. In fact, the next day he hit his third and fourth homeruns, made a circus catch in the outfield, and gunned a runner out at home plate. The next game, he hit a grand slam into the left field seats, a solo homerun, and a game-winning double in the ninth inning. The Braves were winning and attendance was picking up. The Braves were becoming the big ticket in Rome.

He got better every day. By the second month of the season, he was rated by *Baseball America* magazine as one of the top prospects in the South Atlantic League. The Jet called him every week to check on his progress. He hoped he and Paul would become teammates in September, when the Atlanta Braves, like most teams, called up their best rookies to get some playing time.

The odds were slim, though, as very few players climbed the ladder from Single-A to the Major Leagues in the same season.

Paul decided that even if he and Sally would never date, he still wanted her to be part of his life, so the two of them developed a close friendship. They spoke every night on the phone. He told her how he played that day and she told him how her dates went. Paul dated too, but he couldn't help but compare every girl he went out with to Sally. Listening to her talk about the guys that she was meeting was difficult for him but he did it to strengthen their friendship. He found himself putting down every guy she went out with. He told her that she could do better, thinking of himself, of course.

A couple of weeks later, he smacked his twelfth homerun and notched his thirtieth RBI as the Rome Braves took two of three games from the Hickory Crawdads to take over first place in the South Atlantic League. He led the league in homeruns, was second in RBI and had played errorless defense. On June 1 he hit for the cycle—a single, double, triple and homerun in the same game, a feat as rare as a no-hitter. After the game, Coach Thatcher called Paul into his office.

"I've got some good news for you," the coach said, leaning back in the chair behind his desk. "The Braves organization has been impressed with your play. While I'd like to keep you here to help us keep winning, it's time for you to move on. You're going to be playing Double-A baseball, son. Good luck."

Paul couldn't believe it! Double-A was only two steps from the Major Leagues.

Terry and the rest of the team gave him a nice sendoff as he left the Rome locker room for the final time. That night, he told Sally he was being moved up to Double-A and would be moving to Greenville. She wasn't surprised, given his performance and she seemed genuinely happy for him.

"I always knew this day would come," she said on the phone. "I will always think of you."

"Sally, I'm not saying goodbye forever," he said. "We'll still talk on the phone. Hey, Greenville is only a couple of hours north, so if you ever want to come to a game, there will always be a seat reserved for you."

"Thanks Paul, but I don't go to baseball games," she said shortly. "I wish you the best."

Paul was a bit frustrated with Sally but he didn't have time to dwell on it right now, he had other calls to make. He called his parents and had both get on the phone so he could share the news. His mother let out a boisterous "Wahoo!"

"I'm so proud of you, Paul," she practically shrieked into the phone. "By the way, when are we meeting this girlfriend of yours?"

"Mom," he sighed, "I explained to you that Sally and I are just friends."

"She may think of you as just a friend, but I know that you love this girl. If she's that important to you, don't give up," his mother said.

He knew that he had to get over Sally, though. His dream was to play baseball and that required his full attention. Next he called Nurse Johanson, Dr. Knotts and Larry to tell them the good news. They were all very excited that he was not only doing well at the plate but also feeling well physically. His next call was to The Jet, who had already heard the news from his own coaches.

"So I'm only two steps away from being your teammate," Paul boasted.

"Hey, I'll save the locker next to mine," Ricky said with a laugh.

The following night, Sally came over to help him pack. She walked him to his car and gave him a kiss goodbye—a peck on the cheek. Tears were streaming down her face. He was so sad to be leaving her and even sadder to see her crying.

"Our friendship will work out," he told her softly as he held her in his arms. "I will call you every day."

She stood by his car as he got in and suddenly pulled a poster from the back seat of her own car. He read it as he drove away.

You are a bold hero to me. I pull for you.

Next stop, Greenville.

Chapter 32
The Dead Letter

Paul set out for Greenville on June 2. His favorite song, "Eye of the Tiger," played on the radio. He and Garey sang it constantly when they were kids. He rubbed his pendant as he thought of his brother. The song would pump them up no matter what was going wrong. When Paul sang it, he felt like the movie character Rocky, which was the movie the song was from. Rocky, a boxer, defied the odds to live his dreams.

An hour into his drive, Coach Boyer, the Greenville Braves manager, called his cell phone to let him know that he was excited to have him on board, and the team needed a catalyst, since Greenville had a record of twenty wins and forty losses.

Soon after, though, he felt that pulsating pain in his chest again, which he hadn't felt in months. It wasn't really painful but certainly cause for concern. His acid reflux, a heartburn-like condition he'd been diagnosed with several years ago, must have been acting up. He was coughing more than usual, too. He called his father on his cell phone.

"Dad, it's the reflux again. It's acting up. I don't know if my hiatal hernia is the cause of it or what?"

"Go to St. Luke's, Paul," he pleaded. "It might be a bacterial infection. We'll meet you there." As hard as he had worked, it would all mean nothing if he had another long stay at the hospital ahead. He turned his car around, headed back toward Atlanta and called Dr. Knotts to tell him he was coming. He wouldn't be surprised if they rolled out the red carpet, given the money his parents had paid St. Luke's on his hospital bills. He tried to tell himself that what he had was nothing, but he'd been through so much in his life that he worried it was worse than he thought. His mind began to think in worse-case scenarios.

"Did I have a bad bacterial infection? Why was I always sick? Will I ever catch a break?" He probably shouldn't have been operating an automobile at that point. He began speeding more than ninety miles an hour, passing people left and right as he hurried towards St. Luke's. He had to know what was going on and he had to know now.

When he arrived, the attendant asked what doctor he was here to see.

"Dr. Knotts, head of the cystic fibrosis department," he said.

"What is your child's name?" she asked, obviously another in a long line of people who thought people with CF didn't live very long.

"I am the patient," Paul said impatiently. At that moment, Nurse Johanson walked by.

"Lightning!" she shouted. Her hair was now shorter but she still had the look of a swimsuit model. She gave him a long embrace and led him to a room for Dr. Knotts to check him out. Dr. Knotts administered every test he could think of—a pulmonary function test, a blood test and even X-rays. His parents arrived shortly thereafter.

Dr. Knotts asked him to stay overnight so they could figure out the problem. Luckily, the team was okay with him taking an extra day or two to report to Greenville. He called Ricky to let him know the situation.

"I'm not due to pitch for another two days, man, so I'm going to come out there and be with you," said The Jet, who had become like a brother to him. Ricky arrived later that night, as did Sally. He was surprised that she drove all the way up to check on him, but he had called her from the car to tell her he was headed to St. Luke's instead of Greenville. She insisted on coming, probably because she could sense from their conversation how emotionally draining it was for him.

It was awkward for Paul to have Sally meet his parents, especially under these circumstances. He knew his parents were going to treat her like his girlfriend. His mom asked her the usual mix of questions: Where was she from? What did she do? What did she *want* to do with her life? Sally smiled politely and answered each one. His dad nudged him on the shoulder, a gesture of approval. He had to reiterate to both of them that she was not his girlfriend, although he couldn't say he still didn't wish that they were more than friends.

The next morning, Dr. Knotts entered the room a few minutes after his parents and Sally, who had stayed at their house, arrived at the hospital. The Jet had to head to Philadelphia for his next game but told Paul to call him with his test results. Dr. Knotts started with his usual small talk.

"I heard you've been hitting the ball like Chipper Jones lately," he said proudly.

"Yeah, I've been in a pretty good groove lately," he answered lamely. He wasn't much in the mood for small talk—he wanted to get out of there. "So what's wrong with me?"

"In all honesty, we're not sure. It could be just an after-effect of your acid reflux. It could be that you've been overdoing it. All your tests look pretty normal."

"So can I go?" he asked hopefully.

"I think you should take a couple of days away from baseball, rest up and go back on some of your old medications," Dr. Knotts advised. "We're also going to put you on an aggressive steroid called Prednisone so we can knock this infection out pretty swiftly."

"I have to get to Greenville, Doc," he explained. "But I can rest there since the team is idle for the next two days."

"Sounds good to me," Dr. Knotts answered. "Come see me in a month and we'll recheck you."

Paul was so relieved he didn't have to stay in that hospital. He was too focused on his dream to waste any more time at St. Luke's. His life was no longer in jeopardy. Things were going so well, maybe this was just the taste of reality he needed. He hugged Sally goodbye as she departed for Rome. He took the elevator to the third floor where he bumped into Larry.

"You look great," Larry told him as they shook hands. "Still working out? Staying in shape?"

"Absolutely," he said. "I'm still pursuing my dream."

He and Larry spoke for a few more minutes before Paul took the stairs back down to the second floor. As he was leaving the hospital, Nurse Johanson stopped him to get an autograph. He laughed it off but she said she was serious. Every patient on the second floor stood in line behind her holding a baseball for him to autograph. The stories about him in the newspaper had reached his old hospital floor. It seemed he was a hero to these patients, she told him.

"Why am I a hero?" he asked Nurse Johanson.

"Paul, don't you get it?" she said. "You're the patient who made it. That's why you're famous. You're not famous because you might play baseball on television some day, or because your story was in the newspaper. You're famous because you're the one who proved the doctors wrong. That's why kids want your autograph. That's why they admire you."

He never realized how much influence he had just by being brave and walking out those hospital doors. He remembered The Jet telling him that he'd never truly understand how much his success meant to those who needed inspiration. He gave those patients faith that they could conquer their illnesses. He did more good by not being a superhero. He signed Nurse Johanson's as well as each patient's baseball:

Paul Morgan. A superhero needs no cape.

Standing in the middle of the second floor, he addressed the kids.

"All of you have a lot of courage," he told them as they stood, or sat in their wheelchairs, listening attentively. "Never quit, stay strong and cheer me on when I get to the Majors. We're going to find a cure some day for all of the diseases we suffer from—or, I should say, all of the diseases we strive to beat. I'm proud of each and every one of you. The best thing you can do is stay positive."

The patients and physicians applauded. He looked over to see a ten-year-old boy with tubes coming out of his arms sitting in a wheelchair in front of Room 205. When Paul looked his way, he broke into a huge grin. It was as if he was looking at himself twelve years earlier.

That night he stayed at his parents' house. They talked for a while about his plans while he was in Greenville. He told them how he planned to hit the ball even better than he did in Rome. He didn't have time to struggle as he had to make the Major League club by September. They talked about Sally and his parents told him that she was perfect for him. He was so relieved to know they accepted her, although he was still concerned that they'd grow too attached to her and be disappointed if the relationship never progressed beyond mere friendship. After a couple of hours, Sam fell asleep in his recliner to the evening news. Paul and Lilian talked alone for the first time in a long while. She told him she found some letters Garey had written him.

"I don't think you've read them, since he didn't have a chance to mail them. Jennifer's family sent them to us," she said, tears filling her eyes. "I didn't open any of them—I wanted to ask you first if you wanted them."

"Sure, Mom," he said softly. "Thanks."

When she went to bed, he eagerly read one dated September 14. It was hard for him to read a letter from his late brother, but he was still interested to know Garey's thoughts before he died.

Dear Paul,

How is everything going? Mom told me you haven't been feeling well and the doctor is worried. I know they're telling you you're not doing so well but you can't worry about it. They might be able to measure some things but they can never measure the size of your heart. Remember that. Don't worry about our conversation on the phone. I understood that you were upset. Maybe this will motivate you to get better.

I asked Jennifer's dad for her hand in marriage tonight. He was so happy. We talked for about an hour and he gave me his blessing. He actually asked me if I could get him season tickets when I'm a Baltimore Oriole some day. He's a very funny man. You will like him.

I was feeling a little bit tired tonight and I was just going to turn in early. Then Jason told me he really needed to go out, because he wants to get a date with the waitress at the local Greek restaurant. That's how I met Jennifer, remember? She worked at the Chili's in Athens. He just wanted some company I guess. We're leaving in about half an hour. I probably won't get home till around two or three in the morning. You've never met her brother, have you? Jason's great.

I'm going to pop the question to Jennifer in the morning. I'm nervous, but I'm so excited about our future. Hey, I just thought of something. When I throw my first Major League pitch, I'm going to wear a wristband with your initials on it to honor you. That way, we'll both be getting our television exposure. Maybe it will help raise money for cystic fibrosis so they can finally find a cure. Remember, when you're a superhero, don't forget about me.

I love you, Paul.

From your older brother,

Garey Ethan Morgan

That letter was tough to read. Garey never got an opportunity to pop the question to his girlfriend. He was the greatest person Paul had ever known.

He felt bad for the way their last conversation ended but it felt good to know that Garey forgave him for hanging up on him hours before he died. Paul still hadn't been to his gravesite. Maybe part of him wanted to wait until he made it to the Majors to visit him so he could show his brother how his encouragement paid off. Maybe he just hadn't taken the time to drive there, he rationalized. Deep down, he knew the real reason—he just wasn't ready to see his brother's name on a gravestone yet. He was not sure he'd ever be ready for that. He remembered the days when Garey brought in the weightlifting magazines and stood up for him when Biff Goolson bullied him. Garey was always trying to help him. Now, he wanted do something for Garey. He woke his mother up with an idea.

"Mom, do you think the Garey E. Morgan Foundation has a nice ring to it?" he asked her. He decided he wanted to raise funds to fight his disease and honor his brother at the same time. He and his mom stayed up all night coming up with ideas. By 5 a.m., they had a great plan. He told her that when he got settled with the Greenville Braves, he'd follow through with their idea.

As he was trying to fall asleep that morning, he really missed his brother. He cried a lot as he lay there, but not all out of sadness. He remembered those days in the hospital when they ate hotdogs and Cracker Jacks, and watched every pitch of a Braves double-header. He remembered when Garey taught him how to make the perfect hotdog. After an hour of churning memories, he finally fell asleep. He woke up a few hours later and after his morning ritual, packed his stuff again and left for Greenville.

Not long after leaving his parents' house, he found "Eye of the Tiger" playing again on the radio.

He was pumped, and couldn't wait to make a name for himself in Greenville. He was only two steps away from the dream he'd had since the age of ten.

Thirty minutes into his drive up I-85, he saw the sign that read north to Greenville and south to Atlanta. He hoped the next time he headed for Atlanta it would be for his Major League debut rather than a detour to St. Luke's.

Chapter 33
The Greenville Braves

He arrived in Greenville on the team's day off. It was a nice town, but there was little to do compared to Atlanta. He stopped for lunch at the Waffle House before he went to meet the team. His chest was feeling much better now that he was back on his old medications. He had to remember to take them but that was a small price to pay for feeling better.

The player he replaced was sent up to the Triple-A club. Paul knew if he did well in Greenville, he'd be on the road to Richmond also, just one step away from the Major Leagues.

On his drive up to Greenville he made a decision. He wasn't going to call Sally like he did before. He didn't want to talk to her everyday and grow more attached. It hurt him to hear about all the men she was dating. He'd still call her—just not nearly as often. He was in Greenville to focus on baseball and that is what he intended to do.

He arrived at a practice field outside of Greenville Municipal Stadium to meet Coach Boyer. Coach Boyer was short, had a receding hairline and the most humongous forearms he'd ever seen. His nickname around the clubhouse was Popeye because of those massive forearms. He was intense. If he noticed that a player was slacking off or not paying attention to his pre-game talk, he'd have that player doing calisthenics between every half-inning of that day's game. Coach Boyer took Paul into the locker room to meet the rest of the team.

That evening, the team bus picked the players up at the Greenville bus station and took them to their first road series in Orlando, Florida, where they'd be playing the Orlando Rays, an affiliate of the Tampa Bay Devil Rays, the following day. During the bus ride, Paul was introduced to several teammates including his new roommate on the road, Hank Bowers. When he and Hank arrived at the Orlando Holiday Inn, they were assigned room 915. Paul paused to remember Garey.

Hank told him he was an undrafted free agent, which meant he was not chosen in the minor league draft. He made the team via a tryout camp in Charleston, South Carolina. Paul remembered the Atlanta head scout telling him that most players who make the minor league system through tryout camps don't make it to the Majors, yet he and Hank were now top prospects. It was as if that scout was just another doctor to him, telling him he couldn't succeed when he knew he could.

Hank was a good looking guy with short dark brown hair that was frizzy but never moved. He was named after the great Hank Aaron—the all-time leading homerun hitter in Major League history. He was six-feet, three-inches tall, though the Greenville program had him at six-feet, four-inches—an error that he constantly joked about. He said it was a lot easier to tell the women he met that he was six-four because there seemed to be something about that extra inch that attracted the opposite sex. Hank dated throughout the season. He would go out with three different girls a week. Most of the time he would meet them and get their phone numbers in the stadium parking lot before the team bus took off. He once asked out a blonde-haired petite woman in the front row while he was warming up in the on-deck circle. He had the team's batboy fetch her phone number for him. Turns out her boyfriend was at the concession stand getting her a hotdog while all this was happening. While Hank never lacked self-assurance with the opposite sex, his confidence on the field was never more evident than when he stepped in the batter's box.

Hank was the team's leading hitter, with a .345 average and twenty-five homeruns for the season. Paul's start in Greenville, meanwhile, was nothing like his start in Rome. Seventy-five games into his Greenville stint, he was hitting at a .353 clip with fifteen homeruns and ten stolen bases.

During a home stand in August, he finally got up the nerve to float an idea by Coach Boyer. He worried that the coach would veto the idea and tell him to concentrate more on his hitting and less on some marketing scheme. But he was pleasantly surprised when, after he explained his idea of the Garey E.

Morgan Foundation, Coach Boyer set up a meeting for him with the vice president of marketing for the next day. Paul would later discover that Coach Boyer lost a son to cystic fibrosis.

"This foundation is very special and important," Paul shared with the marketing VP and his team. "My brother was my inspiration. He urged me to fight this disease and I want to raise funds for CF in his memory so that even in death, he will continue to inspire others to beat it."

Grown men were tearing up as Paul shared the story of his brother. His pitch worked. The following Wednesday would be Garey E. Morgan Foundation Night at the game—minor league teams were always thirsty for great promotions to draw fans. With the Birmingham Barons in town, he shared the same talk before 10,000 fans. He wasn't that nervous since he didn't have to memorize anything. He simply spoke from his heart.

After sharing the story of Garey and his own struggles with CF, he asked each fan to give one dollar to the Garey E. Morgan Foundation to benefit research for cystic fibrosis. He asked for two dollars if he hit a homerun that night, a nice added bit of pressure for him. He was focused at the plate that night, going 3-for-5 with two homeruns and they raised a grand total of more than $18,000 for the Garey E. Morgan Foundation, for which his mother had already secured non-profit status. From that night of generosity by the Greenville fans, his mother made the foundation her life's work. She was a pretty persuasive fundraiser. She had an even better idea and was eventually able to pull it off. She convinced every minor league baseball team in the United States to give one dollar from each ticket sold to the Garey E. Morgan Foundation during all games on September 15, the anniversary of Garey's passing. She estimated they'd raise over one million dollars for CF research. His brother would have his legacy and Paul's disease would someday have its cure.

The next afternoon, they were in Chattanooga, Tennessee getting ready to play the first-place Chattanooga Lookouts, a Double-A affiliate of the Cincinnati Reds. He and Hank, though competitive, had become inseparable. The two of them went to Burger King that morning, as they usually did on the road. The first night they went to Burger King in Birmingham, Alabama, each of them hit two homeruns that evening against the Birmingham Barons. Being superstitious, as most ballplayers are, they started going to Burger Kings in every city before each game. Paul began to think that Hank was the guy who helped him get the hit in his dream.

The Braves lost to Chattanooga, 8-6, despite Hank going 3-for-4 with a homerun. Paul unfortunately went just 1-for-4 with a double that drove in two runs, breaking the Burger King homerun streak. They had fallen three games behind Chattanooga in their division but the players would be lying if they said that was their biggest concern. They all wanted what was called the "Virginia Telegram," the call from the Triple-A Richmond Braves. Later that night, back in their hotel room, Coach Boyer called, asking for Hank.

"I got the Virginia Telegram! I'm going to Richmond!" Hank yelled as he lowered the phone onto the counter. He looked like he'd just won the lottery, which, in a way, he had.

"That's really great news," Paul said, and he really meant it. He was going to miss Hank, though. He wondered who his new roommate would be. It would probably be a kid promoted from Rome who Paul would need to show the ropes. Still, this was a much easier way to lose a roommate than the way he lost them at St. Luke's.

"Paul, the coach wants to talk to you, too," Hank said, handing him the phone.

He swallowed hard and took the phone. He couldn't help but wonder if he was getting the Virginia Telegram as well.

"Hello, coach," he said, trying to sound casual.

"You and I are on a four-way call with Braves General Manager John Schuerholz, and Phillies General Manager Ed Wade," Coach Boyer said. Paul had no idea why all of these important people wanted to talk to him.

Suddenly, an unfamiliar voice chimed in. "Paul, this is Ed Wade of the Philadelphia Phillies. How would you feel about playing Triple-A baseball for the Scranton-Wilkes-Barre Red Barons up here in Scranton, Pennsylvania?"

Paul was stunned. He was part of a blockbuster trade—the part no one cared about, a minor leaguer no one had ever heard of. Three weeks earlier, the Philadelphia Phillies traded their All-Star centerfielder and a minor league pitcher for an Atlanta Braves relief pitcher and a player to be named later. Mr. Wade told him he was the player to be named later and his scouts had been keenly watching his last couple of games.

Paul's goal was to be promoted to Triple-A all right, but he wanted to go to Richmond, not Scranton-Wilkes-Barre. He'd never even heard of Scranton-Wilkes-Barre! He didn't jump for joy. What was he going to tell The Jet? He wasn't going to be his teammate. What would he tell his parents? His dad was a huge Braves fan. What about Sally? Who was he kidding? She only saw him as a friend—he was sure she wouldn't be too concerned that he was moving farther north.

"I'm looking forward to playing in Scranton, Mr. Wade. Thank you for the opportunity." He put on an Emmy-worthy acting job.

He called everyone that night. The Jet told him trades were part of the business and that the situation with the Phillies favored him, since they no longer had their starting centerfielder.

"You can't ask for a better opportunity to show off your talents," he said warmly. "Listen, there are millions of people who would gladly trade places with you in a second!"

"You are right," Paul said, starting to feel much better. After all, someone wanted him to play Triple-A ball, just one step from the show.

Surprisingly, his parents were overjoyed. They weren't concerned that he'd be playing most of his games in Philadelphia if he made the Major League club. They said they would come to a game any time, regardless of where he was playing. Everyone's support helped him realize this was a promotion and he should appreciate it, not lament it. Next he called Sally. After he told her the news, he waited to hear congratulations in her cheeriest voice but instead, she hesitated for a few moments. She had other concerns.

"How come you don't call me all the time like you used to?" she asked. "You told me you'd call me every day when you left Rome. Or do you not remember that?" she asked, frustration in her voice.

He was a little bit offended by her tone, especially after he'd gotten such good news. So what came out was probably not the best thing he could have said.

"I figured you'd be busy dating some guy anyway."

There was silence. Then finally, "Paul, I can't believe you said that," she said harshly. "I have dated a lot of guys but I'm only seeing one guy now. He's charming, kind and handsome."

"That's great Sally but I love you, and I can't handle just being friends anymore. I never wanted to lose you but what's worse is that I can't hold on to the slight possibility that we will date some day," he blurted out.

Well, there it was. Best to be honest, he presumed, laying his cards on the table.

"I can't date you," she said forcefully. "We can't talk anymore, Paul. Take care. I will miss you."

With that, the phone went dead. He slowly lowered the receiver to the carriage and choked back tears. This was supposed to be one of the happiest days of his life, but it sure wasn't turning out that way.

As hard as it was, he tried to get Sally out of his head and focus on the trip to Scranton. Everyone was okay with the move, except for him. All of his life, he had dreamed of being an Atlanta Brave. The Braves were his favorite team from the time he could hold a baseball. He and Garey watched hundreds of Braves games together. His room at home was a replica of Turner Field. He wanted to have a house in Atlanta and drive to the stadium during home-stands. He always hoped to play where the patients at St. Luke's could come see his games. He wanted to play in the stadium that he watched being built from his hospital room. Instead of playing eighty-one days a year in Atlanta, the Phillies came to Atlanta only eight days each season. Would he get homesick?

He'd taught himself to spin this move into a positive one. He realized he'd have a better chance to make it to the Majors in the Phillies organization, since they were not a playoff contender and would therefore bring up more minor league players at the end of the season. He'd even be more motivated to play against the Braves since they didn't think highly enough to keep him in the organization. He'd show them like he showed the three teams who didn't draft him in tryout camp. He'd show them like he showed Biff Goolson's 0-2 curveball. Regardless of what uniform he wore, he would have a chance to be a Major League baseball player, and that's all he'd ever wanted.

He began thinking back to his dream. In the dream, he wasn't necessarily a member of the Braves. He didn't wear any specific uniform. He'd just always assumed he was a Brave, since he was at Turner Field. So, winning a game at Turner Field in his first at-bat was still possible, though the odds were much lower.

He went to the clubhouse the next day, and gave up the red, white, and navy blue of the Atlanta Braves in exchange for the white with maroon pinstripes of the Philadelphia Phillies. It was like giving his favorite teddy bear to his baby cousin when he was six. He had to give it away but it would always be part of him. It would be strange for Paul to suit up in a Scranton-Wilkes-Barre Red Baron uniform. Coach Boyer and his teammates congratulated him and Hank as they cleaned out their lockers. He and Hank shook hands and agreed they'd see each other again in the Majors. They agreed to call each other to compare batting stats, and get together for the occasional dinner at Burger King, though they joked that the Whoppers weren't helping their waistlines.

The next day he began the journey to Scranton. As he made the long drive up the east coast, he thought back to the days when he was a kickball hero.

That was his first brush with success. Then he recalled being bullied by Biff Goolson and living with a defeatist's attitude in the hospital. Those were his days of failure. Now, he was successful again. He'd been through so much in his twenty-two years, but all of the adversity had made him a much stronger person. He reflected on the people in his life who gave him strength. He thought about his parents, Garey, Larry, The Jet, but most of all he thought about Sally. He wished that he could call her to apologize but the truth was that he loved her and he couldn't apologize for that. He couldn't be sad anymore. He had to stay strong for everyone who believed in him and for those people who would some day need him to prove to them that anything was possible. Most of all, he owed it to Garey to stay tough. He was ready to take the next step to playing Major League Baseball.

Off to Scranton…

Chapter 34
Playing in Scranton

Scranton, Pennsylvania was a quiet town of about seventy-five-thousand people. Paul was accustomed to the hustle and bustle of metro Atlanta, which included about four million residents. But Scranton had as many baseball fields as schools, so right away he knew how much baseball meant to the locals.

Lackawanna City Multi-Purpose Stadium was a step above Greenville as every one of the 10,000 seats had a cup holder and there was a scoreboard in the outfield that updated all of the scores around Triple-A and the Major Leagues. Their minor league championship pennants hung just above the outfield wall.

He walked into the locker room and met some of his new teammates. Alex Brown was a pitcher in his second season at Scranton. He'd bounced around the minor leagues for five seasons. He'd had two reconstructive elbow surgeries, and this was the healthiest he'd been in the last three seasons. The catcher, Jason Villanuevo, was a former first-round draft pick from the University of Southern California and had been in the minors for three seasons. That wasn't uncommon though. Most players spent at least a season in each level of minor league baseball. Paul had played so well out of the gate and had been a part of a trade, so he seemed to be on a faster track than most. Coach Abe Daulton said he was excited to have him in the lineup.

"I've read about you, Morgan," he said, grabbing his shoulder. "I'm going to find a way for you to get to the Majors some day."

"Thank you, Coach," he responded. He hoped some day came sooner than it sounded.

Later that afternoon when he got to his new apartment, the first person he called was The Jet. He was still talking about his near no-hitters, but he also told Paul that he had a dream that Paul had called him and told him that he was playing outfield for the Phillies.

"It would be hard to think that I could go from Single-A to the Majors in one season, Ricky," Paul said with a laugh. The organization had about one-hundred-fifty players in the minors and they would only send two or three up to the Major League club come September, which was only three short weeks away.

After he got off the phone, his father called and asked if Paul had seen the Phillies schedule.

"The Phillies play at Turner Field at the end of the season," Sam told him. "I bought tickets for the three-game set. You never know, Paul. I could be watching my little boy playing centerfield for the visiting team."

Paul could tell that his father was excited that his youngest son could be playing his favorite sport at the highest professional level, but it stressed him out that his dad had spent all that money to see him play in a game that the odds were against him playing in.

"Dad," he explained, "just two or three out of some one-hundred-fifty players make it to the Majors in the fall. Those are long odds, especially for a first-year player."

"You've been beating the odds for a very long time," Sam replied, Paul hearing the smile in his voice. "Doctors thought you might not walk, that you had no chance to beat cystic fibrosis. You've proved them wrong. Your mother and I believe in you. Everyone who meets you knows that you can accomplish anything."

"Dad, that's a lot of money to spend. With all you've paid in hospital bills over the years, I know that our money situation is not..."

"Paul," he interrupted. "I don't care about the money. I want to see my boy play baseball. I want to see him realize his dream. When I was sitting next to you all those months you were in that coma, I promised God that if he gave you a second chance, I would not miss the big moments in your life. Let's face it. I was not the best dad in the world when you were younger. We hardly talked. We were strangers living in the same house. I'm making up for lost time so please let me spend the money to see my boy do what he does best."

Paul appreciated the heart-felt gesture his dad was making. He also realized that his dad was right about something—Paul had to be more positive about his chances. It was just difficult sometimes to stay optimistic. He blamed that on the kickball game several years before. For a few moments, he was a hero and all the kids loved him. Soon after, he was handicapped and didn't have a friend in the world. That time during his life still haunted him whether he wanted to admit it or not. Nevertheless, he was going to try and stay positive this time around.

That night, he had the dream again. This time he saw a little more in the dream. He was sitting in the dugout. It felt as if it was the ninth inning because the crowd was going wild. He was waiting for a chance to bat when the coach finally tapped him on the shoulder. He stood in the on-deck circle and he was pointing up in the air. Why was I pointing up in the air, he wondered? His parents were sitting in their section, cheering him on. He heard his name being called, so he looked up and saw Garey floating through the air like a helium balloon. His turn to bat finally came and the man in the mask walked up and told him how to get a hit. He was trying so hard to see the man's face but he still couldn't make it out. Suddenly, his brother landed a few feet away and shook his head. Why is he shaking his head? Was he disappointed? The noise from the crowd gets louder and louder and...

He woke to shut off his little beeping Sony alarm clock. Again, the dream baffled him.

The following morning, he went to breakfast at Shoney's. He was a big fan of the breakfast bar.

He followed the waitress with a distinct Boston accent to his table just in front of the kitchen. He spotted a familiar guy eating by himself in the corner of the restaurant, maybe thirty feet from him. He was wearing a black baseball cap and a blue Adidas jumpsuit. When he did a double-take, he realized it was his old nemesis, Biff Goolson. What were the odds the two of them would be in the same small town several hundred miles from Atlanta?

Paul wanted to ask him so many questions. Why did he humiliate him when they were kids? Why did he punch him when they were at tryout camp? Did Biff know what he did was wrong? How did it feel to finally lose to The Puzzle? Instead of walking to the breakfast bar, he detoured away from the smell of French toast and towards Biff's table. He was going to let him have it like all those times he'd humiliated him. But just as he was about ten feet from him, a smiling, young woman came over to the table, pushing a stroller. Biff reached into the stroller and pulled out a tiny bundle dressed in pink. He kissed the little bundle and smiled, and then smiled up at the woman across from him.

Paul was shocked. Biff Goolson showing affection to another human being? Biff having a family? Wasn't this the same guy who beat him up? Then he relaxed. Though he'd wanted to know for so long why one kid could bully another, he decided to leave it alone. He realized Biff didn't bother him anymore. Paul had already redeemed himself and proven his point to Biff by winning the pull-up challenge. If he embarrassed him in front of his new family it would be as cruel as, well, putting vanilla pudding in his hair. Biff made some terrible mistakes when he was younger and even as recently as the tryout camp but maybe losing to Paul had changed Biff. Or maybe he just had a softer side that Paul had never seen. He gave Biff the benefit of the doubt. Instead of making a scene, Paul walked past Biff's table and over to the breakfast bar. Biff met his gaze and held it for a minute. They nodded slightly at each other, and Paul saw a tiny smile curl the corners of Biff's mouth. It was as if he'd finally earned Biff's respect. He'd still keep the younger Biff Goolson in his mind, because that bully still motivated him to try and make it to the Major Leagues. But as far as the current Biff Goolson, he wished him well.

That night, he donned a Phillies minor league uniform for the first time. It felt so strange to him. He felt like he wasn't being loyal to the Braves but the Phillies wanted him, so he would need to be loyal to them from then on. He was ready to show the Phillies that he deserved to be on the Triple-A club and would soon be ready to play in Philadelphia. His bat wasn't quite as willing. He went 0-for-4 in his first Triple-A game and struck out three times against the Syracuse Blue Jays. Triple-A seemed a lot tougher than Single or Double-A as these pitchers were throwing harder and had better stuff. He tried to bounce back the next night against the Blue Jays but went 0-for-5 with two more strikeouts. In his first five games, he had gone 1-for-21 without a homerun or an RBI. Why am I hitting so poorly, he repeatedly asked himself? He chalked it up to feeling pressure to make an impression.

To make things worse, Pennsylvania was experiencing an early cold spell in the middle of August. The cold weather caused Paul to have coughing spasms. He'd been so used to playing baseball in the warm weather of the South that the cold weather was adversely affecting his lungs. He grew frustrated fast. When his parents, The Jet, or Nurse Johanson called, he couldn't bear to tell them about his hitting futility. He told them he was doing okay but doubted he'd make the Major League club. His dad called one night and asked if he and his mother could come up to watch one of his games.

"Oh, Dad, thanks for being supportive but please wait for me to be in the big leagues," he said, trying to sound casual. "I'd rather you see my first game as a Phillie in a Major League stadium." During his slump, The Jet sensed his apprehension during their phone conversations.

"What's going on?" he asked one night during one of their many talks. Paul wanted to tell him how badly he was playing and how he felt like he was letting his friends and family down but he kept it to himself. He told him he missed home but things were great in Scranton.

He thought things would improve if he tried to stay positive but, unfortunately, they didn't. After he went 0-for-4 with another strikeout in his sixth game, Coach Daulton benched him.

"You're pressing too much, Morgan," he said simply. "I'm going to give your backup a chance." Paul was so humiliated. He felt desperate too, since the Phillies would be calling up players in about five weeks. They wouldn't take a back-up outfielder. As he sat on the bench that night in Pawtucket, he felt like he was back at gym class in his wheelchair watching the kids play.

"Coach," Paul yelled, "I can play."

"You trying to prove me wrong," Coach Daulton gasped.

"No, sir," Paul replied, as he went back to sulking on the bench.

After his second game riding the pine against the Red Sox, he just snapped.

"Coach!" he shouted, "I can play."

Once again, the coach yelled back, "You trying to prove me wrong, kid?"

"No, sir," Paul said, dejected from all the splinters he was gathering on the bench. After the fourth inning, he stormed back into the clubhouse and threw all his gear into a duffle bag. He decided not to take the team bus back to the hotel. Instead, he walked the entire six miles. It was as if he was having a mid-life crisis, but the truth was that he was questioning his skills as a professional baseball player. He didn't feel like being consoled by his teammates and coaches—he just wanted to pout.

Somewhere along the six miles, he decided to quit the team. He couldn't play at the Triple-A level. And if he couldn't play Triple-A baseball, he certainly couldn't play in the Majors. He had let everyone down. Maybe all those doctors were right when they said he'd be in a hospital most of his life. He was coughing more and more as he walked in the cold night air. He didn't want to call anyone. He just wanted to go back to his hotel room, turn off all the lights, and sulk in bed. He'd call Coach Daulton in the morning and tell him of his decision to leave the team. He would begin his drive down to Atlanta in the morning. He had reached rock-bottom, he felt. He knew he couldn't do any worse than 1-for-25.

After an hour-and-a-half of walking and soul-searching, he arrived at his team's hotel. When he reached the lobby, a guy wearing a gray suit with a navy blue tie was waiting for him. It was The Jet.

"What are you doing here?" Paul asked, surprised.

"Sit down, Paul," he said, leading him over to an ugly couch in the corner of the lobby. "We played an Interleague game in Boston last night. When I returned to the hotel, I had a message from Coach Daulton. He said you're struggling at the plate and stressing over it. He also said that you lost your starting job."

Paul looked at the floor, embarrassed. "Yeah, well, he was right," he said at the floor. "That's why I'm quitting. I can't even start for a Triple-A team."

He didn't want to look into Ricky's eyes but he could sense immediate tension. Ricky was silent for a moment before he sighed and said, "Am I really talking to Paul Morgan? The same guy who sat up in a hospital bed and told me that not only would he walk some day, but he'd play Major League Baseball, too?" Ricky tapped him on the shoulder, summoning Paul to look at him. He could see the dejection in Paul's eyes. "Look, Paul, you're not always going to be the best hitter on the team," he explained. "Remember, a good baseball player hits .300. That means in ten at-bats, you're going to get out plenty more times than you'll reach base."

"But Ricky, I'm 1-for-freaking-25," he confessed sheepishly, feeling like a criminal who had been caught in the act. "I'm not hitting well. I'm never going to make the Major League roster. I feel like I'm letting everyone down, from my parents to Garey, to the entire second floor at St. Luke's. Everyone I know is buying tickets to the Braves-Phillies series at the end of the season. They expect me to be a Phillie by then. I might be back in Single-A or Double-A by that point. At this rate, I may not be in the Phillies system. To make matters worse, the only girl I ever loved broke my heart."

"I can't help you with the girl problems, but I can tell you this. Every ballplayer has slumps. It's only been six games," The Jet implored. "I think you're being too hard on yourself."

"I'm still terrible and I should quit," he shrugged.

"Paul, do you want a shot at your dream?"

He wanted to tell Ricky that it wasn't about *wanting* the dream to come true. It was about *making* the dream come true. Then he thought about when they first met. He had been in a hospital bed. He had been given a death sentence. Did he give up then? No! If he could battle a disease like cystic fibrosis then he could certainly crack the lineup of a Triple-A baseball team.

He had to at least give it another chance. He'd worked too hard to get to this point.

"Well?" The Jet asked again, pressing for an answer.

"Yeah, I want a chance," Paul said, trying to put some conviction in his voice. "Who am I kidding?" he shouted. "I could never give up so easily on something I've wanted so much."

The Jet smiled. "So let's get to work, then. I was able to get a tape from a couple of the locally televised games. Let's look at them and figure out what's not working. We'll get you back in the starting lineup before you know it."

They went to his hotel in Boston, which was a lot fancier than Paul's measly little hotel in Pawtucket. He had a VCR so they could watch his games. He kept pausing the tape and giving advice.

"See, here. See how you're not opening your stance? See how your bat isn't back far enough? That's why you're late on these pitches. See how your stride towards the ball is going too much to the right side? That's why you're fouling balls off. Your head is down. That's why you're popping the ball up." Ricky had him work on his stance in the hotel restroom so he could see the changes in the mirror. Three hours later, a tired Ricky stopped the tape and said, "Paul, that's all I can do. It's your turn to make it happen on the field."

Ricky took him back to his hotel in his rental car. He told Paul he could do anything, but nothing would come easily. He told him that the great quality of a champion is that he or she can win even when dealing with adversity. He also said he shouldn't worry about the pressure everyone else puts on him. They believed in him and would be proud of him regardless of what happened.

"People are more proud of how you fought cystic fibrosis than they could ever be about what you do on the baseball field. It's a game, Paul, and it's supposed to be fun." Once again, Ricky had been a mentor when Paul needed him most.

Before Paul went to sleep that night, he inserted his new workout tape into the tape deck in the hotel room. It played "Eye of the Tiger." His thoughts turned to his brother and Garey's wish for Paul to make it to the big leagues.

He fell asleep feeling positively juiced.

Chapter 35
Red "Hot" Baron

The next morning, he jogged back to McCoy Stadium three hours before the team was supposed to report. He wasn't in the best standing with his coach and teammates for bailing on the team bus, so he had to gain their trust back. He left a message on Coach Daulton's voicemail about being at the ballpark early so the coach knew he was fired up. He spent ninety minutes in the batting cage hitting from the left side and ninety minutes from the right side. By using all of The Jet's tips, he felt really confident at the end of practice. He knocked about ten shots into the bleachers. Each one was deeper than the last. His teammates and coach saw him when they arrived.

"Coach!" he shouted. "I can play!"

"You trying to prove me wrong again Morgan?"

"Yes, sir, I am," Paul shot back.

A gentle smile appeared on Coach Daulton's face as he spit a couple of sunflower seed shells. "It's about time, Morgan!"

Coach Daulton didn't put him in the lineup immediately. After all, his replacement was hitting around .300 since replacing Paul. However, Coach Daulton decided to make a move in the eighth inning after checking the box score to see that his centerfielder was 0-for-3. He rushed up to Paul and said the magic words—"Morgan, you're in."

This time, his name would stay on the lineup card for good.

During his first at-bat he was a little nervous. He had a lot to prove—most of all to himself. He adjusted his batting gloves and his helmet, as was his

ANDY LIPMAN

ritual. He dug his cleats into the dirt, pulled his bat back, and waited for the first pitch from Pawtucket Red Sox southpaw Alvin Smith. He threw a breaking ball on the inside corner, and Paul drilled it high into left field. The Pawtucket left fielder looked up as the ball ricocheted off the top of the eight-foot high wall at the 325 mark.

Paul sprinted around first and slid feet first safely into second base as he'd done hundreds of times in his parents' backyard. He picked himself up and brushed the dirt off his uniform. With a welcome grin on his face, he recalled the dream he'd had for so long—and he fully intended to keep that dream alive!

The Barons lost the game 5-2 but this game wasn't about the box score. It was about Paul and his renewed confidence.

After the game, he took the team bus back to the hotel, still beaming from the double against Pawtucket. When the bus returned to the hotel, Paul grabbed dinner with some teammates and then went straight to his room to get some sleep. As he was brushing his teeth, his phone rang. It must have been Coach Daulton making sure that he was in his room by curfew, so he picked up the extension and said, "Hello," in a silly voice. A soft woman's voice responded.

"Paul," the voice on the other end whispered softly. "Can I come up?"

"Come up?" he asked, confused. "You're…you're here?"

He pinched himself to make sure that he wasn't dreaming. Why was she in Pawtucket? Why did she want to talk to him?

Before he could think any further there was a knock on his door. He opened it and there in the doorway stood a beautiful young woman with khaki slacks and a pink Ann Taylor blouse. Her hair was a little longer than he remembered it but nothing else had changed.

"Hi Sally, how have you been?"

"Hi Paul," she said as she rushed over to hug him and kiss him on the cheek. "I've really missed you," she confessed.

"So where are you living now," he asked, trying not to sound overeager.

"I moved to Scranton, actually," she answered matter-of-factly.

"Scranton, what a coincidence," he said. "I'm still playing there."

"You're probably wondering what I'm doing here, aren't you?"

He shrugged. "The thought did cross my mind."

She sighed and paused, trying to form words that seemed like they were about to mean a lot. "Paul," she said. "I can't deny my feelings for you anymore. I'd like to see where they go."

Paul was turning flips of joy inside but didn't want to give in too easily on the outside. After all, she had been adamant that she would never date baseball players—he didn't want to get into something only to have her change her mind. And wasn't there some other guy she had been dating, he wondered? The one she told him was so good-looking.

"Sally, weren't you with someone?" he asked. Paul didn't want to be the "other man."

She looked at the floor and then back up at him, slightly red-faced. "I wasn't dating anyone. I said that I was seeing someone just because that's all I did," she said. "I saw him every day. His name is Taylor. He is thirty-two and has cystic fibrosis. He lives in Rome and he is a patient in the Cystic Fibrosis Center in Rome."

Paul had no idea where this was going as she continued.

"I met him when I was talking to a doctor there about cystic fibrosis," she continued. "I started talking with Taylor about you, Paul, telling him I was scared I wouldn't be able to handle the disease. Through Taylor, I learned more about the disease, as well as what dating is like from your perspective. I also wasn't completely honest about not dating ballplayers, either," she said timidly.

"You do date ballplayers?"

"I haven't in a long time, since my last boyfriend dumped me after he was promoted but I wasn't really against dating ballplayers."

"So why did you tell me that you didn't?"

Sally took a deep breath and responded, "Really, I just was afraid to tell you the real reason why I didn't want to date you."

"And what was that reason?" he stiffened.

"Because I was scared," she said forcefully. "I was scared that I'd lose you. Because, well, I fell in love with you the moment that I met you and I didn't want to get hurt. Terry told me about your CF before I even met you. I read about CF in the encyclopedia and it gave all these grave statistics. I was afraid that I couldn't handle all the difficult times that come with cystic fibrosis so I lied and told you that I was against dating ballplayers. But after talking to Taylor and some of his friends with CF, I realize that if you love someone, you will do what it takes to be with him."

Sally started to cry. Paul scurried to the bathroom and brought her a box of tissues.

They sat there on one of the hotel twin beds gazing at each other. A part of him wanted to reject her so she knew how he had felt. But he realized that it must have been really tough for her to quit her job, move from the only home she knew and confess her actions to him, exposing her vulnerabilities in the process. Besides, he loved her. He wanted a future with her and he wanted that future to start now.

He was in love with an amazing person. Their love drew them together for a kiss. It was the most wonderful feeling he'd ever experienced. Paul then held her tight the rest of the night. The next morning, he told her to come to his next game in Pawtucket that afternoon and see him play for the first time.

"Actually," she grinned, "I saw all of your games in Rome. I would sit in the back of the stadium and pull out my binoculars whenever you came to the plate." Paul was pleasantly surprised with his new girlfriend and couldn't wait for the next game against the Red Sox.

That afternoon, Sally came to her first Red Baron game. Paul went 2-for-4 with two dingers. The next night, he had three more hits. He was back on Coach Daulton's good side with six more hits in his next three games. He didn't know if he was hitting so well because he was just on a hot streak or because he was in love, or maybe because he was realizing that he did have the talent to make it to the Majors. In the next game, he recognized the same Phillies scout in the stands who saw him in Greenville. He was eyeing Paul especially hard. He called The Jet and told him the scouts were writing a lot on their notepads every time he came to the plate. He'd hoped they weren't just doodling. With only two weeks left in August he knew how important it was to make an impression, as September promotions were just around the corner.

His batting average at that time was .294. He knew if he could get his average over .300 he would have a shot to be called up. For the next two weeks he was the first to arrive at the batting cage and the last to leave after the game to work on his fielding. The extra work paid off. He went on a tear, delivering twenty hits over the next two weeks, five of which were homeruns. His average had climbed to .320, with seven homeruns and nineteen runs batted in.

During those two weeks he led the team in almost every offensive category. He used to keep up with his heroes' stats but now he was keeping up with his own stats, as well as his teammates'. He wished all of them well but in the minor leagues a player wasn't playing for the team as much as trying to get himself to the next level. He felt like he'd put himself in good position to make the Major League team. Now it was up to the Phillies.

After their Tuesday evening game against Syracuse, Coach Daulton called Paul into his office and asked him to close the door behind him. It was never a good sign when the manager asked a player to close the door behind him. He hoped he hadn't been cut because of his rocky start. He couldn't help but notice the clock on Coach Daulton's back wall quickly turning from 9:14 to 9:15. Garey's time. The news had to be good.

Coach Daulton sat back in his chair with a stern look on his face. All Paul kept hoping was that he wasn't about to get cut. He'd do anything to stay in Scranton, a city he dreaded just a month ago. After what felt like five hours, the coach finally started talking.

"Paul, I'm taking you out of the starting lineup this weekend…"

"But coach!" he quickly interrupted, "I've been tearing the cover off the ball the last few weeks. Please give me a second chance. I know I started slow but I'm playing a lot better now."

"Paul, I don't want to take you out of the lineup but I got a call from the general manager of the Philadelphia Phillies today. We have a kid being called up from Reading who is hitting pretty well and he'll be taking your spot in the lineup. He was our number-one draft pick this year, so the organization feels that he's ready to take the next step."

Paul sat there, thinking he might cry at any moment. His dream was about to come to an end.

Coach Daulton continued, "Wade has already called up two players from Reading to go to the show, and now he wants me to select one player from this team who I think has the most Major League ability. Wade wants someone who can be a difference-maker," he said. Paul tried to stand still as he continued. "Over the last week, I've struggled with this decision as I have a couple of guys who deserve to be called up. They've been here a long time and performed admirably."

Where was he going with this, Paul wondered? Was this a demotion or wasn't it?

"Over the last couple of weeks though, you've been in the batting cage earlier than any of the other players and you've worked on your fielding even after practice was over," the coach said. "Your work ethic and your story make you more than a baseball player. They make you a role model and kids in Philadelphia need more of those. Paul, I've never had a player with as much heart as you have. Now, you haven't been the most consistent player but you've really turned it on the last few weeks."

"Thank you, Coach," he gulped, about to burst with anticipation.

"So, son, make sure the Philadelphia Phillies see the player who has risen from the ashes and not the guy who started 1-for-25," he said sternly. "I don't want them telling me I can't judge talent."

Was he telling me what I thought he was telling me, he wondered? Paul could sense his dream coming true but he wanted to hear it in plain English.

"Coach, are you saying I'm going to Philadelphia?"

"I'm saying pack your bags, Paul. You are a difference-maker," he grinned, rushing from behind his desk to shake his hand and slap him on the back. "You have a 3:05 game at The Vet Thursday afternoon against the Mets. Welcome to the big leagues."

His heart had never pounded more ferociously than at that very moment. He tried to hide his trembling hands.

"Good luck, Paul," the bearer of good news said. "Make your dream come true!"

His thumping heart nearly popped the buttons off his uniform. He made it! He made the big leagues. This is why you play the game, he thought. Getting to the Majors was the pinnacle for any minor league ballplayer. He slowly walked to his locker to collect some of his valuables. He didn't make a big deal of it in the locker room because it wasn't polite to celebrate a promotion while the other players had to accept the fact that they wouldn't be going to the bigs just yet. He said goodbye to several of his teammates, all of whom congratulated him. After finally leaving the stadium, he raced to his apartment to tell Sally the good news.

As the elevator ascended to his floor, he couldn't help but recall the days when he couldn't even get out of his hospital bed. He remembered those batboys who told him he had no chance, his early years with Biff Goolson and the day when he almost took his own life. Finally, he thought about his brother. He remembered how hard Garey pushed him, how much he wanted him to succeed. Garey was so close but was robbed of a chance to get to the Major Leagues. Paul knew he wasn't going to Philadelphia alone. Garey Morgan was coming with him.

He burst into the apartment and found Sally folding laundry in the bedroom. "So, Sally, I have a question for you...do you think you could get used to eating Philly cheesesteaks?"

"Wha...?" she started, but then reality sunk in and she realized what he was saying. "Did you make the team? Are you going to the Majors?" she shrieked.

"I am! I made it!" he yelled, tears streaming down both of their cheeks.

After they calmed down a bit, he called everyone to share the good news.

His mom told him that Garey would have been so proud of him. He could hear the rustling of tissues on the other end of the line. It still wasn't easy for his mom to talk about Garey but she knew that the moment required it. Everyone was elated.

It all happened so fast. He and Sally packed their cars with clothes, his therapy machine and baseball equipment that night. He had to be in Philadelphia around eight o'clock Wednesday night. He was a Major League Baseball player! He was going to play against every player he once watched from his hospital bed. His family and friends asked where they could find tickets for his Major League debut in Philadelphia. He told them not to bother showing up for that one because the Phillies had to travel right after the game and he wouldn't have time to celebrate. Actually, he had a more compelling reason why he wanted them to come to his second game rather than his first. It was the start of the last road trip of the year.

Three games at Turner Field!

Chapter 36
Philadelphia Feeling

Paul and Sally arrived in Philadelphia on a crisp, forty-degree September evening. He thought Philadelphia felt even chillier than Scranton. He had some more coughing spasms but he still blamed them on the cold weather. Sally was a little concerned but he convinced her that he would be fine. If he were really sick he'd be out of breath or coughing up yellow or green mucous, he told her. She laughed and said that tidbit might fall in the too much information category, but thanked him for the warning nonetheless. The Phillies had played that afternoon and lost to the Mets, 6-3.

He dropped Sally off around seven o'clock at the hotel and then met with Phillies manager Grant Bowman at his residence, a modest three-story house in the suburbs. The other two September call-ups were also there.

"Welcome to The City of Brotherly Love," he announced as the new players stood there sizing each other up. Paul had forgotten that "The City of Brotherly Love" was Philadelphia's motto. How fitting, since it was his brother's love to play baseball and his dream for Paul to get to the big leagues.

The coach explained that they would be at home tomorrow to play the Mets and then off to Atlanta for the three-game series to end the season. Coach Bowman issued each player his official Phillies cap, which had their numbers on the back. Paul looked at his number—6—wishing that somehow he could talk Bowman and the league into letting him wear 915.

The other two new players there were Shane Scott and Al Parks, who had both been called up from Reading, Pennsylvania, the Phillies' Double-A affiliate. Double-A players didn't get called up as often as Triple-A players but they both had tremendous years with Reading. That night, the three of them went to dinner together and discussed their respective paths to the Major Leagues.

Paul thought his path was tough, but Shane and Al certainly didn't get any free passes either. Shane, the six-foot, two-inch burly infielder, was a number-one pick in the early nineties but languished in the minor leagues for twelve years, nursing four shoulder surgeries and one knee surgery. Paul told him his nickname in grammar school was Puzzle, but maybe it suited him better. Shane found that amusing. Shane had plenty of opportunities to give up on his dream but he loved the game and couldn't see himself doing anything else.

Al had played three years of minor league ball. He had rotator cuff surgery last year and his doctor told him he shouldn't play anymore. Al was tough, though, and refused to give up on his dream. He told Paul that anytime someone said something negative to him, he would write his or her name down on a piece of paper. The day he got the call up to the Majors, he called every person on it to let them know he'd made it. He said he'd never felt more redeemed. Al told Paul that he got his toughness from his grandfather, who was never given the opportunity to play in the big leagues. He played third base in the Negro Leagues, which is where the best African-Americans played until players like Jackie Robinson broke down Major League Baseball's color barrier.

After talking a while, Al mentioned that he played college ball at the University of Georgia. Amazingly, Garey was the one who had showed him around campus when Al was a senior in high school.

"Actually, I called your brother when I was debating whether to go into the Major League draft or play college ball at Georgia," Al told him. "Garey told me that college was a unique experience and that I'd miss out if I went straight to professional baseball. And I never regretted my college years at the University of Georgia."

Hearing how Garey inspired someone else filled Paul with pride. Garey had been a mentor to Al, too, and had urged him to work hard and never give up on his dream of playing Major League Baseball. That sounded exactly like Garey, all right. The strange thing was that this new teammate he had just met actually was so close to his brother that he attended Garey's funeral in Atlanta, while Paul could not.

He told Shane and Al his story and about the dream he'd had since he was ten. They were hanging on every word. When he told them about the masked man, both of them stared in amazement.

"So you don't know who the guy is? You never figure that out?" asked Shane.

"Well, not yet, anyway," he answered.

"And you never get to hit?" Al asked, leaning closer. "You don't know whether you win the game or not?"

"Nope. I guess I'll figure that out at Turner Field in a few days," he smiled at his new friends.

That night, he took his Phillies cap to his hotel room, and tried it on in front of the mirror. Wow! I've really made it to the big leagues, he thought. He took his bat and kept practicing in front of the mirror, envisioning his first Major League hit. He would be his own announcer.

"Here's the 3-2 pitch to Paul Morgan. There's a drive...way back...way back...that ball is gone! Homerun for Paul Morgan and the Phillies win the game, thanks to the rookie out of Atlanta."

Sally joked that he was losing his mind. He probably took practice swings for more than an hour with his brown Louisville Slugger. Since it was the bat he used in his dream, he had no choice but to keep using that brand, no matter how many bats he broke.

Standing before the mirror in his baseball cap and pajamas, he realized how far he'd come. He had gone from the sick kid in Room 205 with a life expectancy of four months to a rookie in the Majors with an unlimited future. He let it sink in. He went to bed wearing his Phillies cap that night, and dreamed again of the masked man at Turner Field.

The next morning, he and Sally signed a lease at Willowmist, an apartment complex about five minutes from Veteran's Stadium. The apartment was small, about double the size of his bedroom at his parents' house. But they were so excited to set up their first home together. They moved in what little stuff they had and then drove down to the stadium for the afternoon game against the New York Mets.

As they got closer, he realized how huge the stadium really was. He'd played in so many small minor league parks where the capacity might be twelve-thousand. Veteran's Stadium held over fifty-five-thousand people. He was going to be playing in the same place where Mike Schmidt hit many of his 548 career homeruns. He was going to be playing on the same diamond where all-time hits leader Pete Rose once played first base. It was a little intimidating but he knew he deserved to be there. As they reached the stadium he kissed Sally goodbye and gave her an upper deck ticket that the Phillies' management had purchased for him. He was told to meet the clubhouse manager, Mathew, at the "G" gate. He arrived around 11:30 when he spotted Mathew, who was wearing a dapper black suit with a Phillies cap.

"Paul Morgan?" asked Mathew, whose Bostonian accent was immediately evident.

"That's me."

"I always get a thrill out of taking rookies to the locker room for the first time," he said as he led Paul into the guts of the stadium. "How long have you been in the minors?"

"A little under a year," he said.

"That's quite fast to be called up," he said. "You must be some player."

Paul had wanted to play Major League Baseball since he was ten years old, so the ride to the big leagues didn't seem that fast to him. He followed Mathew to the elevator. They went down a couple of floors and the doors opened.

"Good luck, Mr. Morgan," he said, pointing him in the direction of the locker room. "Welcome to Philadelphia."

He began walking slowly and deliberately down the spotless corridor. He wanted to take in the entire experience of entering a Major League locker room for the first time. He stood at the door for a couple of moments, breathless, but it had nothing to do with cystic fibrosis. There was no looking back now. He opened the door and was immediately in awe of the place. Everywhere he looked were hulking Phillies getting ready for the game, chatting with each other, playing cards and goofing around. In front of the coach's office, autographing some old bats was Jim Thome, the homerun-hitting first baseman. Ten feet to his right was All-Star shortstop Jimmy Rollins, hanging his suit up in his locker. He noticed Pat Burrell, the power-hitting left fielder, stretching in front of his locker. He recognized everyone—he had several baseball cards of each one of them. And here he was among them, with his own locker.

Coach Bowman was standing in front of his office, which was off to the side of the locker area, talking to one of his players. He perked up when he saw Paul standing there.

"Come on in!" he said as he took him around to meet his new teammates, whom he already felt he knew. He wondered, though, if they weren't as happy to see him as he was to see them. The Phillies were in last place in the division and the young guys were battling the veterans to earn a spot on next year's roster. With just a week left in the regular season, the Phillies had nothing to play for except roster spots. So all of the newbies were threats. Paul tried to maintain a swagger in the clubhouse, as he wanted his new teammates to know that he belonged.

Coach Bowman issued him a white and maroon pinstripe Phillies home uniform to go with his red and blue Phillies cap. Minutes after he arrived, Shane and Al walked through the doors, but they didn't seem nearly as awestruck. Shane said that was because they had gone to spring training and worked out with many of these guys, so the wonder had worn off. A few hours before batting practice, a catering staff brought in barbecued chicken and white rice for the entire team. After their meal, he put on his uniform and walked to the dugout. As soon as he entered the dugout, he beheld the beautiful baseball diamond in front of him. He saw thousands of fans filing in to watch batting practice. He couldn't stop looking around. There were hundreds of billboards. There were tens-of-thousands of fans coming in. He felt a tap on his shoulder. It was Kevin Millwood, the All-Star pitcher.

"Relax, rook." He tried to calm down but that made him even more anxious—Millwood was talking to him! His heart felt like it was thumping the pinstripes off his uniform.

For the next thirty minutes, they took batting practice. He was a little intimidated after watching Thome hit about ten balls over the right field wall including one that had to be close to four-hundred-fifty feet. He took a few cuts in the cage and headed back to the dugout. He went over to look at the lineup card. As he expected, he was not in the lineup. The veterans would probably be offended if a rookie started but he did expect to play later in the game. He was glad he told his parents not to bother coming up for the one game in Philadelphia, since he might not play at all. What if he was wrong, though? Why else would the Phillies bring him up if they weren't going to play him?

Warming the bench took him back to his early days in tryout camp with Coach Tomlinson. Each inning, he kept peering at the manager and patiently waited for him to call his name. He was sure that Sally was in the stands hoping that she'd see her boyfriend hit against Major League pitching for the first time. He knew that since the game was on ESPN, his parents, Nurse Johanson and everyone at St. Luke's would be watching his every move. As the innings progressed, he got more and more antsy. Would he get to play at all?

The fifth, sixth, and seventh innings went by but Coach Bowman never even looked his way. With two outs in the ninth, the Phillies had runners at second and third, trailing 3-2. The manager needed a pinch hitter and looked towards Paul, Shane and Al. If he picked Paul and he got a hit, he would win the game with his first Major League hit. Sure, it wouldn't be at Turner Field and there was no masked man but he would be happy nonetheless just for a chance to win the game. Coach Bowman looked his way and their eyes locked. He had to see passion, grit, and determination. He had to pick him. He just had to. Paul stood up from the bench.

"Julio Gomez, you're up!" shouted Coach Bowman. Paul immediately sat back down, embarrassed that he'd even lifted his rear end from the bench. Julio, a journeyman who was playing on his eighth Major League team, fanned on three pitches and the Phillies lost to the Mets in what was less than a marvelous start to Paul's Major League career. He took solace in the fact that at least his parents weren't out two plane tickets to come see him sit.

Coach Bowman met with Paul and the other two rookies in his office after the game. He could tell that they were agitated about not playing, so he explained how the last three games of the season would go.

"Guys, I've always been loyal to the players who have paid their dues. I find that it's harder to stay in the big leagues than to get here. That's why the veterans play first on my team," he explained. "I know I have to play some of you guys so the team can look toward the future. I have decided that the order in which I'll be playing you in Atlanta will depend on how many years you've logged in the minors. Shane, since you've been a minor-leaguer for twelve years, you'll be the first to play. Al, you'll play second. And Paul, I'll play you if I can but I can't make you any promises. You're third in line, son."

Paul was a little discouraged but there were three more games left in the season and he was sure the Phillies wanted to see if he could help them in the future. He, Shane, and Al joined the rest of the team on the bus and headed to the airport, where they would meet their wives and girlfriends.

Even though Paul didn't know if he'd get to play, he was still excited to be going to his hometown. On the bus he called his mom to make sure that she had some extra medication at home and that the therapy machine was working. She said everything was ready for them and that she and his dad were excited to see him and Sally. One of the dugout coaches overheard him talking about cystic fibrosis and asked what it was.

"It's a disease that affects my lungs, my reproductive system and my digestive system," he explained. "Doctors thought I'd be lucky to live to graduate high school. But here I am."

A lot of the veteran players overheard their discussion. "So, you have this disease and you still play baseball," one asked. "Wow."

"Yeah, man," another player sitting on the other side of the bus agreed. "Good for you."

He could tell that many of them gained admiration for him at that moment, as they smiled and nodded at him, some even coming up to shake his hand. Earning their respect meant a lot to him. Now if he could only get his chance to do it on the field.

His teammates, Sally and Paul boarded the flight to Atlanta. Over the plane's public address system, the pilot told them the distance of the flight: 915 miles. He looked down at the silver "K" on his neck and smiled. He and Garey were headed home.

Chapter 37
A Belated Goodbye

The Phillies touched down in Atlanta at 9:15 p.m. These strange coincidences of seeing the numbers nine, one, and five, the date that Garey died (September 15) were really getting to Paul as he touched his pendant. He and Sally took the team bus to the hotel, where his parents picked them up and took them home. They were overjoyed to have Paul home and asked if he and Sally wanted to go out to breakfast with them in the morning.

"Actually, I have something I need to do in the morning and I'll be leaving early," Paul told them. They didn't push but Sally knew where he was going and she understood that he needed to go alone.

The following morning he woke up and did his therapy. He left the house early. He wouldn't go to the batting cage to practice for tonight's game against the Braves. He wasn't off to St. Luke's. He didn't buy flowers for Sally. He went somewhere he had never been.

Miller Pond Park wasn't the type of park where a person had a picnic and threw a Frisbee. It was the cemetery where his brother was buried. As he eased out of his car with a bouquet of flowers in hand, he couldn't help but wonder what Garey's gravestone looked like. Did it face a tree? Were there flowers growing in front of it? What was engraved on it?

He was given a cemetery map at the front desk of the funeral home and began the long walk to find his brother's grave. Half-way through the walk, a coughing spasm gripped him. He took a few minutes to cough it all out and then continued on his way. He thought the coughing spasms would have stopped after he left the cold weather of Philadelphia but apparently not. Twenty minutes into his walk, he discovered the one site he wished he never had to see.

Garey Ethan Morgan

March 15, 1976-September 15, 1998

"He touched everyone he knew."

As he walked up to Garey's grave, the only sound he heard was twigs crackling under his feet. The grave had no flowers near it but there was a shady oak tree about ten feet behind it. The gravestone was relatively large, about two feet tall. Most people who were buried there had lived into their seventies and eighties. His brother was 22, the age he was now. He even figured out the very day that he would have lived longer than his brother. He wondered if that day would be harder than Garey's birthday or September 15, the day he died. A few tears moistened his cheeks. He took a deep breath and pulled a crinkled piece of paper from his jeans pocket. The night before, he had written a letter to his brother just as Garey had done so many times for him. He hadn't read it aloud until now. He knelt down and began reading it out loud toward the gravestone.

Dear Garey,

I wish you could be here right now. I miss you so much. I never got a chance to apologize to you for hanging up on you that night. I'm even sorrier that I didn't appreciate how much you meant to my life when you were here. You kept me smiling when everything else was falling apart. You were the one who kept my faint dreams alive.

I still dream about winning a game at Turner Field with my first Major League hit. Tonight, I'm going to get my chance. The thing is, I won't be doing it as a Brave. I'm a Philadelphia Phillie now. I wish you could be here to witness all of my at-bats. I wish you could have been here to witness my ride to the Majors. It hasn't been an easy journey but I've worked hard and I know that's what matters to you.

You're probably wondering why I'm here or maybe you're wondering why it took me so long to visit. I don't know. Maybe I'm here because I was in a coma while your funeral was going on and never had a chance to say goodbye. Maybe I'm here because I had to see for myself that you really are gone. Maybe I wanted to believe that you would rise up from the grave and tell me that I'll get that hit. I know that sounds silly but sometimes I wish I could just know that you are around. I guess it took me a long time to see you because I didn't want to see your name etched in stone. I always figured I'd see your name etched on a plaque in the Hall of Fame. When I returned home to Atlanta for this weekend's series, I thought this was a good time to truly say goodbye.

Do you remember what you used to tell me when I was little? You always told me I had to fight. Whether I was getting beaten up by Biff Goolson or getting a bad medical report, you would always tell me I had to fight the battle. I know back then I didn't show much fight, but I fight harder than anyone now. You're my inspiration.

I'll bet you're a superhero right now. In fact, I know you are. Garey, you're my superhero. Don't forget about me.

I love you, Garey.

From your younger brother,

Paul Morgan

Maybe it wasn't so much that he wanted his brother to know he was a fighter. Maybe he needed to remind *himself* he was. Garey didn't have to worry about his little brother anymore. He kissed his finger, and then lowered it down onto Garey's grave. He took the crinkled piece of paper, laid it down on the grass and put a rock on it to keep it from blowing away. He then placed some yellow tulips inside the vase in front of Garey's gravestone.

After a few tearful minutes, he walked back toward his car. It was still hard to believe that his brother was gone but he was relieved that he finally got to say goodbye. As he reached for his keys his chest began to throb in pain. He coughed heavily, too, and each time he coughed, his chest hurt even more. Then came uncontrollable coughing spasms. These spasms were far worse than the ones he was having in Scranton and Philadelphia. He spit up tons of mucous. The phlegm was dark yellow and green, which meant he needed to get it checked. He got to his car and had another fierce spasm. He could barely breathe this time. He called his mom with shaky hands.

"Mom, I'm at Miller Pond Park and I'm having really bad coughing spasms. I can hardly catch my breath. What should I do?" Another spasm kicked in while he was on the phone. His mom could hear it all. "Mom, help!" he screamed.

"Paul, we'll be right over there. Just lie down in the back seat and calm down." He could hear the panic in his mom's voice—the same panic from several years ago when they lost Garey.

He complied and lay in the back seat. He coughed yellow-green gunk all over the phone, dropped it and cried in agony. He bent down in the back seat and began spitting up more mucous. He kept heaving up mucous until he just couldn't throw up anymore. What was happening to him? He struggled to stay conscious. His ribs were throbbing from the non-stop violent coughing.

"Somebody help me!" he croaked. It seemed like an eternity before his parents and Sally arrived.

Chapter 38
A Spectator Once Again

The next time his eyes opened, he looked down to see he was wearing a hospital gown. His arms had IVs in them. A wheelchair sat in the corner of the room. The remote control had his room number on it—205. ESPN's Sportscenter was on the television.

Had everything just been a cruel dream? He was Paul Morgan, the sick kid again. Did he really homer off of Biff Goolson? Had he not made it to the Major Leagues? Was there no Sally? He frantically hit the call button. He needed answers and he needed them quickly.

Moments later, his door opened. It was Sally, who was breathing heavy after sprinting from the waiting room to check on him.

"Paul, you'll be okay. I love you," she said as she kissed him tenderly and leaned over to cover him. "I know you'll be okay."

Seeing her brought him back to reality, which made him feel slightly better. But things weren't good, because Sally looked at him as if the sky was falling. She was buzzing about his room, talking in short, choppy sentences. What was wrong with her? What happened to him? Again, he began coughing and coughing, so much so that his ribs began throbbing. Dr. Knotts soon walked in.

"Hey, Paul," he said softly as he approached the bedside. "Paul, we gave you an anesthesia when you arrived so that you would stop coughing and relax. You've been here for several hours. We did some tests and just got some of the results back. I'd like to tell you that we could release you today but I'd rather wait and see how the rest of the results look. We notified the Phillies of your status."

Sally held his hand and kept telling him it would be ok. He didn't feel like being consoled at that moment. He wanted to know what was happening.

Reduced to a spectator again, he watched the first game of the Phillies-Braves series from his hospital bed. The Braves won, 6-5. The Jet didn't pitch since his turn fell on the last game, Sunday. The Braves had already been eliminated from the playoffs, so they had nothing to play for, either. Paul wanted to play so badly. He looked through his window and saw Turner Field lit up as the crowd filed out. He should have been there living his dream that night—instead he was on his back, living a recurring nightmare. He fell asleep with a resentful heart that night.

The next morning, after his parents and Sally arrived, Dr. Knotts appeared somber at his bedside.

"You have a serious infection in your left lung. It's a staph infection, which is caused by a pretty serious bacterium. We are going to put you on some strong antibiotics and you'll be using your therapy machine twice, rather than once, a day. Your numbers have plummeted into the low seventy-percent range..."

"Doc, can I play this weekend?" Paul interrupted. Dr. Knotts took a deep breath and stalled for a couple of moments before he responded.

"I think it would be smart if you sat out the rest of the season, Paul."

"But, Doc..." Paul tried to plead but the pain in his chest silenced his protest.

"Let's get you better. That's the most important thing," Dr. Knotts said sternly. "I contacted the Phillies this morning and let them know the situation. They wished you well and said you will be invited to spring training next season. Isn't that great news?"

His heart sank. It was terrible news—and Dr. Knotts knew it. Paul felt so empty and alone in a room full of loved ones. Sally tried to comfort him.

"We'll get you through this," she said. "You'll play for the Phillies next season." She kissed him on the forehead.

He just couldn't accept that it was all over. Sally begged him not to play, even if he was able to get out of the hospital quickly. She knew how important the game was to him but, she explained, his health had to come first. She said that he had to look at the future and the damage he could cause himself by going out there. His dad was there, too. He agreed with Sally that he'd be risking too much if he went back out there. After their long discussion, Paul regretfully told Sally and his dad he would follow the doctor's orders and miss the rest of the season. At least he would get better.

Paul's mom was conspicuously missing. He wondered if she was avoiding him like the time Dr. Knotts revealed his slim chances of survival and she didn't have the strength to break it to him.

He couldn't tell Sally or his dad how frustrated he was. As soon as they left he wept, between coughing spasms. He had worked so hard for nothing. He was locked away in the same room he had spent far too much of his childhood in. Nothing had changed except he was on more antibiotics now and was having to do his therapy twice a day rather than once. He couldn't have cared less about spring training next year. He was more concerned with *this* year. All of his friends and family were expecting to come watch him play—now. Everything was in place except his lungs. He couldn't help but wonder what would have happened if he'd had his cough checked out when he was first concerned in Scranton. Maybe he would have been able to overcome the bacteria by now and be playing for the big club.

The Phillies' first game in Atlanta wasn't until six weeks into the season next year. If he made the team out of spring training he'd certainly bat before then. But making the Phillies' roster next year was certainly not a done deal. He may have more lung troubles before then and never play again. He coughed some more. The dream, it seemed, wouldn't come true.

On Saturday he despondently watched as the Braves defeated the Phillies, 2-1, in the next-to-last game of the season. Both Shane and Al saw playing time in the field but neither got to bat. That could have been him playing at Turner Field tonight, Paul thought. It could have been his opportunity to hit in the ninth inning with a chance to win the game and achieve his dream. Again, he looked through his window at the bright lights of Turner Field. Why did he have to be on the other side of the street, he wondered?

Shane called later that night to tell him the team was thinking about him. He told him that they said a prayer before the game, so Paul knew they were genuine because that didn't happen very often. Al and Shane each wore the initials PM on the bills of their caps. They even sent a card to his room signed by the entire team. He was touched by the gesture but still heartbroken that he couldn't play.

After game two of the series he and The Jet talked for an hour on the phone. Ricky was preparing to pitch the final game of his career.

"I'm gonna get that no-hitter, Paul," he said determinedly. "And when I do, I will pitch it in your honor, sign the ball and bring it to your hospital room after the game."

"Thanks, buddy," he said, trying to sound heartened. He conceded it would have been pretty neat if the only no-hitter in The Jet's remarkable career was dedicated to his biggest fan.

The sentiments he heard from fellow players and family members were nice but the truth was that nothing could cheer him up. He reached into his bottom drawer and pulled out one of the magazines his brother had ordered for him to get stronger. His dad had brought them in. Though it should have inspired him, it only upset him because he was letting Garey down. He ripped the magazine in half and threw it on the floor as several pages flew everywhere. He knocked the card sent by the Phillies into his trash can. Why me, he thought to himself? What did I do to deserve this? He turned off the lights, closed his door, and moped in his bed.

Being confined to the hospital, he grew a bit stir crazy. After an hour of self pity in 205, something he was an expert at, he opened the door and strolled through the hall while he rolled his IV pole by his side. He was heading back to his room when he overheard the sounds of *Baseball Tonight* on ESPN coming from room 210. He stuck his head inside.

As if he had seen a ghost, he turned pale. The voice in the room whispered, "Paul? Paul Morgan, is that you?"

Chapter 39
Blast from the Past

Paul couldn't believe it. "No, it couldn't be," he argued to himself. The young man, about his age, with a shaved head and a contagious smile quickly walked towards him.

"Stan? It couldn't be you. You died? Stan, is that you?"

"No, I didn't die," he said calmly as he gave him a quick hug. Paul was too shocked to hug back. He couldn't believe it.

"But Stan, when I came back to the hospital a week after you got really sick, one of your friends told me you died. You never came back. The hospital even had a counselor come see me to check if I was okay."

"Everyone thought I died I guess except my doctors, of course. I was moved to The Northside Hospital Cancer Center, closer to north Atlanta. They didn't think I had much time left, so they probably sent you a counselor thinking that I would pass away. Thanks to some of the specialists I worked with, remarkably, I got better. My cancer was in remission for several years until a few weeks ago when it came back. The specialist that worked with me then is now working at St. Luke's, so he's treating me here. I'm sorry I didn't keep in touch. I kind of blocked out the days I spent in the hospital as it was a really tough time for me."

"I guess it's just like old times," Paul laughed as he gladly embraced his old St. Luke's partner. "I'm glad I can see you again. I'm sorry I was so surprised before. How are you feeling?" he asked.

"You think you're surprised, Paul. When did you start walking? I can't believe you survived our younger days at St. Luke's. I can't believe how great you look. I want to hear everything that's happened to you. As far as me, I've been in chemo for a week now and I finish up my first cycle tomorrow. I felt okay at the beginning of the week but I'm supposed to get really tired and achy tonight and tomorrow. They upgraded me to stable condition the other day. Of course with cancer, you never know. I could be fine one day and on my death bed the next. They think I'm going to be at St. Luke's for a while. I'm a little down, naturally."

"Did you ever become an astronaut?" Paul asked.

"No, I did go to space camp in Alabama, and I loved it but the dream kind of went away like most kids' dreams do. I'm kind of sad about that but dreams don't always come true. What about your dream? Are you playing Major League Baseball?"

He told Stan his story. He told him his goal was to get out of St. Luke's and play baseball for the Phillies this weekend but the doctors, his father and his girlfriend had convinced him that he shouldn't risk it. He told Stan he was trying to remain positive despite the doctor's concerns and that he accepted that the closest he'd get to Turner Field this weekend was turning on the television. The truth, though, was that he wasn't trying to remain positive. He was really frustrated. He'd always heard good things happen to good people. So what did he do wrong, he wondered?

"Paul, do you remember that pact we made when we were kids?"

"Yeah, I remember it," he said. "But Stan, that wasn't really a pact. I was only kidding that if you went to space, I'd play Major League Baseball."

"Paul, I knew you were kidding but I needed something to give me confidence then. Do you remember what I said after that?"

"You said you'd fly over in your space suit to watch my first at-bat."

"Well Paul, I can't very well fly over the stadium to watch you play but I can still turn on the television and root my friend on." He didn't know if Stan was telling him this just because he wanted to see him play and execute his part of the pact, or if Stan just wanted to see his friend escape St. Luke's so he knew that he could, too. Either way, his encouragement was pumping Paul up. But still, he was concerned about his health and upsetting Sally, of course. And a painful coughing spell here and there was a friendly reminder not to overdo it.

He and Stan talked until late that night. Paul told him how depressed he got several years ago and how there were times when he still got depressed because of cystic fibrosis.

"I know, Paul. When we were young, I would say 'When is it going to be my turn?' I felt like I never had a chance to be an astronaut."

"Yeah, I know," Paul replied. "It never seems to be my turn. And just when I think it is, something bad happens. Look at me now, I get promoted to the big leagues and then I get sick and can't even play. When's it going to be my turn?"

"Paul, what I meant to say is I used to think that way but now I realize you have to be ready because you never know when your turn will come. Maybe I had my chance to be an astronaut when I went to space camp. Maybe my turn's passed. Maybe my turn has yet to come. Your turn will never come if you wait for it. You have to make it happen. Your turn might be just around the corner or maybe even across the street."

"Stan, I have to be honest. I worry that I may never get my turn."

Stan put his arm on Paul's shoulder and smiled.

"Never say never, Paul."

They talked about everything that had happened to each of them in the years since they'd seen each other. Stan was now a senior at Georgia Tech. He was making straight A's and still looked forward to being a successful engineer after graduation. He had just parted with his girlfriend of three years and was ready to return to the singles scene when all of a sudden his cancer returned.

Stan was starting to feel really achy as it got late in the evening. He told Paul it was best that he probably go back to his room so he could rest his body. As Paul walked towards the door around midnight, Stan looked at him and asked, "So? You going to be on the television tomorrow or just watching it like me? You going to execute your part of the pact?"

Paul smiled and said, "I guess you'll know in about twelve hours or so, huh?" Stan smiled, turned back toward the bed as Paul turned out his light and closed the door. He wanted to create a little bit of suspense but the truth was that he knew what was going to happen. He was going to disappoint Stan.

Around midnight, he went back to his room and got into bed. He couldn't help but think about Stan and the other sick young people at St. Luke's, and how they all needed hope. He wished that he could be the one to give them faith but that wasn't going to happen—at least not this season. Moments later, there was a soft knock on his door and his mother tip-toed in with a big red box with a blue ribbon on top. She closed the door behind her. It was odd for her to visit so late, and without his dad.

"What's up, Mom?" he asked, concerned. "Is everything ok? It's awfully late. If you're here to tell me not to play Sunday, don't worry about it. Dad, Sally, and Dr. Knotts have made it very clear. I'm not playing." He could almost predict her response. Something along the lines of not over-exerting yourself and paying for your stubbornness now.

"I know you're not playing, son, but I needed to share something with you and I felt this was the appropriate time."

"Well, I'm not much of a listener right now," he told her. "I just talked to an old friend who is battling cancer and I guess I should feel lucky I'm not worse off. But instead, I feel like I'm not only disappointing myself but I'm disappointing the patients here, too. I feel like such a failure. Garey would be really disappointed in me right now."

"Paul, don't ever say that," his mother scolded. "Garey was always very proud of you and I think he still is. In fact, I *know* he is."

"What do you mean?" he asked.

"Your brother's been with you every step of the way," she said firmly. "Haven't you noticed signs that made you think of your brother since he passed away?"

He thought of the continuous sequences of the numbers 9, 1, and 5, which seemed to cross his path at every turn. He didn't think he told his mother about that, so he asked her how she knew he saw things that reminded him of Garey.

"Because I do too, Paul," she responded. "In fact, there is something I should have told you about a long time ago.

Her tone was making him nervous. "What is it, Mom?"

"Do you remember the day when you woke up from the coma?" she asked him.

"Sure, a little," he said. Actually, he had forgotten parts of it but he did remember she had acted odd at one point. He had dropped his magnetic board, after explaining to her his experiences with Gregory Hartman and being The Solution. He had written Gregory's message on the board and it dropped and broke. When she went to pick it up, she had a frightened look on her face, like she had just seen a ghost. But she never mentioned anything and he had forgotten about it until now.

"When I bent over to pick the letters up off of the floor, where you dropped them, I saw something that shocked me. The letters had formed another message that you were supposed to see," his mother said. "I figured when you needed to hear your brother's voice the most, I would tell you what I saw but I decided you needed to see it instead. So I'm going to leave you to open this. You'll see what I mean."

Before his mother left the room, she handed him the box and a letter with Garey's handwriting on the front.

"Read the letter and then open the box," she instructed, then kissed him on the forehead and left. When she closed the door behind her, he ripped the letter out of the envelope and started reading the letter from Garey dated July, 1991, which was about the time that Paul had lost the ability to walk.

Dear Paul,

I know you're scared because you have to use a wheelchair now. Well, don't be. The other day, you and I watched "Superman," and you told me you wanted to be a superhero some day. Since you said that, all I keep imagining is you flying through the air with your super powers. I can really see you being a superhero some day. Don't worry. You'll become a baseball player, too.

You just have to do one thing if you want all of your dreams to come true. You have to fight!

Be a fighter, Paul! Don't let the doctors tell you what you can or cannot do. They can't measure the size of your heart. Nobody can. You are a winner but until you fight, you won't know how big of a winner you really are. When thing seem bleak, you have to gather up the courage to show everyone what my little brother is all about. I will always be there for you. I'm very proud of you.

I love you Paul.

From your older brother,

Garey Ethan Morgan

Enclosed with the letter was a four-inch by six-inch photograph from Paul's tenth birthday. Paul was wearing a blue cape that his brother had given him for his birthday. In the picture, Paul was sitting on Garey's muscular shoulders with his scrawny arms extended, pretending he could fly. Garey's smile demonstrated how important it was for his little brother to believe he could soar through the clouds. A tear rolled off Paul's cheek onto the photo as he reminisced. He couldn't help but think where he'd be without his brother's unconditional support.

He wondered why his mom was giving him a letter that he'd read more than ten years ago. Why would she go to the trouble of finding it? He was even more curious as to what was in the box, so he began to unwrap it.

Inside the box was a magnetic board, but not the blue one she bought for him. Instead, it was the green one she had taken from his room. It wasn't broken at all. Was the fact that it was still intact supposed to shock him? He looked closer.

"Oh my God!"

Before he dropped the board that night long ago, it read, *"You are a bold hero to me. I pull for you. Gregory Vern Hartman."*

Now, the same letters read something totally different.

I love you Paul.

From your older brother

Garey Ethan Morgan

Chapter 40
To Play or Not to Play

His heart pounded inside his chest. But now it wasn't pulsating pain, it was elation. His brother was still there for him. His superhero days were not a dream. All the answers were now coming to him. Gregory told him that the expression "You are a bold hero to me. I pull for you. Gregory Vern Hartman" would help him figure out why he got the wish. Now he knew what he was talking about. When he dropped the board, his mom wasn't supposed to be the one to receive the message. He was!

Then he remembered something that cinched it for him. When he asked Gregory how he knew he liked baseball enough to put a baseball glove on his Solution costume, Gregory said it was because of the baseball-shaped pendant. But Paul had ripped it off just before he went into the coma and his mom had found it under the bed. Gregory never saw the pendant. Gregory knew about his dream to play baseball because he wasn't some stranger from the Make-A-Wish Foundation.

Gregory was really Garey.

Garey wanted Paul to be a superhero and had a carefully crafted plan to set things in motion. He knew that if his little brother ever had a chance to make a wish, he'd want to make his big brother proud and dawn the cape of a superhero, just like he did on his tenth birthday. Garey didn't want Paul to stay The Solution forever. He wanted him to have a taste of what it was like to be successful. He brought Tommy in so that Paul knew that the cape didn't make him a success—his attitude did. Garey wanted to inspire him so that he would some day follow his dream and become a Major League Baseball player. He only asked one thing of Paul—to fight. And that's what his mom wanted to remind him of by giving him Garey's letter.

He took his pendant out of his shirt and looked at the silver K. The 9-1-5 sequences were not coincidences. They were messages from his big brother, always appearing at crucial moments. He was proud of Paul. Even though he didn't get letters from Garey anymore, he knew his big brother would be with him every time he stepped into that batter's box.

With the epiphany of Garey's part in bringing him to this point, Paul now wanted to play more than ever. But, he still had a really bad cough and was short of breath. As he fell asleep, he pondered whether it was really smart to play one game and risk screwing up his entire life. Then again, was it really smart to risk screwing up his entire life by missing this one game?

He had the dream again that night. He stood at the plate staring down the pitcher, his bat poised, when he saw the masked man. Again, he pointed towards the sky when he was in the on-deck circle. Was I trying to call my shot like Babe Ruth or was I pointing to Garey in heaven, he wondered? His parents were cheering in the crowd. Just as he was about to face the pitcher, the blaring sounds of his alarm awakened him.

Just then he remembered something Gregory, or Garey, had told him. When he couldn't fly, he said it wasn't as simple as flapping your arms. He told Paul that he had to visualize himself flying. Their conversation had nothing to do with flying but everything to do about life. If he wanted to be successful at anything, he couldn't just go through the motions while thinking that he had no chance to achieve his goal. He had to see himself being successful. And at that moment, he could see himself with a helmet on his head, cleats on his feet and a Louisville Slugger in his hands. His decision was made. He called Nurse Johanson into his room and asked her to remove the IVs from his arm.

He got out of his hospital bed, got dressed and walked out of his room, with Nurse Johanson following along behind him.

"Paul, where are you going?" she asked, a little concerned.

"Turner Field," he muttered through several coughs.

"Can I do anything for you, Paul?" Nurse Johanson inquired. He asked her to call his mother so he could tell her his decision.

"You can tell her in person," she replied. "Your mom has been in the waiting room all night." He sprinted into the waiting room, still wheezing a bit and sure enough, his mom stood there proudly wearing a maroon blouse and Phillies cap. She saw him and beamed.

"Did you decide?" she asked, expectantly.

He embraced her and professed, "Mom, I promised him I would fight and that's what I'm going to do. Can you take me to the stadium?" She smiled, nodded her head and turned toward her chair to pull something from beneath it. Though not a set of red tights and a blue cape, what she held in her hands made him feel no less heroic. It was his Phillies uniform, which had been delivered to her by Ed Wade. It seemed that everyone was in on Garey's plan for Paul.

"Mom, can I tell you something? You're the last person I expected to tell me to take a chance with my health. I love you for it but I don't understand what changed your mind."

"Paul, after your brother died and I saw his message on the magnetic board, I promised Garey something. I promised that instead of being over-protective of you, I would fight hard to make sure that you lived your dreams. Your brother loved you so much." Lilian's eyes suddenly flooded with tears. He kissed his mom on the cheek and dashed back to his room.

After he put his uniform on, he let his fingertips glide over the word *Phillies* in maroon across his still-burning chest. He glimpsed in the mirror at the name *Morgan* on the back. He slid his hand across his maroon cap with the blue *P* in the center. He buckled his maroon belt. He tucked his batting gloves in his back pocket, put his bat in its case and swung it over his back. He made sure to tuck in his *Pride of St. Luke's* tee shirt that he wore underneath his uniform. He had never looked better.

He was going to show every patient on the second floor that Paul Morgan, now dressed in regulation Phillies gear, was playing tonight. He wanted to inspire them to live their dreams like he was about to live his. He told Dr. Knotts of his intentions to play. The doctor was less than pleased especially after he saw Paul struggle through another coughing spasm.

"You'll be risking a lot if you play, Paul," he warned. "Your pulmonary function scores are down about thirty percent right now and since you have an infection, those numbers can plummet even further. You've lost ten pounds, which means the bacterial infection is fighting your system. And it's not unthinkable that you could go into coughing spasms from the bacteria growing in your lungs. You're really sick, son. I'm concerned what could happen if you go out there."

"I understand, Doc," he said, even though there was no changing his mind. "But I'm more concerned what could happen if I don't go out there."

Dr. Knotts sighed. "I can't promise that you won't need medical attention at the game. I just don't think that playing would be a wise move right now," he said.

Even though Paul knew it was his decision—after all, he was an adult now—he wanted Dr. Knotts to understand why he was making it.

"This is more than just a baseball game to me," he explained passionately. "Each of us has some ultimate dream that drives us throughout our lives. Very few of us get the opportunity to achieve it. That's the opportunity that I'll have tonight. I may never get another chance. And this is my opportunity to show the other patients on this floor that people with CF and other diseases *can* reach their goals. I want to inspire them, too."

Dr. Knotts felt Paul's determination and told him he wouldn't try to talk him out of his decision. But he did offer him lots of advice.

"Do your therapy, drink lots of water and use your inhaler if you need it."

As Paul turned to go, the nurses and doctors applauded. Suddenly, curious faces poked out from behind hospital room doors to see what the commotion was.

"Paul's going to play ball tonight!" hollered Nurse Johanson. "Lightning's going to strike Turner Field!"

"Hit a homerun for us!" shouted one of the younger patients.

He walked into room 210, where an old friend looked him over and smiled. Paul reached into his pocket and handed him a white ball with red laces and a Rawlings logo on the front. The inscription read, "*It's our turn. Your friend always, Paul Morgan.*"

"I know it's not a trip to the moon, but it's a ball that I once hit over the fence to beat my bully," he explained, his voice still hoarse from the coughing and antibiotics. "When you start thinking cancer will bully you forever, put this ball in your hand and remember you can fight back. Maybe your turn has nothing to do with being an astronaut, Stan. Maybe it's proving that you can beat cancer. Maybe that's going to be the amazing thing that you do."

Stan managed a shy smile. "Thank you, Paul," he said groggily. The exhaustion of his battle wore on his face. His eyes were half-shut and his face was as pale as Paul had seen it. The chemo was wearing away at his body. Stan's doctor walked in and attached some more tubes to his arm and forced him to drink an orange liquid. Paul waved goodbye to his friend and prayed for good health.

His parents and Sally met him in the first floor lobby to drive him to the stadium. In the car, Sally showed him the ticket for his first game and told him she was going to put it in her scrapbook after the game. He examined it closely.

Atlanta Braves vs. Philadelphia Phillies
September 15
Turner Field

Some of the excitement drained from his face as he tapped his brother's pendant. He'd almost forgotten what today was. He looked over at his mother.

"Is it okay to play today?"

"Of course," she answered. "You know your body better than anyone."

"That's not what I mean, Mom," he explained. "Would Garey be upset if I played baseball on the day he died?"

She paused for a minute to collect her thoughts before answering him.

"He wouldn't want you to be anywhere else. If you feel like you need to do something for him, then go out there and get a hit for your brother."

As they approached the Fulton Street/Turner Field exit he coughed up a lot of mucous. After he caught his breath, Sally looked at him with a grim expression, unable to mask her concern. He knew she wanted to tell him to call it a day and get some rest but to her credit, Sally kept it to herself. She knew this was his dream and she wasn't about to add another obstacle. She loved him. In the front seat, his parents exchanged uneasy glances. They were all quiet as the stadium came into view. Before they arrived, Sally handed him the morning paper.

"Take a look at the sports section before you play tonight," she said.

They pulled into the massive Turner Field parking lot. His chest still hurt and he still had a slight cough, but he was feeling significantly better than a few days ago. He felt more confident, too, because he didn't feel alone walking into that ballpark. Garey Morgan was coming along for the ride. His dad stepped out of the car and hugged him for a good twenty seconds.

"I love you, pal," he said. He and his dad hardly used the "L" word, but he couldn't think of a more important time to hear it. His mom echoed his sentiments and kissed him on the cheek.

"You're my hero, Paul" she declared.

"Mom, you're my hero, too. Just like little Tommy Stevenson said, 'A superhero needs no cape.'"

"Tommy Stevenson?" she uttered. "Was that the boy's full name from your dream?"

"Yeah, why?" Paul wondered.

"No big deal," his mom laughed. "It's just that Garey's baseball coach at Killer Creek was named Tommy Stevenson. He loved Coach Stevenson."

Paul just stood there for a moment, chuckling, as if he'd finally found the last piece of a jigsaw puzzle.

"Of course, that was his coach. It all makes sense now."

He and Sally stared into each other's eyes for a few seconds. He could tell that she was trying to hide her concern; she knew he needed to hear something positive right now.

"Paul, I know I tried to convince you not to play today but I get it. I wanted you to know that I understand why you have to be out here. I love you and whatever happens, I'm proud of you and Garey's proud of you, too."

They held each other's hands and kissed for a few seconds before he walked off. Friendly faces were everywhere. The first to catch his attention was Larry's, near the front entrance.

"Paul, I'm so happy for you," Larry said, and then winked at him. "Remember that we still have a little bet based on your first at-bat."

"I remember," he laughed. "If I get a hit, I will help you the next time you have a patient who needs motivating. But remember, if I get anything besides a base hit, you lose."

"That's the bet," he said, hugging Paul. Honestly, this was the first bet Paul had ever made that he really wanted to lose. Not only would he love to get a base hit in his first Major League at-bat, but also he wanted to return the same inspiration to someone else who needed it. He knew it still hurt Larry to think about Joey Sakes, the patient he lost with cystic fibrosis. He wanted Larry to remember Paul Morgan, the patient he *saved* with cystic fibrosis.

Before Paul went inside, he remembered The Jet's words the first time he rolled him into the stadium.

"The next time you're on this field, I want you running the bases," Ricky had said. Paul certainly wanted the chance. That's when it struck Paul who was pitching today. The Jet would be on the mound, searching for his first no-hitter in his final start. Paul stopped and looked up at the stadium one more time before he walked in. Through the main gates he saw the seventeen-by-twenty-two foot PlazaVision Board, where the fans could see all of the action going on in the ballpark. He saw the statues of former Braves' greats Phil Niekro and Hank Aaron. On the wall just inside the stadium were all the division pennants that the Braves had won throughout the 1990s and 2000s.

From his hospital room window, he had watched Turner Field being constructed. Now, he looked back across the interstate at St. Luke's and focused on the second set of windows from the bottom—his old floor. He hoped that Stan and the rest of his second-floor friends were staring back at him. So many times he'd been on the other side of the street, dreaming of the day he would get to play Major League Baseball in this stadium. Though he went through rough times and faced several obstacles, he never lost sight of this dream. He walked inside.

He didn't have to dream anymore.

Chapter 41
Walking into Turner Field

Escorted by the club attendant, Paul took the elevator down to the visitor's clubhouse. When he walked into the Phillies' locker room, he was greeted by the shocked faces of Al and Shane.

"What are you doing here?" asked Al.

"I'm not going to let you guys horde all the glory," he said jokingly.

They both smiled and shook his hand. Then they told him about their first Major League experiences.

"My knees locked," Al remembered, laughing. "I couldn't get a key big enough to unlock them while I was in the field. I almost dropped a pop-up."

Shane, despite not getting to bat, called it "the greatest feeling in the world." He only hoped that Paul would get the same opportunity.

Some of the veterans came over to shake Paul's hand and tell him how his strong will inspired them. Coach Bowman usually gave the pre-game pep talk but on this September day, he turned to Paul and asked him to give it, hoping his determination would rub off on the guys. So what did he speak about? He told them about the dream, of course.

"When I was young," he began, "doctors told me that I wouldn't amount to much. As I lay in my hospital bed, I stared across the street at the stadium being built next door. Each day, as it became more magnificent, I became sicklier. Doctors gave me months to live and my attitude wasn't strong enough to doubt them. I tried to end my life and that put me into a coma. This may sound strange, but during my coma, I met a man who told me that I could live the rest of my days in heaven without anymore pain or I could have one more opportunity to live my life, though I'd still have to battle cystic fibrosis. I could have given up then. I could have just coasted up to heaven and enjoyed a pain-free existence. My life had been a complete disaster up to that point, so why would I want a second chance? What was left to motivate me?

"One thing still inspired me," he told the players, whose rapt attention he now held. "A dream I'd been having since I was ten.

"The dream takes place here at Turner Field. I come to bat looking for my first Major League hit to win the game. The dream always ends with me waking up before I could face a pitch. That dream inspired me to come back and live my life. It pushed me when I was a mere 1-for-25 in my first week of Triple-A baseball. It motivated me when doctors told me that my pulmonary function tests were too low for me to get out of bed, much less play in a Major League Baseball game. I'm playing tonight to finish that dream.

"When you're little, you watch television to see your favorite baseball players like Alex Rodriguez or Albert Pujols. They win baseball games and are called heroic. But are they really so courageous? They win baseball games. How is that heroic? To be truly brave, a person must face risks and overcome obstacles. People who fight disease and despair in a hospital day after day, knowing their odds of survival are not very good, are the true heroes. They deal with more risk than some of us can ever imagine. I'm proud to play for those courageous people tonight."

As Paul paused, a smattering of applause came from one side of the room. It grew, like a wave, around the room until all the players were clapping and cheering raucously. When they saw that Paul had more to say, they calmed down to let him continue.

"Let's play hard tonight because I know from personal experience that those people fighting for their lives look to us for inspiration. I used to lie in a hospital bed day after day and the only thing that took my focus off of my terrible circumstances was watching Chipper Jones hit a homerun or seeing The Jet throw a shutout. Tonight, let's not only inspire them with our relentless effort, but let's be inspired by their relentless fight. Now, let's go beat the Braves!"

After hearing the pep talk his inspired teammates cheered, some with tears in their eyes. Veterans and rookies no longer worried about the competition to make next year's team. They saw themselves as role models to sick kids desperate for hope. Tonight was a chance to shine. Al ran over to him.

"Paul, after reading your story this morning, I can honestly say that you are the bravest man I know. Your brother would be proud."

"Reading my story?" Paul said. "What do you mean?"

"You mean you didn't read the paper today, Paul?" Al responded.

It was then that he remembered that Sally wanted him to check out the sports section of the *Atlanta Journal-Constitution*. He flipped to the front page of the sports section and saw a large photograph of himself as a young boy wearing his Braves uniform. To the right of it was the feature's title, *A Superhero Needs No Cape* by Sally Myers. He read both pages of the article. Sally had told his story. It was all there. The last paragraph was the one he remembered most.

Paul is not supposed to play on Sunday and I've told him I don't want him to play and jeopardize his health, but something tells me that Paul will be playing. If a life-threatening disease can't stop him, I don't think an over-protective girlfriend has any chance. Although he'll be wearing a different uniform than our Braves, please take some time to pay homage to a real hero this Sunday.

He was a little embarrassed by the media exposure and some of his teammates even jokingly nicknamed him "GQ" because he was on the cover of the sports section. Still, he was glad that his story was getting out there because he believed that it gave people hope.

Coach Bowman told him he'd try to get him in the game but couldn't make any promises. Some of his teammates told him if he didn't get to bat until the ninth, they'd let him pinch-hit for them in the order. He and his teammates took the field. The grass was the prettiest shade of green that he'd ever seen, with that fresh cut smell missing from Veteran's Stadium's artificial turf. The smell of peanuts and hotdogs wafted through the air. The Braves' logo was in bright red and blue lights above the scoreboard about five-hundred feet up. Fireworks were shooting out of the big Coke bottle behind the leftfield wall. "Centerfield" was blaring from the speakers as it did before every Braves game. The sun was slowly setting behind the stadium as a cool breeze blew past him. He stood right outside the visiting team's dugout for a couple of moments just so he could take it all in. What a perfect night to play baseball!

He strolled into the batting cage to take his practice swings. His first few cuts were a bit weak. It was tough to adjust after being in a hospital bed for a couple of days. After a few foul tips into the net above, he finally got a hold of a pitch and knocked it off the right field wall. That got him into a nice groove and he began stroking the ball into the outfield, pitch after pitch. He looked over at Coach Bowman and grinned, hoping he could see how determined he was to play tonight. He grabbed his glove and a ball, and threw with Shane in the outfield. After a couple of throws, both teams' lineups flashed on the scoreboard above Shane's head. His name was nowhere to be found. Coach Bowman said he might not be able to play him tonight but Paul had hoped that he changed his mind at the last minute and put him in the starting lineup. So much for a chance to face his idol in the last game of his career. Paul was disappointed but hoped there would come a time in the game when Coach Bowman would need his services. He and Shane threw about twenty times before they jogged back to the dugout.

He looked up into the crowd to see if he could find Sally and his parents. They were ten rows above the Phillies dugout, so close he could almost touch them. His mom was pointing at him and smiling, taking pictures with every step he took. His dad waved his "Phillies are number one" foam finger, much to the chagrin of the home fans. Sally, wearing her new Phillies cap, was a bundle of nervous energy, eyes darting about, with her hands locked on the seat in front of her. Sitting next to his parents were Nurse Johanson and Dr. Knotts, minus their customary all-white hospital garb. Behind them sat Larry and Dr. Billingsley, cheering as loud as they could.

He hadn't had a chance to call The Jet to tell him he was suiting up. He didn't want to get his hopes up in case Coach Bowman didn't play him. This was Ricky's last Major League Baseball game and he didn't want to ruin The Jet's focus. Instead, he decided to say a brief hello to him before the game. He figured Ricky would start doing cartwheels when he saw him in his Phillies uniform but when he got to the Braves dugout, the coaches told him The Jet was warming up in the bullpen and couldn't be disturbed. The bullpen was behind closed doors, so Ricky didn't even have the opportunity to see Paul warm up.

He did run into an old friend, though. Hank Bowers, his friend from Greenville, was playing left field for the Braves. He had been promoted from Richmond and already had four hits in his first ten at-bats. The newspapers were referring to him as the next great Braves hitter.

"How do you feel, Paul?" he asked. "I heard you were in the hospital again."

"I'm feeling okay, actually," he said, thanking him for his concern. "I can't believe I'm here wearing a big league uniform."

"I can't believe it, either," said Hank. "Tonight's the night, Paul. Your big chance to get that hit. Are you ready?"

"I sure am, Hank. I can't wait."

"Did you to happen to see the program?" Hank asked.

"No, I sure didn't," Paul said. "Don't tell me. Did they do it again?"

"Yup," laughed Hank. "The program lists me as six-foot, four-inches, just like the Greenville program. That extra inch will make it much easier to date in Atlanta."

Paul and Hank shared a laugh that was suddenly interrupted by another coughing spasm. Hank looked worried, glancing around to see if there was anyone from the medical staff who could help if need be.

"Paul, are you sure you're okay?" he asked as his friend caught his breath.

He swallowed hard and managed a smile. "Yes, Hank, thanks. I'm just fine."

On his way back to the dugout just prior to the National Anthem, a voice called over to him. "Paul," the voiced muttered. "Paul!" the call louder this time. He looked behind the Braves dugout and walking down the steps with an older gentleman, probably a doctor to escort him, was Stan Blue.

"Stan! What are you doing here? You should be in bed." Stan looked tired and a little bit out of it. His eyes were bloodshot. He was wearing a cap to cover his shaved head. He was pale, with several bruises where blood samples had been taken from his body.

"Paul, yesterday was the end of my first chemo cycle…" He took another deep breath. "…and I promised to keep that pact. I promised to be wearing my space suit and come see you play."

He gently tapped on the doctor's shoulder. The doctor grabbed behind him and pulled out a space helmet—the one that Captain McTavish gave to Stan when he was a kid. The doctor removed Stan's cap and put the helmet on his head. Stan, who still looked completely exhausted, waved Paul closer. Paul leaned over to him. Stan took a deep breath and whispered, "I did my part. It's your turn, Paul."

He looked back at Stan. "You're darn right it is."

The doctor helped twist Stan around and steered him towards his seat about twenty rows up, but before he turned around, Paul saw a quick smile emerge on Stan's face. Paul hoped he was inspiring Stan as much as he was being inspired by his astronaut friend.

He had to play today. It was *his* turn.

Chapter 42
Doctor, Doctor—
Give Him the News!

The game began around 7 p.m. The Phillies went down in order in the first three innings—The Jet looked great. He struck out eight of the first nine batters he faced. He had no idea that Paul was available to play tonight. He couldn't see him in the dugout since he was tucked back with the other rookies at the end of the bench, eagerly awaiting an opportunity to display his skills.

In the fourth inning, Paul had another coughing spasm and his chest began to hurt more. He took out his inhaler and sprayed the medication in his lungs. He took a pill to ease the pain from his acid reflux. He felt lousy but he didn't care. He wanted to play. Coach Bowman saw him struggling with his coughing and told him to go into the locker room to get some medical attention. When Paul told him he was okay, Coach Bowman advised him that if he didn't, then he wouldn't consider playing him in the game tonight. That sent him into the clubhouse where he called Dr. Knotts. The good doctor sprinted to the elevator and down to the Phillies clubhouse and met his patient.

"Tell me what's going on," he said as he walked up, quickly ushering Paul into the clubhouse and into a small examining room.

"I'm coughing a lot and having some pain in my chest," he gasped. He feared his chance to play was slipping away by leaving the dugout.

While Dr. Knotts administered treatment, Paul watched the game on the clubhouse television. In the sixth inning, he was done with all his breathing treatments. The rest was up to him. Despite his protests, Dr. Knotts insisted that he lie down on the couch for a while.

The game remained scoreless, Ricky's no-hitter still intact, when the Braves new catcher, Art Jenkins, lined a triple down the right field line. Hank knocked him in with an RBI single to put the Braves ahead, 1-0. The crowd roared its approval.

On TV, Art looked familiar to Paul but he couldn't place him. He picked up the Braves team program and found out that Art was in the Dodger farm system before he was traded to Richmond. That pretty much eliminated any chance that they'd played against each other in the minors.

The Jet clinched his left fist as he retired the side in order in the seventh and was now just six outs away from a no-hitter, his ultimate dream. In the bottom of the seventh, Dr. Knotts let Paul return to the dugout but only to watch. Most of his team was in the field, so it was only Shane, himself, a couple of reserves and some of their starting pitchers sitting in the dugout. After the second out of the inning, one of the kids in the seats above the dugout threw down a baseball to be autographed. The ball bounced off the stairs and ricocheted into Paul's lap.

"Paul, why don't you sign your first autograph as a Major Leaguer?" Shane prodded.

"I doubt he wants my autograph, Shane," Paul said, rolling his eyes.

"Come on, Paul," Shane chided. "Sign it for him."

He took the baseball, signed his name and tossed it up to the kid, who looked about nine or ten years old with wavy dark brown hair. He had a Braves jersey on, so he was not sure he really wanted a Phillies autograph, especially some unknown rookie's. Paul hoped to increase the value of the ball by the end of the night.

When the seventh inning ended, Paul went back to the clubhouse to take a few more drags on his inhaler. From there, he watched the game on television. Dr. Knotts was sitting on a stool next to the lockers, having remained in the clubhouse in case Paul needed more medical attention. He was on his cell phone with a doctor at St. Luke's, discussing another patient's charts.

The Braves were clinging to their 1-0 lead in the top of the eighth when, with one out, Phillies shortstop Jimmy Rollins drove a shot to the warning track that Hank snagged against the wall. Paul tried to root for his team but as he had promised Ricky, he was really rooting for him deep down to get the final four outs. With two outs, he'd resorted to flipping a quarter. Heads, he'd get a chance to reach his dream. Tails, and he wouldn't make it to the batter's box. He flipped it the first time - tails. He decided to go two out of three—tails. One more chance. Three out of five. TAILS! Maybe it just wasn't in the cards for him tonight.

As soon as Dr. Knotts turned off his cell phone, he looked over at his patient. "Paul, this dream, it's really important to you, huh?"

"Yes, doc," he replied. "It meant a lot to my brother…" Paul thought about that statement and quickly included an addendum. "It means the world to me."

"Did I ever tell you that my high school basketball team was in the state championship my senior year?" Dr. Knotts confessed.

Dr. Knotts had never told Paul much about his personal life so, of course, Paul was curious.

"No, Dr. Knotts, you sure haven't."

"I was eighteen years old and the all-city point guard for Dunwoody High School. I'd always had this dream of hitting a shot at the buzzer to win the state title. We were down by one to Redan with ten seconds left. We had the ball and during a timeout the coach looked at me and said, 'Knotts, I want you to shoot the final shot.' Normally, I was cool and collected but this time I panicked. I could hardly swallow. I told the coach to have Johnson, our small forward, shoot the final shot. I couldn't shoot. I was too fearful that I'd miss. I'd scored thirty-two points in that game and Johnson only had six. Johnson got the ball and rimmed out a four-foot jump shot as time expired. We lost the state championship by one point and I didn't realize my dream. Even worse, it was there for the taking and I passed it up. Only a few small schools came to look at me after that game. I became known to the recruiters as the kid who was afraid to take the big shot. It was then that I gave up basketball. I've had a great life but that one moment of fear is the one regret I have."

Paul wasn't sure why his doctor was telling him this story but before he could respond, Coach Bowman's assistant coach came barreling down the steps to check on Paul as the Phillies went down in order in the top of the eighth. Dr. Knotts left the room for a moment to return a page.

"Paul, how are you doing?" he asked.

"I'm okay, I…" he started to say, "I can play…" but another coughing spasm struck just then. This one was the loudest and longest spasm Paul had experienced in years. Dr. Knotts abruptly ended another phone call to the hospital and re-entered the room.

"Dr. Knotts, what do you think?" Coach Ponsino turned toward his doctor.

"Please," Paul tried again. "All I want is my one at-bat. My dream. Doc, please?" he implored. The coach looked from Paul to Dr. Knotts. As was the case so often, his doctor held his life in his hands.

"I don't know, coach," Dr. Knotts said solemnly. "I certainly don't think he's feeling so great." He turned toward his patient and Paul stared right at him, hoping his doctor could see the determination in his glassy, red eyes. Maybe he could bring back memories of those days when Dr. Knotts wasn't sure if he'd last another week. Or maybe, by allowing his patient to achieve his dream, Dr. Knotts would finally hit that jump shot to win the state title. After what seemed like hours, Dr. Knotts gave his assessment. With his left hand gripped around his chin, he turned towards Coach Ponsino.

"Get the kid a bat," Dr. Knotts declared.

Paul couldn't believe it. The coach smiled and grabbed his arm. "Come on, Paul," he said loudly. "Let's get back to the dugout."

On the television, a commercial break had come on between the eighth and ninth innings. As he followed Coach Ponsino out, he looked over at Dr. Knotts and thanked him. He shrugged back at Paul.

"When you were in that coma, just after your brother was killed, I didn't think you'd ever make it out. I kept telling your parents to turn off the ventilator. I'm never doubting you again. I've never seen a person with more fight than you. Get that hit, Paul. Just be back in the hospital tomorrow morning so we can get you well. Good luck!"

At eight the following morning, Paul would return to St. Luke's but at that moment, he was a baseball player. He sprinted up the dugout stairs, still fighting through a slight cough. In the dugout, Coach Bowman approached him. Even if he asked him to fetch some Gatorade, it would at least be something to do. Paul wasn't sure if he was really going to play or if Coach Ponsino wanted to make sure he was available just in case the game went to extra innings.

"Paul, if we get two of the four batters on base in the ninth, I'll let you bat fifth," Coach Bowman explained. "David is one of our best hitters, so I want to lead him off to start a rally. Tyler is hitting .400 in his last ten games, so I think he can help us score some runs too. I could put you in for Shane or Al..."

Paul interrupted, "No, they've been waiting a lot longer than I have. Please don't ask either of them to come out of the lineup. They deserve to hit."

"That's very admirable, Paul. I like any player who puts the team before himself. Look, Thome's foot is bothering him so you can pinch-hit for him and bat clean-up. You would be the fifth hitter in the inning so you're going to need at least two guys to get on."

Paul was excited but to get two runners on in the ninth meant two things: The Jet would probably lose his no-hitter and the Phillies would have to get two baserunners against the best left-handed pitcher of all time. Maybe just getting in the on-deck circle would give hope to the kids at St. Luke's. Maybe he wouldn't even get that far.

The Phillies trailed 1-0 as the ninth inning began. David Bell, the Phillies third baseman, led off the ninth by whiffing on the first two pitches he saw. Then The Jet gave him the eighty-mile per hour change-up. He swung weakly, way ahead of the ball to complete the strikeout. Good ol' Ricky. Two outs away from his dream—two outs from ending Paul's. The strikeout was The Jet's eighteenth of the game, breaking his previous record of seventeen against the San Francisco Giants two seasons ago. Paul remembered that game against the Giants. The Jet allowed one hit that day—a one-out bloop hit in the top of the ninth. If his shortstop had shaded two more feet to the left, Ricky would have had his no-hitter.

Next up was Shane.

Paul could tell he was nervous, but he gave Shane the thumbs up sign as Shane made his way towards a Major League batter's box for the first time in his twelve-year professional career. Shane swung at the first pitch and missed and took a ball on the next. He worked the count to three balls and two strikes. One more ball and the winning run would step to the plate. But The Jet reared back and fired one right down the middle that Shane whiffed at. Two outs! The Jet pumped his left arm as he was one strikeout away from tying the Major League record. Shane walked by Paul and put his hand on his shoulder.

"I'm sorry, Paul," he said, disheartened. "I tried. I wanted nothing more than to help you reach your dream. I can always say that my first at-bat was against the greatest pitcher of all-time. I've never seen a guy with better stuff on the mound. He's un-hittable tonight."

"If it's meant to be, it will happen," Paul said firmly. "If it doesn't happen, I'll be back next year."

Paul *would* be back next year. Regardless of what happened that night, he loved baseball and had plenty of other goals, like making his first All-Star team or winning a World Series. It wouldn't be healthy to limit himself to one dream. He'd accomplished a lot already. Dr. Billingsley taught him that valuable lesson. Of course, this dream had shadowed his whole life and he would certainly be disappointed if he didn't at least get a chance to bat.

Ricky certainly looked to be at his peak. He'd thrown over one-hundred pitches and Paul couldn't see a drop of sweat on him. He had nineteen strikeouts and only three batters had hit a ball to the outfield. The only baserunner he'd allowed was a leadoff walk in the fourth to Jimmy Rollins. The Jet looked fresh enough to throw another three innings.

Paul's only hope now was that Tyler Gramson, the Phillies second baseman, could reach base. The Jet was just one out from a no-hitter. Paul moved into the hole, which meant one batter away from being on-deck. He perched himself on the dugout steps, his batting helmet in hand. The Jet started Tyler with three outside pitches, pushing the count to three balls and no strikes. Then he hurled a fastball right down the middle for a called strike. Tyler fouled off the next pitch. The count was now full: three balls and two strikes. The Jet stared Tyler down, went through his wind up, and tossed a three-two, 101-mile per hour fastball. Tyler couldn't pull the trigger. A strike call would give The Jet his no-hitter and Paul would have to wait another year. His heart rose in his throat. After an agonizing pause, the umpire shouted, "Ball four!" Tyler reached base on a bases-empty walk. The crowd let the umpire have it.

Now Paul's only chance was Al, who still wore Paul's initials on his cap bill, which he wore underneath his helmet. As Al ambled towards the plate for his Major League debut, he grinned at his friend, who had now grabbed a couple of bats and moved into the on-deck circle. The Jet saw his student there and smiled. Paul wondered what must have gone through his head. He was sure The Jet was proud of his pupil for getting this far but he was certain that the no-hitter was still squarely on his mind. Al would be the winning run. Then again, if Al got a hit, The Jet's dream would be over. Paul didn't know who to root for.

Al fouled off the first pitch, sending the ball careening into the Phillies dugout and scattering players like bowling pins. Strike one. Dan and Tim, the batboys who once laughed at Paul's dream, retrieved the ball at his feet. Both of their eyes widened at the sight of him. He remembered the comment Dan had made to him about a year before. He said he'd be landing on the moon before Paul ever played a Major League game. So he looked toward Dan and pointed towards the half-moon above. He never wanted to humiliate anyone but he'd waited for this moment all his life and he never forgot their ridicule. Their faces sagged. Dan looked bitter, as if he'd swallowed a gallon of sour milk. Pointing up reminded Paul of his dream. He thought he was calling his shot or pointing towards his brother in the dream but maybe it had to do with Dan and Tim.

Paul began practicing his hitting stroke. As Dan and Tim walked away from the on-deck circle, he couldn't help but feel a little bit of redemption. He felt thirty-thousand pairs of eyes watching him. They were probably watching Al bat but there was a chance that in the next few moments it would be him. He leaned down to have another coughing fit as yellow phlegm flew out of his mouth.

Al took ball one, high and inside. The crowd booed, thousands of umpires in the stands thinking it was a strike. The noise in the stadium had reached a fever pitch. Everyone was on the edge of their seat, anticipating being part of a no-hitter. Paul looked at The Jet, who focused only on the batter and threw a strike right down the middle.

Strike two. One more pitch and the season was over. He thought about where he'd come from. He went from the sick kid to a superhero to a baseball player one hit away from his dream. He had to prepare himself in case he didn't get the chance to hit. But he had come so far. He couldn't help but envision getting a base hit to win the game, a hit for people like Stan, a hit for Larry. A base hit to honor his brother's memory.

Al took ball two, low and inside. The count was now even. Again, the crowd hissed as they wanted a strikeout to crown The Jet's gem. Paul continued to take his practice swings. He thought of those three months he and The Jet practiced together. He'd only shown him the eighty-mile per hour fastball. No chance he'd show him that pitch on game night. The Jet told him he could never hit his 101-mile per hour fastball. Would this be his first chance to see the barely visible pitch in person?

Ball three, outside. He would do the best he could but his thoughts began to wander. Where was the guy in the mask? Why did his brother shake his head in the dream just before he was ready to bat? Maybe his dream was just a dream. He began to rub pine tar on his bat when suddenly…

Thump!

It wasn't the sound of a baseball smacking the catcher's glove. He looked over to see Al limping up the first base line. Apparently, the Jet's 3-2 fastball hit Al square on the top of his foot. Al was awarded first base, leaving the no-hitter intact. Tyler advanced to second base. The winning run now stood on first base, just two-hundred-seventy feet from scoring. Paul could give his team the lead with a double in the gap. He would get to have his first Major League at-bat. And it would be against The Jet!

Or would it?

The Braves' manager, Bobby Cox, walked out to the mound, along with the entire infield. Cox usually didn't come out unless he was making a pitching change. The fans began chanting, "Let's Go Braves," as was the message that flashed repeatedly over the giant scoreboard in centerfield. Part of Paul wanted to face The Jet. Another part of him didn't want to face his idol because it would be difficult to get his first hit off of him. Plus, he didn't want to ruin the no-hitter. What a Catch 22! Cox took a moment to talk to The Jet. He doubted that The Jet would agree to be taken out, just one out short of his dream in his final game. But the Braves had John Smoltz warming up in the bullpen, ready to come in. He had fifty saves as the Braves closer and he was as close to automatic as a relief pitcher could be. While everyone was meeting at the mound, the Phillies trainer was checking on Al at first base. Al was fine, so the trainer jogged back to the dugout but before he got there, he passed by Paul.

"How's his foot?" Paul asked.

"Paul, it's pretty bad. But he said he isn't coming out of the game with you at the plate. He knows he's the winning run and he knows about your dream. He could have been shot and he'd still be at first base. He's going to run like a race horse for you."

Paul smiled and looked over at Al. He could see him wincing and grabbing his foot but he looked over at Paul and gave him the thumbs-up sign.

After he'd had his say, Cox returned to the dugout without making a change. The crowd went wild, still rooting for The Jet's first no-hitter.

Paul and The Jet stood face to face, like two roadblocks in front of each other's destiny. Turner Field. Ninth inning. The last game of The Jet's career but the first game of Paul's. It would be a confrontation that neither man would soon forget.

Chapter 43
The At-Bat

If The Jet got him out, Ricky would have his dream of a no-hitter in his last big league game. If Paul hit a double, triple or homer, he would win the game and accomplish his dream. Paul and The Jet were the only two people in the stadium—in the world even—with any knowledge of this bittersweet irony. He could no longer worry about The Jet's dream. He had to focus on the job at hand, and that job was to get a base hit and drive both runners home, no matter who was pitching.

He made his way to the plate. The crowd came to its feet, clamoring for Ricky to close out the no-hitter. The PA announcer was barely audible against the crowd noise.

"Now pinch-hitting for the Phillies, number 6, Paul Morgan."

The Jet looked at the rookie clean-up hitter, smiled for a moment, and then put his game face back on. Paul had waited a lifetime to hear his name called out by the Turner Field public address announcer. The crowd roared even louder, not for Paul but for The Jet to get his no-hitter. Paul glanced into the seats behind the Phillies' dugout and saw Sally, his parents, Nurse Johanson and Dr. Knotts sitting just ten rows up. Larry and Dr. Billingsley were sitting one row behind them. He looked the other way and saw his friend, Stan, leaning back on the seat gripping the space helmet on his lap. For Paul, it was like a "this is your life" party. So many people sitting in the stands tonight had played a role in getting him here. His mom held up a sign reading "The Morgans believe in dreams."

Paul was pumped but at the same time very nervous. He kept telling himself just to make contact. He didn't want to embarrass himself in front of his family and friends. He wondered if his mom could hear his heart beating from her seat. He went into another coughing fit, barely able to breathe, so he took another second before he stepped in the batter's box. On the Jumbotron, he saw his huge face, as did everyone in the park, along with his statistics.

Batting Average: .000
Homeruns: 0
Runs Batted In: 0
Runs Scored: 0
Games Played: 0

He wanted to add another statistic to the board.

Heart: PLENTY

Fittingly, he noticed that the scoreboard clock read 9:15 p.m. He rubbed his pendant as he made his way to the box. Before he could take his stance, Art Jenkins again called time out and went to the mound to talk with The Jet. The Jet looked up and flashed another grin Paul's way. He then resumed focus as he talked to the catcher. Paul figured they were meeting because he was a rookie and Art was worried The Jet had no scouting report on him. He couldn't have been further from the truth. He and The Jet had faced each other hundreds of times on the grass of Piedmont Park, but never with so much at stake. Would he pitch around him? No way. Would he try and strike him out? Paul had no idea what they were discussing. Finally, the umpire walked out to the mound and broke up the meeting.

The rookie looked into the outfield and saw the likes of Andruw Jones and Gary Sheffield, two players he'd grown up watching on television. The moment seemed so surreal. The crowd again roared for The Jet to get the last out. Art walked back behind the plate and Paul assumed his stance. Before crouching down, Art whispered something to Paul.

"Hey rookie, The Jet wanted to let you know he'll be taking you out to the ballgame on the first pitch. He's going to strike you out."

"Oh my God!" Paul whispered to himself, shocked. "The Jet told me he nicknamed his pitches. 'Take me out to the ballgame' was what The Jet hummed when he was preparing to strike out a player with his mid-range fastball! He's tipped off his pitch to me."

236

The Jet had always told Paul he would never tip a pitch to his opponent. He was going to throw his student his eighty-mile per hour fastball, the pitch he'd seen and hit a number of times during their Piedmont Park practices. Paul looked back at Art again as he crouched. Art had no idea that he just told his opponent what pitch was coming. Now, Paul knew why Art looked so familiar. They never met in the minor leagues. Art was the masked man. The masked man in his dream who told him how to get the game-winning hit. Paul never realized that the mask in his dream was a catcher's mask and that the guy telling him what was being thrown would do it unintentionally. His dream was beginning to make sense but he still didn't know what was going to happen.

The Jet must've cared more about Paul's dream than his own. As he stepped on the rubber, he looked at Paul and gave a subtle smile. Paul remembered the first time The Jet steered his wheelchair around the Turner Field bases and told him he'd run around those bases some day. He also remembered how The Jet told him nothing would be given to him.

Paul had been in a position to win a game three times in his life. The last time was his first minor league game in which he struck out after being ahead in the count, three balls and no strikes. The second time was when he hit that blast off Biff Goolson. But the one he couldn't get out of his head was twelve years ago when he faced Josh Wilson during a "meaningless" kickball game. It was the first time he became a hero. What was once a moment of glory for him had become a negative memory now. He depended on Bobby Jarvis that day to help him beat The Human Highlight, and afterwards kept depending on people to come through for him instead of coming through for himself. He never wanted that to happen again.

He knew he could line Ricky's pitch for a base hit as he had done so many times in practice but would a hit like that be truly heroic? Just then, he remembered the part of his dream where his brother shook his head at him. He knew what he had to do.

The Jet came set on the mound. Paul batted right-handed since he was about to face the greatest left-handed pitcher of all time. He adjusted his helmet and batting gloves, then dug his cleats into the ground. The Jet checked first and second base to keep Al and Tyler close, then threw Paul his eighty-mile per hour fastball right down the middle. The ball popped into Art's glove.

"Strike One!" the umpire called.

Al and Tyler were running on the pitch, so Art popped up and fired a laser to third base. The ball beat Tyler there but sailed a little high. Tyler tried to slip his foot just underneath the tag. The umpire waited a moment, stretched his arms away from his body and screamed "Safe!" In an aggressive but risky move, Coach Bowman now had his runners at second and third with two outs. The winning run was now just one-hundred-eighty feet away. Now all Paul needed was a single to the outfield. Two runs would score and he would be even closer to fulfilling his vision.

The Jet wasn't phased by the runners advancing, though. He expected them to go. He was more puzzled by Paul watching the easiest pitch he'd ever see in his Major League career pass him by. His eyes met Paul's. Paul could see the question in his eyes: "Why didn't you swing?" He stepped out of the batter's box and stared back. He wasn't going to make The Jet another Josh Wilson. He shook his head at Ricky and, with his eyes, implored him to bring on his best shot. Art and the umpire must have thought the rookie was crazy. The Jet nodded. He understood what Paul was asking for and why.

Years ago, lying in his hospital bed, Paul would have paid any amount of money for that situation—knowing what pitch he was about to get, hitting it, and being a hero. Now he wanted to earn that hit. The Jet had said so many times that nothing would be given to him. Now, each man had his own dream within reach and no one was going to hand it to either of them. It would be earned, one way or the other.

All of a sudden, Art came out of his stance and trotted to the mound again since the runners were now ninety feet closer to scoring. The crowd relaxed in the lull. During the time out, the public address announcer played "Eye of the Tiger" throughout the stadium.

The song was supposed to motivate the thirty-thousand home fans but it had more of an effect on the young rookie batter wearing the visiting uniform.

Art returned to the plate. This time he ignored Paul and crouched down behind the plate. The Jet set himself on the mound. He knew what Paul wanted. If he struck out, then he just out-pitched him but if Paul got a hit, it would be earned. Ricky looked in and shook his head until Art changed the signs. He checked both runners' leads. From behind the plate, Art issued Paul a warning.

"You're going down, rookie."

The crowd was on their feet again, rooting for the no-hitter, the only jewel missing from a Hall-of-Fame résumé. The crowd noise was deafening. Paul felt the ground shake as the fans were stomping on the bleachers above him. He heard some fan from behind home plate scream, "Strike the rookie out!"

238

The Jet threw to second to keep Al closer to the bag. He was the winning run and the bigger his lead was, the better chance he would score on a base hit to the outfield. Paul stood outside the batter's box for a moment and endured another coughing spasm. His chest was hurting again but he got back in there. He looked at his fans in section ten. Sally had her hands over her head, screaming out his name. His dad was pumping his fists and Paul could read his lips saying, "Come on, Paul!" His mom held up the poster again. He looked at his Phillies teammates lined up along the dugout stairs, eager to see how this drama would play out. He imagined that many of his "other" teammates were glued to their television sets at St. Luke's, just the way he used to focus when watching The Jet. Though he'd dreamed many times of getting to bat in this situation, he'd never faced a single pitch in any of those dreams. Whenever he saw the masked man, he'd wake up. There was no alarm clock to wake him this time. After twelve long years, he was finally about to find out how the dream ended.

Sweat dripped off his chin as he stepped into the box. He pulled his maroon and gray wristbands tightly around his arms. He rubbed his "K" pendant one more time. He straightened the Phillies helmet on his head and then adjusted his batting gloves. His eyes widened to focus on the pitch. His hands clutched and re-clutched his dark brown Louisville Slugger and then pulled it back behind him. He dug his cleats into the dirt. The runners took their leads from second and third. The Jet set himself and then checked the runners.

Soon the distractions from the stands faded to silence in his mind. Paul focused so intensely that he may as well have been in the school library during study hall. The only thing he was worried about was hitting the white orb with red laces that would soon be hurled his way from The Jet's left hand. Would he throw him another eighty-mile per hour fastball? He doubted it. He was pretty sure he would get Ricky's best pitch, the 101-mile per hour jet!

Finally, The Jet threw the 0-1 pitch. The ball shot off his fingers like a bullet fired from a gun. It flew towards the plate with such velocity that Paul could barely see it. He swung with all his might.

Crack!

He made the slightest contact, fouling the ball back against the padded wall behind home plate. "Strike two!" shouted the umpire.

That was his first encounter with The Jet's number one pitch. Even in practice, he didn't throw it to him because he assumed Paul couldn't hit it. Most veteran hitters would ask for contract extensions if they made contact with the 101-mile-per-hour fastball. Art chuckled as he threw a new ball back to Ricky.

"You are never going to hit that ball, rook!"

Another coughing spasm struck. Paul wiped the sweat from his brow with his wristband. He stepped away from the batter's box, knelt down to the ground and spat some of the phlegm from his throat. Coach Bowman shouted from the dugout.

"Paul, you alright? You need a pinch-hitter?"

Paul looked over and could tell by the grim look on his manager's face that he was concerned. "No," he shouted back. "I'm okay." He got back into the batter's box. He was in some pain and he was congested, but nothing was going to keep him from his dream.

He looked towards The Jet. He'd seen him pitch about a thousand times on television and he knew that when Ricky faced a batter who had trouble hitting his 101-mile per hour fastball, he was apt to throw it again. The Jet got set at the mound and checked both the base runners. The crowd grew the loudest it had been all night. "Let's go Braves!" flashed on the matrix board behind the centerfield wall. The Jet looked down at Art who Paul imagined was flashing signs of what pitch The Jet would throw next. The Jet let go of another heater and this time Paul took the pitch about six inches outside.

"Ball One," shouted the umpire. A chorus of boos showered the ump.

"Ump, you're a bum!" yelled a spectator behind the on-deck circle. "Hey, blue, you're missing a good game!" another heckler chimed in.

Paul took a moment to straighten his wristbands and got right back in the box. He didn't know what pitch The Jet would be throwing but he had confidence that whatever it was, he could hit it. The Jet set himself again at the mound. He checked both runners from the stretch and then turned toward the batter. As he released another 101-mile-per-hour fastball, Paul closed his eyes for a split second and there appeared his brother's smiling face, telling him the same thing he had written to him in letters since he was little: *"I love you Paul."* Right then he felt a squeeze from above. It was Garey rooting him on.

Suddenly he opened his eyes, found the ball scorching towards the catcher's mitt and swung with everything he had left.

Bam!

He started running toward first. He'd pulled the ball towards left field. The ball continued to climb. He knew he'd put a charge in it but how far would it go? He sprinted around first base hoping that the ball had eyes and would elude any Braves' players. His old friend, Hank Bowers, back-pedaled all the way to the wall and braced himself to jump. He was the only one left who could foil his old roommate's dream. He leapt as high as he could go, his glove outstretched. If anyone could bring the ball back into play, it was Hank, but not this time. The ball cleared his glove by about an inch and disappeared behind the left field wall.

Homerun!!!

He did it! He'd homered off of The Jet's best pitch! He pumped his fists in the air and looked up into the crowd. Everyone was quiet except for section ten. He looked up to see his parents and Sally jumping up and down, exchanging hugs. Larry was giving high fives to Dr. Knotts and Nurse Johanson.

As he circled the bases, he realized how one hit affected so many lives. As he rounded second base, he thought of the people at St. Luke's who'd asked him to homer for them. This would surely inspire Stan, who he glanced and winked at as he approached third base. As he stepped on third, he thought of Larry and how he'd be helping one of his patients some day soon. When he stepped on home plate, he thought of the person who he was happiest to homer for. In fact, he scratched *915* in the dirt next to home plate with his cleat and rubbed the K on his chest.

His teammates picked him up and carried him to the dugout. Shane and Al each gave him a hug. He finally sat down with a grin from ear to ear. He could hardly catch his breath so he took a couple of puffs on his inhaler. He poured a bottle of water over his head to prevent him from getting over-heated. His heart was beating a million times a minute. He coughed a little from the long trot around the bases but he didn't care. The dugout buzzed with excitement, while the crowd sat in silent shock. You could've heard a pin drop at Turner Field.

Slowly though, the crowd started to make noise again. Thirty seconds later, the crowd was as deafening as they'd been all night. The Jet tipped his cap, as the fans realized that not many people get within one pitch of a no-hitter. Even after he tipped his cap, part of the crowd continued to yell. They began to chant. Paul couldn't understand what they were saying. It sounded like *"Whi-Ting, Whi-Ting, Whi-Ting."* He had no idea. Finally, Coach Bowman came over to him.

"Ever done a curtain call before?" he asked.

"No, why?" Paul gasped.

"Cause I don't think this game is gonna go on unless you get out there and tip your helmet."

That's when he picked up what the crowd was chanting. *"Light-Ning, Light-Ning, Light-Ning."* The rest of the crowd took part. It seemed the *Atlanta Journal-Constitution* was pretty popular that day. The story of the local boy who had overcome impossible odds had spread throughout the stadium. He jumped up on the dugout steps and tipped his hat to the fans. The crowd erupted and moments later settled down. It was the first and only time a visiting player received a curtain call at Turner Field.

Pat Burrell batted next and struck out on three pitches as The Jet struck out his twentieth batter, tying the Major League record. The crowd erupted once again and gave the future Hall of Fame pitcher another standing ovation as he walked off the field, unbeknownst to anyone except Paul, for the last time. As The Jet walked back to the dugout with a one-hitter, Paul wondered what he was feeling. He would always be indebted to his hero for getting him to this point. He knew his mentor was disappointed that he didn't get his no-hitter but he hoped a part of him was proud of his pupil for accomplishing his dream. But then again, Paul was still three outs from achieving his dream.

Three long outs…

Chapter 44
Trying to Get Defensive

In the bottom of the ninth, Coach Bowman let Paul replace Jason Michaels in centerfield. He dashed from the dugout to center as fast as his legs could take him. Though he was physically drained, the adrenaline rush kept him pumped. As he ran out to his position, he noticed a message on the matrix board behind the centerfield wall.

Now playing CF, Paul Morgan

Though the Turner Field scoreboard operator meant centerfield, Paul's first thought, of course, was the other CF—the disease that had played him most of his young life. For the first time, he was no longer being played by CF. He was, in fact, playing CF—and not just on the baseball field.

Playing defense on a Major League field for the first time helped him overlook how exhausted he was. He took his place in the outfield and turned to face home plate. Philadelphia's closer, Billy Wagner, overpowered the first two batters with high fastballs. One out away now from the dream coming true.

The left-handed Wagner now had to face the heart of the Braves' lineup. Chipper Jones came up next and lined a shot into the leftfield corner. Burrell threw the ball back in as Jones coasted into second base.

The tying run came to the plate in Adam LaRoche, the talented first baseman for the Braves. He had twenty-six homeruns for the season and was a leading candidate for player of the month in September as he'd already hit eight homeruns in the month. LaRoche took strike one on the outside corner. Paul was two strikes from his dream.

"Strike two!" shouted the umpire as LaRoche swung and missed a ball in the dirt. The next pitch was a little high for ball one. Wagner reached back for some heat and threw the ball in on LaRoche's hands. He swung and broke his bat. The ball, along with several pieces of wood, dribbled down the third base line. Bell, the Phillies Gold Glove third baseman, barehanded the ball and threw it to first base all in one fluid motion.

"Saaaaaafe!" shouted the umpire. LaRoche beat it by a step. Jones advanced to third on the play. Coach Bowman walked towards the mound to meet with his closer and catcher. A few seconds later, he was back in the dugout and Wagner was still out there. No one was in the Phillies bullpen. It was Wagner's game to save or lose. Batting next was Art Jenkins, the guy from Paul's dream. Paul was concerned. He could see his dream slipping away. Art's triple resulted in the Braves first run. He already had a single and a double and was a homer away from hitting for the cycle. A homer would also win the game for the Braves and crush Paul's dream. Wagner looked at his catcher, who stuck his glove towards the third base line. The Phillies were walking Art intentionally to get to the rookie batting behind him—Hank Bowers.

Paul sensed the irony. He had told Hank his dream countless times about having a chance to win a game in his first at-bat at Turner Field and now Hank could win the game himself with just one hit. The crowd booed, as was customary when one of the home team's best players was walked intentionally. It was considered a cowardly move by the visiting team.

Paul patted his glove and waited as finally Hank, nicknamed Hank the Tank by his adoring fans, stepped in. The crowd roared again—the game rested on this match-up. A section of Hank's fans, who were seated in the upper deck wearing Braves military garb, began chanting "Hank the Tank!" over and over until the rest of the crowd eventually joined in.

Wagner checked the base runners and blew a ninety-eight-mile per hour blur right by Hank for strike one. Hank took a ball high on the next pitch and then a ball low on the next one. The noise in the stadium was deafening, again. Wagner set himself at the mound and threw a 2-1 fastball.

Hank *crushed* it to deep centerfield!

Paul turned and sprinted toward the wall. He ran faster and faster, his breathing becoming heavier with each step. The ball was like a guided missile whose primary target was the centerfield stands. Paul could hear the thirty-thousand fans getting louder as he moved closer to the 401 sign on the dead-centerfield wall. He stutter-stepped at the base of the eight-foot tall blue fence, jumped as high as he could go, and extended his glove over the wall. At first, his cleats stuck to the padded wall but then he slipped and fell to the warning track. Hank pumped his fist and trotted around second base. The crowd went absolutely crazy, throwing red foam tomahawks onto the field, and exchanging high-fives. The umpire waved his hand in a circular motion, indicating a homerun. The scoreboard, in Biff Goolson-like fashion, flashed—

GAME OVER!

His uniform covered with dirt, Paul sat up against the fence, took a moment to catch his breath and thought of the kids at St. Luke's who wanted him to accomplish his dream. Maybe it was good enough that he beat cystic fibrosis. Perhaps they'd be satisfied that he got to the Major Leagues. Maybe those kids would be okay with him not reaching his dream that night. After a moment or two of pondering, the answer translated in Paul's head.

"I didn't come this far to fail. This is *my* time."

He stood up, dusted himself off and dropped from his glove what appeared to be a magical spherical object because the red-laced ball turned a deafening crowd into a bunch of mimes. Paul had not only hit the game-winning homerun, but his spectacular catch over the fence had saved the game for the Phillies.

The umpire changed his call and put a fist in the air indicating the third out. Hank stopped dead in his tracks as he rounded third base. His jaw dropped wide-open; his face had a look of bewilderment. No one in section ten could believe it, either.

Lilian and Sam started jumping up and down, waving their hands in the air until they finally embraced. Larry began playfully taunting the Braves fans behind him.

"I told you my boy was a hero! I told you!"

A warm smile flashed across Sally's face as her boyfriend heroically sprinted to the dugout. The scoreboard was right. The game was over. Paul's dream had come true.

Phillies 3, Braves 1.

Chapter 45
Fatherly Advice

Eighteen years after that at-bat against The Jet, Paul remembered it like it was yesterday. He could still smell the cotton candy from the stands of Turner Field and hear the screaming from section ten when he hit the homerun. As he finished telling his story, Greg looked at his father with a newfound admiration. He hadn't seen much of his father's baseball career except on old videotapes and classic sports channels. It was obvious the story had an effect on Greg. Paul hoped that it had the same effect on Greg as many of Garey's talks had on him.

"Wow, Dad," Greg said, as they sat in the stands at Turner Field, watching Hank take his final at-bat before being replaced in the outfield by a fresh-faced minor league call-up. "Is that why you always say that Hank Bowers is six-feet, three-inches and not six-feet, four-inches like the program says?"

"Right on the money, Greg. I told you something as small as an inch can change someone's life. If Hank is really six-four and catches that ball, the dream I'd had most of my life would not come true. The point is, every little thing in life matters. Never take anything for granted."

"When you say a little thing, you mean not making the baseball team, right dad?"

"You got it, son."

Greg embraced his father. "Dad, thank you for telling me that story. I'm really proud of you and I'm going to make you so proud of me. Can we start practicing tomorrow? I'm going to try and make the middle school team next year."

"Absolutely, Greg," he said, happy to see Greg's renewed confidence. "And you don't have to try and impress me. I'm already proud of you."

Suddenly, the strange man who'd been staring at Paul and his son throughout the entire time it took Paul to tell Greg his story began walking towards them. Greg began to tremble. The man had shoulder length brown hair, looked about ten years younger than Paul and noticeably kept his right hand in his pocket.

"Mr. Morgan," the man began.

"Yes."

"You don't know me. I'm Richard Cohen, and my son and I are very big fans." He shook Paul's hand and summoned his nine-year-old son over to meet Paul. "Seth, this is Paul Morgan. He's the player I've been telling you about." The man removed a shiny white baseball from his pocket and gave it to his son.

"Would you like an autograph, Seth?" asked Paul. Paul seldom gave autographs these days as many of the young fans did not know who he was.

"No, thank you, Mr. Morgan, sir," the boy replied.

"Oh, okay," Paul responded, a little bit confused as to what the man wanted.

"What my son means is we already have your autograph. Show him the ball, Seth." Seth flipped the ball around and sure enough, Paul's signature was on there with his motto, *A superhero needs no cape*. "I got it from you at a game when I was a little boy about my son's age," Mr. Cohen said.

Paul gave lots of autographs so he wasn't sure he would remember the moment as much as the strange man.

"You see Mr. Morgan, I was at your first game. I tossed a ball in the dugout and you signed it for me. You hit a homerun in that game to give your team the lead and then you won the game with an acrobatic catch in center. You're my idol, sir. I wanted my son to know who I looked up to. I wanted to thank you for being a good role model to many of us young baseball fans. Enjoy tonight's game."

Paul smiled. "Mr. Cohen, I do remember signing that ball for you. I'm glad I made a difference in your life."

As the man walked away, Greg could only smile, so proud of his father. He had so many questions now.

"Dad, does that happen to you often? Do people just come up to you and thank you?"

"Sometimes, Greg. That homerun changed my life."

"By the way, did you and The Jet talk after the game?" Greg asked. "Did he ever tell you why he tipped you off on the first pitch?"

"The Jet and I spoke right after the game prior to his press conference in which he announced his retirement. He said the only reason he tipped off the first pitch was that he believed my dream was more important because it meant a lot to so many people who needed hope in their lives through my inspiration. Days later, a nurse who was on duty the night of the game said there wasn't a television on the second floor that wasn't tuned to that game. She'd never seen those kids happier than the moment I homered off of The Jet. She told me patients were screaming at the top of their lungs. After that game, Nurse Johanson said the work ethic amongst the patients had gone through the roof. The patients began to believe they could do anything."

"What about Stan?" Greg asked, suddenly concerned. "Is he still alive? How about Larry, Dr. Knotts and Nurse Johanson? What happened to them?"

"Stan beat cancer, left St. Luke's and he just got married about a year ago. The cancer has come back a few times but he keeps fending it off. He sent me a letter about six months ago telling me that my one at-bat changed his entire outlook on life. He now speaks on cancer awareness about ten times a year, and he still keeps the baseball I gave him in a glass case on the mantle above his fireplace. Oh, and even though he said he'd given up on his dream of being an astronaut, he is doing the next best thing. He is an engineer for NASA and is a big help to the space program."

"Dad, what about Nurse Johanson, Dr. Knotts, and Larry?"

"I'm getting to that. They actually still work at the hospital. Nurse Johanson is still beautiful and Dr. Knotts, although set to retire next year, is still cracking corny jokes. After lobbying the hospital for months, they were able to turn Room 205 into 'The Lightning Lounge,' named after the nickname Nurse Johanson had given me when I started walking and jogging around the hospital to inspire the other patients. The room has several pictures of me hitting the baseball. There are also pictures of other patients, like Stan, who escaped St. Luke's and succeeded in life. The room's purpose was to give patients a place to dream and find hope even under adverse circumstances.

"Larry, who hadn't put a picture on the wall since he lost his first CF patient, framed my picture and put it on his wall the day after my homerun. And, as promised, every time my team visited Atlanta I came by his office to motivate his kids, just like The Jet once did for me. Three seasons after my debut with the Phillies, I signed a free agent deal with the Braves and was able to visit Larry's patients a lot more frequently."

Greg had a lot of questions and Paul was proud and happy to answer every one of them. After all, the baseball field was where they always did their best bonding.

"Do you still have the baseball that you hit off The Jet?" he asked. "I bet it's your most prized possession."

"Yes, it was my most prized possession, but no, I don't still have it," he answered. Greg seemed puzzled how a souvenir so valuable to his father was not in his possession.

"After his press conference, The Jet showered and, in his street clothes, walked over to me while I was packing up my stuff. He reached into his brown leather jacket and handed me the ball which I'd blasted over the fence about an hour earlier. I stared at it for a moment. There was still a fresh scuff mark underneath the *Rawlings* logo where the sweet spot of my bat had made perfect contact with it. I ran my fingers along the red stitching. It meant a lot to me that he went out of his way to make sure I got that baseball. He'd planned to pitch a no-hitter and bring the ball to me in the hospital, but I think he was happier with the way things turned out. I know I was.

"Ricky asked me if I was going to put it in my trophy case but actually, I had a better idea. The next morning, I paid a visit to Miller Pond Park and left it at my brother's grave. He was someone who would have appreciated it more than anyone. I even wrote the storyline on the baseball. I figured Garey had given me so many baseballs from his games that it was about time I returned the favor."

"I had no idea how much Uncle Garey meant to you until you told me the story," Greg said in awe. "So you named me after him in a way—the name that he used when he turned you into a superhero?"

"Yes, you were named after your uncle," he explained. "You were born at 9:15 a.m., so it was only fitting that you were named Gregory Hartman Morgan."

"Why didn't you just name me Garey?"

"We could have named you Garey, but my father intended that name to go to only one person, because he wanted Garey to know that there was no one else like him—and he could not have been more right," Paul answered as his eyes grew a little moist. He always got choked up when he talked about his big brother.

Suddenly Paul looked up and walking toward them was the other love of his life, his wife, Sally. He still couldn't take his eyes off of her.

"Sorry, I'm late," she said breathlessly, as she tousled Greg's hair, kissed her husband on the lips and sat down between them. "I was finishing up a story for the paper."

Paul turned his attention to Turner Field. No matter how many times he came here, he was still in awe of the stadium and its history. He looked over at the big Coke bottle in left field. It was about fifty feet high and fireworks shot out of it when a Brave homered or the Braves won the game. On the field, the Dodgers, in their blue caps and gray uniforms, were lined up in the visitor's dugout. The Braves, in their blue caps and white uniforms, were lined up in the home team's dugout. It was a battle of last place teams.

He looked toward the left field rafters at the number nine that would display eternally on the ring of fame at Turner Field, the famous nine worn by Ricky during his Hall of Fame career. Next to his number were the numbers of Spahn, Mathews, Aaron, Niekro, Smoltz, Glavine, Maddux, Jones, and Murphy—all Braves' Hall-of-Famers. Soon, Hank Bowers would join that list.

Paul had a pretty ordinary career in his eight seasons, three with the Phillies and five with the Braves. People loved the way he played the game, though. He sprinted to first even on a base on balls. He ran out pop-ups, took the extra base and had more cuts and bruises from sliding than any other player in the Major Leagues. He'd even been named to the National League All-Star team his third year in Philadelphia and won a World Series with the Braves three years later. He'd gained a few blue-collar fans in his eight-year career. He still saw a few adults and kids wearing his number six jersey. No matter how many times he saw people wearing his number, it still felt like the ultimate compliment. His shining moment in baseball was still probably his first at-bat. When he had trouble sleeping late at night, Paul would sneak over to the television and insert the game tape in the DVD player so he could hear Harry Kalas, legendary voice of the Phillies, call his first at-bat one more time:

"The youngster steps back into the batter's box. The Jet sets at the mound. The runners lead from second and third. Here's the 1-2 pitch to Morgan...swing and a drive, Bowers back to the wall. He leaps...it's outta here! The Phillies take the lead. Morgan socks a clutch three-run homer in his first at-bat as a big leaguer. What a debut for the hometown kid!"

Back in the present, Paul thought about how tomorrow was a big day and it had nothing to do with baseball. The Garey E. Morgan Foundation, of which Paul was now chairman, had raised fifteen million dollars for cystic fibrosis research. Thanks to the Foundation's work, Paul would begin a treatment called pulmonary inhalation therapy. In six weeks, he, like thousands of others, would be cured of cystic fibrosis. Soon he'd have to find another job, because there would be no more need for the Garey E. Morgan Foundation. It would be a glorious job search, knowing that no one ever need die from cystic fibrosis again.

He never thought he'd see the day when he'd be cured of cystic fibrosis. He thought of all the doubters, from doctors to classmates to even the young naïve kid who used to call Room 205 home. No more chest therapy. No more meds. No more specialists. He was going to live a normal life. He would have his wish from his childhood granted and he didn't even have to be "The Solution" to get it. But because of his experiences, he would always have such an appreciation for life and never take it for granted. Unfortunately, most "normal" people didn't do that.

His only regret was that his parents would not see the day when their son was cured of this awful disease. Lilian passed away just six months after his game-winning homerun after a bout with breast cancer. She told him that she was grateful that she got to see her son's dream come true. Sam, who was in amazing shape, suffered a stroke ten years later and the doctors were unable to save him. Paul was thankful that his father got to know his grandson before he passed away. Although his parents would not be present physically, Paul knew their spirit, along with his big brother's, would always be with him.

He looked into the crowd again. It was then when he swore that he saw him, Garey, just as he remembered him: Braves hat on, snacking on some Cracker Jacks and a hotdog. He was certain that was him, but he quickly looked back and he was gone. Paul saw him every now and then, sometimes when he was at the gym or when he was closing his eyes while listening to "Eye of the Tiger." When he needed motivation, his brother was usually there. But it was the night of his famous homerun when he spoke to his brother.

Paul fell asleep that night and awoke to see Garey, in his Braves uniform, patting a baseball in his glove, standing on the mound at Turner Field, coaxing his little brother to step up to the plate. When Paul stepped into the batter's box, Louisville Slugger in hand, Garey dropped the ball at the mound and asked, "Do you remember the best pitch I ever gave you?"

Paul laughed. "In all our years, you never threw me a pitch. I certainly would have remembered."

"Yes, I did," Garey countered. "The best pitch I ever gave you was when I pitched to you to never give up and to always fight. Because you fought to win the game of life, you will always be hitting 1.000 in my book." Garey picked up the ball and bounced it over to his little brother on three hops. Paul barehanded the ball and noticed an inscription.

Goodbye, little brother. I love you and I'm very proud of you.

At that moment, Garey smiled at Paul, turned around, and walked off the mound for the very last time. The back of his jersey became smaller and smaller until he disappeared into the centerfield fog. That would be the last conversation the two brothers would ever have.

Paul woke up to rub his pendant. He would always be grateful to his big brother for showing him that the key to accomplishing any dream is visualizing success.

Paul looked again at the Hall of Fame numbers on the wall. His name would never be up there but that was okay. He already felt like a Hall-of-Famer, not just because he was going to be cured of cystic fibrosis, but also because thanks to breakthroughs in fertility medicine, he was a dad. He was going to pass on a lifetime of advice to his son. He was going to see him go to prom. He was going to see him drive his first car, get married and have a family. For a while, he didn't even think he'd see his own sixteenth birthday.

Prior to the seventh inning stretch, he and Greg ran into Charlie, the concession stand vendor, again.

"I'm here for my hotdog and Cracker Jacks, Charlie," Paul chuckled.

"Amazing, Mr. M., 9:15 on the nose for dinner. Every game it's the exact same thing."

Paul shrugged his shoulders. "I don't know, Charlie. That is quite strange." Although, he knew it was far more than coincidental. Greg, now understanding Garey's significance in his father's life, looked up at his dad and smiled.

Charlie handed Paul his hotdog and Cracker Jacks and Paul escorted Greg over to the condiments table across from the concession stand. He asked Greg to dress his dog while he took his medication. Greg sprayed some ketchup all over it. The hotdog had vanished under the red dressing.

"Wait a minute," his dad said. "That's not how you make a juicy hotdog taste better."

He wiped it off with a napkin. From there, he showed him step by step how Garey had taught him to make a tasty ballpark frank. When he finished, he asked Greg to take a bite.

Greg stuffed a good-sized chunk in his mouth and smiled. "Best hotdog I've ever had, dad," he said after chewing enough to talk again.

Paul smiled as he thought back to that day in the hospital when Garey first taught him how to make the perfect hotdog. His brother would have been proud to know that Paul's son knew a secret that previously only he and Garey shared.

After the game, Paul, Sally, and Greg packed up their things and drove home. Paul and Sally were chatting about the inhalation therapy he'd be starting tomorrow as they drove out of the parking lot when suddenly they both noticed how quiet it was in the backseat. Sally turned her head toward the back.

"Greg, you weren't very talkative most of the game," she said. "Is everything okay, honey?"

"Yeah, Mom, I guess so," he said, a look of concentration on his face, as if he was trying to figure out the biggest jigsaw puzzle in the world.

"What is it, Greg?" his dad asked. "What's on your mind?"

"Dad, when you were younger, you were sick a lot. Doctors didn't give you much of a chance to live a normal life," he stated.

"Yes, that's true." he looked over at Sally, who was tearing up. It didn't take much to bring back the pain of his early life. The struggles of his youth often saddened her because she knew that it had been such a difficult time for him. Paul couldn't help but think back to his childhood at that moment.

His parents were told he'd be lucky to live ten years. When he was ten, he lost the ability to walk. Dr. Knotts doubted he'd be strong enough to wean himself off the ventilator. His life had turned out better than he could ever have imagined it. And it wasn't just because he was lucky nor was it because he had Garey for a guardian angel. He defied the odds because he knew that he could, and that could be directly attributed to his positive attitude.

Greg interrupted his father's inner thoughts with concerns of his own.

"I want to make the baseball team so badly, but I know that I have to improve to get there," Greg began. "You were on the verge of dying and yet you still made it to the big leagues. I know you need to have a good attitude but was there something in particular that motivated you to be better? Something that wouldn't let you give up? What inspired you, Dad?"

Paul thought for a moment and suddenly noticed the glow of a well-lit Turner Field in the rearview mirror. His thoughts again returned to his childhood. The answer became relatively clear.

"Well, son," he said as he gazed at the stadium, and then at his boy. "It all starts with a dream."